P9-CKS-905

TELL ME
A SECRET

ALSO BY SAMANTHA HAYES

In Too Deep
You Belong to Me
Before You Die
No Way Out
Until You're Mine
The Reunion

TELL ME
A SECRET

SAMANTHA HAYES

bookouture

Published by Bookouture in 2018

An imprint of StoryFire Ltd.

Carmelite House
50 Victoria Embankment
London EC4Y 0DZ

www.bookouture.com

Copyright © Samantha Hayes, 2018

Samantha Hayes has asserted her right to be identified
as the author of this work.

All rights reserved. No part of this publication may be reproduced,
stored in any retrieval system, or transmitted, in any form or by
any means, electronic, mechanical, photocopying, recording or
otherwise, without the prior written permission of the publishers.

ISBN: 978-1-78681-420-3
eBook ISBN: 978-1-78681-419-7

This book is a work of fiction. Names, characters, businesses,
organizations, places and events other than those clearly in the
public domain, are either the product of the author's imagination
or are used fictitiously. Any resemblance to actual persons, living or
dead, events or locales is entirely coincidental.

~~This one's for…~~

Actually, this one's for me

Three may keep a secret, if two of them are dead

Benjamin Franklin

PROLOGUE

1983

I didn't realise it was an actual dead body at first. I thought he was just standing there, his feet hovering off the ground. His torso was round-shouldered and sagging, with his head limp and bent to one side. Not much different to when I'd seen him drunk and lolling about. For a moment, I even thought he was hunched over his workbench, pondering a woodwork project or poring over some sketches for a new bookcase. He was always making things; always tinkering, as Mum said.

But he'd never done it naked before.

He'd been on a shoot several days before and was surrounded by pheasants and ducks, perhaps a partridge or two, their plucked bodies all skinny and pale like his, as they hung on wires from the ceiling of the workshop. One or two still had iridescent greeny-blue feathers on their wings. But while the birds were meant to be dead, suspended by their claws, making them look as though they were nosediving mid-flight, Dad wasn't. He was hanging by his neck.

I screamed.

I cupped my hands over my mouth, my body shuddering. I couldn't take it in: a smashed-up jigsaw puzzle with a thousand muddled pieces. The radio was on – he always had music playing when he was out in his shed – and I jiggled about, but not to the music. I was trying to stop the pee trickling down my legs. But I couldn't. It dribbled hot down to my ankles, soaking into my slippers.

I blinked hard, unable to take my eyes off him.

My father was hanging by an electrical cable from a crossbeam in his shed wearing only his watch. I'd only ever seen his *thing* down there once before when I'd gone into his room late one night a few weeks ago. Mum was away for a long weekend with her sister, and Dad had sent me to bed early because I wasn't feeling very well. He'd insisted I stay there. But I'd been sick in my bed, and my body was sweating and cramping, so I'd got up and crept across the landing. There were noises coming from his bedroom. Noises that made me wonder if he was poorly too – all those grunts and moans.

But when I'd gone in, it turned out Dad wasn't sick at all. Paula, the woman who rented a room from us, was in there with him, both of them naked. Her face was pressed sideways against the wall, and he was standing right up close behind her, ramming his hips against her and smacking her bum like she'd been naughty. But then I realised it was because Dad *liked* her. I'd seen people doing it on the telly enough times to know what was going on. Mum always told me to close my eyes and look away, but some-times I'd peek between my fingers.

I knew Mum wouldn't like it; knew that Paula shouldn't be in there, that they shouldn't be naked together. I was just about to creep back to bed, pretend I'd never seen them, but then Dad made this really big roaring sound, the tendons standing out on his neck, his face all screwed-up. And that's when he saw me standing in the doorway in my sicky pyjamas.

Fuck… fucking hell… but his words were all mixed up with groans.

I covered my face, but the next thing I knew his hand was tight around my arm, grabbing me, pulling me into the room.

'What the hell are you doing, spying on us?' Sweat was running down his bare chest.

He shoved me down on the bed, and I buried my face in the sheets. They smelt funny, maybe of Paula. I was scared.

'I wasn't spying, honest,' I said, daring to look up, stifling a sob. Then my eyes flicked down to his *thing*, all big and angry. 'I don't feel well.' Then I sobbed again, but it turned into a retch and sick came up into my mouth, spilling down my front.

Dad pulled on his shirt and hopped into his jeans, cursing the whole time. Paula grabbed Mum's gown from the back of the door and wrapped herself in it. Her breasts were huge, and her body was slim, nothing like Mum's spongy middle. The gown swallowed her up.

'Jesus Christ,' Dad said, pacing about, red-faced and seething. 'You should be asleep, not snooping, you little wretch.' Then he punched the door, his fist lashing out over and over until his knuckles bled and there was a hole in the wood. Dad liked punching things.

Tears and snot were streaming down my face.

'Leave it, Jeff,' Paula said, touching Dad's shoulder. 'She didn't know.' She was kind, even though I hated her now – hated that she lived in our house because my parents needed the money. Hated what she was doing with my dad. I bet Mum didn't even know.

Dad came right up close to me then, breathing heavily. 'OK. You *were* in bed, *weren't* you? You didn't see anything at all, did you? *Did* you?'

I shook my head again, snivelling.

'*Did you?*' he yelled.

'No,' I whispered.

'Pardon?'

'No, I didn't see anything, Dad.'

He hauled me up and marched me through to my bedroom, swearing when he saw the pool of sick on my sheets. He shoved me into bed.

'Clean this up in the morning,' he said, crouching down next to me as I huddled under the duvet. 'You don't tell *anyone* about what you saw tonight, right? Nothing. You understand?'

I nodded.

'You never woke up, you never came into my bedroom, and you never saw Paula in there.' His voice was quiet now but intense, driving into me. Veins stood out on his temples. When Dad was this angry, he meant it. He prodded my shoulder.

That was when I knew he loved Paula way more than me. I loathed her as much as I now loathed him.

I nodded until I thought my head would fall off. He stared at me, scrutinising my face, deciding if he believed me or not. After what seemed like ages, he stood up and left. Then I heard voices, footsteps on the stairs, and the front door eventually opening and closing.

Afterwards, I lay awake all night, shaking, crying, forcing myself to forget. But I couldn't. I'd been so very, very bad.

Another scream tore out of me as I stood in the workshop, my father's body only feet away, hanging from the beam, the bright yellow cable digging into his neck. His face was ghostly pale, his eyes bulging open while his tongue was purple and poking out. The skin on his body was mottled with red patches, getting darker and darker right down to his feet, which were blown up like angry balloons.

But it was his *thing* – standing upright again, just like it was when he'd been with Paula – that I couldn't take my eyes off. It was as though it was the only part of him left alive.

Then I was thinking about it all again. I couldn't help it. Her smarting bottom, Dad's moaning, the straps of muscle across his back, her huge bobbing breasts, even the taste of sick in my mouth and the smell of his breath as he yelled up close in my face. It wouldn't go away.

Then a few days afterwards, Mum and Dad had had their biggest fight ever. That's when everything got worse.

I swear I didn't mean to tell her, but she forced it out of me like a madwoman – said I must have been in the house when it happened, that she could see it written all over my face, that I was nothing more than a dirty whore like Paula for keeping secrets. She made me tell her everything. She drank gin as she listened, smashing the empty bottle against the wall when I'd finished.

'This was all *your* fault!' she yelled at me. Her hysteria doubled her up, making her stagger as the tears and rage poured out. She went upstairs, yanked her towelling gown off the back of her bedroom door and chucked it in the incinerator outside, dousing it in lighter fuel. When she threw in a match, it lit up the entire garden. The next day, my mother was gone. Packed up and left without a word. After everything, I ended up staying with my aunt and didn't see Mum for months.

And then I vomited again, spewing mess all over the feather-strewn workshop floor at the sight of my naked father hanging, swaying gently as Elton John's 'Tiny Dancer' played on the radio. I'd always loved that song, imagining it was me at my dance class on a Wednesday. I began to sway and move to the music, my feet slipping in all the stinky wood oil spilling from an overturned can on the floor, whispering the words as best I could – anything to take away the sight of my father. Anything to make things normal.

Even though they weren't.

As sure as the hot piss running down my legs, I knew that my father had done this to himself because of what had happened.

Because of me.

And then I spotted the note on the workbench, surrounded by his tools and sitting in a sea of sawdust. It had my name on it.

This is what happens when you watch people, when you tell secrets. It's your shame now...

A neighbour burst through the shed door. He'd heard my screams and come running. He stood frozen for a moment before swearing and grabbing a Stanley knife from the workbench. He stood on a wooden box and hacked at the electrical cable, jumping back as my father's body dropped to the floor. Then, frantically, he sliced the cable away from his neck as I watched in horror.

My nine-year-old body then did what bodies do best – it protected me. Or so I thought. I don't remember who found me passed out on the floor, my face slick from lying in the oil when I woke, or anything about what happened right afterwards. It was missing time. Everything locked away. Where it belonged.

Guess Dad was right in the end. Watching people is what I do. But telling secrets?

Never.

CHAPTER ONE

Lorna

March 2018

I'm awake. I glance at the clock. It's 4.02 a.m. and won't be light for a couple of hours yet. I take a long, slow breath in, counting to seven. Then I let it out, counting to eleven. I repeat this ten times, relaxing my body at the same time.

I'm still awake.

Still tense.

Mark lies beside me, the soft purr of sleep escaping his lips. I envy his oblivion, but then I remind myself that it's my fault I can't sleep, that I haven't been able to for months.

I slide from between the sheets – changed yesterday because I always do the beds on a Friday – and tiptoe across the room. There's only one creaky floorboard between here and the bathroom, and I know how to avoid it. I don't want to wake Mark, don't want him asking why I can't sleep yet again. He wouldn't understand.

Afterwards, I don't flush. Instead, I stare at the basin, desperately wanting to wash my hands but knowing the tap will make too much noise. I catch sight of the unexpected smile on my unmade-up face in the mirror – a smile that has very little right to be there. Perhaps it's more a grimace.

I slip back into bed, my fingers still itching to be washed. It doesn't feel right, things not being done a certain way. Leaves too much room for catastrophe. Mark stirs, turning over and draping his arm across my middle, weighing down on my ribs, making it hard to breathe. I try to shift it, but he grumbles so I leave it where it is. I daren't disturb him.

For the next two hours I lie awake, watching it get light. When my thoughts go places they shouldn't – the forbidden landscape of last year – I force myself to think about the mundane, the everyday, the little things that keep me sane. I consider going for my run early, to get it out of the way, but I couldn't do it on an empty stomach and the juicer would wake the whole street, let alone Mark. Besides, it's way too early yet. My Saturday run is always at 8 a.m.

'Do you *have* to do that, Jack?' My stepson scrapes burnt toast over the sink, specks of black showering the white porcelain. I don't like nagging him, but sometimes it's necessary. And I know Mark won't like the mess. 'Just chuck it out and make some more, love,' I say less sternly.

Jack turns, staring at me over his shoulder for a moment before starting to scrape again. He doesn't say a word.

I open the window and back door, flicking on the extractor fan before checking my phone to see if there are any texts from Annie, Lilly's mum. I tell myself that's what I'm checking for, anyway, but old habits die hard. The screen is blank. Freya's not been keen on sleepovers lately but agreed to stay with her best friend after school yesterday. I'm worried that she's become so clingy, that something's troubling her.

Jack shoves the blackened knife into the peanut butter jar, watching my expression as he slathers it on the toast. He's blank-faced, waiting for me to say something, expecting the criticism

that he knows is stinging the back of my throat. I turn back to
the juicer, jiggling the components, trying to make it fit together
properly. It won't turn on.

'People are starving, you know,' Jack says, perfectly timed for
Mark to hear as he comes in the kitchen. 'Waste not, want not.'
He chokes out a laugh – his not-so-long-ago little boy voice now
a manly growl.

'Not sure *anyone* would want that,' I say, my cheeks flushing as
I tussle further with the juicer. I flick the switch back and forth,
feeling tears welling as the stupid machine remains lifeless. It was
already in the kitchen when I moved in, and we could really do
with a new one, but Mark insists that this one, the one that Maria
bought years ago, works fine. Anyway, right now I need the noise
of it to drown out my thoughts way more than I need the juice.
He'd said that once, the comment Jack just made, as he'd grinned
and forked up the chips I'd left on my plate. *People are starving,
you know…*

'Mark, what's wrong with it?' I give the juicer a shove, making
it wobble, hoping he can't read my face. He knows every nuance,
every line and blemish, every shade of blue my eyes take on
depending what's on my mind. I glance at the clock. Nearly eight.
I'll be late leaving for my run at this rate, then the whole day will
be thrown out of kilter.

'You need a mechanic?' he says, coming over and grinning as
he fiddles with the machine. He knocks a carrot onto the floor,
inspecting every inch of the juicer carefully as if it's a patient in
for a check-up. I lunge for the carrot.

'That should do it,' he says, squeezing me around the waist. I
love him. For always mending things. For always keeping things
going. For keeping *me* going even though he doesn't know he is.

'Genius,' I say above the noise, shoving a load of carrots into
the chute, adding in an apple, a stick of celery and a knuckle of
turmeric. I pour it out, sitting down to join Mark and Jack at the

table. 'What?' I say, giving a little smile, noticing their conspiratorial looks. Though Jack's is more scornful than anything. I wipe the bottom of the glass, so it doesn't drip on my white robe. Mark's trying not to grin, while Jack shoves a fistful of burnt toast into his mouth, his usual doleful stare boring out from beneath his too-long fringe.

'*What?*'

'Helps if it's switched on at the wall, love.' Mark puts a hand on my arm.

Jack sprays out toast through a laugh, though I can't tell if it's mocking or not. I manage a little laugh myself amidst this normal, happy family scene, closing my eyes as I sip my juice. But I quickly open them again when, inside my mind, all I can see is *him*.

CHAPTER TWO

Lorna

It's twenty past eight when I tie back my hair, then fiddle with my trainer laces because they don't feel right. I set my Fitbit, making a note of calories burned over the week. I've lost weight these last few months – not that I needed to. I watched it fall away without even trying. Stress will do that. But then *he's* on my mind again as I wonder what he'd say if he saw me now, if he'd like me like this, still find me attractive. I try not to think about him but can't help it.

I set off, closing the front gate, breathing in the chilly morning air. Spring is here, but that's not good to think about either – the bulbs in the park, the cold but sunny afternoons, the handmade chocolates *he* gave me last Easter. *Switch the channel*, I tell myself as my feet pound the pavement. *Change your thoughts!*

Then work is on my mind – which isn't much better because everything leads back to *him* in some way. I try not to think about the clinic at weekends, but I'll take anything as a distraction right now. Besides, it's not the kind of job that stays put in the office. Cases are always on my mind. I suck on my water bottle, turning up the volume of my very carefully selected playlist, tripping on a raised paving slab. I stumble for a few paces, getting myself back in time with the beat, turning my thoughts back to yesterday.

Our weekly team meeting was cancelled, what with one partner being sick and another needed as part of a crisis intervention team.

Then I had two no-shows after lunch, which was when Sandy, our receptionist, told me about a potential client who'd been calling all day, wanting an appointment with me and *only* me. She explained to him about my waiting list.

Why only me?

The insistence unsettled me, of course, made me on edge and out of sorts for the rest of Friday. Perhaps that's the reason for my lack of sleep last night, the uncertainty, what it represented. It was exactly the sort of thing *he* would have done – the urgency, the demands. I felt rattled by it. Still do.

But at least we have dinner with Ed and Annie to look forward to this evening, I think, leaping over a puddle. Running is a good way to work things through, to process feral thoughts. And feral has no place in my life any more.

My breathing kicks up, burning my throat as I press on, speeding up the pace, heading downhill. It's the route I always take on a Saturday – predictable, safe, a known path. My thigh muscles are aching and heavy already, even though I've only run half a mile.

But it's back on my mind again.

'Unrelenting is the word I'd use,' Sandy had told me, her voice slow and cautious as if she didn't want to worry me. 'When I told him you had a waiting list, well that's when…' She'd looked perplexed for a moment, which was unlike her. Sandy pretty much held the clinic together. Nothing harried or fazed her. 'Well, there was silence on the line for a while. Then I just kept hearing the same thing over and over again. "I want an appointment with Lorna Wright, please. As soon as possible."'

I'd nodded, listening, allowing her to finish. She was sitting at her desk in the waiting area, fresh flowers and pleasant lighting doing nothing to allay the look of concern on her face, even though she was quite used to dealing with difficult or emotional clients. 'I told him he could have an appointment in a month's time and that I'd put him on your cancellation list. But…'

'Go on.'

'… but it fell on deaf ears.' She shook her head, her neat bob haircut swaying at her neck. She looked embarrassed. 'So I said I'd have a word with you and I'd call him back.' She tapped her message pad where she'd written his number. 'Sorry, Lorna. I know your list is full, but it was the only way to get rid of him. I didn't want to be rude.'

'It's fine,' I'd said, smiling and tearing the number off the pad. Even as I did it, I could hear myself screaming out to myself not to, that I'd knowingly set the ball of boundary-breaking in motion. Mistake number one. 'I'll sort it.'

Sandy's mouth opened and closed several times and, even though she didn't say anything, she didn't need to. In our practice, and most others, therapists never contact clients outside of the therapy room. It's a violation of our professional code of ethics. That's why we have people like Sandy – to act as a buffer.

I glanced at the name on the paper – David Carter – though Sandy's writing wasn't the most legible. The name didn't mean anything to me. 'No problem,' I said, giving her a cheery smile. She didn't reciprocate. Rather she looked concerned, as if she'd failed at her job. As if I'd failed at mine.

At my desk, I stared at the number. I didn't recognise that either. I also stared at the stack of notes that needed writing up from earlier clients. I'd only been working at the Grove Clinic for ten months, though I'd fitted in so well it was like I'd been here forever. The practice was efficient and friendly, with four full-time therapists – each of us adhering to a strict code of professional ethics, yet maintaining a camaraderie between colleagues that kept us going.

I looked at the name and number again, doodling on the corner of the note, trying to work out what was bothering me about it. Did it make me feel wanted and in demand because I'd been personally requested? At least I had enough self-awareness to see that – to see that my ego was inflated just a little bit bigger than the stack of papers on my desk. But what worried me more was what I was trying to recreate. What feelings I was trying to… well, *feel* again. It was dangerous ground.

I opened a file to get on with some work, but old addictions die hard, so I dialled the number. Just to see what happened, to prove to myself that it was nothing. That I was still in control.

After six rings a generic voicemail kicked in. I left a message. 'Hi, it's Lorna Wright here from the Grove Clinic. If you call me back, I'll see what I can do to fit you in.' I hung up, staring at my phone. Mistake number two – a complete violation of client–counsellor boundaries, not to mention preferential treatment. Well, mistake number three really, given that I'd called the number in the first place. I really hadn't thought this through, acting impulsively for selfish reasons. And whoever David Carter was, he now had my personal mobile number.

I smiled at the background picture of Mark on my phone – the boys' sailing holiday that he and Jack went on ages ago. It's years old now, and I should probably have updated it with a more recent one, but it was very soon after that things got serious between us. It had taken him ages to fully commit. But after everything he'd been through, I understood he needed to take things slowly. So each new phone I have, the picture's come too; my lucky charm. I tucked it back in my bag and set to writing up my clinical notes before the end of the day.

I keep running, my feet slipping into time with my heartbeat at last. What I did yesterday sits at the back of my mind like a dormant seed that's just been given the tiniest amount of soil, water and light. Which is why I'm pounding it out on the pavement now, each footfall hammering home my stupidity.

The tarmac changes to grass as I enter the common, bracing myself for the incline. If I'm called out on it, if anyone – especially Joe, my supervisor – finds out, I'll just say I was helping Sandy, that the client had been giving her a hard time, that she was rushed off her feet.

I put my head down, flicking the music volume up to max, running faster and faster, needing to punish myself. Then, without having any idea why, I break with routine and veer left at the fork, missing the point where I usually stop for thirty squats, some water, a dozen push-ups. I run on, completely off course now, heading down a path I've never taken before.

It was just a trigger, I tell myself over and over. *A silly, inconsequential trigger.* Thing is, I know better than most that when the trigger's pulled, the emotional gunshot is never far behind.

CHAPTER THREE

Lorna

'You're kidding?' I say as Mark hangs up. 'Tonsillitis? Poor Emma.'

He nods, rolling his eyes. Our babysitter is sick, and we're all dressed up with nowhere to go.

'Ed and Annie will be in the taxi on their way to the restaurant by now,' I say, pulling a face and taking off my coat again.

'Shall I ask them over here instead?' he suggests, nosediving into the fridge to see what we have. 'You could whip something up perhaps?'

I glance at my phone. Nothing on the screen apart from a reminder to give Annie back the book I borrowed. I'm not sure if I'm relieved or disappointed.

'Lorn?'

'Sorry, love…' I smile, grabbing his hand. 'Sure, let's ask them over here. We can just chill, listen to that new band you like.' He gives me a peck on the lips. 'And let's send out for a Thai instead.' I squeeze him. 'Will you call Ed to let them know? I'm just going upstairs.'

Mark hesitates – a brief frown – but then smiles, those warm eyes of his creasing at the corners. His smile was one of the things that attracted me to him most – the way his whole face lights up with kindness. 'Will do,' he says, tapping my bum as I go. 'Can't waste you looking so good. I love seeing you in that dress.'

And I can't stand to break from routine, I think, heading up the stairs. Tonight was all planned out, everything in my life designed to fill large gaps of time. The danger zones. Breaking the habit. Twice a month, on a Friday night, it's just Mark and me. We don't like to call it 'date night', but I suppose that's what it is. We'll try a new restaurant or go to the cinema, maybe a gallery preview, or a concert depending what's on. Monday is Mark's sports night – usually squash, followed by a curry with the lads, while I catch up with things around the house or, if I can't be bothered with boring jobs, I'll do my nails or write in my journal. It's more important than ever for me to keep up with that. I'll be honest, Mondays are tricky.

Tuesday evenings are filled with an online food shop and anything else we need ordering, then Mark and I will hit Netflix if we're not too tired. Wednesday evening is book club – always a laugh – while Thursday is Pilates, and Saturday is all about friends. Letting our hair down with some drinks, decent food, a good catch-up. Other than that, I'm either at work, ferrying kids around to various activities, or cooking and cleaning.

Halfway up the stairs I stop, feeling a pang as I realise my life has become nothing more than a timetable. Spontaneity, surprises and spur-of-the-moment decisions are a thing of the past. Holding on tight is the only way I know how to cope, to get through the months, to avoid slipping through the cracks.

Damn him to hell!

After I've checked on Freya – she was fine, happily doing a jigsaw in her room – and, of course, checked my phone again, I come back down. 'All cleared with Annie and Ed,' Mark says, giving me a thumbs up. 'Smudge in bed?'

'About to brush her teeth,' I say with a smile. He's always called her that, because of the little birthmark that looks smudged on the back of her neck. I take a bottle of Pinot from the fridge. 'Though when I told her Annie and Ed were maybe coming here, she assumed Lilly was coming too and got all excited.'

'But *their* babysitter didn't cancel.' Mark takes the wine I pour for him. 'So they can have a kid-free evening.'

I admit that, at seven, Freya's my little baby. My *only* baby. Jack is Mark's son from his first marriage and never got to know his real mum, Maria. Mark was widowed before we met, and Jack was only three. He has no memories of her.

Even now, it's hard not to think of Maria as the 'competition'. Mark loves me dearly, of course, and we're a family now, but it's tough to know that, given the choice, he'd rather she was still alive, that they were all together. I can't help feeling like the consolation prize. He once told me that they'd had plans for a big family, perhaps a move to the countryside, maybe even a holiday home abroad. It was hard to hear. I know Mark would love us to have more children, but I often wonder if it seems the same for him second time round with me. If I live up.

If I'm as good a wife as Maria.

As good a lover.

Truth is, since *him*, these feelings have got worse. My fears have been confirmed. Guilt will do that.

The doorbell rings and I hear a squeal as Freya comes running down the stairs.

'Careful, Frey, slow down or you'll trip.' It's a bit dim in the hallway. I still haven't found a replacement lamp for the one that got smashed last year.

Proves you vacuum, at least, Mark had said, when I'd told him I'd knocked it off the side table when hoovering. I didn't know what to say back; wasn't sure if he was joking.

He answers the door to Annie and Ed while I try to damp down my daughter's excitement. 'I told you, sweetie, Lilly's not coming this time. It's a grown-up night tonight.' I go to cuddle her, but she ducks away. 'We'll fix up a play date soon, OK?' She stomps back upstairs again, her arms folded across her pyjamas.

'Annie,' I grin, opening my arms and pulling my best friend close as they come in out of the rain. A waft of chilly air comes in with them. 'It's so good to see you both. Sorry about the babysitting fail.'

I take their coats, propping wet umbrellas in the porch, and we all get settled in the living room, each of them proclaiming not to mind about the change of plan. Mark puts some music on while I fetch the drinks. I hear him telling Ed how he first heard the electro swing band live in the Old Picture House, the place that's been converted into a music venue, how he can't get enough of their stuff.

'Here, help yourself,' I say, putting out some olives and mini stuffed peppers as well as a couple of takeaway menus to browse. I flop down next to Annie on one of the floor cushions. She prises off her shoes, exposing perfectly painted toenails, and spreads her long flowing skirt around her. It's peach and purple – something Mark would never allow me to wear – but it suits Annie. Free, easy, unafraid.

'These are lovely,' she says, patting the cushions. 'Though white's a brave choice. Tell me you're not turning into Charlotte?' She whispers the last bit, about Mark's house-proud sister. 'Lilly would trash these within a day with ice cream and paint.'

'I think the covers will wash pretty well,' I say. 'Anyway, Freya knows she isn't allowed anything messy in the living room. Mark wouldn't allow that.' I glance over at him, worried he might have heard. Even though I've been living here nearly nine years now, it still feels like his place, his rules. And I'm OK with that. 'How's the new head teacher working out?' I ask, wanting to change the subject.

'*So* much better than Daggers already,' she says, pulling a face. 'She's acting head for now but is applying for permanent for next year.'

'The shit hit the fan like you thought, then?'

'Yep. Thankfully, the governors took it seriously. Anyway, let's not talk about that. Our school is brilliant, and we lanced a boil.'

'Maybe I'll think about moving Freya there now,' I say. It's been on my mind since Freya's seemed… well, unsettled. The timing is no coincidence. Another wave of guilt hits me.

Annie shifts on her cushion, pulling up her knees and sipping more wine. She takes a stuffed pepper. 'But I thought she loved her school?' she says, chewing. Mark turns up the volume on his favourite track.

'She used to,' I say, wishing I could pour out my heart. But not even my best friend knows what I've done. 'I think she's a bit bored there.' It's partly the truth.

'But you can walk from here,' Annie says. 'You really want to have to drive?'

I laugh. 'We *rarely* walk. That's the irony. If I'm driving to work, I drop her off on my way and the childminder picks her up in her car. It would be just as easy to drive to your school.'

And then drive past *his* place just around the corner, I think, to see if his car is there, perhaps get a glimpse of him. Or *her*. I never once went inside.

Then, with perfect timing, my phone buzzes in my pocket. It's a call, not a text, so I let it go to voicemail, trying not to seem too distracted. If it was Jack, he'd call Mark first, not me. That alone hurts, that I'll never be as good as his real mum, the one he turns to first. For a long while he even refused to put my number into his phone, saying he wouldn't ever need it, that there was no point when he'd got Mark's. It was only after he broke his arm, and his school couldn't get hold of Mark that his dad insisted he have my number. I can count on one hand how many times he's used it.

The buzzing stops, and I wait for a voicemail notification, but none comes. I can see by the look on Annie's face that she heard the call too, but she says nothing.

'Anyway, it would be great knowing you're there, to watch her back.' I smile, refocusing on our conversation. Annie is Freya's godmother. She was there at her birth. If anything ever happened to me and Mark, I'd trust her implicitly to take care of our little girl. She and Lilly are like sisters anyway.

'Does she need her back watching, then?' Annie looks concerned.

My phone buzzes again, this time indicating a text.

'I… I'm not sure,' I say, pulling a face that tells her I don't want to talk about it now. I've not mentioned anything to Mark yet.

Annie gives me a knowing nod. 'We'll discuss it another time,' she says, topping up my wine as I feel my phone vibrate yet again. I close my eyes briefly.

'Right, what are we ordering?' I pass a menu to Annie and, while she reads over it, I steal a quick look at the screen. A missed call and two text messages from a number I don't recognise. Then another text alert flashes up from the same number.

'Everything OK?' Annie asks.

'Yeah, sorry,' I say, slipping my phone back in my pocket without reading the messages. I stare at the menu, even though my eyes won't take it in. Random texts from an unknown number is feast enough, filling me up, sating me – a time-slip back to how things were, even though I know it's not *him*. Couldn't possibly be. I never gave him this number. 'Shall we get one of the banquets to share?' I suggest, not feeling hungry any more.

'Good idea,' Mark agrees as he and Ed sort through a load of vinyl from his collection. 'Call it through, would you, love? Serious business going on here.' He grins, holding up a T. Rex disc, gently wiping it before placing it on the turntable. He crouches down low, squinting as he drops the stylus. Then my phone vibrates again and, while Mark's back is turned, I decline the call.

'Someone really wants you,' Annie says in a silly voice, without the men hearing. She gives me a look, nudging me.

'Bloody work,' I say, rolling my eyes, though she knows as well as I do that the clinic would never contact me on a Saturday night. I call through the food order, then switch off my phone, putting it in the kitchen drawer for the rest of the night. Just knowing it's there, with all those unread messages, is some kind of comfort. Some kind of cheap thrill. Even though it's not *him*.

Three boozy hours later and Annie and Ed stumble out to their taxi. 'Good luck next week, mate,' Mark says to Ed, patting him on the back. He's going on some family law training course.

'And enjoy your week,' I say to Annie, giving her a hug. She feels full and healthy beneath her woollen shawl, as though her body matches her personality. What does mine say about me, I wonder, wrapping my arms around myself, feeling my ribs, the cold air making me shiver?

'You coming Wednesday?' she asks. Book club is really just an excuse to meet up with wine and no husbands or kids.

'Sure am. Cath's place this time, isn't it?' Another evening checked off. Another night filled up, not spent thinking about *him*.

She nods. 'And don't overwork yourself,' she calls out. I'd already filled her in on my hectic week, how packed my client list is, not to mention the professional development course I have to attend. 'Get through till Wednesday and we'll recharge.' She stumbles and giggles. 'You know what Cath's like.'

'And don't think *we* don't know what she's like too,' Ed chips in with a grin, getting into the taxi.

Cath is the only single one in our group of friends, eternally dating and convinced 'the one' is out there. So far she's had no luck, attracting married guys, emotionally unavailable guys, and guys who just want one thing. But Cath still believes in love and is resolute about finding it.

'We'll fix her up with someone from the real world one of these days,' I say, feigning a swoon with the back of my hand. 'Not some moron with a fake profile online.'

Annie gets into the cab and we wave them off before going back inside, Mark locking up and putting the chain on before taking it off again. 'Just in case Jack decides not to stop over at the party,' he says.

Secretly, I hope that he doesn't come home in the small hours, waking us up, disturbing my already fragile sleep. My relationship with him has always felt fractured – a tentative dance, each of us unsure of the other. I've tried to make things OK, but sometimes it feels like I just make it worse.

'You're not my real mum,' he said once, aged ten. 'You can't tell me what to do.' I'd recoiled from his words. The expression on his face said it all. *He hated me.*

'But you can't do that in here, Jack,' I'd said, glancing at my watch. 'Please…' It wasn't long until Mark would be home, and Jack had decided to bring in a load of his dad's dirty tools from the shed. They were spread out on the pale living room carpet, along with his broken bicycle chain. There were grease and oil stains smeared everywhere. I begged him to pack it all away, that I'd help clean up the stains, but he refused.

'Dad won't mind. He's chilled and you're not,' he said, giving me a look I'd not seen on a child before.

Half an hour later he went out to play football, leaving the mess everywhere. I was scrubbing at the oil when Mark came home, breathless with worry.

'God, I'm so sorry, love,' I said, kneeling, scrubbing, rubber gloves on. It was coming off, but slowly. I told him I'd had an accident with the hearth blackener while I was cleaning but didn't realise that Jack was standing in the doorway, listening, watching, saying nothing. I'd hoped it would help me get onside with him, show him he could trust me, but all it did was make him act up more. He knew what he could get away with.

But I won't give up trying to reach out to him, to be something even vaguely close to the mother he never had. We went through a good patch when he was in his early teens, and I'd hoped things had settled, but recently, like Freya's, his mood has changed again.

It makes me wonder why. If it's me.

Kids pick up on adults' behaviour.

'That was a really lovely evening,' I say, leaning back against the wall.

'Mmm,' Mark confirms, pressing up against me. 'Lovely indeed.' He looks me up and down with boozy eyes, grabbing hold of me.

'I should clear up,' I say after he's kissed me. I pull away and head back into the living room to gather the foil cartons and plates.

'Let's leave it until the morning,' he says, his hand settling on my bum as I bend down.

'That's not like you,' I say, winking. 'Mr Shipshape. It won't take me a moment.' I wipe up the spilt food with a napkin, gathering up some plates and glasses. 'Anyway, Freya has Sunday school first thing, so we need some sleep.'

'Can't she miss it for once?'

'It was your idea she go in the first place,' I remind him.

Then the sigh, virtually imperceptible, although I know what it means. I close my eyes. 'OK,' I say, forcing a smile. 'Let's leave it until morning.' I dump the plates in the kitchen sink and turn off the lights. After everything, I can't deny him what he wants. I give him a slow wink, but Mark hesitates a second, his eyes narrowing before the small smile comes. Then he takes my hand and leads me upstairs.

Afterwards, I lie awake listening to Mark's breathing. All I can think of is my phone secreted in the kitchen drawer, the unread messages, the missed calls. All I can think of is *him*.

CHAPTER FOUR

Nikki

From where I'm sitting, the world is full of happy, contented, fulfilled women. Women quick-marching down the street, phones pressed to their ears, cups of steaming coffee to hand, laughter lines stretching their made-up faces. Women with purpose, women with zest, women with children, with loves, with jobs, with families – all painted nails and swishy hair, and those clippety-clip patent heels striding along the pavement, all in such a hurry to get where they're going.

Women like that know how to avoid the cracks. Me, I tread on them with every footfall.

Today is a watching day. It's either that or a shift with Denny in the burger van, the day ending with greasy skin and my hair smelling of onions. I have a usual bench, where I'm sitting now, overlooking the playground from a safe enough distance but still close enough to observe. Since lunchtime, it's been filling up with young mums and toddlers – some in buggies, some running free, one in a baby sling rounding its mother's shoulders as she struggles with its weight. If I were a man sitting here as often as I do, someone would have called the police by now. But being a woman, a book or newspaper to hand, I'm safe. No one suspects anything. To anyone who notices me, I'm just another mum watching her children play, an auntie fondly looking after her niece or nephew, or maybe even a woman waiting for her secret lover. Now there's a thought.

But I am none of these things.

The playground equipment is brightly painted, with noisy kids swinging, dangling, climbing and squealing. Grubby jeans, mittens on strings, baby dolls and toy cars fill the scene. One mother is on all fours filling a bucket with sand, while another pushes two swings at once. Other mums are chatting, huddled in groups, warming their hands on coffee cups, laughing and smiling.

And then there's me, my eyes stinging with tears.

I'm feeling especially brave today, so I get up and walk down to the spongy-tarmac play area. Close to where the children are. Close to where *she* stands with her friend, laughing, chatting, her white teeth flashing, their two little girls squealing together on the swings. I lean on the black metal railings surrounding the area, kicking my foot against them.

Thud, thud, thud...

It looks an awful lot like a prison, though I have no idea if I'm on the inside or the outside.

CHAPTER FIVE

Lorna

I lean over the reception desk to sign in, my bag falling off my shoulder as I write, making my name wonky – pretty much how I feel after another night of little sleep.

'Good weekend?' Sandy asks.

Her question makes me defensive – as if she knows something, when of course she doesn't. 'Yes. Lovely, thanks,' I reply, wondering if she'll notice how my expression doesn't quite match my words, or if she'll spot the tremor in my hand as I try to get the pen back in its holder. 'You?' I drop it down on the desk. *You've done nothing wrong*, I tell myself for the hundredth time since yesterday morning. Even though I have.

'Glad to get back to work, frankly,' she says. 'The in-laws came to stay so it's good to be back with sane people.' She gives a silly laugh before answering the phone, switching to her serious yet compassionate receptionist's voice.

Sane people, I think, heading through to my consulting room which, until Friday, felt like a sanctuary, a safe place, a space where I help people, a room where I focus on my clients as well as taking time out for myself, working on my own self-development – crucial for a good therapist. But today it feels as though work has seeped out of it, is bleeding under the door. As if I'm cupping water in my hands.

It was just a trigger, I tell myself. *A throwback… It's over now…*

I flick on the main lights as well as the two side lamps. It's gloomy outside – cool and overcast. I like things to feel warm and welcoming for my clients. *My* clients, I think, glancing at the clock on the wall – the clock that only I can see during sessions with barely a flicker of my eyes. My stomach churns. None of them actually belong to me.

At my desk, I take a deep breath. 'Sandy, hi,' I say, buzzing through to reception, knowing I need to just get this out of the way. I was too ashamed to do it face-to-face. 'I have a new client coming for an assessment at one o'clock today.' I pause, swallowing. 'In my lunch break.'

'Oh. Is this a self-referral?' she asks.

I clear my throat. 'Yes. Yes, it is,' I say. 'It's actually the person who kept calling on Friday, remember? Could you put him in the system, please?' Treating one client differently to another is not in the rulebook, let alone contacting them directly, especially in a practice such as this.

'Oh,' she says again. 'OK.' She knows it's odd but doesn't say anything. It's not her place to question me. That's *my* job, questioning myself, my professional behaviour. I know I should take this to a supervision session, to work out my feelings, but I also know I won't. Not about this. Not when, at its core, it's all about *him*.

I lean back in my office chair, sighing. I didn't get a chance to read those text messages from Saturday night until late yesterday morning. Mark and I went out for breakfast after we'd dropped Freya at Sunday school, and my phone was still in the kitchen drawer. The battery was flat when we came home so I charged it, but then Mark was with me for several hours as we flicked through the newspapers together, drinking coffee, chatting about the kitchen extension we've been considering. Besides, it was the anticipation I was after – nothing else. Just knowing the messages were there was enough. It was nothing to do with the content or even the sender – that was irrelevant, because it wasn't *him*. And besides, for the full effect, just this once, I wanted to read them alone. Gorge on illicit texts, which these most definitely were. It was an addiction. *He* was an addiction. It was a methadone situation.

But then we'd had a brief panic about Jack's whereabouts. He wasn't home and hadn't contacted Mark since the party on Saturday night. We couldn't reach him anywhere and his mates weren't sure where he was. It wasn't like him to not get in touch, so we drove around looking for him. But by midday he'd come back, sauntering through the door saying his phone was dead, that he'd gone for a walk to think about stuff and that it was no big deal. It was a big deal for us, though, and Mark let him know it in no uncertain terms. I know Jack's had stuff on his mind lately, that he's keeping things bottled up. I just don't know what. It doesn't feel right for me to push him, as if there's this unspoken buffer between us. After that, Jack sloped off upstairs for a while.

But a short time later he seemed OK again and was chatting with his dad in the kitchen as normal. I finally unplugged my phone, slipping it in my jeans pocket, heading down to the end of the garden. My heart was thumping and my throat tight and dry. I savoured every moment of it, pretending I was going to look for something in the shed even though no one batted an eyelid at me going outside. *I'm just popping to the shops... just taking a long bath... just going for a walk...to the cinema... the gym...* Echoes of the not-so-distant past.

And of course I still despise myself for it. Still despise *him* for being inside my head after all this time. To be the wife Mark deserves, the mother Freya and Jack need, I need him gone.

At the end of the garden, I held the phone in my hands, imagining, fantasising that if it was actually *him* who'd texted, what would he say? Maybe just a two-worder: *Love you* or *Miss you.* Or the promise of a meet – *Usual place, 6 p.m.* – or a cute emoji, or even a string of them to make a cryptic message like we used to do. Or perhaps one of the many soul-ripping exchanges we had, leaving me upset and edgy during the days of silence that would inevitably follow: *I can't do this any more… You don't understand… It's over…*

'You're a class A drug,' I whispered, glancing back up to the house. It looked warm and inviting inside the kitchen – Mark sitting at the table, his grey T-shirt stretching across his broad back, laughing with Jack, who was staring out of the kitchen window directly down the garden. I quickly ducked behind the shed.

I tapped my screen, looking at the notifications. The little white number sitting fat in its red globe looked like a ripe cherry. Full of promise and excitement. All those unread messages, little nuggets of delicious time snatched to read them, to savour the words, to type out a reply to him. I stared up at the sky, blinking back tears. Streaky mascara would raise questions and I wasn't ready for those.

It should never have happened.

And I still don't know why it did.

'Fucking, *fucking* hell,' I whispered, my head resting back against the wood. Over those few short months, there'd been thousands of messages between us – enough to gouge a planet-sized hole inside me. And here I was using the neediness of an innocent client that I'd never met to plug it up. To recreate the dangerous high.

I quickly opened the texts, holding my breath as I imagined what I *wanted* them to say, rather than what they actually said, which turned out to be mundane and intrusive, making me want to stamp on my phone.

It wasn't him.

Of course it wasn't him.

I'd like to arrange an appointment with you. Please phone back. David
Then…

Let me know asap. Monday preferred. David

Then…

You were recommended. Pls contact me with a time.

'And this is why we don't give out our fucking personal numbers,' I muttered, clenching the phone in my fist. The effect was not what I was hoping for. Nothing to work with. There was no thrill, no fire in my heart, no head pounding with guilt that screamed out good sense while my body ignited from his words. And I already didn't like this David person, being so demanding and needy, especially over the weekend. But whoever he was, whether he ended up being my client or not, he was already different from the others. I'd made sure of that by contacting him personally.

I can see you at 1 p.m. Monday, I texted back, my fingers shaking. But in my mind, I was typing *I love you too…*
My phone pings in my bag under my desk.

Squash cancelled. Dinner?

I smile, tucking it away again. I sit and stare at the pot plant in the corner, a palm of some type that could do with watering. A couple of leaves are brown and crisp at the edges, though it still manages to unfurl a new frond from the centre every month or so. The life force within, that driving essence behind all living things, never giving up, making the best of what's available. It's what makes people come to therapy amidst their hopelessness. I take a pair of scissors from the desk drawer and snip off the brown bits, tossing them in the bin.

Do I want dinner with my husband?

I take a breath, putting the scissors back in the drawer in exactly the same place.

That would be lovely. See you later x

I shake my head, chasing the thoughts away by straightening the papers on my desk. Order, order, *order*! My first appointment isn't until 9 a.m. so I still have time for a coffee and to review this morning's three clients.

Back in reception, several people are already in the waiting area. 'Sandy,' I say quietly. 'If you're popping down to the deli later, would you be able to pick me up a salad? I won't get a lunch break today because…'

She glances up, giving me a look. 'Of course,' she says, one eyebrow raised. She taps away at her computer, no doubt still curious why I contacted a client myself.

'Morn, Lorn.' Joe comes out of the back room carrying a mug of coffee. He gives me a wink, a pat on the arm.

'Hey,' I reply, all of us aware there are two clients waiting already. There's none of our usual chatter, nor the bear hug Joe would have given me had it been private. He's the only one of my colleagues to do this and, while we're all neatly boxed up within our professional boundaries as soon as we step inside the clinic, somehow it doesn't seem wrong coming from him.

Or maybe it's just me who's boxed up.

'I need one of those,' I say, pointing at his coffee.

'Lorna,' Joe says, following me into the staffroom. 'Have you got a moment?' He closes the door behind us.

'Sure,' I say. Can he read the guilt on my face? As my supervisor, Joe has my best interests at heart and we have regular sessions to discuss my clients and their progress, as well as my own issues. Supervision is a bit like therapy for the therapist. 'What's up?'

'Sit down,' he says, a serious look on his face.

CHAPTER SIX

Lorna

Tom is fifteen minutes late and, by the time he arrives, I've downed another cup of coffee and written a couple of referral reports. I'm swigging the last drop when Sandy buzzes me to tell me he's in the waiting area. I go out to greet him, immediately spotting from the way he walks, the way he holds his head, that he's not had a good week.

'Have a seat, Tom,' I say, closing the door behind us. He chucks his bomber jacket on the end of the sofa and drops down onto the dark grey fabric. There's water on the side table in case he wants it, though he never does, and a box of tissues within easy reach. Plus, I brought in the small, nameless plant that Freya gave me for Mother's Day yesterday to brighten the room a little, to remind me of my little girl while I work.

Then I think of my own mother and the gift she was reluctant to accept from me. I thought I was doing the right thing for once. Even as a child, she seemed to despise everything I did, made me feel guilty for even breathing. 'You know I can't leave your father for that long,' she said, staring at the voucher. After taking Freya to the park yesterday afternoon, I'd popped over to see her. 'What do I want with a new hairdo anyway?'

'I thought you deserved a treat,' I told her, glancing at my father as he sat in the chair. He didn't comment, of course. 'And Dad will be fine for a couple of hours. Won't you, Dad?' I said, glancing at Mum, hoping she'd accept.

'See?' she said, shrugging. 'I can tell he's not happy about it.'

'Dad doesn't mind, Mum. He'll barely notice you're gone. Anyway, I can always come over and sit with him while you go to the salon. You'll enjoy getting out, chatting with people.'

Mum put the voucher on the mantelpiece, at least, which showed a glimmer of hope that she might actually use it, treat herself. Being stuck inside with Dad all the time wasn't healthy, but it had been that way for years. She'd pretty much turned into a recluse apart from when she came over to us – sometimes with Dad, sometimes without.

'How are things?' I ask Tom, settling into the chair opposite him. It's just the right distance away – not too intimate, yet not so far away I seem detached. I cross my legs, making sure my skirt stays at knee level.

He shrugs.

'OK,' I say. 'You seem a bit like you don't know, or maybe don't want to say?'

Another shrug, though he's looking at me, almost as if he wants me to guess. I hold his gaze, aware of him wringing his hands in his lap.

'How have you been sleeping?'

Tom shakes his head. 'Not great.'

'You sound exhausted.'

He nods. 'It's more than tiredness. It's like my body's giving up on things, you know? I thought I could deal with it, get back on track, but it's getting worse.'

'OK, so you don't feel like you're functioning properly?'

'Nope. Especially not on Mondays.'

'Sunday night sleep is still the worst?'

'Yes. Sunday nights I can never sleep. Not a second, literally.' He stares at his fingers. 'It's, like, hardwired into me, as if my body knows it can't relax or let go on a Sunday night.'

'So it's become a pattern for you, that you can't relax on Sundays?'

'Yeah,' he says. 'Aren't you supposed to just tell me how to fix it?'

It's only our third session, so I'm not expecting much yet. I'm still trying to connect with him, forge our relationship, but he constantly shuts me out. 'I'm hoping that we'll be able to discover together what's going on for you, Tom. It's not simply a case of you telling me that you can't sleep and me giving you the answers.' I give him a small smile as he pushes his hands through bleached hair. The roots are black and greasy. 'With my help, with you sharing your feelings, I'm confident you'll be able to find your own answers.'

'But my parents are paying you for advice. Can't you just tell me what to do?'

Tom is only nineteen, studying at university, and has been falling behind with his work. His OCD is virtually at the point where he can't leave the house, and he finds it difficult to form and maintain relationships with people his own age. His tutor has given him a final warning, and he smokes weed from the moment he gets up.

I make a little sound to show I've heard him. 'Well, firstly, I don't give advice. But the way you say it, it makes me think you want "advice" to appease your parents rather than to be of benefit to you?'

Tom shrugs again and sighs heavily. 'They're only doing this to cover their guilt. They don't really give a shit. They just want me and my problems to go away. They hate me.' He slides down in his chair, chin resting on his breastbone, fingers clasped across his chest. His legs are spread wide. 'And I hate them. Especially my mother.'

'So by paying for your sessions, you think your parents hate you?'

He's silent for a while, then takes a tin out of his jacket pocket. He pulls out a ready-rolled joint and a lighter. 'That's what it feels like, yes.'

'I'm afraid you can't smoke in here, Tom.'

He puts it between his lips. 'That other shrink used to let me.'

'For a start I'm not a shrink, I'm a psychotherapist,' I say with a slight smile. 'And I'm afraid this building is completely no smoking. You can go outside if you want, but you'll be wasting more of your session.' He's testing me, I know, but if he chooses to go outside to smoke, I will show that, within our allotted time, I'll still be here waiting for him when he comes back inside. It's all about boundaries, him knowing where he stands. It's unlikely he'll have experienced such a relationship before.

And then *he's* on my mind again… swooping in at just the wrong moment.

'Fuck it,' he says, throwing the joint down beside him. 'I don't even know what to say any more. It's like my feelings are all dried up.'

'I get that,' I tell him. 'I get how hard it is sometimes to say the things we most need to. Like they're stuck – or dried up, as you say.' I hold a loose fist against my throat.

Tom nods, his cheeks reddening as he turns away. 'It was like, when I was eight, I stopped sleeping. Mainly on Sundays but other days too. Back then, I never knew when it was all right to sleep. It was like, if I didn't, then everything was fine. Even though it wasn't.'

'OK…' I shift my position, leaning forward slightly. 'So it sounds like you almost felt afraid to sleep, that if you kept awake, everything would be all right?'

'Yeah, that's it exactly,' he says, staring straight at me. For the remainder of our session, Tom talks about how he's ruined his parents' lives, how they never wanted him, how he was an accident and should have been aborted. He says he hates himself. He doesn't cry, but he's close to it.

After our session ends, Tom's mum is waiting in reception to drive him home. She doesn't look at me as I say goodbye, telling him I'll book him in for the same time next week.

'Chicken salad OK?' Sandy asks, squaring up a stack of client files on her desk. I sense a different tone to her voice but could be imagining it.

'Thanks,' I say. 'Can you book Tom in for his regular slot again, please?' I head back to my office to make a few quick notes, then go to collect my next client from the waiting area. She's always on time and never tries to run over the end of our session like some.

After that, I only have one more appointment booked for this morning – Brian, a long-term client – but Sandy tells me he cancelled half an hour ago. 'He apologises profusely and says he'll come next week.'

'Thanks, Sandy,' I say, feeling slightly thrown. Or maybe it's because I'm concerned that she's still curious about my unusual lunchtime booking, my guilt rearing up again. But I can hardly tell her that I only did it to make me feel alive again, that I only broke strict ethical guidelines for selfish reasons, just to feel the high, to get a fix. To feel close to *him* again even just for a second.

Back in my office, I tap my pen on my desk, staring at the clock, sighing. There's still an hour before the new client comes – the poor, unwitting person I'm projecting my mess onto. I'm already thinking up excuses to explain why I texted him directly, how it's not normal practice, how we won't be doing it again. I'm terrified he'll make a complaint.

That's what *he* said once, when we had a big fight. *One* of our big fights. That he'd report me, have me struck off. Then he stormed out, leaving me reeling. Leaving me shrunken and fearful, terrified of the consequences.

'Heard you'd got a no-show,' Joe says, poking his head round the door, making me jump. 'Fancy an early bite of lunch?' There's none of the earlier concern in his voice, nothing that gives away that he thinks I'm losing it. In the staffroom earlier, I did a good job of convincing him that all was fine, that I didn't need extra supervision, that my workload was manageable and there was nothing extraordinary on my mind. But it made me suspect that Sandy had said something to him about what I'd done.

How could I have been so stupid?

'It's just that you've seemed a bit distant these last couple of weeks, Lorn,' he'd said earlier. 'Want to talk about it?' A therapist who's not there for herself isn't going to be there for anyone else either, and that's part of Joe's job – to flag any issues with the clinical team, to offer support and help.

'Have I?' I'd replied, sipping my coffee. 'Really, I'm fine.'

Not fine.

'Everything OK at home?' he'd asked, taking me by surprise. It's not the sort of thing he'd usually broach unless I brought it up.

'Sure.' I shrugged, trying to look perplexed.

He'd smiled then, that wide, beaming Joe smile that shifted the geography of his face upwards. 'Good,' he said, though I didn't fail to notice the little twitch at the corner of his eye.

'Er, paging Lorna…?' Joe says from the doorway. 'I said, do you fancy some lunch?' He grins, one hand toying with his beard.

'Oh God, sorry, Joe. You caught me in deep thought. I've got an assessment soon and I really should catch up with some notes right now, plus I have some reading to get through for my course and—'

'It's OK,' he says, holding up a hand. 'If you change your mind in the next half-hour, let me know.' He pauses, as though he's going to say something else, but then shuts the door behind him.

In truth, there's nothing I'd like more than to go for lunch with Joe, have him listen to me, hear the whole sorry story, spew it out instead of leaving it to rot inside me. I imagine his expression slowly changing as I drip-feed him, bit by sordid bit – his eager smile transforming into a tight frown as he realises what I've done. But I can't do that. I'll *never* do that. Even therapists have secrets.

CHAPTER SEVEN

Nikki

I stretch out in bed, forcing myself awake, wondering if today is the day. I sense it's not. Not yet.

I didn't sleep well last night. Usually sleep comes easily – an escape, a respite. Perhaps it's because I know the time is drawing closer, my mind unable to switch off, running over how it's going to happen, what I'm going to do. My plan is sketchy, but when I do finally meet her, I'm concerned all she's going to notice are the dark circles under my eyes, my twisted mouth biting back everything I want to say. I know she'll pity me, think I'm crazy, send me on my way feeling smug and oh-so grateful she's not me.

After I drag myself out of bed and wash myself down in the tiny shower across the creaky landing, I rub a towel over my short hair. The mirror is dirty, the foxing on it overlaying my skin to make me appear twenty years older, all freckles and distortions. She'd like that, I think – if I was old and past it. No competition for her in her perfect life. Complete with her *lover*. I'm determined to look my best when we finally meet. I found a scarlet lipstick dropped outside the burger van last week, so I shoved it in my pocket. I can't afford things like that for myself.

I dab some on my lips now, puckering up, deciding I'll wear it when I meet her. A scarlet woman. That's what she'll think as I laugh like a witch, when really she's no better herself. Her do-good therapy crap won't fix me. Besides, she'll need a few sessions herself after she hears what I've got to say.

Sometime after ten, I lock up my room and head out. I'm just a lodger, holed up on the top floor of a wonky old house with a tiny bathroom and a kitchen shared with the landlord.

The landlord and the lodger. Such a cliché.

It should be a hundred and fifty pounds a week, but I pay a lot less. I've been here two years now, the longest I've stayed anywhere for ages. 'Bye,' I call out from the hallway. My landlord smiles, mumbling something from the kitchen, something about an appointment later, that he'll be out for a while and could I take a delivery of paint and brushes for him.

'Sure,' I say, flicking him a wave, not knowing if I'll be back or not. It's often unpredictable where I'll end up.

The cool morning air makes my nostrils flare as I step outside, breathing it in. I take the familiar route to where Denny's had the van parked recently, dumping my jacket and bag under the tiny counter. No doubt we'll get moved on soon. First thing I do is open up the hatch, heat up the hotplates and get the coffee on.

'Nice lipstick, chick,' Denny says, rasping out a laugh that ends in a smoker's cough.

'Thanks,' I say, opening up the freezer compartment to pull out two boxes of burgers. I glance at the grease-stained clock above the small sink. Seven hours to go. Seven hours to fill with buns and onions and cans of pop. And, when she leaves work, I'll be waiting, watching her every step.

CHAPTER EIGHT

Lorna

A few minutes before one o'clock, Sandy buzzes me to let me know that my new client has arrived. Any thrill from his texts has long since gone. Like any good therapist, I'm aware of my feelings. Nothing goes unnoticed or unused in this job.

Cath says I overthink everything, that I analyse stuff to death and see things that no one else would pick up on. But it's second nature to me – noticing every single word someone uses, every muscle twitch and look, and every movement made and awkward silence.

'You'd bloody well read something into the angle the postman drops the letters through the door, you would,' she said, laughing, last time we met. But I took it on board, thought about it lots – *of course* – and I laughed along with them too. Cath, Annie, Megan, Charlotte – none of my friends know anything about what happened last year. Keeping secrets is part of my job.

Cupping water in my hands... I think, shaking my head as I gather up the rubbish from my lunchtime salad, chucking it in the bin. I check there's a clean glass on the table and enough tissues in the box, glancing in the mirror to fix my hair. I like to collect my clients exactly two minutes before their session begins. This allows them time to come into my office, take off their coat, settle down and catch their breath before we begin. But, just as

I'm leaving the room, my phone pings. I turn back, grabbing it from my bag. Even now, ten months on, the sound still gets me.

Jack's agreed to babysit Freya, so we have a whole evening's pass. Dinner then a movie? xx

I stare at it for a moment, frowning, before flicking it onto silent. Mark knows I usually I do other things on a Monday – calling friends, doing my nails, reading, taking a candlelit bath, journaling. All those self-care things I preach to others but despise doing myself. It's only for distraction. To fill a void. But then my mind swerves onto what I *used* to be doing on Monday nights a year ago and my cheeks burn, my heart races. I hold on to the desk, taking a deep breath.

'Get a fucking grip,' I whisper to myself, glancing at my watch. A minute past one already. *Dammit.*

Sandy glances up as I come into reception, the sound of my footfall changing as I tread from soft carpet to tiles. There are two people waiting. A woman, facing me, and a man, dark-haired, with his back to me. I don't immediately notice the lurch in my stomach. It's more of an undercurrent, but it soon turns into something I can't ignore. The looming rise of a tsunami.

'Hello,' I say, walking up behind him. The odd feeling grows, creeping up my throat, choking me, even though I don't know what it means. Habit makes me offer my usual kind, welcoming smile, but it quickly falls away when he turns around.

Him.
Shit.
No!
'David…?'
My new client.
Not David.
Andrew.

I can't breathe.

I can't run.

He's staring up at me. His shoulders square and firm, his hair cropped short at his neckline, longer on top. The scar forking out from his top lip.

Then I feel the full force of the fear in my stomach, like I've been kicked. A crunching twist in my guts as he stands. Taller than me, of course. Looming and present. My body screams out at me. Betrays me. I'm shaking inside, the tremors vibrating from deep within – through my heart, my chest, my legs, arms, shoulders and right down to my fingertips. Everything's numb, yet I feel on fire. I grip on to the back of a chair.

A year dissolves into nothing.

Speak, Lorna!

'Hello, um, hello David.' My voice is thin and unconvincing.

He gives a small nod, blank-faced, waiting for me to continue. His strong features hold fast. Exactly how I remember.

I'm drowning.

'Please, come through.' I look away. I can't hold his eyes any longer.

I know Sandy's watching, scrutinising. All my senses are in overdrive: a dog barking outside sounds as if it's trapped inside my head, the tick of the clock is like a hammer, passing cars are an earthquake and a mother calling out to a child in the street is a fire alarm. The lilies on the reception desk smell of paint, making me want to retch, and the tiles beneath my feet are like walking on shards of glass. Even my clothes hurt.

Walk!

I force my feet to move, one in front of the other. Click. Click. Click. I see my hand reaching out for the big old brass knob on the door to my office. My feet sink into the plush green carpet as I step inside, making me feel as though I'm sinking in quicksand.

All I want now is numbness. Detachment. Dissociation. Monday nights.

But, thank God, something inside me takes over. Ingrained habit from seeing thousands of clients over the years – a second nature kicking in. Whatever it is, I'm grateful. I swing around, holding the door as he follows me in, gesturing towards the sofa with my arm.

'Please, take a seat.' It's more of a croak, not quite proper words.

He says nothing. His jacket – *oh how I remember that jacket* – slips off his shoulders in one easy move. He drapes it on the sofa, lowering himself down, hitching up the legs of his jeans, adjusting a cushion. All the time his eyes are on me – I can feel the heat on my skin.

I want to scream, punch something, but instead I close the door, manage to go to my desk and pick up my notepad and pen even though there's no way in hell I can go through with this assessment. I sit down, trembling, thinking how to get out of it.

'Why are you *here*?' I whisper, leaning forward and glancing at the door. My voice is deep and low now. It doesn't sound like me.

He stares at me. 'I miss you.'

That voice.

For a moment I think I must be going crazy, that I'm in the middle of one of my dreams – the ones where he and Mark meet by mistake – or that I'm perhaps in a psychiatric hospital: the sectioned therapist, drugged on medication.

'You shouldn't have come here.'

'I'm paying for it.' That look. Those eyes.

No, *I'm* paying for it, I think. Paying for my stupidity.

'You know that's not what I mean.'

'I need your help,' he says, relaxing his shoulders, making my heart slow to a steadier pace for a couple of beats – *he needs me*. It's just muscle memory, I think, forcing it to kick up again. It's fight or flight I need right now, not to be lulled by his smooth words and charm. 'I'd like to start up therapy again.'

I fight the urge to laugh. It would come out as hysteria. 'It's impossible,' I say. 'Unethical.' I clear my throat. 'But of course I can get you an appointment with a different therapist. You'll still have a full assessment.' I wait but he says nothing. 'Though I think under the circumstances, another practice entirely would be best.'

'But it's *you* I want to see, Lorna.'

I close my eyes briefly.

'How did you find me?' I take my glasses off. Put them on again.

Hearing him say my name makes me melt inside. It's been ten long months. Each one bound up with tight routine, making sure each day is stuffed to the brim with work, activities for Freya or other scheduled evening pastimes. No space to think about how things used to be. It was because of *him* that I changed jobs last June. I keep telling myself that I never asked for any of it.

'Answer my question – how did you find me?'

Thing is, I know it's not hard. Not hard to find me at all. Moving jobs wasn't so much to run away from him, but rather to escape the fear. The longer I stayed at my old clinic, the Medway, the more likely it was that I'd have slipped up, been found out, not to mention what could have happened if things had turned nasty between us. My career would have been finished.

He laughs, shaking his head, looking around my office, drinking it all in as if he's just catching up with me over a coffee. Him assessing *me*.

'I like it when you're bossy,' he says, ruffling his hair and rolling up his shirt sleeves. I can't help the glance at his forearms. Strong, muscled, just the right amount of hair. I hate what he does to me. What he's always done to me, from the moment I first laid eyes on him. I still don't understand it. It's not for want of soul-searching.

Then thoughts of how it was, how things used to be for those few intense months, ransack my mind, trying to protect me – second phones secreted away, a car cruising slowly by my house late at night checking who's home. Thousands of texts, missed calls, scuppered meets because Freya was ill, or Annie asking why she never saw me any more. Mark puzzled but patient, concerned for me when I told him my odd mood was probably just hormonal, or that I was stressed at work. All the cheap hotels with the late-afternoon sun streaking across our sweaty bodies. Lunchtime hangovers and hidden gifts. Cancelled clients, fake doctor's appointments, explanations, excuses, excitement and lies… Exhausting doesn't come close. Exhilarating, intoxicating and wrong only touch the surface. I exposed my soul, gave it away.

I still haven't got it back.

And Mark. In all of this there was Mark – kind, generous, loving, devoted and hard-working. He doesn't deserve someone like me. It's true. I *am* second best.

'How did you find me?' I repeat, my voice quiet.

'Lorna,' he says, leaning forward, his dark eyes drawing me in. 'I never lost you.'

CHAPTER NINE

Lorna

I wipe my lips and scrunch up my napkin, placing it on the table. My pasta was delicious – Mark's choice, of course. He always knows what I like, what's best. The restaurant, our usual Italian place, was busy when we arrived, but Mark wangled a spot. Wherever he goes, he's able to work his way around people, getting what he wants with a smile, witty quips and a promise to return the favour one day. It's what I like about him, that he looks out for us, for *me*, for my happiness. Never taking no for an answer. And he seems happy tonight, which makes me glad. Eases the guilt by the most minuscule amount. He pulls my hand across the table, our fingers meshing like familiar pieces of a puzzle, reminding me how much I love him. How much he loves me.

'How was work today?' I ask.

He stares at me, an appreciative look in his eye. In truth, it's probably been a long time since I've shown an interest.

'Really busy. How about you?'

'Ditto,' I say, and we exchange a fond look – the look that says we're both remembering. "Ditto" was what I replied to Mark the first time he told me he loved me. I'd explained that *Ghost* was my favourite movie ever, where I'd got it from. He'd never seen it, but now, every time I say "ditto", it's an unspoken reminder of how much we're in love.

'The day flashed by,' he goes on, taking the last piece of garlic ciabatta. 'Surgery for most of the morning,' he says, chewing. 'A bloody tough extraction.' He swigs some of his beer. 'Fractured root canal, and this one was a bitch. Upper right three that is, not the patient.' He laughs at his own joke. 'Mind you, she did honestly think she was going to die, especially when I was drilling into her bone for the implant.' He rolls his eyes, a small smile curling one side of his mouth. 'I love dealing with the nervous ones,' he says, something flaring in his eyes.

'Well, I sympathise with her,' I say, pulling a silly face. 'You know what I was like before I met you.' It's true, I was terrified of going to the dentist before Mark. But soon after we got together, he had my teeth straightened, whitened – gleaming and flawless. Not that they were bad in the first place. Far from it, in fact. But he liked his women perfect, he told me; liked them to be the best they could be. That he thought me so worthy of the finishing touches, the gentle way he'd treated me during the treatment, I admit, it made me fall for him all the more. I wanted to be the best I could be for him. I still do.

'Then it was mostly routine stuff this afternoon. Guilty mothers justifying why their kids' mouths were full of rot.' Mark drains his beer before stretching back in his chair. 'Fine by me,' he says. 'Keeps me in business.'

'Messed-up mouths and messed-up minds,' I say quietly, wondering what that says about the pair of us.

The cinema is virtually empty, probably because the movie has been out for a few weeks and didn't get great reviews anyway. But Mark wanted to see it, insisted he was a fan of the main actor, though having just seen the lead female actress, part of me bristles that she's the real reason he wanted to come. Thirty minutes in and she's barely worn clothes.

I have no right to feel this way.

'Just going to the loo,' I say, leaning in to whisper.

'You always do that,' he replies, giving me a look.

'Sorry,' I say quietly, getting up and following the floor lights out into the corridor. The toilets are empty, so I whip my phone from my bag, my heart thumping as I check the screen. Nothing.

I shove it back in my bag and go into a cubicle. Back then, he never had my main phone number. We were way more careful than that. But now, because of my stupidity, he does. Mark and I freely access each other's phones, always have done, which is why I used a second phone last year – an old one I'd kept after upgrading. The rabbit hole had got deeper and deeper.

I sigh, leaning back against the wall, not particularly wanting to sit through an hour and a half of car chases and a helpless, half-naked woman. Bombs, explosions and Bond-style shenanigans aren't my cup of tea. Especially not the punch-ups. And despite all my lone trips to the cinema last year, telling Mark I needed 'me' time, self-care time, I never actually went. I never saw one single movie. Instead I was holed-up in a cheap hotel with *him*.

I wash my hands, noticing the shiver, the shudder, as I think of the person I was, who I'd become without even realising it. The woman I vowed never to become again. I love Mark and he deserves all of me – the woman he fell in love with years ago.

'Oh God, *why…*' I say, almost in tears, trailing off as a girl comes into the toilets. She gives me a strange look and goes into a cubicle. Then I give myself a similar look in the mirror above the sink. A stern look. A look that tells me to watch it, that I'm dangerously close to veering off the straight and narrow.

'Fuck, fuck, *fuck* him to hell,' I whisper, staring at the drawn, tired woman I've become.

Back in my seat, I take hold of Mark's arm, curling mine around his and pressing my head against his shoulder. It feels safe. He reaches through and holds my other hand, reminding me of when we were dating and all over each other – of all the dinners he bought me, the romantic walks, kissing in the rain, cooking for each other, sizing up each other's food likes and dislikes. Eventually, we became a *thing* – a couple – though it took a long while. I'd worked out he was likely still grieving for Maria when we met, judging by the way he so rarely mentioned her. And when he did, there was always a look of regret about him, that perhaps he wished I was her. It was ages before he could even hint to me how she died, but I liked that it wasn't rushed between us, that he took his time, that we were able to get to know each other gradually, thoroughly, deeply.

Mark and Lorna. Lorna and Mark.

Lorna and *him*.

I stare at the screen but have lost track of what's going on. Then Cath is on my mind again – all her dating stories. Her loves, her hates, her successes and her heartbreaks. There have been dozens over the last year or two, and it makes me so grateful to have Mark. I know he's my forever man, which makes what I did even harder to understand. Poor Cath came out of a long-term relationship and hasn't properly healed. As a therapist, it's obvious she's still on the rebound, though she won't admit it. And as her friend, there's not a damn thing I can do apart from be there as she crawls through the wormholes of Tinder and various other dating sites she's always showing us all, Mark and Ed included. I think she hopes they'll have some single mates she can meet.

I jump, suddenly screaming. A bomb just exploded, making my ears ring and the floor vibrate.

'Didn't see that one coming,' I say into Mark's ear, laughing.

He looks at me, perhaps for a moment too long. 'That's because you weren't paying attention,' he whispers back.

'You like her, don't you?' I say playfully. It's pure projection, of course. We're in the car, Mark driving. He pulls out of the car park, swinging onto the main road. 'Go on, admit it.' He knows I'm winding him up, making a silly thing out of it, but he doesn't know why. Doesn't know that I actually want him to confess to it, that I *want* him to hurt me. Payback.

'Who do I like?'

'That blond actress, what's-her-name in the movie...'

I wait for his response but he's concentrating on the round-about. It's dark as we head back into Fulham from south of the river. We rarely go into central London these days, preferring the more local cinemas and restaurants.

'Don't you?' I press again.

It was something he said way back, not long after we met – something so small and insignificant that I should probably have laughed it off. I frown, not wanting to make a thing out of it now, but equally I do. I want to make a thing so big, so vile and offensive that Mark has no choice but to pull over, yell at me, spit in my face and hit me for being a complete bitch.

And there's Cath in my head again. *God, stop overthinking everything, will you, Lorn? You're a fecking nightmare...*

'What are you chuckling at?' Mark says.

Cath does that, brings a smile to everyone's face even when she's hurting inside. 'You've definitely got a thing for that actress, haven't you?'

'I've got a thing for *you*,' he says, sliding his hand onto my thigh.

'Stop it, you,' I say, taking his hand and sliding it under my skirt. I hold it there, warm against my skin, making us both just want to get home.

But those words, those words from way back about a month after we met. At the time, he'd not even introduced me to his family or friends – that came way later – and perhaps he was only trying to be complimentary, make me feel good. What he said has haunted me ever since, made me feel second best even more.

'You know what, Lorn?' he'd said. We were on the balcony of my flat, sipping wine on a warm night. I'd not been to his place at that point. He'd got his hands on my hips and we were pressed close, swaying to the music playing inside. 'I've always had a thing for busty blondes...'

He stared at me, drinking me up, pressing the length of his body against mine. I didn't have a chance to react before he spoke again. 'But I think I've just got myself a new type...' His mouth came down on mine then, one hand pushing through my long dark hair, the other feeling out the leanness of my athletic body, my small breasts.

He'd made me feel like the most special woman in the world, while also making me feel like the most ugly and unwanted, planting a make-believe woman in my mind. Almost as if she'd been there all along.

'Hey, Jack,' Mark calls out as we go inside. 'All OK, mate?' I squeeze his arm, giggling, telling him to shush or he'll wake Freya. Last thing I need is a grumpy daughter in the morning because she didn't get enough sleep. She's been acting up enough recently as it is. I hate seeing my little girl fractious; hate it that it's likely my fault because I've not given her the attention she deserves lately.

Jack's sprawled on the sofa, laptop on his legs, headphones clamped across his head. He raises a hand, which Mark high-fives as he walks past.

'Freya's fine,' he says, turning off his music. 'She was asleep by eight. Have a good evening, you two?'

You *two*. It doesn't go unnoticed and neither does the almost warm look he gives me. I smile in return, feeling, for just a moment, something like his real mother. It's hard to live up to someone he doesn't even remember. Mark's always been considerate and doesn't like to mention Maria if I'm around, and he's never been one for talking much about her, but he did tell me she was killed in an accident. I know all too well from my job how tragedy weaves into the psyche. I hoped in time he'd open up about it more, and I once suggested he get some grief counselling, perhaps with Jack, but he was reluctant. I didn't pressure him, gave him the space he wanted. It doesn't take a therapist to work out that he blames himself for what happened.

'Hungry?' I ask Jack.

'Nah, Frey and I ordered in pizza. I'm stuffed.' He turns back to his computer for a second but then looks up again. 'But thanks. There's some left if you fancy a slice.'

I nod, giving him another little smile before joining Mark in the kitchen. It's the small breakthroughs that mean the most.

'Bed, then?' he says, taking me by the hips and inching up my skirt little by little. His mouth is against mine, the vibrations of his words tingling my lips.

'Definitely,' I reply, hoping it will help get rid of the ghosts in my head. My phone pings in my bag on the table, then twice more in quick succession.

'Someone wants you,' Mark says, pulling back from me.

'Yeah, well, they can wait,' I say, reaching inside my bag and switching it off.

Later, with Mark softly snoring beside me – not enough of an annoyance to make me him roll over, but just enough to show me that he's satisfied, content, in a deep sleep – I lie awake, staring at the ceiling.

Three messages. *Three*. At eleven o'clock at night.

Cath, perhaps, or Annie. Or… *him*.

Another wakeful hour later, with Mark so deeply asleep I doubt even the smoke alarms would rouse him, I get out of bed and tread softly down the stairs.

CHAPTER TEN

Lorna's Journal

Reading back over old therapy journals is cathartic, they say, the whole point of writing them in the first place – which is why I'm doing exactly that. Hoping that by going back over old ground, the events of last year, it will throw light on how I need to act now, what I need to do to put an end to the situation I've found myself in. It wasn't something I ever intended on doing, reading this, and it almost feels as if I'm prying into the life of a different woman, someone I don't even recognise any more. But perhaps that will help me make sense of what I need to do to make everything right in this family. Put it back to how it was. Back when I was in control.

19 January 2017

It's been a while since I put pen to paper. Hardly surprising with all the Christmas shopping, arrangements, entertaining, cramming in clients before the break and having Freya on school holidays. Mark had to stay late at the surgery a few nights, sometimes not coming home until after ten. I felt so sorry for him. Most of the festive arrangements fell to me, but that's OK as he was so exhausted. Over the break it was nice to see him doing very little apart from hang out with the kids and relax. I know it's a tough time of year for him.

Sometimes it feels like there's a hole inside him and I'm the wrong shape to fill it.

Though I didn't help matters when I came back with the Christmas food shop. Writing it down here makes me feel a tiny bit less guilty. It wasn't my intention to upset Mark, but it was murder in the supermarket, and I was so behind with preparations. I hoped he'd be happy when I showed him my grocery haul. But he just stared at everything as he poured himself a whisky and ginger.

'What's that?' he said, watching me unpack.

'It's organic,' I said, patting the turkey. 'I was lucky. It was the last one. Another woman was going for it, but I just got in first.' I laughed as I put it in the fridge along with everything else. How I'd got all those bags home alone, including all the bottles, beats me. I hadn't had a chance to eat all day.

'But Maria always cooked goose,' he said. 'You know that.'

I stopped, the fridge door open, my back to Mark. I closed my eyes. 'I'm sorry, but...' I blinked away the tears. '... but there weren't any geese left,' I said, turning, smiling. 'I thought we could have turkey this year.'

Mark nodded. Truth was, I'd stood staring at the geese in the supermarket for ages, thinking about Maria, wondering how she would have prepared it, if she'd have made the traditional apple sauce herself, crisping up the roast potatoes in the goose fat. Day to day, I'm pretty good at not thinking about her when I use the kitchen, the things she'd have used too. Some of the stuff is mine, of course, from when I moved in, but when the Christmas crockery comes out once a year, somehow she seems to be standing over me, watching, folding her arms and shaking her head. Anyway, it's probably just me being oversensitive. I know the psychology behind it all, of course, but knowing it is one thing. Feeling it is quite another.

As it turned out, everyone loved the turkey on Christmas Day, especially Mark, thank God. He ate so much of it! And he got through the day remarkably well, considering how loaded it must be for him. I think I did a good job of making everyone happy. And he gave me the most beautiful necklace – white gold with a teardrop diamond pendant. I love it!

But that's not why I'm writing here again (heaven forbid if anyone reads this entry). My last supervision session reminded me how important journaling is for a therapist, and not just during training. God, that seems such a long time ago now – these ten years have flown by. A counsellor's self-awareness is so important if I'm to help my clients. There's something about the process of putting ink on paper that's cleansing, a place to expunge myself, to get stuff out of my brain. During training, our journals formed part of the degree, allowed us a deeper insight into ourselves; though, of course, they were never read by the tutors. As a therapist, it's my responsibility to be congruent and honest with myself. I once tried writing an online journal, secured with a password, but it felt too impersonal, just wasn't the same. Besides, there was none of the thrill of finding a hiding place, stashing it away until next time, opening up the pages and reading my previous thoughts and feelings, noticing what had changed.

Anyway, Mark is the only one likely to come across it and, to be honest, I wouldn't really mind if he read it anyway. I share everything with him.

Nearly everything.

But maybe not now. I wouldn't want him to read this entry. It's too personal. Hurting him is the last thing I want to do, but I have to get this out. And I have to remind myself that I haven't done anything wrong, as well as remembering that it happens to the best of us in this job. Most in this line of work have experienced it. I know from chatting to colleagues. I'll take it to supervision with Chrissie next week. It's her job. And I must remember what mine is.

OK... so there was this client today (my hand is shaking, my writing turning into scrawl now). He was self-referred, and he arrived on time... nothing unusual there. I went to fetch him from the waiting room (wish they'd make it more welcoming at the Medway. Even a pot plant would help!) and Nat was on reception. She's OK – people grumble about her, but she does her job.

Anyway, when I saw him, something fired off in my brain and body – one of those indefinable moments I don't want to dwell on. I have no idea why or where it came from. A trigger, perhaps, but of what? Thinking back, it was his scent I noticed first – sandalwood, musk – something alluring yet dangerous. It got to me. Drew me to him like a moth to a flame before he'd even spoken a word. Attraction to a client occasionally happens, of course, and it's certainly very common the other way around – a client falling for their therapist. Even women fall for me sometimes. It's the unique relationship that does it. A good therapist is genuine, empathic and non-judgemental, providing a safe and unconditional space for the client to open up. What's not to fall for? It's a relationship like no other and sometimes clients have never experienced these feelings before. It's this security that gives them the space to grow, to change, to empower themselves. To fall in love.

But a therapist doesn't cross the line with a client. <u>Ever.</u>

It was when he stood up and turned around, when we were face-to-face, that it really started. And I know he sensed it too.

(Note to self: next journal entry will show this very differently once I've worked through this. Supervision + self-awareness = sorted. ~~Go me!~~)

But then all that physical response stuff came. My body couldn't help it. My heart was suddenly freewheeling at the sight of him, my pupils dilating, my cheeks colouring up, not to mention all the thoughts flying around my head. (Yes, I've had a glass of wine or two writing this. Mark's out with Ed at a gig so it's OK – I'm allowed to chill. But I must remember, when I read this back, I was just getting it out, expunging. It doesn't mean anything. It's just words. ~~They can't harm anyone, right?~~)

So he came into my office, sat down, and I knew, just knew, *he was thinking the same. Fucking hell. It was so weird. A bolt from the*

*blue. Our eyes wouldn't let go of each other – his were particularly…
well, kind-looking. Warm. Jade green with a rare depth to them. I
could barely speak. But what was I supposed to say? 'Actually, sir, I'm
afraid I can't see you professionally because I fancy the bloody pants
off you?' The attraction was instant.*

*I dealt with it the right way, of course, saying and doing nothing
out of the ordinary. Instead, I hit the refresh button on my boundaries.
I started the assessment, went over the client–therapist contract, letting
him know how I work, the session timings, payment, confidentiality,
client safety and all that. Like everyone, he probably just wanted to
get on with telling me why he was there. (Note to self again: have had
three glasses of wine now so 'scuse crap writing and spelling ha ha).*

*He signed the contract and we got going. At least I'd managed
to reel in my stampeding heart (a little) and the flush had subsided,
though I know I kept fiddling with my hair. Barely took my eyes off
him. But when he started talking – oh, his voice! I really don't think
I was listening to him properly. Rather I was soaking up the timbre of
his words, absorbing the rich sound rather than what he was actually
saying. In all my years as a therapist, I'd only need one or two fingers
to count the number of times I've #listeningfailed a client. And he
sensed it. Like he knew he had this power over me. It was when he
gave that smile – just the one side of his mouth lifting a little, his eyes
narrowing and inquisitive – he just* knew *the effect he was having.
And all this twelve minutes into knowing him.*

~~*Nice work, Lorna.*~~

*So by the end of the first session all I knew was that his name was
Andrew, he was forty-five, had no kids, had never been married,
and that he was an artist who lived in a rambling terraced house
that needed repairing, with a lodger to help pay the bills. Oh, and he
occasionally played golf. I didn't think he looked the type. When he
told me about his house, describing the renovation work it needed, I'd
even imagined myself in his kitchen. Watching him whip up a meal
for us both while I sipped a glass of wine, some music playing, the*

conversation effortless. He was simply the most gorgeous and perfect man I'd ever laid eyes on. I have no idea why he affected me so much. Me, Lorna, a happily married woman with a wonderful husband. The only other thing I recall him saying during the session was something about him being at a crossroads in life, that things hadn't turned out the way he'd imagined or hoped. That he needed something more.

But I'd not listened. Not truly listened because I spent the rest of the session hoping that 'something' was me.

Good therapy works, Lorna.

But sometimes it goes horribly wrong.

CHAPTER ELEVEN

Lorna

'Annie's here,' I say, getting up to press the button on Cath's entry system. On the black and white screen I see her outside the building's main door, standing on the old stone steps with a bottle of wine tucked under her arm. Megan comes back from the kitchen carrying some pâté, and cheese and crackers. She puts them on the coffee table. A moment later, Annie is knocking on Cath's flat door and I let her in, pulling her close for a hug.

'Sorry. Bloody parents' evening ran over. Some stroppy father wouldn't accept that his son is a little—'

'Shhh,' I say, placing a finger over her lips. 'Sit, wine, food,' I tell her, leading her through. Cath's only been living in the flat a few weeks, but already it's oozing her individual style – crammed full of knick-knacks and clutter and stuff she doesn't need but can't bear to part with. The high ceilings, the decorative architraves, the wooden floors, the mismatched kitchen cupboards are the perfect backdrop for her weirdness – from her taxidermy, her eclectic paintings bought from junk shops, her 1970s tasselled lampshades, and a huge collection of ornate mirrors that make the place look twice its size. Much of it is still in packing boxes stacked up in corners. Cath never seems to get organised.

'What did everyone think of the book, then?' Megan asks, perching on the arm of a shabby red velvet sofa. An assortment of brightly coloured cushions makes it almost impossible to sit down. She taps the novel she's holding, its cover slightly torn. She's a few years younger than the rest of us and quite new to the group. She works in the shop with Cath.

'Oops,' I say, pouring more wine, eyeing Annie.

'Er, what book would that be?' Annie says, laughing.

'Fecking useless, the lot of you,' Cath chips in, carrying two trays of hot pizza from the kitchen. 'I read it, Meg, and I thought it was actually quite good. Though it made me bawl into my pillow and hate myself even more.'

I watch as she sits down, curling her legs up underneath her. Her cherry-red toenails peek out from her spotty slippers. The smile stays on her face even though I know she's hurting inside.

'I thought it was quite romantic,' Megan says sweetly. She's slim and blonde, her long legs crossing over each other as she struggles to get comfortable.

'Sit here,' I say, moving up. She does but stays on the edge of the sofa, reaching forward for a single crisp. I take a slice of pizza, lifting it high, the cheese strings refusing to break. It's the first thing I've eaten all day. In fact, it's pretty much the first thing I've eaten since *he* came into the clinic on Monday. I've barely been able to function since.

'That's actually *not* romance,' Cath says. 'It was some guy being a bastard to a vulnerable woman until she caved in and gave him what he wanted.' She drinks a large mouthful of wine, grabbing her phone as it sounds an alert. 'Hey up,' she says, her eyes lighting up. 'What have we got here, then?'

'And you think *that's* romantic?' Annie says, laughing. 'Some dating app? You'll get used to her, Meg.'

'Oh, I already am,' Megan replies, warming up a little. 'Don't forget I work with her all day every day.' She tips back her head, laughing, exposing her long white neck. She's wearing one of the necklaces from Cath's shop, but it looks too large and chunky on her small frame.

'And she's like this all the time?' I say, trying to join in, trying to sound normal even though I don't feel it. Rattled sums me up right now.

'Yep.' Meg leans closer to me, grinning and pretending to make it so Cath can't hear. 'One guy she's been chatting to online actually found out where she worked and came into the shop the other day. He'd stalked her.'

'Creepy as,' I say, frowning as I'm reminded of *him*. Though with Andrew it wasn't creepy, as such. More like pure passion – him frustrated that we'd met at the wrong time in our lives, and me, well, I was driven by something I've still not worked out.

'Fuck off, you lot. I'm not made of wood.' Cath holds up her phone with a guy's picture on the screen. 'What do you reckon? Hot or not?'

'Definitely hot,' Annie says. I can't help catching an eyeful of a semi-naked man standing on a surfboard. 'Hell yeah to those abs.'

Cath passes round her phone, and it ends up in my hands. 'OK,' I say, trying to sound enthusiastic. 'So what does Mr Surfer-dude actually have to say for himself…' I scan the text. '"Discreet daytime meets only. Can you take your punishment like a…"' I hesitate, the words swimming out of focus. '"…like a good girl?"' I finish reading, my voice wavering. 'Jesus, Cath, and you've actually matched with him? What were you thinking, swiping right?'

'Duh…' she says, rolling her eyes.

'He might be hot, but he wants to slap your arse on a Tuesday afternoon while his missus changes his kids' nappies and cleans his house.' I toss her phone back, angry. Something bites deep inside. 'Do you *have* to go on that bloody app? It's unhealthy.'

'I don't always go on it,' she says, tapping the screen. 'There, he's gone. Unmatched. Despite what you lot think, I don't want hook-ups. I do want to meet a decent guy.'

'Then find one the bloody normal way,' I say, immediately regretting sounding so harsh.

'It's not that easy,' Cath replies, a pensive look on her face. 'Anyway, all the good ones are taken. By you bloody lot,' she adds, rolling her now teary eyes.

'And I'm not sharing mine,' Annie chimes, sloshing more wine into everyone's glasses. 'I knew Ed was a good 'un from the start.' We all know that Annie and Ed sweat love for each other.

'How about you, Lorn?' Cath asks. 'Did you feel that about Mark when you first met?'

'Oh God, yes,' I say, hesitating. Truth is, when I first encountered Mark, I thought he was a bit of an arrogant sod. He soon won me round, though, with his constant messaging, his romantic gestures – red roses sent to my flat every day for a week – the pictures of himself he'd text me (some quite revealing, but it turns out that's what I liked about him – his boldness, his confidence), the theatre tickets, the snatched weekends away. All this after only meeting briefly at a mutual friend's party. He'd begged the host for my number.

'I always get what I want,' he'd told me at the end of our first date, smiling, tilting my chin up with his finger. I thought about that for a long while after, wondering what happened after he'd got it.

'Love at first sight?' Megan asks.

'Oh. Yeah, definitely,' I reply. 'How about you?'

'Gary and I started slow. You know, a few dates here and there. Nothing too heavy. After a couple of years and we were serious, it seemed sensible to move in together, especially when I started work at Cath's shop. His place is only round the corner. We've been together three years now and…' She waves her left hand about. 'Watch this space,' she adds, sticking up her empty ring finger.

'You lot make me totally sick,' Cath says, hurling herself back against the cushions, diva-like, folding her arms and pouting.

Her phone pings again, but Annie grabs it first, laughing. 'You must have been swiping hard today, hon. Another match.'

'Let me see,' Cath says, lunging for her phone but knocking over her wine instead. While she's fetching a cloth, Annie checks it out.

'He's not great,' I say, peering over her shoulder, actually beginning to enjoy myself, to forget. 'Looks a bit boring. She can do way better.'

'Do better than what?' Cath says, mopping up the spillage.

'Him,' Annie says, flashing her a quick look.

Cath pulls a face. 'I don't even remember swiping on him,' she says, going back to the kitchen. 'Check out the other dating app I have on there and see what you think,' she calls out. 'You can actually search for interests and stuff. It's one of the most popular apps now.'

'We should *delete* all her apps, more like,' I say, wishing I could fill the gaping hole in Cath's heart. She tries to cover it up with humour, act like she doesn't care, but I know she does. Since Matt left a couple of years ago, it's been tough for her. Especially when she found out he'd married the woman he ran off with. She was crushed. And it doesn't help that all her friends are in happy relationships.

'OK, look, here it is,' Annie says. 'Double Take. She's shown us this one a hundred times already,' she says, rolling her eyes and thumbing through various lists.

I peer over her shoulder, hoping we'll find Mr Right for Cath here and now, get it sorted once and for all. But I know that's not how love happens – that sometimes it hits in the most random of ways and for the most unlikely reasons. And sometimes for *no* reason. I hug my arms around myself, refusing to think about it. Refusing to think about *him*.

'These are the people she's already contacted,' I say. 'And these are the guys who've messaged her. Some of them look OK.'

'Agreed,' Annie says. 'I'll do a search and see if there's anyone decent in the area. Best we take control here, eh girls?'

Cath comes back and sits down again. 'Go for it, you lot. You can personally vet them all for me. Remember that guy I met last week? Turns out he had some kind of live porn channel and wanted me to be on it. He was basically using the dating site as a perverted employment agency.' She laughs, but I can still see the look in her eyes. 'It was annoying as he was actually really nice. Great-looking, fun to be with, we had loads in common—'

'Except he wanted to be your pimp,' Annie says. 'Leave this to us, Cath.' She rubs her hands together.

'Then there was the one who wasn't over his ex,' Cath goes on, cradling her wine and talking to no one in particular. 'Unknown to me, he got me to have my hair done the same way as hers, saying it would suit me, even convincing me to wear the same style clothes as her. I truly thought he was "the one" until I found a picture of his ex. She looked just like me, and he was still sending her hundreds of messages a day.' She scowls, trying to appear defiant even though I know she's not. 'And don't get me started on the guy who wanted us to be exclusive but then replied to other Tinder messages while we were together. Or the one who asked if I'd date him until someone better came along. And not forgetting the guy who wanted a fuck-buddy. He came armed with a contract, paragraph two clearly stating he refused to use condoms. Plus, there were at least three who were married or in relationships, a couple who were looking for naughty fun, and then there are all the scammers from—'

'Cath, love,' Annie says, touching a finger to her lips. 'Hush, sweetie. We're going to sort this.'

'Even if you find Brad bloody Pitt on there, he'll turn out to be a twat.' She pours more wine, but secretly I can tell she's glad we're trying to help. Book club nights are always like this – not so much to do with books but rather us muddling through our lives, helping each other however we can, whether it's to do with work or kids or love or health. We've all got a listening ear, can all offer advice, somehow turning our worries into a laugh. It's the opposite of therapy, but therapy nonetheless.

But I can never tell them about *him*.

'Right,' Annie says, scrolling through a list of mug shots and ages. 'No, no, no, yuk, Christ no, hmm maybe…' She clicks a link but then sees he's only five foot three. 'No way,' she says, going back to the list and scrolling through at least another thirty or so profiles.

'Slim pickings when you narrow it down,' I say, reaching for my wine, grateful for the distraction. Grateful I have Mark. Megan is peering over our shoulders now, while Cath feigns indifference.

'It's always the same old faces,' she says. 'I'm sick of it. You can delete them all for all I care. I'm going to join a nunnery.'

'Oh *wow!*' Annie suddenly says, her mouth dropping open. 'Take a look at *him*.' She halts her scrolling, tapping on a profile. 'Let's not be too hasty here.' She gives Cath a wink, nodding as she goes through his pictures. Curiosity gets the better of me, so I lean in to take a proper look.

And that's when my world falls apart for the second time in a week.

CHAPTER TWELVE

Nikki

It's raining. A fine drizzle that's not enough for an umbrella – if I even owned one – but enough to wet my lashes and cheeks, stick my hair to my head. But I don't care what I look like. No one will see me. Not today. The hedge is tall and good cover to lurk behind. There's a convenient gap to peer through – just wide enough to get a view of the clinic door yet not big enough for her to spot me. And even if she did, it doesn't matter. She wouldn't know my pale, unmade-up features, my gaunt look. Though it strikes me that she might recognise the pain etched on my face.

I retreat back into the small green area at the centre of the crescent – woven with geometric paths and low box greenery, a cluster of twiggy, pruned roses in the centre bed. There are four wooden benches – one at each edge of the square – with several trees also forming a boundary along with the hedge. I sit back down on my usual bench. She rarely leaves before 5 p.m.

'Got a light, love?'

I swing round. A man looms over me, but I don't feel scared. He looks the same as me – broken, lost, waiting for something though he's not sure what.

'Sure,' I say, fishing in my pocket. I've seen him a couple of times before, sleeping on one of the benches, his clothes filthy and his head resting on his backpack. 'Here you go.'

'You ain't got a fag too, have ya?' He fidgets from one foot to the other, glancing around nervously. He's not wearing any socks, his thin white ankles showing between the hem of his frayed jeans and battered trainers.

'Take these,' I say, handing him the packet. I have another one in my bag. 'I'll have my lighter back, though.' I laugh, the first time I've heard myself do that in a while.

'You sure, missus?' He opens the pack, looking incredulous.

'Certain,' I say. 'And it's not missus.'

He nods, lighting the cigarette and handing me back my lighter. He goes to the bench opposite, pulling a large plastic bottle of cider from his backpack, swigging from it. He leans forward on his elbows, the bottle propped between his feet and the cigarette dangling from his hand. Every so often, he takes a drag or a swig, his eyes still focused on the ground. He breathes out in long, heavy sighs.

I light a cigarette myself, checking my watch again before going back behind the hedge, just in case. Her office lights are still on. Rain or shine, she always has those lamps on – one by the window, another over near where she sits. A warm glow spills out of the Georgian sash window, making the street scene look autumnal even though it's early spring.

'What you looking at?' His voice makes me jump again.

'Oh…' Cigarette man is standing close. I can smell his breath. 'I'm just waiting for someone.' I kick myself for explaining when I don't need to. It's reminiscent. Making excuses that weren't needed. I shudder.

'Who you waiting for?' he says, coming closer. I press my shoulder bag against my body, stepping back. The hedge is right behind me.

'A friend,' I say, glancing nervously behind him.

'So why you hiding here, then?' His face relaxes into a smile, his expression earnest.

'Who says I'm hiding?'

'Cos I know the signs. And you're doing them.' He laughs, exposing rotting and missing teeth.

'Well, you're wrong.' But I can't help wondering if he's got a point. Perhaps the very act of hiding is making me more conspicuous. What if she's already spotted me on one of the countless afternoons I've been here? What if she calls the police? Does she sense me watching when she comes down the steps of her office, tracking her towards the main road if it's a bus day, or the other way if she's heading to the car park? I always hang back a few seconds before following.

Cigarette man nods. 'I seen you round here a few times. You wanna be less obvious. So go on, then, who you hiding from?'

'Like I said, I'm just waiting for a friend.' I sidestep him and go back to the bench, dropping my cigarette to the ground, squashing it with my foot.

He sits down beside me. 'Look, I ain't gonna tell no one or nothing.'

I give a little nod, glancing sideways at him, trying not to catch his eye. His hair was probably once a vibrant red, but now it looks weathered and dull, more a flat, rusty tone as if he's been outside too long. His skin is ruddy and freckled, with deep lines around his eyes and mouth. I suspect he's only early twenties but looks much older. Maybe telling him everything would help.

'You ain't a spy, is you?'

'No,' I laugh, thinking that's not so far from the truth.

'You got a place to live?'

For a second I'm not sure what he means, but then I realise why he's asking. My hair isn't in much better condition than his and my skin is sallow and dull. My clothes, all from charity shops, never quite fit, and my one pair of shoes are scuffed and old-fashioned – chunky brown loafers with one of the tassels missing. I hate them.

'Have *you* got a place to live?' I ask, avoiding his question. Next thing he'll be wanting somewhere to stay.

Cigarette man shrugs. 'Not no more.'

'So where do you sleep?'

He points at the bench. 'Sometimes here. Sometimes the shelter.' He wipes his hand across his nose, pinching the tip with his fingers. 'I'm hoping to get my own flat again soon.'

'That's tough,' I say, as we each light another cigarette. He offers me the bottle of cider. Stringy, milky stuff is floating in it. 'I'm OK, thanks.'

'I used to have a home,' he goes on. 'A nice home.' He jiggles his skinny leg, leaning forward on his knees. The cider sloshes in time with his movements.

'What happened?' Talking to him helps pass the time, though my attention is focused beyond the hedge, waiting for her to come out of the office, to trit-trot down the stone steps in her court shoes, stepping out onto the street. Oblivious.

Cigarette man shrugs. 'Had a job in a warehouse picking orders a couple of years ago. Then the girlfriend got sick, so I had to take time off to look after her. We had a right nice flat, like with a washing machine and everything. I earned good money and she had a job before she got ill.'

'I'm sorry to hear that.'

'I ended up losing my job, losing the flat. Losing my girl.'

'I'm sorry…'

'She didn't die or nuffing. Just like we got in each other's faces and that, so I moved out. Stayed on mates' sofas for a while. Got in with the wrong crowd, you know. But I ain't no bludger.'

'I'm sure you're not,' I say, distracted, wondering if I should check the clinic again.

'I had to sleep rough for a few nights, and then it became kind of a habit.'

I nod, half listening to him, one eye on my watch. Not long to go.

'You don't see it coming. You really don't,' he says, shaking his head. 'I got a kid too, but they won't let me see him.'

I stare at him, suddenly wishing he'd go away. I stand up, slipping back behind the hedge, shifting nervously from one foot to the other. 'That's… that's really tough,' I say, hesitating, feeling bad for him even so. But Cigarette Man is gathering up his pack from the bench opposite and doesn't hear me.

When I look through the gap, I see someone standing outside the clinic, slightly out of view. A man. Tall, wearing a jacket and jeans, his shoulders hunched against the drizzle, hands in his front pockets, his cap pulled low. I'm not sure if he's just come out, if he's going in, or is simply waiting. I can't see his face.

Then the main door opens, and *she* comes out – a little earlier than usual. I hold my breath. She's wearing a navy dress today, slightly above the knee with black leather boots, a dark jacket on top, a red scarf wound around her neck. Her hair is swept up in a messy but stylish knot. To begin with, her face is calm, neutral, not giving anything away as she swings out of the big black-painted door, hitching her bag on her shoulder, flicking back a strand of stray hair.

But then she freezes on the top step, stopping in her tracks when she sees him – one foot poised to go down, pointed like a ballerina.

Her expression changes.

He seems to say something to her then, but I can't be sure as his face is still hidden from view. She looks back towards the door, as if she wants to run back inside again. She touches her forehead, frowning, as if she doesn't know which way to turn or what to do. She looks afraid. Then he says something else, gesturing with his arms, and, for a moment, she half smiles, narrows her eyes as if she can't help herself. But then she shakes her head, comes down the remaining steps and slips quickly past him, striding off down the street. He goes after her, his collar up, his back still turned to me as they head off.

I wait thirty seconds before leaving the little square, following in her wake. A couple of blocks up ahead, she crosses over the high street and lingers outside the florist's shop, browsing the metal buckets stuffed with bouquets, glancing back over her shoulder. There's no sign of the man now – he veered off a few streets back without me getting a proper look at him, but she still looks nervous, somehow disappointed that he's gone.

She picks out several bunches of daffodils and white tulips and goes inside to pay, glancing over her shoulder again. She emerges a couple of minutes later with an expectant look on her face, scanning around until her expression falls flat. Then she half walks, half runs to the bus stop a short way down the street. A double-decker is just pulling up, and I watch as she gets on, taking a window seat downstairs.

My heart thumps as I edge closer to the road, closer to the bus as it pulls away, driving towards me. As it passes, it's the nearest I've ever been to her, and I swear she catches my eye through the window, swear I see a tear rolling down her cheek.

CHAPTER THIRTEEN

Lorna

I cradle the flowers on my knee as the bus leaves the stop. I'm tempted to pick off all the tulip petals one by one... *He loves me, he loves me not.* The cold drizzle has given me a headache, though it could be from the wine last night at Cath's place.

As often happens, we all drank a bit too much – especially me after seeing *his* profile on that Double Take app.

'Bloody hell, Cath,' Annie had said, holding out the phone. 'Take a look at him.' Cath was unable to hide the gasp, making her silly selfie pout face as she looked at his photos. I'd already glimpsed his picture, of course, was still in shock; couldn't unsee it.

'I'd be punching there,' Cath said. 'He's way out of my league.'

'Nonsense,' Annie said, grabbing the phone back. 'I'm going to message him for you. What do you normally say in these things?'

Cath was laughing nervously, clearly excited, going along with Annie's recklessness. I hadn't seen all his photos but just the one was enough to know. Enough to feel the crushing weight bearing down on me, twisting my insides when it had no right to.

Megan was also looking, peering at the phone, giggling, egging Annie on. 'Artist seeks muse,' she read out in a silly voice. 'Loyal, kind, honest to the core, I'm looking for a woman to challenge me in every way. Not satisfied with normal, I'm seeking someone adventurous, quirky, spontaneous and creative. Join me on my journey and let's make new memories together.'

'He sounds a bit conceited, if you ask me,' I said, feeling sick. My voice was a croak, my throat tight. I couldn't stand to look again.

'You serious?' Annie said, rolling her eyes. She shoved the phone up close to my face. 'Just *look* at him! He's bloody well worth cheating on Ed for.'

'Yeah. He's pretty,' I said, turning away while trying to appear normal. I didn't want to see.

'Says he's never been married, has no kids. Perfect!' Annie went on.

'Those are red flags, if you ask me,' I said. The others stared at me, raising their eyebrows. 'Commitment-phobic,' I added, but they ignored me.

'So, what shall I type?' Annie asked, finger poised.

'How about "Hi, how are you?"' Cath said.

'It's no wonder you're single if that's your best chat-up line,' Annie replied, typing something. She stared at the ceiling for a moment, then carried on tapping. 'How about this? "Hi, it's your loyal muse here… I'm Cath, an interior designer. Quirky is my middle name. Would love to connect to see if we can challenge each other… in a good way." Oh, and I added a winky-face emoji too. Might as well.' She looked to Cath for approval but then decided not to wait. 'Too slow. It's sent.' She reached for her wine. 'To Cath's new love,' she said, clinking everyone's glasses. 'And a future wedding, girls.'

The bus slows again, pulling to a stop. A few people get off, some more get on. I'm still shaking from the encounter just now outside the office, praying Sandy didn't see or hear any of it, even though I know that from her desk it's impossible to view the street. And I'm pretty sure the door had swung closed by the time I'd spotted him. But Sandy has a way of knowing everything that's going on at the clinic, a sixth sense that perhaps comes from working in a therapists' office for so long.

I shake my head and close my eyes. How on earth did I not fall down the steps when I saw him waiting on the pavement? How did I even manage to say a word without throwing up, manage to walk past him, hold a straight path down the street until I reached the flower shop? Truth is, I don't even remember buying the flowers. It was a distraction, a means of escape, something else to fill my head. I can still hear his words, still feel his hand as he reached out and touched my arm as I slipped past him.

'Lorna… we need to talk.'

'We can't,' I told him. 'Not outside of therapy. And we shouldn't be doing it *inside* therapy either.' It was the hardest thing to say when all I wanted was for him to hold me, take me in his arms, tell me it was all going to be OK. But I couldn't.

'Please, wait…' he called out as I walked off, but I carried on, not stopping.

'Don't follow me,' I said over my shoulder, though I know he did for a little way. I could feel the heat of his stare on my back.

I lean my forehead against the glass, allowing the vibrations of the bus to hammer into my headache, thinking back to last night again.

'Has he replied yet?' Cath had said impatiently. We'd not even got on to talking about the book yet, probably because Charlotte, Mark's younger sister, wasn't there. She's the one who usually leads discussions, drawing us deeper into explorations of what we've read, but she was away on yet another holiday.

Annie glanced at Cath's phone again, having taken charge of it for the evening. I was holding my breath, desperately hoping he hadn't messaged back, but also wanting nothing more than to have Annie read out his words. *His actual words*. Andrew hadn't mentioned anything about being on a dating site in our assessment session. The betrayal had no right to cut deep.

'Nothing back yet,' she said. 'But once he sees your profile, I'm sure he'll reply.' Then a concerned look swept over Annie's face. 'Tell me you've got a good profile, Cath?' She made a show of shaking her head, rolling her eyes. 'Great photos and an enticing blurb?'

'Well, I think so,' Cath said. 'It's hard to get it right, though.'

'Oh God, let me look.' Annie was back on Cath's phone then, her face gradually changing from blank to incredulous. 'Oh dear, hon. No, no, this won't do.' She held up the phone, flashing a few photographs at us. 'And how old is *that* picture?'

Cath laughed and shrugged. 'I dunno. A few years, maybe?'

'But you look *way* better now. You've lost a ton of weight, your hair's different, and these pics are blurry and all… *selfies*.' She whispered the word 'selfies'.

'So?'

'Frankly, it makes you look like Billy No-Mates.' Then she read out the words, skimming over Cath's profile. 'And you sound dull as fuck. "Likes baking, TV and reading?"' She shook her head. 'Leave this to me, my lovely,' Annie said. Then she spent a few minutes typing while we hoovered up pizza and sank more wine. Well, *I* sank the wine while they all chatted and ate. My mind was elsewhere.

'Right,' Annie said. 'Photo time, girls.'

'What?' Cath put her hands up to shield herself, laughing. 'No, I look like shit.'

'You look fine. Better than in these pics. Get your wine glasses, everyone. We're having a group photo.' Annie stood, dragging Cath up by the arm. 'Let's all get near that stuffed pheasant with the huge painting in the background. They're good talking points for when he messages you back. Lorn? Get yourself up here.'

I barely heard her. I was frozen – my legs, body, arms unable to move. It was all I could do to keep hold of my wine glass. I couldn't let *him* see me on that site, even if it was just for a friend's profile. It didn't seem right. Didn't seem… *professional*.

'You need to loosen up tonight, Lorn,' Annie said, sloshing more wine into my glass. Then the pull of her hand on my arm. 'C'mon, we're doing this for Cath. And we need to be quick before Hot Guy looks at her photos.'

Hot Guy…

'I… I don't feel so great.' I think that's what I said.

'Well, you *look* great and that's what Cath needs right now. A bunch of gorgeous friends around her to make it seem as though she has the best social life ever. How could any guy resist us lot?'

Megan was laughing. 'I totally agree. Come on, Lorn. Take one for the team.'

'Pretty please?' Cath said, getting into it now. Perhaps I could somehow hide behind them in the photo, bow my face at the right moment or bend down to pick something up.

'Sure, sorry,' I said, trying to force a smile. I joined the back of the group, ending up behind Annie, who's about five inches shorter than me. I tried to shuffle behind Cath but Megan, the tallest of all of us, had taken that spot. They were fluffing up their hair, pouting, angling their best sides forward, raising their glasses. I couldn't do it.

'Make sure you get Archie in,' Cath said, referring to the dead pheasant on the mantelpiece. Right now, I wished I was dead and stuffed. I felt the heat of the standard lamp to my left highlighting my face when all I wanted to do was disappear.

'Ready?' Annie said, holding Cath's phone at arm's length and angling it to get us all in. I heard her snapping dozens of shots. 'Work it, girls,' she said, laughing while the others shaped themselves into different poses. I stood stock-still, staring at my feet, allowing my hair to fall over my face. 'Lorna!' Cath said. 'Fuck's sake, look at the camera, will you? And smile. You're meant to be having fun, remember?'

'Sorry,' I whispered, on the verge of throwing up. Then Megan prodded me several times in the side, hitting a spot between my ribs. I yelped, wide-eyed, throwing back my head, unable to help the grin as the helpless laughter set in.

He teased me about being so ticklish, used it to his best advantage in bed.

'Nice!' Annie said, snapping a dozen more quick-fire shots before I composed myself. 'That'll do for starters,' she went on. 'Now, we need to look back in our pics from that night out a couple of weeks ago. Send me any good ones of Cath. We got your back, hon.'

I sat down again. The others were in fits of giggles.

'He's still not read the message, so work fast, girls,' Annie went on. Then she took some more pictures of Cath on her own, posing by her artwork, in her kitchen pretending to cook, on her balcony with some fairy lights picking out the pretty highlights in her hair that she'd had done recently. In the meantime, I just sat, numb, downing my wine.

Shortly after, Annie had finished. New photos were up, and she'd written an enticing blurb with just enough detail to tempt any halfway decent guy. I had to admit, she'd done a good job. But I couldn't resist looking when she showed me the group photos. I had to see for myself. And there I was, fully visible, a white smile glowing wide across my face, wine glass inadvertently raised as the lamp lit me up brighter than the others. Cath looked good, but I didn't suppose that's who *he'd* be interested in when he saw the picture. *If* he saw the picture. Of course, there was still a chance he wouldn't bother clicking on the profile of an eccentric woman who professed to be his muse. I prayed Cath wasn't his type.

Ten minutes later, I get off the bus and walk slowly down my street, clutching the flowers to my chest. A few petals fall to the pavement along the way as my mind floods with last year.

Does he love me, or love me not…?

CHAPTER FOURTEEN

Lorna

'So what made you change your mind?' he says. His face gives nothing away, though beneath his defensive look, I can still see kindness. His eyes betray that much. It's been a week since the initial assessment, not that much assessing went on. 'About seeing me?'

I stare at him. Sun streams in through the tall window, casting a golden bridge between us on the carpet. It's as if no time at all has passed – since last week or, indeed, last year.

'You said you needed my help. It's my job to help people.' I clear my throat. While it's the truth, we both know it's not the real reason I agreed to schedule him in for a further appointment. The pull of seeing him again was simply too great. Or, more to the point, I was afraid of the consequences if I didn't. Of him reporting me.

He nods a couple of times, the corners of his mouth turning up, as though he knows he's already won.

'This has to be a short-term arrangement, you understand,' I continue. 'An agreed number of sessions.' My boundaries were already shot by seeing him for the first appointment, let alone a second. But I tell myself that this is different, a one-off, something I need to do. Closure. I'll record it as a further assessment and, to anyone looking at the file, that's how it will seem before I refer him on. Nothing suspicious.

Justifying, always justifying…

'Do you say that to all your clients?'

He knows how it works, knows the rules.

'No, not always, but I'm saying it now. It's for the best.'

'You know it's wrong to see me at all,' he says. His voice is provocative, testing me. 'But I'm glad you are.'

'It almost sounds as if you *want* it to be wrong,' I say, floundering, not being authentic or genuine. Not counselling. My heart thumps. It's not stopped racing since he was last sitting opposite me.

'We could look at it as closure,' he says, as if he's read my mind. His voice is deep and slow. Just how I remembered it, washing over me as I'd lie with my head nestled in the crook of his shoulder, breathing in the scent of our sex, him stroking my hair, wanting the moment to last forever. Knowing it couldn't. He told me he loved me many times.

But I never said it back.

'So, you feel as though you need closure?'

'Don't you?'

I shake my head briefly, wishing I hadn't. 'This isn't about me… Andrew.' I can hardly call him David, the false name he booked under. 'It's your time to explore your feelings. Your safe space.' The irony of it sticks in my throat, makes me want to choke.

'Safe space?' he says, knowing exactly how to get to me.

'Yes. To get some understanding of the issues that brought you here in the first place.'

Every word is killing me. Why the *hell* did I agree to see him again? When did my resolve crack? Was it at the end of the assessment last Monday, after he'd left, and I felt so empty and alone, as though our affair had just ended all over again?

On my journey home, I'd wondered if it might be abandonment issues that I wasn't even aware of, but I couldn't fathom what. I examined every part of myself, overthought everything until I yelled at myself in the rear-view mirror to shut up with all the psychobabble. Cath would have been proud.

Or maybe was it several days later on Thursday that did it, when he was waiting outside the clinic? Or perhaps it was at 3 a.m. the other night when I sneaked downstairs to check my phone. The texts were from him, of course. Just one or two words. The *right* words. Words he knew would bore into my heart. And all the more dangerous because they'd come to my regular phone. I didn't reply.

But by Friday he'd called the clinic reception again, still posing as David. Sandy had passed his message on to me, asking for a further appointment. To refuse him would have aroused suspicion, perhaps even got Joe involved as to why I wasn't taking on a client. The 'yes' slipped off my tongue before I could think.

'Answer my question,' he says. 'Why did you change your mind about seeing me?'

He always had a knack of turning things around, getting me to say what he wanted to hear. Except the one thing he *needed* to hear. That I loved him.

'I treat all my clients the same,' I say, looking away. 'And seeing clients again for more sessions after a few months, or even years, have passed is not uncommon. Sometimes people need to talk again.'

'You disappeared,' he said.

'I got a different job.'

'I know you changed your mind about this appointment because you're still in love with me. That you're secretly pleased I came to see you.'

It's a kick in the face.

'No, Andrew,' I say, feeling sick, but only because he's right. 'I can't treat you differently to my other clients. It's not eth—'

'Not ethical?' He laughs again. Not a nasty laugh – far from it – but a laugh that shows me he knows what I'm thinking, that he's got to me. I can't let him do this again.

'Look,' I say, leaning forward, lowering my voice. 'You know as well as I do that nothing about our previous client–counsellor relationship was ethical. It couldn't have been *less* ethical.' If I'm not careful, I'll be right back where I was last year and looking for a new job. Or worse, getting struck off. And then Mark is on my mind again – the man who loves me, trusts me, would protect me with his life. I want to throw up.

'Agreed,' he says, sitting back on the sofa. 'You know you did wrong.'

Me? I feel like hitting him. Reaching out with a heavy book and swiping him around the head, watching him fall sideways, unconscious. But I also want him to take me in his arms, wrap me up, make me feel how he did last year – the best I ever have with a man.

'Turning this round is not helpful, Andrew. Maybe there's some reframing work to be done here.' I swallow, pulling out the most basic of counselling skills to get me through. 'I can offer you three sessions maximum and a referral on to another therapist who can help. Does that sound fair?' It's a play to keep things calm, to appease him until I can figure out what to do.

'Is that how long you think it'll be before we're fucking again?'

I can't help the sudden intake of breath, can't help that my head tips back slightly and I close my eyes for a beat too long. 'We've both moved on. You know it can't be like that any more.'

'Have we?' he says. 'Can't it?'

'Sounds like you maybe feel stuck?' I say, composing myself for the tenth time. But then it slips out. 'Have you been seeing anyone… anyone new?' I dig my nails into my palm. 'Oh, apart from… well, you know,' I add sarcastically, just to let him know I haven't forgotten her. In fact, I'm grateful to her now. Without the insane jealousy she roused in me, I'd probably still be seeing him, getting myself deeper and deeper into trouble, living a double and dangerous life. In fact, I'd like the chance to shake her hand.

'Not been seeing anyone apart from… *well, you know?*' he says, smiling, his teeth on show – that one slightly jagged canine endearing yet dangerous as ever. Since I've known Mark, I notice people's teeth. The scar just above Andrew's top lip creases upwards. It's as endearing as it is sinister, and I have no idea why. But it was one of the things that made me find him so insanely attractive. 'There was no "you know" about it. I told you the truth. You chose not to believe me.'

I look away, feeling my jaw tighten. 'OK, so it sounds as though you've not moved on at all, then, in terms of seeing anyone new? Perhaps that's how these sessions can help you.' There needs to be a reason for him being here, apart from me.

Then I'm mentally back in Cath's flat, his image on her phone – the sight of his profile ripping me apart. I can almost hear Annie giggling beside me, flicking through his photographs, making appreciative sounds.

Artist seeks muse… Loyal, kind, honest to the core…

'So, you're feeling stuck?' I suggest. *At a crossroads…* were his words during our very first session last year. Before everything went wrong.

'Perhaps *you* feel stuck,' he says. Then that smile again.

'Andrew, I really get the impression you're not ready to engage with therapy. Especially not with me. I also feel I've made a terrible mistake by agreeing to further sessions with you. It's not going to be helpful for you to see me as a counsellor and it's highly—'

'Highly unethical? Yes, I know. You've said many times.' He reaches over to the side table and pours himself a glass of water. 'Nice new office, by the way. So much nicer than the old place.'

'Yes, it is,' I say. 'To both of those things.'

'OK,' he says, standing up. 'I'll go.' He lifts his jacket off the sofa and goes to put it on. I see the hard lines of his shoulders standing proud through his white shirt. I look away. 'You're right. This isn't going to work.'

A stab of panic shoots through me.

'I'm sensing avoidance now.' I hate it that my voice shakes, not wanting him to go. But it's what he always did if I had doubts or questioned his actions or we'd had words about each of our situations. He'd up and go – me second-guessing his next move, if he was going to punish me by reporting me to the clinic, impose a week's silence or, worse, tell Mark. I know it was because he felt hurt, that we couldn't be together properly. 'You still have plenty of time left,' I say. Him cutting a session short won't look good, even if it's just Sandy that notices him going. Word will soon get back to Joe.

Andrew slowly sits down again, looking at me all the while, making a show of taking his jacket off. I feel the breath I didn't know I'd been holding release.

'No, in answer to your question,' he says.

I raise my eyebrows.

'I'm not seeing anyone new.'

'OK,' I say slowly. 'So you're still with *her*? Or have you been looking for someone new?' I'm pushing it too far – partly because I don't believe him, and also because I have no idea if he's seen Cath's dating site message or our group photo.

'Does it worry you if I am?'

'I'm not worried,' I say, hiding my bitterness. But it's killing me not to know.

'Oh, the irony,' he says calmly.

We're two feral cats sizing each other up, pacing around a cage, uttering throaty warning growls, claws out. When all we really want is to tear each other's clothes off.

'But you were – *are* – living with a woman?' I hedge my bets at it still being current. *Although it can't be much of a relationship if you're on a bloody dating site!* I want to scream.

'And you were – *are* – living with a man, Lorna.'

'She's your lodger. Your girlfriend. Your *lover* for fuck's sake.'

'And he is your *husband.*'

I swallow, flicking my eyes at the clock behind him. Never before has a session run so slowly.

CHAPTER FIFTEEN

Lorna's Journal

I don't have long this time, but I need to read more of this, to throw some light on what's going on for me now. I feel guilty snatching these moments to myself, but I convince myself it's for the best, that it will help repair things, to help me do what's right, to stop my family falling apart. I couldn't stand for that to happen. Not after everything. I'll do whatever it takes to keep Freya and Jack happy, my relationship alive. Thank God these words are here for me to look back on, to learn from, to reflect on until I figure out a plan. Because something needs to be done. I can't carry on like this.

25 January 2017

It's been nearly a week since I last wrote here. Mark's downstairs watching something on Netflix, Freya's been asleep for several hours and the kitchen is all tidy. It's one of the things I've always loved about Mark, that he likes everything shipshape for the morning. It makes things so much easier with busy family life. It's a trait inherited from his military father, I think, though I hardly know Geoff, what with him and Margie living up in Durham. I didn't meet them until I'd been living with Mark for at least a year and I know his relationship with them has always been a bit tense, but he told me especially so since Maria died. I'd hoped I could help build bridges for him, that we'd go and visit often, take the kids, but Mark is stubborn. His grief in the early days drove a wedge between him and most of his family and friends. He needed to mourn alone, turn in on himself, and I understood that. I've seen it enough times with clients. But long term, it's not healthy. I wanted – want – to help him somehow.

I still sometimes wonder if he's ashamed of me, that I don't quite fill Maria's shoes, and that's why we don't see his family very often. But I have to remember that I came with my own footwear, that hers couldn't possibly fit. Though God knows, I keep trying to shoehorn myself in.

Anyway, I was quite happy to clear up the kitchen just now while Mark chilled with that new series he loves. He'd had a hard week so we're not going out tonight. What was it he said? 'I don't deserve someone like you, you angel…' It made me smile. So now I've come upstairs 'for a bath', as I told him, which is why I'm running one, even though I have no intention of taking it. I just need to write, to get it all out, to clear my head.

Andrew's next appointment – only the second time I've ever seen this man in my life – was at three o'clock today. But he didn't actually arrive at the clinic until three twenty-five. I thought he wasn't coming. Felt so disappointed that he'd not called to cancel or say he'd be late. In fact, I felt panic-stricken. Bereft! Gutted! When he finally did arrive, he apologised of course, looking flustered, telling me about issues at home, stuff going on with his lodger. But I didn't really hear him. Not as I should have done. I was just giddy to see him, as if he were someone I knew from the past and had missed terribly. (~~Giddy? Can't believe I actually wrote that.~~)

I agreed to continue with the remainder of the appointment – he was still within his session time, after all, and had thirty-five minutes left – which is all I should have given him. Boundaries etc. But I let him run way over until four thirty. Rewarding his tardiness. The reality is, I broke a basic contracting rule for my own pleasure – the pleasure of being in his company. He was a delight to look at and I was still entranced by him – his kind voice, his warm and genuine words.

It was easy to justify because I didn't have any other appointments that day, was only planning on writing up notes afterwards, making some referrals. But I never got round to doing any of those things. Rather, afterwards, I sat staring out of the window, thinking about him. Thinking about everything. Trying to work out why he'd affected me so much. What it was about him that chimed with me. I still have no idea. Except that it's something. I've never felt like this before.

'I think we'd better end here,' I'd said finally as the clock ticked on, making a point of glancing at my watch.

He just stared at me, gave me that smile – the one I'm slowly coming to know, even though I've only spent a total of two hours with him. A part of me believes that he knows what I'm thinking – a sort of wry flicker that gently tugs the corners of his mouth, flexes the scar above his lip. And, of course, I'm curious where the scar came from. It doesn't look recent. But it does something to me. Something I can't explain.

'Shame,' he replied, which tied in perfectly with what was in my head. 'I was just getting warmed up.'

Warmed up. I wondered what he meant by that, but seeing as I'd not truly focused on anything specific he'd said that last hour – rather just got lost in his presence again – it was difficult to know. He wasn't pushy, though. Nothing to suggest he wasn't completely self-possessed. Unlike me.

(Writing's getting messy again. I need to be able to read this back. And I still haven't bloody well spoken to Chrissie to arrange a supervision session!)

'Life has a habit of… changing,' he'd said as he stood to leave.

I felt a chill then. Head to toe shivers as I showed him to the door, reaching out for the handle to open it, everything in slow motion, my hand not even looking like mine. As though I were someone else entirely, someone I didn't recognise. I'll be honest, I hated that he was leaving, hated that there was stuff I wanted to say even though that's not the point of therapy. Then that scent again – the scent I'd noticed last week.

I felt dizzy, insane, upside down and inside out. I wondered if he knew.

He was beside me at the door, almost touching me as I stood frozen to the spot.

'Just when you least expect it,' I'd replied stupidly, looking directly at him, my cheeks flushing. His eyes drilled into mine for the shortest time, but long enough for a second wave of shivers. Then that smile. Melting me. Drowning me in… kindness. As though he was wrapping me up, taking care of me, rather than there being any chance of me actually helping him. 'Maybe we can talk about that next session,' I said, wanting nothing more than him to bend forward and kiss me.

And in my mind, he did.

CHAPTER SIXTEEN

Lorna

'Cath, hi, it's me.'

'Oh… Lorna, what's up?' She sounds groggy, as though I've woken her.

I imagine her looking at the clock beside her bed, wondering why I'm calling at 7.21 a.m. on a Saturday morning. I pace about the kitchen. Mark has just popped out to get milk, and Freya's up in her room playing. Jack won't surface for hours yet.

'I… I was just wondering if you'd heard back from, you know, that guy on Double Take.' I slug a big mouthful of coffee. I don't feel like my usual protein shake. And I certainly don't feel like a run either. I shouldn't have had that extra glass of wine last night, but my mind wouldn't switch off.

'Wow,' Cath says with a throaty laugh followed by a cough. 'I'm so glad you care… at the crack of dawn.' She groans loudly.

'But did you?'

'Fuck knows, Lorn,' she says. I hear noises as though she's sitting up in bed, shifting into a comfortable position. 'Why do you want to know?' She makes a groggy sound again.

'I was… I was just concerned for you, that's all. You seemed sad about it last time I saw you.'

'You should have come to book club this Wednesday, then, to find out the next exciting instalment…' She manages a laugh, having woken up a bit.

'I'm sorry, Cath. You know I had to work late.' Which was true. I stayed on at the clinic until nearly 9 p.m., catching up on all the things I'd let slip since Monday – since my second appointment with *him*. My mind had been in other places. Dark places. Places that I never wanted to visit again. Mark was understanding, as ever. I told him that we were short-staffed, that I'd been asked to help out. I hate myself for lying. For my tight routine slipping. Slipping because of the very person I implemented it for in the first place.

'So, did you?' I ask.

'What?'

'Hear back from that guy.'

'I've been messaging several guys, actually,' she admits in a flirty voice. 'It gets hard keeping track of who's who, to be fair. But Annie was right, improving my profile worked wonders. I've had loads of messages.' Cath giggles and then I hear her footsteps, followed by the sound of her running the tap. 'But I have to be realistic. It's probably just because my hot friends are in some of the photos.'

'Can you check?'

'Check what?' She gulps down water. 'God, I'm thirsty. Overdid it a bit last night.'

'Check your messages, Cath!' I don't mean to sound so on edge.

'Yeah, I will later.'

'Can you do it now?'

'Now?'

'Yes. Now.'

'Blimey, you really *do* care, don't you?' She laughs again. Good-natured Cath. I can't tell her that it's my marriage and family I care about more.

Me and Mark and Freya and Jack.

'OK, hang on,' she says. 'You're on speaker now so I can go on the app.'

I hear her breathing, the sound of her finger lightly tapping the screen. She hums for a moment while I go into the living room, glancing out of the window. There's no sign of Mark.

'Oh wow, I've had three new messages overnight,' she says with a chirp. 'Mmm, he looks nice…'

'Cath, what about *that* guy, though – did you hear from him?'

'Sorry, what was his name again?'

That's a good question. I didn't see if he'd used his real name or some other user name. 'I don't know,' I say. 'You'll remember him if you see him. He's the tall one with the dark hair, green eyes. And the scar above his top lip.' A shudder runs through me, a familiar wave of dizziness.

'Lorn…' Cath says, drawing out my name into a long, accusatory syllable. 'You remembered he had a scar. And green eyes. Oh my God, *you're* into him, aren't you?'

'*Hell* no! Don't be so stupid. I mean, he's good-looking, sure, but I'm with Mark for God's sake. Why would you even say such a thing?'

'Lorn, I was joking. Chill.' Then silence while she checks through the app. 'OK, I see the guy you mean. His username is Andy_jag.'

That figures, I think. I once read an online interview he'd given, and he mentioned his love of Jaguar cars, how he'd always wanted to own a classic.

'No, no message back from him,' Cath says. 'Oh, but wait…'

'What is it?' Someone is coming down the stairs – Freya, most likely. I go back into the kitchen.

'I can see he's viewed my profile.'

'Really?' My heart thumps. In that case, he's seen me too.

'Yeah, actually about twenty times by the looks of it.'

'You can tell how many times?' I say, ruffling Freya's hair as she pulls the chocolate milk from the fridge.

'Yes… I can,' she says thoughtfully. 'In fact, it's way more than twenty. He's viewed my profile about twenty times a *day* since Annie sent him that message. But there's no reply from him.'

'Oh well,' I say, trying to sound casual even though my throat is closing up. 'Can't win 'em all.'

'He's fit, but I reckon he knows it, if you ask me. He has that certain look in his eye, a bit cocksure. Frankly, I find it a bit creepy he's been stalking me. Think I'll block and delete him.'

'No!' I shriek, making Freya slosh milk on the counter. Instinctively, I reach for the cloth by the sink, my hand shaking as I wipe up the mess. 'No, don't delete him.'

'Too late,' she says. 'Already done.'

And with those few words, the rest of my weekend is ruined.

I'd know Joe's knock anywhere – three raps followed by a quick double tap.

'Come in,' I sing out, propping my glasses on my head. 'Hey,' I say, smiling. 'It's OK, my next one's not due until three.' I glance at the clock. Still half an hour. Half an hour before *he* comes. Joe sits down at the chair the other side of my desk.

'Good weekend?' he asks.

'Yeah, not bad. You?' It's a lie.

'Ah, you know,' he says. 'The usual. Footie training for the kids. Shopping. Chores. Errands.' He pushes back a clump of curly blond hair that's fallen across his forehead. It's a habit he has, an endearing one that suits his casual but academic look – an open-neck pale blue shirt, light trousers, loafers without socks – it makes him seem approachable yet still professional for his clients.

'Goes in a flash,' I say, rolling my eyes. After I'd spoken to Cath early on Saturday morning, I was agitated for the rest of the day. Mark and I had planned to go shopping for a new sofa in the afternoon, but I told him I didn't feel like it. I would have liked to replace the old one with something we'd chosen together, but my heart wouldn't have been in it. I felt bad. We were also meant to go out that night to meet his work colleague and wife for dinner, but I feigned a headache way worse than just the nagging sensation pressing on my temples. Stupidly, I'd had one too many glasses of wine the night before and couldn't face the chit-chat, the pleasantries – not with *him* on my mind. Mark didn't grumble, but I could tell he was disappointed. I need to make it up to him somehow.

After months of hard work on myself, a solid ten months of not contacting him, of letting go, of healing the pain that had burnt through me, of trying not to allow a single thought about him to enter my head by fixing on a rigid routine that had reached OCD proportions, he'd burst his way back inside my mind. It was as though he'd never gone away.

Maybe he hadn't.

Maybe he'd always been there, even way before I'd met him.

I stare at Joe, all these things rushing through my mind.

'Is everything OK, Lorna?' he asks.

'Sure,' I reply. 'Why?'

He watches me, pauses, sizing me up. Then comes his empathic face, as if he knows something's up but isn't going to drill it out of me.

'I dunno, you just seem…'

I raise my eyebrows.

'Maybe a little stressed, distant perhaps?'

I shake my head, grabbing my reading glasses as they dislodge. 'No, not at all.' I clear my throat.

The dimple in Joe's chin puckers as he pulls a face. 'Come on, Lorn. You can talk to me. Anything you want to bring to supervision?'

'Oh, well actually, yes,' I say, appreciating the diversion. 'There are a couple of cases I'd like to talk about. One in particular.

I'm seeing a lad called Tom. He's nineteen. I think there may be historical abuse. Not certain yet but I'd like to get your take on it.'

'Sure, no problem,' Joe says. 'You're booked to see me Friday, but we can bring that forward if you like. Just in case there's anything else on your mind too?' He's not letting up.

'Friday's fine,' I tell him, when in reality I want nothing more than to open my heart, pour everything out right now. But I can't. There are some things therapists never reveal in supervision – not if they want to keep their jobs, anyway.

'Certain?' He clasps his hands across his chest.

'Certain,' I say, shrugging, trying to look vague.

Joe nods, watching me.

I clear my throat, straightening a stack of files. 'How's Sarah, anyway?' I've only met his wife a couple of times.

That smile again. He leans forward, ignoring my question. 'OK, look Lorna, I'll be straight with you. Sandy mentioned something to me the other day, and I was wondering if you'd like to discuss it. About client booking arrangements.'

I feel the first flush of my cheeks as the burn begins to spread, radiating down to my neck and chest. I'm nodding a little, my mouth slightly open. 'Oh, yeah.' I give an awkward smile.

'Sandy handles all the appointments, as you know, and obviously I don't need to say anything about therapist–client contact outside of session.'

'No, no, of course not,' I say. My mouth has gone dry, but I daren't reach for my water because my hand would shake too much.

'She was just a bit concerned, that's all.' He pauses. 'And frankly, I am too. She said that you took a client's phone number from her desk a couple of weeks ago.' He laughs, trying to dispel any tension in his usual Joe way, rubbing his beard. 'In fact, she said that you *snatched* the client's number from her pad, but I couldn't imagine you doing that.'

I stare at the ceiling, pretending to recall what he's talking about. 'Ah, yes. I think I remember now. There was a client who was very demanding with Sandy, phoning all the time, giving her hassle. She seemed really upset about it.'

'OK, so it sounds like you were trying to help her?'

'Absolutely,' I say. 'Some people can be so rude.'

Joe nods. 'Thing is, Lorna, a client is a client. Sandy knows how to handle the bookings, how to deal with the awkward ones.'

'I know. I'm sorry.'

'Did you make contact with the person directly?'

'Well, hardly,' I say. 'Just to fix up an assessment.'

Joe sighs, leaning back in the chair, slowly rolling his eyes to the ceiling. 'And he came for the assessment?'

I give a tiny nod, unable to speak.

'Then I'd like to see your notes from that session and any subsequent appointments.'

'Of course,' I say, making a pained face. 'Is tomorrow OK?' I don't reveal that he's actually my next client.

'Sure.' He waits for what seems like an age before standing and going to the door. Hand on the knob, he turns, looking back at me. 'You know where I am if you want to talk, Lorna.'

CHAPTER SEVENTEEN

Lorna

'Thank you for seeing me again,' he says as we go into my office. As ever, it's his scent that hits me – that familiar mix of spices and danger hanging in the air, making me feel light-headed as I lead him through.

'No problem,' I say, businesslike, closing the door, sealing us in for a third time. Though in reality, it *is* a problem. He's the worst kind of addiction. The worst kind of danger.

'I offered you the three sessions, Andrew, and I don't renege on clients.' What I really mean is that I'm too scared of the consequences.

We both sit down – me wearing grey trousers and a cream long-sleeve blouse to keep myself as covered up as possible – and him in jeans and a plain black T-shirt with a dark jacket over the top. I remember his brown leather shoes, remember once commenting on their quality. All these tiny things. Little triggers.

'So, how have things been this last week?' I try to make it sound the same as it does to all my other clients – interested but not pressuring, empathic and genuine without being patronising. But with Andrew, it comes out trite and awkward.

'Fine, thank you. Really good in fact.' His confidence makes me believe him, makes me hate him that things are so wonderful for him when they're the opposite for me. Since he came back.

'Good?'

'Sure,' he says again, shrugging and giving an amused smile. 'You sound surprised.'

I pause, looking at him, trying to keep a neutral look, trying not to let it turn into anything more than engaged eye contact. Trying not to show my longing.

'I'm a therapist, Andrew, and usually people come to see me when they have problems.' I wait for his response, but he says nothing. 'This is our second actual session now, not counting your initial assessment, and I'm still not clear why you're here. You have one appointment left after this, so now's your chance to share anything you'd like to explore with me.'

'Three sessions isn't a lot,' he says, his tone suddenly serious, regretful.

'Perhaps you'd like to talk about your personal life,' I say. 'It was the reason you came to see me last year, after all. Maybe a recap would be useful for you?' Or useful for me, I think. Even though I've tried to forget him, I've been desperate to know what's been going on with him, who he's seeing. If he misses me.

'Sure,' he says, folding his arms across his chest and grinning. His scar creases upwards. 'Ask me anything you like.'

'Thing is, Andrew, therapy doesn't really work like twenty questions. I'm here to help you help yourself.'

'Help myself... to what?' he says with almost a wink.

I look away, trying not to let the smile come. What is it about him, after everything, that still makes me want him? It's as though a loved one has come back from the dead, as if he's filling a void I never knew existed.

'You know what I mean,' I say. 'And you know how I work.' I just need to get through the next hour.

'I can't forget you, Lorna,' he says, knocking me off balance. 'What we had was—'

'Have you tried dating since I last saw you?' I can't let him go there, taunting me, sparking old feelings. 'It might help.'

'You mean since we last fucked?'

'Andrew—'

'You're curious, aren't you, in a twist-the-knife-in kind of way?'

'Is that what you think?' I laugh, feeling my cheeks burning. 'You're the one who came to see *me*, remember?'

'Anyway, "dating" sounds too much like teens at a high school prom,' he says. 'We didn't *date*, Lorna. We had sex.'

I close my eyes for a moment too long. 'Sounds like you're feeling a bit cynical about the whole idea of meeting new people?' I force myself to stay focused.

Andrew shrugs, pulling a face as if I've struck a nerve.

'Have you tried any dating sites? That could be a good way to meet new people.' I'm pushing hard, I know, but I need to know if he spotted me on Cath's profile. 'It might help you to move on.'

'Christ, no,' he says. 'Absolutely not.'

I nod slowly, knowing for sure that he's lying. My heart clenches. Such a basic lie confirms that he was no doubt lying about that woman too, his lodger – that he was doing the same with her as he was with me. I hate that I'm in no position to feel as jealous as I do.

'You seem pretty adamant about that,' I say, testing.

'Why do you think I came back to see you, Lorna?'

'Really, I have no idea. It's what I've been trying to establish.' I try not to sound scared, even though I am.

Scared of loving him again.

'It's simple. I wanted to see you,' he says. 'No other reason.'

He sounds genuine.

'But… but why *now*? And why like this?' My heart relaxes, unable to keep up its frantic pace, as though the toughened outer layers that have formed these last ten months are dissolving. Peeling away as my blood warms.

'I told you, it's simple. I miss you.'

I look away – towards the window, across at my desk, scanning all the psychotherapy books I have on the shelf behind it, the neat stack of files on my desk… anything. Anything to ground myself, to stop the feelings igniting.

'Andrew,' I say, uncrossing my legs, then crossing them again. 'I'm in a very *happy* marriage and I want it to stay that way. I can't explain what happened last year any more than you can. Yes, it was intense, and yes, it was unexpected. But we only met because I was your therapist—'

'*Are* my therapist.'

'No… no, I'm *not* your therapist. Don't you see? A therapist having *any* kind of relationship with a client is strictly forbidden. Let alone a married one.' I turn away again, closing my eyes and covering my face with my hands.

'Did your husband ever find out?'

'No,' I whisper from between my fingers, feeling the tears prickling in my eyes.

Oh God, Mark, I'm so sorry…

'Then he won't find out about us this time either.'

I turn round again to find Andrew in front of me, crouching down, his hands resting lightly on my knees. Our eyes are locked in that fragile moment between something happening and me stopping it. My heart races, pulsing in my throat as his fingers work slowly up my legs, veering off at my thighs as he takes hold of my hands. He lifts them to his lips.

'Andrew—'

'I want you, Lorna. I still love you. I've always loved you.'

'Please…' I try to pull away, but he holds me tighter.

If someone comes in and sees us, I'm finished. I tense, finally sliding out from between him and my chair, going over to the window. I take a few deep breaths, pushing my fingers through my hair, sweeping it back off my face. I stare out of the window at the small square opposite, shaking, trying to ground myself.

The same homeless guy is there, as ever, lying on the bench. And there's a woman there too, smoking, looking agitated. She turns quickly away when she sees me watching.

Suddenly, I feel light-headed, as if the floor's fallen away and I'm floating. I make it over to my desk, holding on to the edge to steady myself, putting a hand on my temple as the ringing in my ears grows louder. I don't feel well. Don't feel like me.

'Lorna?' Andrew says, coming over. 'Are you OK?'

I shake my head, which makes him go more out of focus until he transforms into someone I don't even recognise, as though he's someone from long ago. All I can focus on is his scar, while breathing in the strange, spicy smell. He holds me, guiding me back to my chair, pouring me some water. As I sip, the room gradually comes right again, and he turns back into Andrew.

'I'm sorry,' I say, feeling a cold sweat break out. 'I… I don't know what happened.'

He crouches down beside me, his hand on my legs again. 'You'll have to try harder than that to get rid of me,' he says, his face deadly serious.

CHAPTER EIGHTEEN

Lorna

'You know me so well,' he says, coming up behind me and pressing himself against my back. He nuzzles my neck, making me close my eyes. 'My favourite.'

'I'll have to beat you off with my wooden spoon,' I say, waving it in the air as he slides his hands down my body, across my hips and around to the front.

'You don't want to go upstairs quickly before dinner?' Mark takes the spoon from me, dipping it in the saucepan, tasting it. 'Oh God, scratch that. This trumps sex.' He licks his lips.

'Oh. Thanks a lot,' I say, laughing. 'Second best to fish curry, am I?' I spin around, grabbing him.

'A very close second,' he replies, making me think of what – or *who* – else I fall short of.

'Anyway, I made it because I wanted to do something nice for you. You deserve it.'

'I do?' He kisses me, tasting of Thai spices. 'It's not even my birthday.'

'Does it have to be?' I kiss him back, this afternoon's session with Andrew still thrumming in my head as though there are three of us in this kitchen. Then my phone pings in my bag on the table, making me stop, mid-kiss. Frozen. I turn back to the hob feeling the colour rise in my cheeks even though it's probably just Annie or Cath texting about something or other. Then it pings again. And again.

'Miss Popular,' Mark says. 'Want me to get that for you?' He reaches for my bag.

'No. No, that's fine. It can wait.' I screw up my eyes, stirring the curry.

'Sure,' he says quietly, and I hear him hanging it on a hook on the door. 'I'll set the table, then.'

After we've all eaten, I busy myself with washing up – plus scraping Freya's virtually untouched meal into the bin. I hate it that she's not eaten properly, and she didn't say much when Mark asked her about her day either – checking how her reading book was going, coaxing her to do her piano practice later. She shrugged an evasive reply, nibbling a piece of fish and complaining the sauce was too spicy. Jack wolfed his down, not saying much either before making excuses to get back upstairs to his coursework.

A normal dinner. A normal family. A normal wife and husband, except the wife has unread text messages on her phone burning into her heart. The last ten months' work on myself may as well have not happened.

'Want to carry on with that Netflix thing?' Mark says when I'm finished. 'I'm too knackered to play squash tonight.' He's already told me about his tough day.

'Tempting,' I say. 'But I ought to listen to Freya reading first. There was a note from her teacher in her school bag last week, asking me to make sure I do it with her every night.' I pause for a moment. 'Then I'll need to chase her into the bath, help her tidy her room.'

'I'll watch the news until you're done, then,' he says, giving me a squeeze. When he's gone from the kitchen, I slip my phone from my bag and go upstairs.

'Frey-frey,' I say from the landing. 'You reading your school book?'

'Uh-huh,' comes the vague reply from her bedroom.

I poke my head around the door to find her lying on top of the bed, her tablet propped in front of her. She quickly pauses the movie when she sees me, a guilty look on her face. I make a silly face in response. 'Run yourself a bath soon, then, you monkey.'

She nods gratefully, making me curl my toes into the carpet and close my eyes for a second. I shut the door behind me and head up the narrow staircase into the loft spare room – the room Mark and I both use as an office. We converted it not long after I moved in, and there's a sofa bed for guests up here too. It's a bit cramped, but there's enough space for us to catch up with work if necessary.

I sit down at my desk, stubbing my foot on a box underneath. 'Oww,' I say, scowling. It's the last of Maria's personal stuff – a few things that Mark still can't – or won't – let go of. I don't mind him keeping it, but we could do with the extra space these days. I've gently mentioned charity shops a couple of times, but his blank stare stopped me bringing it up again.

I pull the dusty carton out from under the desk. The flap pops open, allowing me a glimpse of some of her clothes, a jewellery box, a few scarves and a couple of books – none of it very neatly packed. I stare at the contents for a moment, wondering whether to dig deeper, but decide to seal it up with tape instead. I don't want to pry. I slide it across the floor under Mark's desk, along with the couple of others he's got stashed there.

I drop down on the sofa, closing my eyes, allowing my head to fall back.

I remember the first time he invited me here, a little while after we'd started seeing each other. Maria's stuff was still everywhere, as though she'd just popped out to the shops even though she'd died a couple of years earlier. I was surprised, but knew it was because he wasn't grieving properly, not moving on. Bringing me into the house for only a couple of hours was hard for him, let alone considering us moving in together. He needed to accept that she really wasn't coming back, but I knew it was going to take time. I just wasn't sure how long.

In the end, it was another eighteen months before he finally asked me to move in. Most of her stuff was gone by then, with the sentimental things he couldn't let go of packed away. I know he gets them out occasionally to look at with Jack, to tell him stuff about his mum he wouldn't otherwise know. I try to keep out of the way, understanding it's part of the process. It was a big change for him, bringing me into his life, and it wasn't long after I moved in that I fell pregnant with Freya. This loft conversion was me wanting to put my stamp on the house, wanting to make it feel more like mine and Mark's. My nesting instinct. It was all worth the wait.

I turn my phone over and over, still not knowing if the messages are from *him*. Savouring the moment. In reality, it's probably nothing more than a silly YouTube link from Cath, or a message from my mum about coming to visit at the weekend for Easter or, more likely, something about Dad. When I finally pluck up the courage to unlock it, my finger shakes.

Meet me.
Tomorrow morning.
Shots 10.30.

'Shots,' I whisper, thinking back to that morning last year, when everything was OK. When I was just hanging on. I still don't know if it was coincidence or a set-up by him – I'd only stopped at the café to grab a quick takeout coffee, and I was already running late for the office.

'Lorna?' someone behind me in the queue said, touching my shoulder. I swung around to see a man's face.

'Oh… I, um…' I tucked my hair behind my ear.

My eyes locked onto his as they drew me in, his very presence stripping me of coherent words. He had exactly the same effect on me there as he had done in the few therapy sessions we'd had so far. I hated myself for it. And it wasn't getting any easier.

Shit, I'd thought, reeling myself in, stepping back a little. There's a protocol for bumping into clients outside of a session, but all good sense seemed to dissolve in an instant. I couldn't help it.

'Oh, Andrew, hi,' I said, trying to sound casual. My smile came automatically, and he reciprocated with a bigger one. 'After a caffeine fix too?' I joked, putting my hand on his arm. *His arm.* Three rules broken – only acknowledge a client if they acknowledge you, but certainly don't use their name in public. And definitely don't ask questions or prolong the conversation. As for *touching* them…

He looked down at my hand, so I whipped it away, pulling my purse from my bag, head down, as we edged forward in the queue. I knew some of my colleagues from the Medway came into the café sometimes. I'd have a lot of explaining to do if I was caught chatting to a client.

'Essential to get the creative juices flowing,' he'd said. 'What's your poison? My treat.' He'd already told me in session he was an artist.

'Oh,' I said, caught off guard again. However small a gesture it was, it would make me indebted to him – and not just financially. In therapy, it's all about balance of power – in that there should be no disparity between client and counsellor. It's an equal relationship. Accepting gifts, however small, is against the rules. 'That's very kind,' I replied, knowing I should have made my excuses, left the café. 'Thank you. A soy latte would be great. With an extra shot.' I dug my nails into my palms, praying no one I knew would come in.

'Good girl,' he said. 'I like a woman who takes it strong.' He winked then, though I couldn't be sure because all I heard was *good girl* ringing in my ears a thousand times. The ground seemed to fall away, and I went woozy, almost as if I was drunk. All I could manage was a laugh – a stupid little girl laugh that dissolved the last of my boundaries.

He ordered, paid and we went outside. 'Cheers,' he said, raising his paper cup.

'Yeah, um, cheers. And thanks,' I replied, cupping my hands around my drink. It all felt so wrong, yet ridiculously right too.

Looking back, I hate it that Mark was nowhere in my mind.

'I'd like to buy you a proper drink sometime, if you're free one evening,' he said as I was about to leave, wrong-footing me again. By then, I was punch-drunk.

'Oh, well...' I said. 'It's not really, you know...'

'Ethical?' he said, so I didn't have to.

'Yeah.' I pulled a silly face, stepping from one foot to the other. It was freezing. 'I shouldn't even really be talking to you now, truth be known,' I admitted, which, in hindsight was stupid. But those eyes, his lips, the scar, the stubble on his jaw disappearing down beneath the black scarf he wore... I didn't think I'd ever seen a man I found more attractive. Or if I had, it hadn't felt anything like this.

'But you are, though,' he said, staring right into my eyes. 'Talking to me.'

We held the gaze for what seemed like forever – one of those heartfelt movie moments where you just know what's going to happen. Except it didn't. Not then.

'Right, I'd better go,' I said, giving him a nod, a last look, a mumbled thank you, before turning and walking down the street in completely the wrong direction.

Are you still living with her? I text back with shaking hands, ignoring his message about meeting tomorrow morning. Within moments, my phone pings again. I switch it to silent, so no one hears.

It's not what you think.

I squeeze my phone, wanting to fling it across the room. If I reply, it just prolongs the agony. If I don't... well, that's agony too. My phone vibrates again.

You know she's just my lodger. Meet me tomorrow.

Typo? Lover, you mean. Then I write *No* and hit send.

I can see within a few seconds that he's read my message, but he doesn't reply. 'Fuck,' I say, throwing my phone down on the sofa beside me. I wait. Fifteen minutes pass. Nothing. I begin typing another message but delete it. Mark calls up to me, asking if I want a cup of tea.

'No, thanks,' I shout back from the top of the stairs. Loud music suddenly booms below me in Jack's room as I begin typing another message, hoping to see the little bubbles of Andrew typing back meantime. But there's nothing. I don't send mine.

'Fuck, fuck, *fuck*,' I say under my breath, pacing around the attic room. I lean my forehead against the slope of the ceiling, catching sight of a couple of stars through the Velux window. Then that time on the houseboat is on my mind, how he rented it just for a night through Airbnb. We lay on rugs on the deck drinking champagne, watching the few stars visible in the London sky. All such a cliché. Except it was beautiful and romantic. Temporarily perfect.

I'd pretended to Mark that I'd gone away on a work conference, almost believing it myself so I didn't feel quite so wretched. By this time, I excused my behaviour to myself as a disease or a mental health issue, as though I simply couldn't help what I was doing. Plenty of people have told me about their affairs in therapy. And I was only human too, I convinced myself.

Hear from that guy yet? I text to Cath, partly to stop me texting something to *him* that I'll regret, and partly to check if she really did block him. Not knowing what he's doing is killing me, yet knowing anything about him is killing me too. Ten months of no contact, ten months of being clean, being off my drug, was the only way I got through. A tight, ordered existence with no room for intrusive thoughts. Now I've fallen off the wagon.

Lol no, I deleted him, remember? Cath replies quickly.

Oh yeah, I text. *His loss. How're things?* I add, to sound vaguely normal.

Then she gives me a rundown of her day over several messages and, as I'm about to reply, Andrew texts again. *Meet me tomorrow. Please.* He's not giving up.

I sit on the couch, staring blindly at the desk opposite me – the desk with my laptop on it. It's then I know what I have to do.

After a few more minutes battling with myself, my mind's made up. I can't help it that I dash downstairs, apologising to Mark that I have some urgent work notes to write up for tomorrow, that he'd better go ahead and watch the Netflix series without me. Can't help it at all that on the way back up to the study, I tell Freya that she can skip her bath if she wants, that she should just put her pyjamas on and get into bed.

And I completely can't help it that, back at my desk, I open up my laptop and go straight to the Double Take website. I can't help anything any more.

CHAPTER NINETEEN

Lorna

My fingers hover over the keys as I stare at the pink and yellow website. I take a sip of the neat whisky I brought back up with me in the hope it will slow my heart, ease my guilt. Surely just looking at it for a few minutes can't hurt?

Can it?

That's all I'm going to do.

'Log in' or 'Register', it says in the top right corner of the screen. My eyes flick over the collage of photographs of paired-off, exceptionally good-looking men and women in the centre of the page – a collection of individuals unlikely to be on this website if the examples on Cath's phone app were anything to go by. I hover the mouse over them but there's no link, no search button anywhere on the home screen. Just happy, shiny couples. The FAQs tell me I have to register to view members.

'Damn,' I whisper, tapping my fingernails on my glass. All I wanted was a quick look, a glimpse of his profile to see what it says, to see his other pictures. He's already lied about being on there; doesn't know that I know.

I click on 'Register' and a basic form pops up. Username, email address, male or female, date of birth, what gender I'm looking for... 'Damn again,' I say again, allowing the whisky to burn down my throat. What would happen if I were to quickly register, just take a peek, then never look again? But I can hardly use my work email address because they're monitored, and Mark and I have access to each other's home email addresses – we always have done, trusting each other implicitly. It was his idea, and I've always loved how open and honest he is about stuff like that. Changing my password would arouse suspicion. My stomach knots at the thought.

I'm hardly aware of opening another tab, going to Gmail, clicking on 'create account' and speeding through the form, quickly making up a name formed from the first and last names of several of my current clients – Abbi Foster. Within a couple of minutes, I have a fresh new email account. Back on the dating site, I enter the details and think up a username ... nothing *he* would ever connect with me, but something I can remember too. I settle on Abbi74 – the year of my birth and also the number of our house. I fill out the other boxes, click enter and then I'm faced with a raft of questions about my likes and dislikes, my hobbies, my education. I go through them all at speed, not thinking much about the answers.

'Enter a description of yourself... oh God,' I say, trying to bypass this bit. But it won't let me. I've come this far, so I quickly make up a blurb about Abbi Foster, the woman who is not me.

Kind, good listener, spirited but easy-going, I'm a professional lady looking for a decent guy. If you love walks along the river, drinking wine by candlelight and kissing in the rain, then send me a message... What could possibly go wrong?

It'll do, I think, figuring it's generic and trite enough to look genuine, but with a bit of humour thrown in. I click 'next', only to be faced with a photo upload screen. 'Great,' I mutter. I can hardly use a picture of myself. Then I hear a noise. 'Freya, love, is that you?' Nothing. I go to the top of the stairs. 'Frey-frey?'

'What, Mummy?' comes my daughter's reply from her room.

'Nothing, sweet—'

'It was me, love,' Mark says. 'Just getting something.' I see him on the landing below, the book he's reading tucked under his arm. 'You nearly done up there?' he asks, pausing, leaning on the banister, looking up at me.

'I… well, I've got a fair bit to do yet,' I say. 'Joe needs these reports first thing. Sorry,' I add, making a pained face. My stomach churns – warning me, reminding me – but I ignore it.

Mark gives me an understanding nod and goes back downstairs.

'I'll try to be quick,' I call out, feeling a surge of guilt. Back at my desk, I wonder what to do about a photograph. It's not as if I'm going to contact him.

Is it?

My guts twist in knots as I do a Google image search for pictures of women about my age. Halfway down the page, there's a photo of a woman who's very attractive, yet not brash or obvious about it. Her hair is much lighter than mine, her figure curvier. I don't want anyone vaguely resembling me. I click on it, ending up on some fashion blog in the States. There are plenty more pictures of her here.

I right-click on a few of them, saving them to a locked work folder on my laptop – somewhere Mark would never look, even if he borrowed my computer. He respects how confidential my client files are.

'OK, OK…' I say, uploading three photos of the unsuspecting American woman. My hands are shaking and my breathing erratic. 'It's fine,' I tell myself. 'She'll never see them… I'll be deleting the account in ten minutes anyway.'

Congratulations! pops up on my screen. *You're now ready to start searching for love!*

I take a deep breath, ignoring how wrong this all is.

'Right, let's do this…' I whisper, filling out a few search criteria to help locate my 'dream man', as the site suggests.

To help find *him*.

I tap in his specific age – nothing more, nothing less – as well as his exact height, eye colour and all the other minutiae that will lead me to him, while also keeping one ear open for anyone coming upstairs. My heart is thumping. It feels as though I'm creeping up the front path of his house – the house he never let me visit because of *her* – and peeking through his front window, watching him, spying on him. Maybe even seeing them together.

A long list of profiles flashes onto my screen, ordered by 'last online'. I scroll down, scanning all the dark-haired men who are six foot one, not recognising any of them. A couple of alerts suddenly pop up – *Your profile has just been viewed by KingKong72… Prairie_dog1 likes your profile… chatty_guyw12 wants to meet you…*

'*Meet* me?' I whisper incredulously. 'But you don't even *know* me.' It suddenly feels as though I'm standing naked in a noisy bar, surrounded by lecherous guys all closing in on me. But none of them are *him*. It feels dangerous, as if I've stepped into a fantasy world as Abbi74. I'm half expecting to be sniffed out at any moment, as if a message might pop up saying 'Lorna, fancy seeing you here! Does Mark know you're on a dating site?'

It's all in my head, I tell myself, sipping more whisky. No one knows… Even *he* won't know.

I keep scrolling down the list, about to give up when I stop suddenly, almost choking on my drink.

It's *him*.

It's Andrew.

His profile stands out from the rest like a punch in the face. I stifle a gasp, as if I've been caught red-handed peeking through his window.

'Hi,' I say softly, touching his image on the screen with a shaking finger, stroking his hair, tracing the line of his jaw. Judging by the notifications I'm getting in the corner of my screen, if I click on his profile he's going to get an alert showing that I viewed him.

I take a deep breath and do it anyway.

Clicked. Done.

It's as if I'm actually inside his living room now.

'He won't know it's you,' I tell myself over and over as my eyes greedily soak up all the information on his profile. His pictures fill the top left corner of the screen, then it shows his likes, interests, marital status and what he's seeking listed below.

One by one, I scroll through the pictures he's put up – pictures I know only too well. Him at an art gallery opening, another shot of him that was in the local papers when he was commissioned by someone famous, another one of him from a school's website showing him mentoring A level art students. I cover my face again, unable to help the sob. Seeing all these details about him – his love for fine wines, for cooking, for art, for river walks, for old books and rummaging through flea markets… it's killing me.

Why not send Andy_jag a message? the box says, the cursor blinking at me, tempting me.

'Why *not*?' I whisper, my head filling up with a thousand reasons why not. But I still click in the blank space, still begin typing words that don't seem to be coming from me, as if my hands have been taken over by someone else. I stare at what I've typed, my mouth dry, my eye sockets aching, my heart on fire.

Hi Andy, are those your paintings behind you in the photo? Exquisite…

I know they are his. It's the word I used to describe his work the first time I saw his pictures – an array of nudes in bright, unnatural colours displayed on a slate grey wall. He'd played with the female form in a way I'd never seen before – making their bodies seem both beautiful and grotesque. It made me love him all the more.

'I'll paint you one day,' he once told me.

Someone is coming up the stairs.

'Shall I tuck Freya into bed, Lorn?' Mark says from halfway up. 'It's getting late.'

I freeze, my mouth hanging open. Then, without thinking, without considering the consequences, I click send. My message flies off the screen with a congratulatory pop-up window telling me that I'm on my way to finding true love.

'Sure. Thanks, love,' I call back. 'I'll be down in a moment.'

Then, knocking back the rest of my whisky, I log out of the site and close my laptop. I sit with my head in my hands for the next few minutes before going down to Freya's room to give her a kiss. I pick her crumpled school skirt up off the floor, then stop, staring out of the window, trying to work out why I'm hell-bent on destroying everything I hold dear.

The figure standing on the pavement in the shadows makes me catch my breath – someone across the street is staring up at me in the cold, dank evening. Their hood and collar shield their face and the drizzle snaking down the panes makes it impossible to tell if it's a man or a woman. Within seconds, they disappear into the darkness.

'Was that *you*?' I whisper softly, fogging the glass with my breath. '*Andrew*…?' I write an X in the mist, hating myself even more, before pulling the curtains closed.

CHAPTER TWENTY

Nikki

I hate her, though I shouldn't. It's hardly her fault, after all. She doesn't know anything.

Yet.

I stare at her house – middle class and perfect with its two bay trees in pots guarding either side of the front door. The black railings, the brass door knocker, the stylish wooden shutters in the window giving me sliver-sized glimpses of her happy life, her happy husband, happy children.

It's a far cry from my childhood home – dirty and unwelcoming after my father died. My mother blamed me, punishing me by transforming our once joyous domain into a wasteland of blame, fags and alcohol. Or perhaps she was punishing herself.

It's cold and dark out here on the street, but also where I feel most comfortable, lurking in the shadows – my hood up, the collar of my coat turned against the wind. With my hands in my pockets, my face down, I steal furtive glances at the lit-up, three-storey brick terrace. Worth what around here now – one and a half million? I shake my head, pacing about and glancing at my watch whenever anyone walks past, making it look as if I'm waiting for someone.

I cross the road and go up to number seventy-four, trailing my hand along the cold railings, sending tremors up my fingers, along my arm and straight into my heart. Reigniting it, as if I'm slowly recharging.

When I reach the end of the street, I turn around and walk back again. This time, when I reach her house, I dare to go up the front path – lit up by a coach lamp above the door. I pull the little spray of spring flowers from my pocket. I picked them earlier in the park. They're a bit wilted and crumpled now, but still pretty. I breathe in their scent, before laying them down on the front doorstep. Leaving my mark.

Flowers on a grave.

I cross the street again, standing in the shadows. There's a broken flower head in my pocket so I crush it between my fingers, grinding off the petals one by one. And that's when I see her at the upstairs window, staring out, looking down on me.

I dart backwards, wondering if she saw me, if she's even aware I exist. I doubt she knows anything about me – the lodger who fits all her worldly possessions into a single holdall, who works in a greasy burger van for cash in hand. *He* won't have told her anything about me. He's good at keeping secrets.

I turn to leave, taking one last glance at the upstairs window. Her forehead is resting against the glass before she touches it with her finger. Then she snaps the curtains closed.

Shutting me out.

My hand shakes as I put the key in the lock, letting myself into the place I call home. It's where I've been the longest these last few years. I saw the advert in a shop window a couple of years ago, handwritten in the most beautiful, artistic writing – cursive, unselfconscious pen strokes and such heartfelt words:

I don't want a lodger, I want a friend. Come and share my home, my food, my wine and good company. There's a garden for you to sunbathe or smoke in. A log fire for you to keep warm by. Rental terms flexible for the right person.

Flexible, I thought, wondering what that meant, writing down the phone number. There were a couple of grainy photographs attached – it was old-fashioned but looked like a real home, with everything from clutter on the shelves to a fridge with curious photographs stuck to the front. I could see immediately that it had soul. And, most of all, it was in the right location. He sounded like the sort of landlord who wouldn't mind taking cash, who wouldn't ask questions. Who'd do me a deal.

'Hi,' he calls out from the kitchen as I creep past the door. I'm not in the mood for talking, for pretending everything's OK. And not in the mood for anything else either. 'Want some food?'

I halt, one foot on the bottom of the stairs. 'Sorry, I'm not really hungry,' I say, hoping that will be enough.

'Plenty here. Come on, Nikki,' he replies, coming into the hallway. 'You've not been yourself recently. What's going on?' He draws up close beside me as I stand frozen on the first step.

'I'm fine,' I say, shrugging. I need him to believe everything is normal between us, need him to not suspect a thing. I don't want to be homeless before I'm ready.

He takes my arm, not gently but not roughly either. 'No, really I *insist*,' he says, his other hand on my bum.

Something flares in my mind – an instinct, something defensive and protective from way back. An inner voice that once kept me alive. I want to lash out, hit him, scream and bite him, but I don't. My mind feels dirty and clogged, filled with stirred-up silt, making me not think straight. Then that feeling of déjà vu sweeps through me and I'm thinking about *her* again, if this is what she has to endure. Does she comply in the same way? Does she smile sweetly, obeying his every word, caught up in his charm, his lies, his fake sincerity? Does she hate herself for it, like me? He's played the both of us.

'Come on. Come and eat,' he tells me, sitting me down at the kitchen table. 'You've lost weight, skinny girl.'

I force a smile and do as I'm told. The room is big but dated – high ceilings and 1970s-style worktops with aluminium handles on the cupboards, a lino floor, a limescale-encrusted metal sink. I pull the crumpled primrose head from my pocket, rolling it round and round between my fingers. 'I'm eating just fine.'

'Well, you could have fooled me,' he says, lifting the lid from a steaming pan. He grabs two plates from the cupboard – brown and orange chinaware. I remember my gran owning similar. And then my dad's on my mind – Gran's only son. I was the first to find him. I should have tried to save him instead of gawping and screaming at his lifeless body.

The dizziness comes again then, and not from lack of food. I'm neck deep in freezing water, paralysed, the cold gripping me by the throat, pulling me down. The numbness taking over.

At first, I didn't know what it was. Didn't recognise the signs. But years ago, I had time on my hands, so I went to the library, read all about it, used the computers to research PTSD and all the vile, pernicious tendrils that permeate my life. Knowing what it was gave me some kind of comfort. Almost helped me feel alive again.

'You treat me too well,' I say, watching him serve out ribbons of creamy pasta, wondering if he can hear my thoughts. I slide out of my coat, while he glances at me from the corner of his eye, a little smile forming through the steam. I go up behind him, slipping my hands around his waist, my chin resting on his shoulder. 'You're the best landlord.'

'And you're the best lodger,' he says, swinging round to kiss me.

CHAPTER TWENTY-ONE

Lorna's Journal

More sneaking about, but it's just the way my life is going these days, finding snatched moments to read, leafing through the handwritten pages as fast as I can, trying to make sense of what went on. Except there is no sense. No sense at all because it's all kicking off again. I know it. I feel it. Sometimes you have to trust your gut.

This time I have the house to myself, everyone is out. But it won't be long before the front door bursts open and the others are home, the house filled with noise and chatter, the chaos of the evening beginning. And I'll have to behave normally again, as if nothing's going on, as if I haven't done anything wrong, or been sneaking about, or registered a fake account on a dating site. I open the notebook, remembering where I got to, knowing where to pick up.

30 January 2017

I hate to admit it, but I dressed up for him this week. I tried on three different outfits this morning before settling on a dress. A dress! When did I last wear one of those to work? Mark commented, asked who I was trying to impress. Then he grabbed me, dragging me close, kissing me, telling me how good I looked. Part of me wished we could each take the day off work, stay in bed. But the other part was desperate to see him.

'Just fancied a change,' I replied, making sure I had that lipstick in my bag, plus my other make-up for a touch-up before his appointment.

'Mmm, I approve,' he said, holding me at arm's length, looking me up and down. I suddenly felt self-conscious; in the couple of photos I'd seen of Maria, she was always impeccably dressed. That one of her and Mark at a friend's wedding has always stuck in my mind – the clingy red fabric and plunging neckline making her figure look... well, not like mine.

But I appreciated Mark's comment, that he liked my outfit, and tried to take it at face value. I'm not Maria, and Mark knows that. I just need to acknowledge it too.

'Oh...' I'd said, about to leave. 'What are you doing?'

Mark was rummaging through my handbag. He didn't stop when I questioned him. 'Just looking,' he said, without glancing up.

I waited a moment, in case I'd got it wrong. He was perhaps just after a tissue. Some change. But he opened every compartment, pulling stuff out, as though he was looking for something in particular.

'For what?'

He stopped then, dropping my oversized bag on the bed. 'Anything,' was his matter-of-fact reply. I didn't understand. 'We're both at work five days a week, Lorna. That's a lot of time apart.' It didn't make sense. And to be honest, as I'm writing, it still doesn't. What was he expecting to find?

So Andrew was on time this week (his lateness last week unsettled me and I was nervous he'd do it again). I didn't bother saying his name when I collected him from the waiting room, rather I just waited for the eye contact I knew would draw him to me when he sensed me standing close. He was engrossed in something on his phone but looked up as soon as I was beside him. That little smile exchanged; the smile that said there was something else between us now, something else outside of the therapy office – those few illicit moments shared in the coffee shop.

'I never expected to be alone at this time of my life,' he said after he'd settled on the sofa, after we'd exchanged a few overly long glances that didn't need words. I asked him how his week had been, how he'd been feeling, what had been going on with him. Kudos to me for not leaping out of my chair and punching the air when he implied he was single.

'You sound a bit sad about that, Andrew. As if you don't like living alone,' I said. 'As if perhaps you had other expectations?'

'I don't do expectations,' he replied with conviction. 'And actually, I don't live alone,' he said, switching my brief excitement to disappointment. Anger, even.

'Oh,' I said, trying not to betray my feelings. 'So… so there's a relationship that's gone stale? Are you lonely?'

That would be OK, I thought. Something to work with. After all, I'm not exactly unattached.

Anyway, I still wasn't clear why he'd come for therapy. Relationship issues, I supposed, even though he'd not actually said. In fact, he wasn't saying much at all about his reasons for being there. But sometimes it goes like that. Half a dozen sessions passing before the real issues surface. Bad relationship choices turning out to be childhood abuse; sleeping problems and anxiety at the core of complex PTSD. Things are rarely what they seem.

'Yes, I live with a woman,' he said then – the equivalent to a kick in the guts. (~~I'm so pathetic~~). He'd sort of laughed – a laugh that made me think he was hiding something, as if he had a secret. As if he wanted me to find out. To work for it.

~~Or is it~~ me ~~with the secret?~~

'She's my lodger, actually.'

I felt physically sick then. Sick and stupid. Sick I'd bothered with the dress that showed off my figure, sick I'd freshened up before he arrived, applying the peach shimmer lipstick I'd chosen especially. Sick

I'd bought fresh lilies for my office. The flower of death, I'd thought, as I arranged them on the side table. But sick for another reason too. One I couldn't quite reach, something stuck deep inside. And I felt stupid... well, fucking stupid for everything.

I love Mark.

'I see,' I said, not liking one bit that his lodger was a 'she'. 'So you have a lodger who you're in a relationship with but you're lonely.' I was making too many assumptions, of course. Telling him his own feelings. There's no room for that in a therapy session.

He made an odd face then, as though in his mind the two things weren't linked. I flagged it, at least, but I wasn't truly hearing him. I was too caught up in my own stupidity.

'Yeah, yeah kind of.' He rubbed the stubble on his jaw, looking pained. 'But it's more complicated than that. Or perhaps, actually, it's really simple. What it is...' he continued, but stopped short because I interrupted him by drawing in a huge breath, ready to speak. So he paused, gentle smile lines forming around his eyes, as though he was the therapist and I was about to pour my heart out to him. I wanted that more than anything. To tell him how I felt – that he was the most attractive man I'd ever laid eyes on, that already he made me feel safe, wanted, secure. Childlike. I had no idea why. I just knew it. Felt it.

'Sorry,' I said, laughing nervously, rolling my eyes in a sort of cute apology. 'Carry on.'

'No, no, really it's fine,' he said. 'I was just going to say that in relationships generally, no one ever lives up. And look, don't get me wrong. Loads of people I know have lodgers these days. It's easy money, really. Plus the tax breaks.'

'OK,' I said. 'Lives up... as in?'

'Expectations again,' he said. Then an embarrassed laugh, almost as though he had something to be ashamed of.

A switch flicked in me then and I pretty much did everything right after that point. Thank fuck some professionalism finally kicked in once I realised he was involved with a woman, that he wasn't interested *in me. At least one of us had morals. But I couldn't forget that he'd bought me a coffee, that he'd asked me out for a drink as we were standing outside Shots. Then Mark flashed into my mind at just the right time, as if he was there, watching over me, reading my thoughts. It was all so crazy and mixed up.*

After that, I had to fight back the tears for the rest of the session – tears of self-loathing, mainly – especially when Andrew mentioned a couple of past relationships. I hated that, though I hated it more when he mentioned his lodger again. Everything seemed to come back to her. I even wondered if he did it on purpose, to make me jealous. I convinced myself he did. Because that would have meant he liked me.

'So the woman who lives with you...' I continued relentlessly. He'd not mentioned her name yet, as if he wanted to protect her. 'I'm sensing something underlying there, some kind of... I don't know, tension, perhaps?'

'Maybe,' he said, staring at me until I felt forced to look away.

But the real shock today isn't that I didn't listen to him without judgement as a good therapist should, or even provide him with any kind of useful help. Nor was it much of a shock that, as he was leaving, with his hand settled in the small of my back, he again asked to meet me for a drink. No, the real shock here is that I actually said yes.

CHAPTER TWENTY-TWO

Lorna

I didn't sleep, of course. Not after what I did last night. Seeing his pictures on Double Take was one thing, but actually sending him a message, pretending to be someone else, was pure insanity. Mark was already in bed when I slid between the sheets: softly snoring, oblivious. After I'd said goodnight to Freya, I was downstairs for the rest of the evening, checking my phone, unsettled, pacing about, splashing surreptitious shots of whisky into my glass and sucking mints so Mark didn't notice the smell on my breath.

I'd stared at the app store on my phone, my finger hovering over the install button for Double Take, convincing myself I could get rid of it at any time, that it would just be a quicker and easier way to check if he'd replied. But when Mark came into the room, I stopped.

'I'm going to bed, I'm knackered,' he'd said, sounding flat. I'd nodded and flicked a wave at him along with a half-smile. He looked at me for a second before heading upstairs, leaving me mindlessly flicking through channels, then staring at the wall, wondering what the fuck I was going to do.

He'd come back into my life, stirring up everything, and there wasn't a damn thing I could do about it. Eventually, I climbed into bed next to Mark, sleeping fitfully for a couple of hours, watching the clock, waiting for morning.

'Mark?' I whisper, touching his shoulder. It's 5.45 a.m. – less than an hour before I need to get up. 'You awake?' He stirs beside me, flopping his arm across my waist. His breathing is steady, content, so I slip the weight of his arm off me and ease myself out of bed, watching him for a moment. When he doesn't move, I tiptoe across the room and go up the stairs into the attic room, leaving the light off.

With shaking hands, I open up my laptop and log into the site. Alerts immediately pop up, showing me my profile has been viewed thirty-six times and that I have five new messages. I click on the inbox icon, my eyes scanning the list of senders. None of them are him.

'Mum-*mee*...' Freya says, shoving her cereal bowl away and folding her arms. 'I hate muesli.'

'Please eat something, Frey,' I say, passing her a banana. Her little mouth puckers as she peels the underripe fruit, her face following suit when she bites into it. I put a tangerine, a packet of crisps and a chocolate bar into her lunchbox alongside the Marmite sandwiches – the only thing she seems to eat these days – and stuff the plastic tub into her backpack. Her PE kit is still in there from last week, crumpled and in need of a wash. I close my eyes for a moment.

'I don't want to go to school,' she says, kicking the chair and ducking her head as Jack comes in, ruffling her hair. 'It's boring. I want to stay with you.'

'S'up, Smudge?' he says, sitting down beside her. He pulls her untouched cereal bowl towards him, shovelling up the muesli for himself. Normally, this would make her grab it back and eat, but Freya just sits there, picking at her fingers.

I watch her for a moment, wondering why my little girl has dark rings under her eyes, but there's no time to ask, barely time for me to gulp down my coffee and grab my work bag.

'C'mon,' I call out. 'Time to leave.' I open the front door, watching as Jack stuffs his feet into trainers and heads off to the bus for college, leaping over the threshold as he goes. There's no kiss but at least he calls out a goodbye.

Freya does her laces meticulously, sighing as she grabs her pack off the bottom of the stairs, dragging her feet. She walks out beneath my arm as I hold the door wide, but stops on the top step, bending down to pick something up.

'Look, Mummy,' she says, holding up a bunch of wilted flowers. I take them from her, puzzled. They look handpicked – their stalks are all different lengths – and they're not tied together, just left loose and drooping. A few lilac primroses, some narcissus, something else pale blue that I don't recognise, flop over my hand as I hold them. They look as though they've been there all night. I'm surprised Mark missed them earlier when he left first thing for his meeting.

'How odd,' I say, glancing up and down the street. I peer into next door's garden to see if there's anything similar, but there isn't.

'Maybe it was the fairies that left them,' Freya says excitedly. 'Or perhaps there's a boyfriend that loves you,' she giggles.

'Cheeky monkey,' I say, forcing a laugh, dumping the flowers on the hall table, wondering if perhaps she's right.

The usual five-minute car journey takes twenty, though it seems like ten times that. 'Come on, come *on*,' I mutter, angry at myself for spending too long up in the study earlier, poring over who'd viewed my profile, making us late.

Not him, I think, feeling abandoned, let down, rejected. Some of the lewd messages I, or rather *Abbi74*, received flash through my mind. No wonder Cath's having such a hard time finding someone decent.

We pull up outside the school gates and Freya slowly opens the car door. 'No kiss?' I say, swinging round, but she just looks at me with sad eyes, slowly opening the door. I reach out my hand to at least touch her, but she's out on the pavement, giving me one last glance and a little smile before the teacher standing at the gates ushers her inside.

Tom sits opposite me, his arms folded across his chest, his expression giving nothing away.

'So you want to make Tuesday your regular slot now?' I ask.

He gives a small nod, not looking at me.

'You're still struggling with Mondays, then?'

'Always will,' he says. 'Don't do anything on Mondays. Makes it easier. Kind of.'

'But I'm sensing it's not Mondays that are the problem, Tom. You've already talked about Sundays, that you couldn't sleep.'

He nods again. 'But Mondays are filled with Sundays,' he tells me. 'The aftermath.'

I pause, trying to absorb what he's telling me, what he's trying to admit to himself. But my mind is elsewhere – on the Double Take app that I plucked up the courage to install on my phone just before Tom's session began. Because of this, I was five minutes late collecting him from the waiting room. Sandy gave me a look as she glanced up from her screen.

'The aftermath,' I repeat. 'That sounds like what someone might say about an accident…' I say, hoping it will open something for him.

'It wasn't an accident. Accidents aren't on purpose.'

I hear my phone vibrate in my bag under my chair. Normally, I leave it in my desk drawer well out of earshot, or even turn it off completely. Even a phone buzz can be distracting and unsettling to a client, as if I'm not fully present with them, as if I'm more interested in my life outside the therapy room.

My mouth goes dry as a repeat buzz sounds a few moments later. I ease my foot back so if it happens again, I'll feel it against my skin. Feel a physical connection, just in case.

'What wasn't an accident, Tom?' It's more direct than I usually am, but my mind is elsewhere.

He covers his face, scratching his nails down skin that already looks tormented by lack of sleep, by worry, by alcohol and weed and whatever else he uses to numb the pain.

'I'm going to quit uni,' he says. 'It's not for people like me.'

'People like you?' My phone vibrates again, buzzing against my ankle. I close my eyes for a second.

'Yeah, people like—'

'Would you just excuse me a moment, Tom? There's something I need to check.' He stares at me as I reach down to my bag, unaware that I'm blowing apart everything I've ever held dear about my job, breaching my code of ethics. 'Sorry,' I say, sitting up again. 'I'm expecting a message.' Which effectively shows him that whoever I'm waiting to hear from is more important than him. I check the screen.

Two texts.

From *him*.

It's all the therapy I need.

CHAPTER TWENTY-THREE

Lorna

'See you next week, then, Tom,' I say at the reception desk as Sandy books him in. Joe is bent double beside her, delving through the filing cabinet.

'Thanks,' Tom says, gripping his fingers, agitated. 'And don't worry about checking your phone again next session either, miss. I don't mind.' He gives me a little smile.

'Oh, I… um…' I freeze, not knowing what to say. Sandy's eyes are suddenly on me and I sense that Joe's certainly are. He's standing up now, hands on hips, listening. 'There's no need to call me miss, Tom. Lorna is fine.' I smile, hoping that's deflection enough, but I know it won't be. It will have been an exploding can of red paint for Joe.

'Thanks, Lorna. Thanks again for today,' Tom says, sounding an ounce lighter than when he came in. He has no idea what he's just done.

His mother is hovering nearby, frowning, walking off beside him, mumbling something under her breath… *Checking her phone? I don't pay good money for that…*

Once they're gone, I turn to go back to my office, head down. I don't have any clients for the next half-hour.

'Lorna, a word please,' Joe says, stopping me in my tracks. When I look round, he's holding the door to the staffroom wide open. I nod, expressionless, catching Sandy's raised eyebrows and almost sympathetic smile.

'OK, Lorn,' Joe says once we're inside and he's closed the door. 'What was all that about?' There's no one else in there – just the smell of stale coffee that was made several hours ago now burning on the machine. Joe flicks it off, folding his arms and facing me, leaning against the counter. I stand, guiltily, in the middle of the room, my arms dangling by my sides.

'God, I'm sorry, Joe.' I hang my head, thinking quickly. 'It's not how it sounds,' I say, knowing it's exactly how it sounds. Probably worse. 'Freya's not well. Not well at all, actually. I dropped her at the school gates this morning and she was coughing and felt really poorly. I thought she was going to throw up. I shouldn't have left her. During Tom's session, I heard my phone buzzing in my bag and figured it was probably the school calling to tell me to fetch her.' I make the most apologetic expression I can, while my guts twist in knots.

'You answered your phone in a session?'

'No, no, of course not,' I add quickly. 'I didn't answer it. I… I just checked to see who it was. Tom said he didn't mind.'

'You gave him a choice?'

'Not exactly, but—'

'And was it Freya's school calling?' I've never seen Joe's face so stony.

'Yes, yes, it was.' I look down, fiddling with my fingers, hating the lie. 'It was Freya's school.'

Joe sighs. 'I don't need to tell you what's wrong with this, Lorna. But it makes me concerned for you. Your adherence to basic ethics recently, well, it's making me wonder what else is going on with you.' He waits, allowing me to speak. But I don't. 'Do you not have arrangements in place for assisting with childcare issues while you're working?'

'Not really,' I say quietly, wishing my mother was up to the job. But she's so preoccupied with Dad. 'There's the childminder, but she's not well either,' I lie. 'And Mark would have been busy with patients.'

'Just like you're busy with clients,' he adds, raising his eyebrows. 'Look, sorry to sound like I'm telling you off, Lorna, but you know the score. What you did was...' he trails off, shaking his head, knowing he doesn't need to tell me.

'I know. I'm so sorry. It won't happen again.'

'I'll have to note this on your file, Lorna. You know I have no choice, especially after the other day, with you contacting a client directly. If there are any complaints, we'll need to have a record of everything. I'm sorry but what you did is wholly unacceptable.' He hates doing this to me, I know he does. 'Your client just now... was he the one you brought to supervision at the end of last week?' He looks to the ceiling, thinking for a second. 'Tom, isn't it?'

'Yes, that's Tom.'

'The client you believe to be vulnerable?'

I nod, hanging my head in shame again. Tom managed to talk to me about the abuse today, about his humiliation, his hatred of himself. He brought it up just before the session ended, just before my phone buzzed in my hand yet again.

'How's he doing?' Joe asks.

'We had a doorknob moment,' I say, relieved to be off the subject of my wrongdoing.

'OK-aay,' Joe says thoughtfully. 'And how did you manage it?'

'Like I would any other client,' I say. 'I told him it was interesting that he was only mentioning this at the end of our session, just as I was showing him out.'

Joe nods.

'I checked that he was safe to leave, where his thoughts were going, if he felt able to save it until next week, how his mood seemed after the revelation but...'

'But you'd figured you'd broken enough boundaries already to break another one by running over time?'

'I wouldn't have run over anyway, Joe. That's unfair.' But I'm in no position to defend myself.

'And what exactly was his doorknob moment, Lorna?' Joe's tone is frosty, quite unlike the colleague I've come to know these last ten months.

'He told me that he was abused by his father every Sunday night since he was eight years old. His mother knew from the start.'

'Christ,' Joe says, unfolding his arms and taking hold of the chair in front of him, leaning forward. He shakes his head slowly, his breath out heavy and prolonged. 'What the *hell* did you think you were doing, Lorna?'

I close the door of my office and lean back against it, screwing up my eyes, still able to hear Tom's words as he was about to leave the session – a session where I'd given very little of myself to a vulnerable young man. I'd kept hold of my phone as more messages came in from *him*. I didn't read them, but seeing the alerts was distraction enough.

'He made me touch him,' Tom had whispered, his face burning scarlet from shame. He told me that it had gone on for years, that the only person who knew was his mother because she'd caught them. 'She blamed me,' he said, matter-of-factly, at the door. 'Said I must never speak of it, that she was washing her hands of me.' He made a hand-washing gesture then, before heading for the door. Clients often drop bombshells just as the session ends.

I glance at my watch, swiping my bag from under my chair and dumping it on my desk. I whip out my phone, as if it's to blame for what's happened, and see that there are some new alerts from the Double Take app – people viewing me, liking me, wanting to meet me, messaging me. I should just delete the stupid thing now, I think, my finger hovering over it. But something stops me, and I open it up, going to my inbox.

Another slew of messages awaits – some just saying 'hi' and others cutting straight to what it is they want to do to poor Abbi74. I shudder on her behalf. All she wants is for *him* to reply. But he hasn't, and he hasn't even read my message yet.

Then I read the text messages he sent me during the session with Tom, bracing myself as I open them. I'm only a blink away from two career-finishing complaints.

> *I miss you,* Andrew says.
> *Please meet me*
> *I will keep coming to see you until you agree*
> *Don't give up on me*

My thumbs hover over the keys as I tap out three different replies – *No, I can't… Please don't contact me again… It's over, Andrew* – but I delete each one. Then I type *When?* and quickly hit send.

'I'm just popping to the deli. Want anything?' Getting on Sandy's good side can only be to my benefit right now.

She takes off her glasses, leaning forward on her elbows. Another look sweeps across her face but I'm not sure what it is. 'Are you OK, Lorna?' she says. 'Sorry if I'm wrong, but… but you seem out of sorts. I'm worried about you.'

Thankfully, the waiting room is empty. 'No, I'm fine,' I say, leaning over the counter. I give her my best smile. 'Why?'

'Woman's intuition,' she says. 'You don't sit here five days a week and not pick up on things.'

'Well…'

'Someone's been hanging around, you know,' she says, raising her eyebrows.

'Oh?' My heart pounds.

'Outside. Late in the afternoon, mainly.'

'You should have been a detective,' I say, forcing a laugh that comes out as a croak. He's been waiting for me again.

She pauses, raising her eyebrows even higher. 'I'd love a chicken and avocado bagel, please,' she adds, reaching into her bag for her purse. 'An orange juice too.' She hands me a ten-pound note.

'Sure,' I say, about to leave. But I stop, my coat half on, turning to face her again. 'What did he look like?' I ask, unable to help myself.

Sandy looks surprised but also satisfied, as if she's the keeper of all secrets. 'Oh, it wasn't a man,' she says, before turning to answer the phone.

CHAPTER TWENTY-FOUR

Lorna

'Why did Nana go funny?' Freya asks later that evening, smashing a fish finger up with her fork. Some peas and chips shoot onto the floor. It was all I had in the freezer. Jack is eating at a mate's house and Mark said we may as well order in a Chinese later, which suits me. I can't face cooking. Plus, there's nothing much in the fridge.

'That's an odd question,' I reply, sitting down next to her. Mark gives me a look. 'What do you mean by funny, sweetheart?'

'You know,' she says, kicking the chair leg over and over. 'Mental. Weird in the head.'

'That's not a very nice thing to say about your nana, Frey,' Mark says, flipping the top off a beer. He pinches a chip off her plate.

'Nana's had some troubles,' I tell her, not knowing what else to say. It's never seemed the right time to explain. Besides, Mark and I decided she's still too young to know.

Freya pulls a face, thinking about this. 'Jack said she's not all there,' she says, tapping the side of her head before diving under the table to pick up her dropped food. 'He says she's a nutter.'

Mark shoots me a look – a look that says *You're the therapist, you deal with it*.

'That's not really the right way to describe someone with mental health issues, Freya,' I tell her. 'It's a bit rude, OK?'

She shrugs, playing with her food again. 'So are you going to become a nutter too?' she asks. 'And then will I? Jack told me "like mother, like daughter" and I don't like it. I'm scared.' She squirts a load more ketchup on her chips, looking at me with big eyes. 'I don't want to be mental.'

I pull her in for a hug, giving Mark a quick look. His son started this, but I daren't say anything. 'No, darling,' I say, kissing her head, wondering if this has anything to do with her reluctance to go to school lately, her strange mood. 'Nana's been through some tough times,' I tell her, hoping that will suffice. 'And sometimes it makes her act a bit… well, funny.'

Freya nods, forking up some peas. Only a couple make it into her mouth. 'Is it because of Granddad?'

I give a little nod, deciding to leave it at that. She doesn't need to know about my father, what happened. Explaining would mean admitting that *I'm* not sure either – not great for a therapist. So I fetch her dessert from the fridge instead.

'What was all that about, do you think?' Mark says after Freya's gone upstairs. I said she could have half an hour watching cartoons on the iPad before her bath. Another night without listening to her read. And a far cry from the usual tightly scheduled evenings of piano practice and schoolwork. I promised her we'd catch up with it all soon. Mark wraps his arms around me, one hand making contact with my phone in my back pocket just as it vibrates. 'Something's upset her,' he says.

Yes, your son, I want to say, but bite my tongue. 'It was bound to come up at some point, seeing Dad like that all the time. She knows it's not normal. And to be honest…' I hesitate, not wanting to cause an argument. 'It sounds as if she and Jack have been discussing it.'

'I'll have a word with him,' Mark says. I love him for that, for caring, for trying to join us all up. It makes me feel one ounce more like a mother to his son.

'It's probably nothing. Just the pair of them chatting away like they do.' And it's true – they've always been close, despite the age difference. With Jack almost taking on the role of uncle rather than brother, and Freya using every opportunity to exploit that – mainly for sweets and treats, late nights and extra pizza.

Like mother, like daughter… I think, shuddering at what Jack has been saying to her, wondering if he's actually right.

'Thanks, love,' I say. Then my phone buzzes again.

'You going to check that or what?' He pats my bum.

'It'll just be Cath,' I say. 'It can wait. What are we going to order, then?'

'A shitload from Waitrose, I reckon, judging by this,' he says, going over to the fridge and pulling the door open. The shelves are mostly empty. 'Don't you usually do the shopping tonight?'

Another casualty of my broken routine. 'Sorry, I'll get my laptop and do an order for tomorrow.'

I dash up the two flights of stairs and return, breathless, with my computer, opening it up at the kitchen table. Mark's already on the phone to the Happy Dragon. He knows what I always have – the same he always orders for me. 'The least likely to pile on the pounds,' he once told me, poking my thigh playfully. I know he's right. 'And extra prawn crackers too,' he adds for himself. I know how much he loves them.

I open a Google tab in my browser and, as usual, a list of recently visited links appears in the middle of the screen below the main logo – shortcut icons revealing my history.

Mark stands behind me, taking hold of my shoulders, pressing his fingers deep into my muscles. 'Make sure you get some of those little chicken skewer things,' he says, pressing harder as I react to his touch.

'Mmm, sure will,' I say, melting into his hands. 'Any other requests?'

My eyes flick about, looking for the supermarket link – it's usually there on my home screen… There's Facebook, my favourite clothes website, the BBC, the electricity company… and then I see it.

The pink and yellow Double Take logo.

My mouth drops open, my finger skidding uselessly around the trackpad as I try to get rid of it, trying to find the x to make it go away. To my horror, I accidentally click on the link and the login screen appears in front of me. Abbi's username is already displayed from last time, ready for me to enter the password.

I make a little noise, shaking as I get rid of it. I turn to look up at Mark.

'No, just get the usual stuff,' he says, smiling, bending down so his mouth is on the back of my neck, trailing his lips across my skin. 'You're so tense,' he whispers in my ear. 'Your shoulders are like rock.'

My hands are trembling, my heart thumping, the sick feeling rising up inside me. I have no idea if he saw it.

CHAPTER TWENTY-FIVE

Lorna

The house is quiet. We've eaten the Chinese – or rather I picked at mine – and Freya went to bed an hour ago. Jack is home and upstairs catching up with his studies, while Mark has gone out for a pint with Ed. He promised he wouldn't be long, promised he'd rub my back properly when he returned. I hated myself for telling him not to rush, to take his time chatting with Ed about a trip they're planning to Berlin in a couple of months to see their favourite band. I still haven't finished the online shopping.

Instead, I've been sitting rigid at the kitchen table, my head bent down on folded arms, heavy sighs escaping my lungs. I can feel myself falling.

Finally, unable to resist any longer, I grab my phone. The sight of the notifications sets my mind alight. A fix.

I attended a lecture recently about the psychological effects of text messages, social media likes and comments on our brains – how the more we get, the more we want, never feeling satisfied, constantly seeking validation and attention. It provides a dopamine hit. In fact, it's the anticipation that's actually the addictive part. That's what I tell myself, anyway – that it's my brain chemistry's fault, just how I'm made. That I can't help it.

'Andrew,' I whisper. It doesn't say Andrew on my screen, of course, because his contact is stored in my phone as Andrea – that one letter change making it somehow safe, acceptable. Three messages… three bites of desire. I open them up.

I need to see you.
Thursday morning.
Shots at 10 a.m. Please…

Please, he says, as if it will change my mind, as if he's begging. Or worse, insisting. He's capable of doing that, of forcing my hand in just a few unspoken words, a thinly veiled threat. Even just a look.

OK, I reply before deleting all his messages, including those I've sent.

I go back to my laptop, adding butter, juice, toilet paper and cat food to my shopping basket, not bothering to hunt around for the special offers or look out for the three-for-twos as I usually do. I mindlessly shove some chicken, two packs of minced beef, a load of our usual vegetables and salad into my basket, along with snacks and cereal, tea, coffee, milk and wine. I skim down the list of my usual purchases, clicking furiously, the mundanity of it making me want to scream.

'Shampoo for Freya,' I say to myself, suddenly remembering, seeking out the brand that doesn't make her head itch. I think about what she said about my mum. She's probably been dwelling on it for a while, chewing it over in her mind, wondering why her nana is different to her friends' grandparents. Kids pick up on things, even if husbands don't.

I quickly add the satay chicken skewers that Mark wanted and head to the checkout. One hundred and twenty-three pounds eighty-seven pence. Just as I'm confirming the delivery time, another text comes in.

Looking forward to it.

Me too, I fire back, unable to help myself, wondering how the hell I will get out of work to meet him. But I daren't risk upsetting him. Since he turned up at the clinic, it's as though the detonator of a hand grenade has been pulled. It's not *if* it explodes, it's *when.*

Once the grocery order is confirmed, I open up a new browser tab and go to the Double Take site, logging in. The usual raft of notifications and inane comments are waiting – at least twenty messages – but I don't bother to read them. I keep scrolling down the list, stopping suddenly as I see a familiar profile picture no bigger than a postage stamp.

It's *him.*

Andy_jag has finally replied to Abbi74.

'Fuck, fuck, *fuck*,' I whisper, my finger barely able to move on the mouse pad.

I creep out into the hallway, listening up the stairs. There's the tinny beat of Jack's music, turned down low so he doesn't wake Freya, and a sliver of light flickering out from underneath his door. Freya's door is still set just how she likes it – about six inches open with the landing lamp on in case she wakes up in the night. She's never liked the dark.

Back in the kitchen, I pour myself a shot of cooking brandy for courage. Mark won't notice the level; I keep the bottle in the cupboard next to the stove. I take a slug, enjoying the warmth of it searing down my throat. Then I open the message, hoovering it up in one greedy gulp.

Yes, they are my paintings – and thank you. How are you finding this site? Having much luck? I'm not. (PS your photos are stunning.)

I read it at least twenty times – each time trying to work a new meaning into it. Analysing each syllable, every punctuation mark.

Then Cath's in my head, about overthinking everything, how I see things that don't really exist apart from in my own tortuous mind.

He thinks my profile photos are stunning. Andrew likes the face and body of a random woman I plucked off the internet and named Abbi. I feel pathetic. But I still click in the box to reply.

You're very talented, I type. *Are the paintings of anyone in particular?* He never admitted to that – whose gentle curves, angular features, swathes of hair he'd spent hours and hours brush-stroking into wild and disturbing representations of women's bodies. I'd tried to find out, of course, wondering if any were of *her*, the lodger, if she'd sat for him, nude, while he studied the intricacies of her shape. But he'd never given me a straight answer, always deflecting with something else, implying I was in no position to be jealous or questioning.

And thanks for the compliment, I add, feeling sick. *What are you looking for here? Ditto about having no luck*, I say, thinking at least that's true. I sip more brandy, wondering what else I can type that will elicit information, unravel the man I once loved.

'*Love*,' I whisper, hating myself.

Then a little green dot suddenly appears beside his profile photo, showing Andy_jag is online. It's as though he's right here in my kitchen.

'Oh Christ,' I say, knowing he'll see I'm online too. I quickly finish typing my message – *Hope to hear back from you soon* – and click send, trying to convince myself that I'm not breaking any laws, that I'm just trying to get deeper inside his mind. 'As any good therapist would,' I whisper, knocking back the rest of my drink.

CHAPTER TWENTY-SIX

Lorna's Journal

While I'm alone, I get out the journal again, picking up where I left off, filling my head with the past, trying to reconcile it with the now. Trying to make sense of it, figure out what I should do. I feel numb reading it, as if I don't even know the person it's written about, as if she was someone else entirely, like I never knew her. And it makes me not *want* to know her any more. But then, that's the point of a therapist's journal – to grow, to become self-aware, to reflect.

I'm sitting on the floor in Freya's room with about twenty minutes before the front door bursts open, everyone coming home. But I'm ready. Ready to stash it away again in the secret hiding place. Ready to pretend none of it ever happened. To carry on as normal. For how long I can do that, I'm not sure.

17 February 2017

I'm only going to write about the kiss, then I'm going to tear this up. Destroy it. Burn the paper before swallowing the ashes. Get rid of my shame. Now I'm imagining myself doing that – forking up the remains of my deepest, most secret thoughts, shoving them down my throat. Choking. But then they mutate and spread throughout my body so that every time I speak, all that comes out of my mouth are charred lies.

It was cold. So cold that I'm shivering even remembering it, my hand shaking, making it hard to write fast. I'd hoped yesterday's chill would keep the park empty. I'd not seen many people about, just the most hardened dog walkers. And I'd checked a thousand times that no one was close or hidden behind a bush watching. He'd told me not to be silly, so paranoid, that two people who had feelings for each other were allowed to kiss in the park. No one knew who we were, he tried to convince me, while I tried to convince myself that I didn't have feelings for him. And that if I did, they weren't normal feelings. Not like those I have for Mark or the kids. It was all so very wrong.

'It's not that simple, Andrew,' I told him. Then the shudder, running the full length of my spine, as though someone's eyes were on me. Always feeling watched. Though it was probably my own conscience keeping tabs.

'What is that cologne you wear?' I asked him, managing a smile, beating my gloved hands together – a muffled, slow clap – as though Mark was applauding my stupidity.

Bravo, Lorna! Encore! *he'd say. It sounds the same as my guilt.*

I screwed up my eyes then, drinking in that pervasive scent – the zesty notes of sandalwood, spices and something else that set me alight. I tried to unravel the puzzle, almost as if it were mathematical, but I wasn't coming up with answers. Answers – it's always about answers and logic with me, formulating and figuring people out.

Except with him, I couldn't.

Perhaps that was part of the intrigue, the allure. The reason I craved him more than anything else in the world, as if he was the missing piece to an ancient puzzle.

If we were caught or spotted, I planned on saying it was eco-therapy, that I was counselling in a natural setting to help unlock some powerful issues my client seemed unable to talk about indoors. I know a therapist who works like that. All part of the service, I'd say, even though it wasn't.

So I breathed him in deeply again, unable to decide if I loved the smell or hated it. All I knew was that it did something to me. Took me to a place I'd not been in a long time, as though I'd been transported somewhere long forgotten. ~~Was it the start of me loving him?~~

He drew me close again, edging me backwards towards the tree, my body stiff and resisting as he pulled me closer. That was when I felt as though I was floating, watching those two lone figures, the river snaking its way past in the background, flashes of sunlight glinting a warning off its surface.

He pulled off my left glove then, slowly, seductively, a finger at a time, as if he were slipping off all my clothes. Unzipping, unbuttoning – gently at first, but then resorting to ripping and grappling, desperate to get to my skin.

He took hold of my bare hand, stroking my fourth finger, sliding off my ring.

'You're not married now,' he said, keeping hold of my hand.

'Don't, Andrew…' I said, putting it on again. 'Mark and I have been together a long time, we have a daughter. And I have a stepson—' I was about to say that I loved Mark, but stopped. It didn't seem right bringing him between us. Anyway, he took off his scarf then, wrapping it gently around my neck. The drunk feeling got worse.

'Keep it,' he'd said, pulling me even closer. 'To remind you.'

'I can't,' I replied, wanting nothing more. There would be no explaining away a man's scarf.

Then the warmth of Andrew's mouth – no, the heat of his mouth – as his lips pressed down on mine. Silencing me. Filling me with something I'd not experienced in… well, forever. I can recall every tiny detail – how his lips felt unfamiliar, a different shape and taste to what I'm used to, yet somehow I instinctively knew the geography of them, the layout of his mouth.

I was completely helpless as he consumed me, as though he was in my blood, flowing through my veins. He'd unlocked something, and it already felt addictive.

Finally, he pulled back, holding me at arm's length, inspecting his work, what he'd done to me. He saw it simmering in my eyes – the way I stared at him with a drugged look. He knew he'd got to me.

'That wasn't supposed to happen,' I said.

'Yes, it was,' he whispered, cupping my face in his hands as he drew me in again. I had absolutely no chance of escaping, even if I'd wanted to. No chance of doing the right thing, running away and never looking back. He'd got inside my mind, my psyche, when, really, it was my job to get inside his.

~~Now burn this. Burn it!~~

CHAPTER TWENTY-SEVEN

Nikki

It's cold tonight. She's already gone out, but the others are inside still – Mark, Freya. Jack. A lot can be gleaned from going through someone's rubbish. Old bills, junk mail, food wrappers and cartons, doodles the little kid has scrawled on the backs of envelopes, on scraps of paper, practising writing her name, making up little poems. I've seen it all, feel as though I know them well.

I pace up and down, sucking on a cigarette. I have two choices – stay here, snatching glances of the cosy scene inside their living room, perhaps sneak around the back of the house, down the alley at the bottom of their garden. If I stand on the wooden crate behind the wall, I can see into their kitchen. Or, I can head off to her friend's house and check out what's going on there instead. She seems to alternate between different friends' places every Wednesday. It'll be Annie's tonight. Another name discovered in a dustbin. They have some kind of meeting each week – wine and chatter, like women do.

Women like *them*.

I chuck the cigarette in the gutter, making my decision. It's only a short bus ride to Annie's house and I'm feeling bolder. Anyway, I always have excuses at the ready: *'Have you seen my little cat? She's been missing for three days now…'* Or *'Is this George's house? No? Oh, I'm so sorry…'* People believe what you tell them.

But, just as I turn to leave, the front door of number seventy-four opens and Jack comes out, banging it closed behind him. My heart pounds, making a whooshing sound in my ears as he stops at the front gate. He fishes around in his bomber jacket pockets, one side then the other before patting down his jeans. His shoulders drop as he makes an annoyed face, going back up the path and checking under a flowerpot, nodding at what he finds there, dropping it down again.

Keys.

He heads off, stopping at the end of the front path to tap something on his phone, before pulling a packet of cigarettes from his jacket. The flare of the lighter gives me an eerie glimpse of him – a light covering of youthful stubble and a frown too old for his young face. He shoves his hands in his pockets, the cigarette dangling from his lips, and walks off, shoulders hunched, his back to me. I decide to follow him instead.

Keeping a good way back, I keep pace until he reaches a small park – dark and secluded at this time of the evening. He turns in through the gate, looking up and down the street.

I stay close to the railings and the cover of the bushes as he heads down to the small play area where there are some other lads about his age waiting, sitting on the swings, their trainers scuffing the ground. They exchange brief greetings – fists knocking, bumping, clenching – before one of the other boys pulls something from his pocket and gives it to Jack. A swift and barely noticeable transaction before it gets stuffed in Jack's pocket, but I still catch sight of the little bag, the cash handed back in exchange.

I drop my head for a second, sighing – a proxy reaction for Lorna, worried on her behalf, even though she's oblivious. Then the anger bubbles up – where is his father, why isn't he keeping tabs on his son? It's hardly my place to question.

But it makes me do something stupid.

'Hi,' I say, heading down to the lads. They all look up at once, falling silent, probably thinking I'm homeless from the state of me. 'Know where I can get a smoke?'

None of them say anything. Instead, they glance behind me, checking out who might be watching, worried I'm a cop about to bust them. It's only because I want the company, I tell myself. Just wanted to speak to someone. Even though I know that's not entirely true.

'How much you need?' one of the lads says. The one who dealt with Jack.

'Just a quick smoke,' I say, knowing he'll want to sell me more. 'I don't have much money.'

The boy rolls his eyes, giving a throaty laugh. 'You can finish this, if you like,' he says, passing me his nearly burnt-out joint. 'On the house.'

I look at him for a moment, making eye contact with each of the others in turn, ending up on Jack, holding his gaze for way longer than I should. My heart is thumping, my mouth dry.

'Thanks,' I say. 'What you lads up to?'

'What *you* up to?' dealer boy says. 'Creeping about. I saw you up there.'

My cheeks burn. I suck on the joint, feeling the wetness of it on my lips. 'Not much,' I reply. 'Just out for a walk.' They want me to go, I can tell. But I'm not going to. Not yet. 'You live around here?'

A couple of them shrug.

'Where do *you* live?' dealer boy asks. The leader of the pack, I think, wondering why it's not Jack. Wondering why he's silent, kicking at the ground, looking awkward, taking a couple of paces away from the group.

'I've lived in all sorts of places,' I tell them.

'What sort of places?' Jack says, the sound of his voice making me more light-headed than the weed. I turn to him, taking in his big eyes.

'I lived in Scotland once,' I tell him with a nervous smile. 'In a really remote place you won't have heard of.'

'Cool,' he says, shrugging. 'It's cold up there, innit?'

'Can be,' I say. 'You live far away?'

'Look, lady, we're like, having a private meeting here, yeah?' dealer boy says, interrupting before Jack can reply.

'Sure,' I say, pulling my scarf up over my chin and cheeks, wanting nothing more than to hide again, slink back into the shadows where I'm comfortable. 'Thanks for this,' I say, holding up the dog-end before dropping it on the ground. I turn to go, tears stinging hot in my eyes.

'Bye,' Jack calls out as I walk off, his voice following me through the darkness. I don't look back.

Twenty minutes later and I'm there, outside, watching, cursing myself, feeling stupid for what I just did.

I pace about, agitated. Hiding outside Annie's house isn't as easy as lurking outside the clinic, with the secluded green opposite, the benches and the cover of the hedge. Or, indeed, Lorna's house, where the street is darker. But it's a busy road here, at least, with lots of passers-by, allowing me to blend in. A group of lads come past, taking up the full width of the pavement, forcing me to step back against a wall, making me do a double take in case it's the boys from the park. But, of course, it's not.

A bus pulls up and, when everyone gets on, I sit down at the empty stop. It's pretty much right opposite Annie's house. She's married to Ed, the couple Lorna and Mark see every week or two. Annie is all smiles and soft curves, her hair falling across her face, her skirts long and flowing. She looks like a social worker or nurse. Someone who cares. The man, Ed, has a short beard and isn't much taller than her. He looks the type to lecture in a university – perhaps maths or astronomy or quantum physics, something clever, something he doesn't talk about much because no one understands.

I see them all sitting inside – cosy, chatting, laughing. I imagine that I'm their friend too, that they invite me to their girlie nights to drink wine with them. What stories I could tell them, I think, staring at Annie's lit-up front window, the curtains wide open. Lorna's husband doesn't know about *him*. Yet.

CHAPTER TWENTY-EIGHT

Lorna

'Calling Lorna… hello?' Cath says, tucking her legs up on the sofa. 'Christ's sake, woman, did you read *any* of the book?'

'Sorry?' I say, looking up from my phone. 'Yes, yes, of course I did,' I tell her. 'I just need to plug in. Is there a power point?' I scan the skirting board. 'Actually, no, I didn't read the book.' Somehow, being honest about the small things eases my guilt. Helps me breathe.

'Just put your phone down,' Charlotte says, offering me some nuts. 'You've been glued to it since you arrived.'

'It's work stuff,' I say, searching around for power. Reluctantly, I leave my phone plugged in on a table over by the window. 'Shall I draw the curtains?' I say, reaching out to close them.

'God no, don't do that. You'll bring the whole lot down,' Annie says. 'Christ knows how many times I've asked Ed to fix the pole. It's hanging on by a thread. I keep threatening to call a man in, but he won't hear of it. Meantime, the whole street gets to see what's going on in my living room.'

I sit on the sofa again, conscious of my screen lighting up a couple of times before I've even settled down. I've already received four text messages from *him* since I arrived. I feel sick at the thought of meeting up, yet insanely excited.

'So,' Charlotte, says flicking her hair back over her shoulder. I've not seen her for a couple of weeks – one or other of us not making it to book club for various reasons. 'How did we all find this read, then? That ending was, like, *oh my God!* But I have to say, I saw it coming a mile off. Clever though.' She places the book on her lap, patting it, her expression conveying her smugness. I like Charlotte, but everything in her life is perfect. As perfect as I try to make mine except she really does it. Me, as soon as I patch up one crack, another one appears.

'I thought it was OK,' Megan says. Then she goes on to describe how she hated the woman in it, how she couldn't get her head round someone messing up her life so comprehensively, how she didn't believe anyone could get herself into such a mess without knowing the consequences. 'She must literally be evil, to behave like that. Or stupid.'

'Evil?' I say. 'That's a bit harsh.'

'But you can see *why* she did it,' Annie chips in, rolling her eyes when my phone pings yet another alert – the sound of the Double Take app. I get up, but Cath's hand is suddenly on my arm.

'Chill,' she says. 'Work can wait.' She puts my glass of wine in my hand and shoves a bowl of corn chips on my lap.

'No, no, you don't understand,' I say, my eyes wide, my heart thumping. 'I need to check my... my emails.' They all exchange glances.

Cath draws in close, while the others chat about the book again. 'That's not an email alert, though, is it?' she whispers.

I stare at her. 'What do you mean?'

She rests her hand on my wrist, giving me one of *those* looks. 'We've both got iPhones, Lorn. I'd know that sound anywhere.' She's so close I can smell the red wine on her. 'It's the default tone for...' she hesitates.

'I don't know what you're talking about.' I look her in the eye, pulling my hand away. 'I have a client in crisis right now, Cath, and I'm liaising with the intervention team to make sure she's getting the care she needs. There's every chance she'll be admitted to the psych ward later and they're going to need input from me.' I put my wine on the table. 'I can hardly ignore it.' I force a brief smile.

'Sure, sorry,' she replies, letting me get up this time.

I grab my phone, my hands shaking, my back to the room as I cradle it to my chest. A message from Andy_jag. I hear my own breathing – short, shallow asthmatic gasps – while Megan debates with Charlotte about the wrongdoings of the woman in the book, her shrill laughter drowning out my guilt.

She's just a friend… the message says, confusing me for a moment. *I like to paint her.* Then I realise he's referring to the woman in the pictures that I asked him about. I can't help the surge of jealousy. It *must* be her, then. The lodger. He never once painted me.

And I'm looking for a very special person, he continues. *So you've not found anyone either? ;-)*

Someone very special? It makes me want to throw my phone through the window. But instead, I tap out a reply, trying to sound light and normal. *Sadly, no. Still waiting for a special person too.* My fingers are trembling, mistyping every word. *Perhaps we should meet*, I add, wanting to test him, to push him. He's still online so I send it quickly, before I change my mind.

'Work, eh?' Charlotte says over my shoulder, giving me a playful poke in the ribs. 'You OK, Lorn? You seem a bit distracted.'

'I'm fine,' I say, shielding my phone, switching it to silent. I slip it in my pocket now that it's got a bit of charge. 'Like I said, there's a crisis.' It's not far from the truth. I slide past Charlotte, ignoring her doubting look, and pick up my wine again, drinking half of it in one gulp.

'Anyway,' Megan says. 'Whatever her problems and history, what that woman in the book did was wrong. She had an affair and that's that. Excuses or not, she deserved what she had coming to her.'

'Meggie!' Cath says loudly. 'No one deserves to get murdered, you tit-brain. Not even someone like her.' She shoves her playfully, making her slosh her drink. For a moment, Megan looks affronted but then laughs, carrying on chatting about the characters, who she liked and who she didn't.

'It's just a bloody book,' I whisper under my breath, my shoulders and neck tense as I sit down. My phone vibrates again, but no one takes any notice.

CHAPTER TWENTY-NINE

Lorna

It's not long before the conversation drifts onto other things in our lives. For Charlotte, that's the agony of her favourite cruise ship being booked solid for the next year and having to make do with a hotel in the Caribbean. Megan is worried because her boyfriend wants a dog, but she doesn't, while Annie extols the new head at her school, telling us how much happier everyone is at work now, not to mention the pupils, since the new timetable kicked in.

'You'll never guess what,' Cath says. 'I had a super-hot date two nights ago.' The evening usually ends up on Cath's love life, as though it has its own gravitational pull.

'You're welcome,' Annie chips in. 'Feel free to thank me in your wedding speech.'

'Who was it?' I ask quickly. She said she deleted and blocked him, but I can't be sure she really did. He's messaging Abbi74, so who knows what else he's up to? I've no right to be feeling this way – jealousy knotting up my veins.

'He's really nice,' Cath goes on.

'Is it… is it *that* guy?' I say, trying to sound happy for her. The others wait for me to explain. 'You know, the one Annie messaged for you?'

Cath shakes her head slowly, making a pitying face. In fact, they've all got the same look on their faces. No one speaks.

'What?' I say, looking at each of them. '*What?*'

'Oh, hon, shouldn't we be asking *you* that?' Charlotte squashes up next to me, her arm looping around my shoulders, pulling me close. The fingers of her other hand wipe under my eyes and down my cheeks, smudging away tears I didn't even know were there. Annie dives in with a tissue as their soothing voices rain down on me, making me feel as if I'm drowning. As if I can't breathe. As if I'm going mad.

'What's the matter, Lorn?' Charlotte says. Her perfectly made-up face is close, her lips puckered up in a concerned way that makes me feel about eight years old. I reach out, gripping onto her arms, feeling dizzy, as if the ground's falling away. I don't feel real.

'Shit, *Lorn*...?' That's Cath's voice, I think, though I can't be sure. All my senses are failing. Then my phone vibrates again, making me pull it from my pocket, clutching it between my palms, pressing it to my chest. I stand up, feeling wobbly, staggering.

'Sit down,' someone says. 'You've gone really pale. You don't look well.'

'I... I need the loo,' I hear myself saying, raising my hands as Charlotte follows me into the hallway. 'I'm fine, really,' I say, faking it until I get in there, shutting the door behind me and sliding the lock home. I slump down onto the seat, cradling my head in my hands, hoping that whatever's happening will pass. My vision's blurry and there's a ringing in my ears. It feels as though I'm going to pass out, but I have no idea why.

It's stress, I tell myself. *A panic attack and stress... Breathe, Lorna, breathe...*

Then I check Double Take. I can hardly see the screen.

Sure, I'd love to meet up, Abbi. Are you free tomorrow morning?

The vomit comes into my mouth, but I swallow it back down, coughing and choking. I spit out into the basin, turning on the tap to drown out the noise of my gags.

Andy_jag wants to meet Abbi in the morning. I let out a silent sob. But he's meant to be meeting *me* in the morning. I thump my fist against the wall, sending pain shooting up to my elbow.

I flick back to the texts from Andrew to make sure I've not made a mistake. It's true. He asked me – no, *begged* me – to meet tomorrow.

I swill out my mouth, my hands shaking as I dry them, my mind all over the place. On the Double Take app, I tap out a reply from Abbi, hardly able to get the words out. *I'd love to meet you tomorrow morning. What time and where?* Then I send Andrew a text message from me, just to confirm. *Looking forward to seeing you.* I add an X before sending.

'You OK in there?' Annie calls out, knocking on the door.

'I'm… I'm fine,' I say back.

I stare into the mirror above the basin. I'm Mark's *wife*, dammit, Freya's mother, Jack's stepmum, and currently therapist to over twenty-four clients, not to mention the hundreds and hundreds I've helped over the years. I'm an accredited member of the BACP, on the PTA at Freya's school, I have good, respectable friends, a husband who's a dentist with a good reputation to uphold, a comfortable home in Fulham and I drive a Mercedes four-wheel drive. I shop at John Lewis, for fuck's sake.

But, as I stare at the woman looking back at me, I have no idea who I really am, who she is, what all these things mean. What secrets lie behind her tormented eyes. She's becoming a stranger in a body I barely recognise.

When I unlock the door and go out, Annie is standing there, wringing her hands.

'Stop the bullshit,' she says, leading me into the kitchen. My phone vibrates again as she pours me a glass of water, making me drink. 'What's going on? You're glued to that bloody phone. You're not yourself. Talk to me.'

My head shakes, my shoulders shrugging and tense. I sip the water. 'I'm just a bit worried about Freya, that's all.'

'Go on,' Annie says. 'School stuff?'

I nod, latching on to anything that seems plausible. 'Partly,' I say, not wanting to admit that what's bothering her is closer to home.

'You still thinking about moving her to my school?'

'It's been on my mind,' I say. 'Some of the other kids have been teasing her about…' I trail off. It's hard to talk about. 'One of her so-called friends was round to play a couple of weeks ago. Mum was there. With Dad. It was bad timing.'

'Ah,' Annie says.

'You know what it's like. I try to keep her away when the kids have friends over, but it's not always possible. This girl Rosie was teasing Freya about how Mum is, not to mention what Dad's like. Now all her friends are making fun of her too, saying she's weird. Plus, she's worried that I'll end up the same as Mum. And that she'll follow suit,' I add, remembering what Jack said.

'OK…' Annie says thoughtfully. 'That's tough. But if it makes you feel any better, most kids can be little buggers at times. They speak without thinking. Have you told Freya why her nana's…' Annie stops. No one really knows how to describe it.

'How can I?' I say, picturing her worried face. 'She'll only ask more questions.'

'You need to talk to her, Lorn. Kids aren't stupid. You have to tell her something eventually, and about your dad too.' Annie places her hands on my shoulders, tilting up my chin with her finger. 'Thing is, Lorn, I know there's other stuff going on with you. We all do. We just don't know what.'

'Oh, that's great,' I say, pulling away, scowling. 'You've all been discussing me behind my back? Talking about the messed-up therapist. Thanks, Annie.' I put the glass down beside the sink harder than I intended. 'I should go now. It's been a long day.' I swing round, but she grabs my arm.

'Just tell me, is everything OK between you and Mark?' She stares directly at me, not allowing me to dodge her gaze.

I open my mouth to speak, but when nothing comes out, I run back to the living room, grab my bag and coat and leave without saying another word.

CHAPTER THIRTY

Nikki

She's running out of the house, the door swinging wide behind her, her coat slung over her arm and her bag bouncing against her hip as she comes down the path and crosses over the road, heading right towards me at the bus stop. Her friends are standing in the doorway, calling out to her, while one of them – Annie – follows her across the road. I freeze, unable to move. They are only a couple of feet away from me. I turn the other way.

'Lorn, what on earth's got into you?' I hear Annie panting, seeing that she's not wearing any shoes when I glance down – just black tights under her long skirt.

'Nothing. I told you I'm fine,' Lorna replies. I feel the bench seat jog as she sits down.

'Come back inside. I'll call you a cab.'

'What, and face the third degree from you lot? I'm getting the bus,' she says just as one comes in to view. I keep my head down when she stands up, flagging it down, insisting to Annie that she's OK, that nothing's wrong, that she's just tired.

When she gets on, I get on too, completely unnoticed, taking the seat right behind her – so close I could reach out and touch her. See what *he* feels when he's stroking her hair, the soft skin on her neck.

But of course, I don't. I stare out of the window, watching the passing street scene, the drizzle that's started up, snaking down the window. It's like being underwater.

I screw up my eyes, fighting away the images, shutting down my feelings. I'm getting better at it, but sometimes the fear seeps out. The noise still haunts me, still wakes me at night.

'Trauma takes a lot of work, a lot of therapy,' someone once told me. 'Your brain needs to process stuff.'

But what I didn't tell them is that therapy isn't for people like me. Perhaps not until now.

Fifteen minutes later and Lorna stands up, her hand grabbing the bars as she makes her way to the front of the bus, waiting as it slows and pulls over at her stop. At the last minute, I stand and follow her, tracking her at a safe distance as she heads for home – far enough away for her not to notice me, but still close enough for me to hear her stifled sobs.

CHAPTER THIRTY-ONE

Lorna

'Freya…?' My daughter sits there, refusing to unbuckle her seatbelt, refusing to get out of the car. 'You'll be late for school, darling.' I stretch around to the back, unable to reach her hand. Instead, I touch her knee, hating that she flinches.

'Not going,' she says through brewing tears. 'I want to go home.'

Oh God, please not today. Not today of all days. 'If you're late again, there'll be no chance of getting the attendance award. Isn't it being presented in final assembly today? Anyway, it's the last day of term, then you have two weeks off. We'll do some fun stuff together.'

'I don't care about a stupid award,' she says, staring out of the window. 'I don't feel very well.'

'Freya,' I sigh, hating myself for feeling annoyed with her. 'How about I come in with you, help you hang up your stuff, take you to your classroom?'

She shakes her head vigorously. 'Then they'll tease me even more.'

I get out of the car and climb into the back seat beside her, trying to pull her close for a hug. But she stiffens. 'Frey-frey, talk to me, sweetie. Tell me what's upsetting you.' I sigh, stroking her soft hair, noticing the food stain down her red sweatshirt. I should have put some washing on last night, had it ready for the morning, but when I got back from Annie's, I was preoccupied with checking my phone, with trying to sound normal to Mark, wondering if he was a bit aloof or if it was my imagination. 'Is it to do with what you mentioned the other night? About Nana?'

She shrugs, not denying it.

'So you're worried in case I go like…' I close my eyes for a beat. 'In case I get upset like Nana sometimes does?' It's the best I can do for now.

Freya gives a barely perceptible nod, a fresh stream of tears rolling down her cheeks.

'Oh darling,' I say, pulling her close again, feeling her loosen as she rests against me. 'That's not going to happen, OK? I promise. I'm still the same mummy I've always been.' I swallow hard. 'I'll always look after you and love you. And I'm not ever going to be like poor Nana. Do you trust me?' That sticks in my throat too.

'But that's not what Jack told me,' she says, leaning away from me, wiping her eyes with the backs of her hands. She scowls as I pull a tissue from my pocket and go to dry her cheeks. She takes it from me, doing it herself. 'He told me stuff. And he told me that people lie, especially grown-ups.'

I study her face, trying to fathom what she's thinking, what Jack's 'stuff' is. 'Well, maybe you heard him wrong,' I say, trying not to sound angry at him, even though I am.

'I didn't,' she says, hauling up her backpack before opening the door and sliding out. She stares at me from the pavement. 'Anyway, you already *are* like Nana.' Then she shuts the car door, her words and the rush of cold air hitting me square in the face.

Slowly I get out, watching her go inside the school gates, my mouth hanging open. She's no doubt the last pupil to arrive as usual. As she goes into the building, she gives one last look back and gives a little wave before disappearing inside. I blow her a kiss.

Back in the driver's seat, I glance at my watch. It's just after ten to nine. I reach for my bag and pull out my phone, dialling the number to make the call I've been dreading.

'Sandy, hi. It's me, Lorna. Look, I'm so sorry to do this to you at such short notice but the hospital just called with an appointment for Freya. They had a cancellation. She's been having trouble with her ears, remember? Mark can't take her, so I'll have to. Would you cancel and reschedule my clients this morning? I know… I'm so sorry. But I can't turn it down or she'll have to wait months. She's often in pain… Thanks, Sandy. I owe you one.'

After I hang up, my skin clammy with sweat, I turn off my phone and drop it back inside my bag. I don't want anyone to reach me.

I get to the park ten minutes early, waiting under a tree not far from the river, fidgeting from one foot to the other. A couple of runners pass by, the sound of their tinny music hissing from their earphones. My body tenses as I scan around the park. It was the only place I could think of to meet. *Our* park. Shots café would be far too busy at this time and they know my face. There's no way I could risk it.

A male figure approaches in the distance but, as he draws closer, I can see it's not him. What if he doesn't even come, I think, already feeling the ache inside? What if he's trying to fix up a meet with 'Abbi' right this moment, or worse, he's with *her*, his lodger? Still, I keep my phone switched off.

'Hi,' comes the low voice from behind, making me jump. He's close, so close it makes me wonder how I didn't hear him approaching. 'You're looking good, Lorna.' I feel his hands drawing me closer. His confidence and assertiveness were always so attractive. Like he owned me, wanted me all for himself. To care for me.

'Hi,' I say softly, my eyes flicking from his eyes to the scar on his lip. 'You came.' As ever, my heart kicks up at the sight of him.

'You thought I wouldn't?' He laughs, leaning forward to kiss me. I pull back, conscious of being in public. Of it all starting up again. That's not why I came.

'No, I just…' I can't mention Abbi. I sweep back my hair, lowering my eyes. 'Don't kiss me here. Someone might see.'

'Is that an invitation to go somewhere private?'

'No, Andrew, it's not.' We start walking, tracking the path through the trees that runs parallel with the river. The air is fresh and cool, springlike and untainted by our illicit presence. 'I thought we should talk. And not in one of those hotels. They made me feel like a dirty little secret. I hated that I couldn't come to your place.'

'But the whole *thing* was a dirty little secret,' he says, flashing a smile. 'Wasn't that the point? Anyway, I'd rather talk about the future. About us. What happens next.'

'Andrew, I don't think you really understand.' I stop, turning to face him, the same strange feeling from last night hitting me.

'Then explain,' he says, trying to draw me in for a kiss again. I shy away.

'Look, I'm not doing this a second time, Andrew. I want you, but I don't want you. I was moving on, but now this…' I look up into his eyes.

'Is it because of your family?'

'Of *course* it's because of my family,' I say. 'But how is that any different to you putting your… your *lodger* first, or…' I only just stop myself from mentioning Abbi and all the other women he's no doubt chatting with on Double Take.

His face changes then, as if I've overstepped the line. 'Lorna, *Lorna*,' he says, reaching out for me. 'Why are you so hung up on her? This should be about us. No one else. I want us to have a future together.'

'Hung *up*?' I say loudly. 'Hung up on the woman you're living with, that you lied to me about?' My hand goes to my forehead as I hear myself sounding crazy. I feel as though I'm stumbling through thick fog, searching for something except I don't know what.

'I've told you before, but you never listen. It's as though you don't *want* to hear.' He laughs then, setting my already raw nerves on fire. 'Anyway, you're in no position to lecture me.'

'But I didn't *lie* to you about Mark. I've always been honest about it. Not proud, but at least honest. You just won't... won't even admit what's going on, like you *want* to torture me.' I walk off, shaking, scuffing the ground until he catches up, grabs me and swings me round.

'OK, I'll be honest then. We had a thing, but it was ages ago. Before you and I even met.'

'So you *are* fucking your lodger, and you lied about it. Lied to your *therapist*.'

'You're *not* my therapist any more, remember?' Even though I can see the hurt in his eyes, it feels as though he's mocking me, playing with me, making me feel like a naughty child. Right now, I hate him.

Love him.

'I *was* your therapist, before you decided to... to...' I cover my face, angry and frustrated. 'How long before we met was it going on with her?' I hate how I sound – desperate, needy, as though an unplugged hole in me needs filling with reassurance. This isn't how this morning was meant to go. I wanted a calm ending, closure, a chance to get on with my life.

Then the panic again – ringing in my ears, blurring my vision, making me doubt everything.

'I don't know exactly,' he says, shrugging as if it's no big deal. 'Why can't this just be about us, Lorna?'

'Because there *is* no us,' I say. 'Answer me. How long before we met were you with her?'

'You're obsessed. She means nothing to me, can't you under-stand?' That's when his mouth comes down on mine – his lips all-consuming, his scent becoming a taste now too. I try to pull away but can't, and I have no idea if it's because he's forcing me or because I don't want to.

'A few months maybe,' he whispers, the words resonating in my mouth, as if he's chanting them down my throat. 'Maybe a few days, I can't even remember… Who cares?'

'*I* care,' I say, kissing him back, holding his face, touching the cleft above his lip with my thumb.

'Look, Lorna, she's not even that attractive. She's all alone and has nowhere else to go. She works a crap job that doesn't pay much. I have to… to subsidise her sometimes. I can't just chuck her out. You want me to be heartless?'

I stare at him, narrowing my eyes before they turn to saucers. I'm filled with fear. 'Oh God…' I whisper, his face swimming in front of me. 'It's all my fault… *all my fault*…' The scar transforms from something rugged and attractive into a grotesque, open wound.

'Lorna?' Andrew says. 'Are you OK? You're not making sense.' He holds me by the shoulders.

My palms are flat against his chest. I can't even see Andrew any more. He's turned into someone else. My hands smack against him, gradually picking up a beat as I clench my fists and thump him over and over again. He grabs my wrists, trying to stop me, but I carry on hitting him as hard as I can, swaying from side to side, my hair getting in my mouth as I shake my head, crying out, spit and tears flying everywhere.

'Lorna, stop!'

I stiffen, my elbows bent against his chest, his hands clamped around each of my wrists as I sob and heave. 'It's all my fault… it's all my fault…' I'm not even making sense to myself. Images of naked women and bright colours swirl through my head, and the taste of sick in my mouth makes me want to throw up.

'Lorna, calm down. If it's what you want, if it'll make things OK between us, I'll ask her to leave. She's been thinking about it anyway, I reckon, acting odd. Let me sort it.' He puts a finger under my chin, lifting it up. His voice is low and calming as he leads us over to a bench. 'Are you OK? You look really pale.'

I stand there, trying to slow my breathing, shivering and shaking, trying to focus on him, but I can't. It's getting worse.

'Lorna,' he says, kissing me again. I'm vaguely conscious of his hand slipping inside my coat, down beneath the loose V-neck of my top. His fingers feel cool against my skin.

'Do you want me?' he says, though I can't be sure, because the ringing in my ears finally drowns everything out. My heart races and my limbs are heavy and weak. I can hardly hold myself up.

Then there's nothing. Just blackness.

CHAPTER THIRTY-TWO

Lorna

'Lorna… Christ, Lorna, are you OK?'

I groan, touching my face. There's blood on my fingers.

'Talk to me, Lorna… please. Tell me you're OK. What happened?'

Is it Andrew's voice? I'm not sure. In my mind, it's mixed up with someone else. The sun glares through a gap in the clouds, turning him into a fuzzy silhouette.

'I… I don't feel well.'

I try to sit up, but my muscles won't work. His arms are around my body, helping me up. I go with it, allowing myself to be lifted and pulled onto a bench. My head wants to float off my shoulders.

'Where am I?' I flop sideways, lying down on the wood. I can't hold myself up.

'You're in the park, Lorna. You fainted. Just lie there for a bit, let the blood go back to your head.' He pulls off his coat, draping it over me, crouching down beside the bench so our faces are close. 'You've cut your lip.' He dabs at my mouth with a tissue, making me flinch.

'I feel sick,' I say, trying to sit up again.

'Stay lying down,' he says. 'Do you want me to call someone?'

It takes me a moment to think who he might call. The only person I can think of is Mark. 'No,' I say, managing to sit up. 'What a mess.' I cradle my head in my hands, elbows resting on my knees as I fight the urge to throw up. 'This has got to stop, Andrew. I was moving on, trying to get on with my life. Nothing we've done or ever could do is right.' My voice is weak, but I've never meant anything so much.

'I know,' he says. 'And I'm sorry.' His words are soft and low as he takes my face in his hands. 'It'll be OK. We'll be OK. Just know that I love you.'

I shake my head, not allowing myself to hear him. If this is what love feels like, then I don't want it. 'Where's my bag?' I need my car keys. I need to go.

'Here,' he says, passing it to me. I pull out my phone, switching it on with trembling hands. I have to call work, tell them I'll be in shortly, try to put my life back where it was. I had one foot over the precipice again, nearly took another step. It's not too late to change, to make things better, to get back on track. 'Ow… my head,' I say, touching my forehead. I delve in my bag, finding a blister pack of paracetamol. I take a couple, swallowing them without water.

Then the alerts on my phone start coming in. Missed calls, texts, WhatsApp messages, several voicemails and a couple of notifications from Double Take. Those won't be from Andrew, at least, my muzzy brain tells me as I angle the screen away from him. But it's all the other alerts that concern me.

'Shit,' I say, reading the messages from Mark.

Lorn, where are you? School called me when they couldn't reach you

Call me back asap. Trouble with Freya. Where are you?

Clinic has called me. They said you're not in work. You with Freya yet?

Lorna, where are you?

What's going on?

I scroll through all the other messages, hardly believing what I'm reading. 'Oh Christ, no…' I listen to the voicemails – three from Mark, sounding more and more concerned about me and, eventually, annoyed – plus several from work and Freya's school.

'You've gone really pale again, Lorna. What's wrong?'

'What's *wrong*?' I say, standing up, wobbling, my face twisted with anger at him, even though I know it's myself I'm mad at. 'The one time I turn off my phone, *ever*, the entire world has been trying to reach me. It's Freya. Something's happened.' I rummage in my bag, pulling out my keys. 'I love Mark,' I tell him. 'I love my family. I can't do this any more. Please don't contact me again.'

I walk away, my footsteps fast and unsteady, unable to stop the tears. When I hear his voice calling out to me, I don't turn back. I get in the car, locking the doors, fastening my seatbelt. As the engine roars to life, as I speed out of the car park, I vow to myself that I'll never see him again.

'Mark, hi, it's me. What's going on?'

'I should be asking you that,' he says down the line quietly, as though he's with someone. I grip the steering wheel, cursing the traffic as I head towards Freya's school.

'I'm sorry, my battery died. I forgot to plug in last night.' I swallow down the lie. 'Is Freya ill? She told me she was feeling poorly this morning.' I almost choke on the guilt, for sending my little girl into school when she didn't want to go. I swerve, narrowly missing the back wheel of a bicycle. The car in the next lane hoots. 'Mark?' Silence. 'Where are you?'

'Again, shouldn't I be asking you that?' He sounds louder now, as if he's moved somewhere where he can talk.

'I'm on my way to school,' I say. 'I got the secretary's messages, but she didn't say what was wrong.' Panic builds, layered upon the dread of what I've done. I'm tempted to put my foot down and drive into a lamp post.

'Where have you been, Lorna? No one could reach you. I was worried.'

'I'll tell you when I see you,' I say, hoping to have thought up a plausible excuse by then. A plausible *lie*.

'No, tell me now.' There's something in Mark's voice I haven't heard in a long while.

'I… I wasn't feeling well. I went to the doctor, OK?' He doesn't reply so I carry on. 'I blacked out. I cut my lip.' I glance in the rear-view mirror, thankful that where I hit my mouth has now swollen and split, corroborating my story.

'But Sandy at the clinic said something about you taking Freya to hospital? I don't understand why she's at school.'

'I didn't want to tell work I'd passed out,' I say, my mouth dry to the point of not being able to speak. I indicate right to turn down the road the school is on, drumming my fingers on the wheel as a stream of traffic passes slowly. 'I was embarrassed. It happened just after I dropped Freya off, and when I came round, I decided to tell work something else. I wasn't thinking straight.'

'Lorn, you don't think you're…' I hear the hope in Mark's voice, a thread of forgiveness if what he suspects is true.

'It's crossed my mind,' I say, hating myself even more. 'The last time I got light-headed was when I found out I was pregnant with Freya.' I pray it's diversion enough. 'Look, I'm nearly at the school now. Where are you?'

There's a lengthy silence before he says, 'I'm already there. I had to cancel patients because of this. Freya's in with the head.'

I pull up outside the school gates, parking illegally, scraping the wheel along the kerb as I reverse back at speed, bumping into the car behind me. 'Christ,' I say, pulling forward again. I grab my phone, turning it off hands-free, checking the paintwork after I get out. There's no damage. I'm shaking, still dizzy and nauseous as I dash into the playground to find Mark pacing about, his phone pressed to his ear.

'I'm here,' I say, just as he turns round. We each hang up, me coming close, him instantly noticing the cut on my lip. His eyes narrow before locking onto mine.

'Freya attacked a classmate,' he tells me, blank-faced apart from a small twitch on his jaw.

'Attacked a *classmate*? That can't be true. She wouldn't do that.' I dash towards the entrance. I don't want him to see my face, read the guilt. I hear him following behind, and I also hear my phone ping in my hand. Unable to help myself, I glance at the screen as I stride down the long corridor, the smell of school dinners making me feel even more like throwing up.

You're proving popular today! The alert says. *You have a new message from Andy_jag.*

I screw up my eyes as I reach for the door handle, going straight into the head's office. My little girl is sitting in a chair, her legs dangling, her head down. 'Frey-frey…' I say, crouching next to her, curling my arms around her as Mark draws up. 'I'm here now, darling,' I whisper. 'We'll sort this out, don't you worry.' Mrs McBride clears her throat.

Freya stares at her fingers, picking the skin around her nails. Finally, she looks up, her icy-blue eyes boring into mine – eyes I don't even recognise as my daughter's. It's as though she's not in there, not the Freya I know.

She slides off the chair and goes up to Mark, pushing herself against his side, resting her head against him. He wraps an arm around her, stroking her hair. It's only because I have the good sense to drop down into the chair, to put my head between my knees, that I don't pass out for a second time that day.

CHAPTER THIRTY-THREE

Lorna

Afterwards, when we're all outside, I go to give Freya a kiss, a hug, anything to make her connect with me, but she's still clinging on to Mark, sidling further behind his legs. 'We'll sort this out later,' he says, touching my arm. 'It's best you get to work now, Lorna. Freya can come with me and sit in the office. That OK, Smudge?' he says, looking down at her, ruffling her hair. 'You can do some colouring.'

I give a small nod, all I can manage, and watch Mark stride away across the playground holding on to Freya's hand. Neither of them looks back. When they're out of sight, I head slowly towards the school gates, my handbag slipping off my shoulder, my coat flapping open and tears pouring down my face.

In the car, I rest my head on the steering wheel, forcing myself to breathe steadily… counting to seven on the way in, eleven on the way out. I can't do it, my shallow rasps barely making it to three. How can my daughter be suspended from school? Even if it is on the last day of term, it'll no doubt go on her record, perhaps carry forward to high school that she attacked another pupil – a friend – with a pencil.

'The teacher saw everything,' Mrs McBride told us. 'She was in the middle of reading out a passage from a book and Freya got up, walked right over to Rosie and jabbed at her face with a pencil, narrowly missing her eye. The school nurse attended to her and recommended that she be taken to A & E in case she needed stitches or a tetanus shot.'

'Oh, *Freya*,' I'd said, but she refused to look at me. 'Why would you do such a thing, and to one of your nice friends? Rosie's been round to play.' All I'd got from her was a shrug before she looked at Mark, her big eyes swollen with tears.

'Mrs McBride, I can assure you that Freya is the kindest, most gentle girl I know. I can't ever imagine her doing anything like this, not without a very good reason.' Of course, in my mind I was scrambling about for motives, for justification, for *anything* to explain why my daughter would attack a classmate unprovoked. But really, I knew – knew how it's entirely possible to do something dangerous, reckless and life-changing for no reason whatsoever. Not consciously, anyway.

I start the engine and drive off, allowing the traffic to swallow me, not switching lanes or taking short cuts or doing anything to hasten the journey to work. When I've parked, my feet feel heavy as I head to the clinic, my skin prickling with shame as Sandy looks up from reception. She doesn't say anything until after I've signed in.

'Lorna, your face…' She half stands up, wanting to help in some way.

'It's not been a great morning,' I say, raising my hand to let her know I don't want to talk about it.

'Is Freya OK? Her school called several times and… well, I thought you were taking her to the hospital?' When I don't reply, she says, 'Do you want me to put off your next appointment?'

'No, no thanks. That's OK,' I say, going straight to the staff toilets. Thankfully, no one is in here as I dump my bag beside the basin, pulling out my make-up bag and hairbrush. In the mirror I see a woman I don't recognise, not least because of the angry welt on my lip. I touch it, wincing, before wetting a paper towel and dabbing at the dried blood. I reapply my make-up, getting rid of the mascara streaks under my eyes, and brush my hair. The mud on the side of my skirt has dried in crusty streaks so I wipe at it with another dampened paper towel. I look just about presentable enough for clients.

I lean on the sink, closing my eyes, but there's no escape – my mind consumed by thoughts that don't make sense – past and present knotted into a tangled mess. I don't understand any of it; don't understand what's real and what's made up. Don't understand anything any more.

I pack my stuff away but my bag tumbles off the ledge and onto the floor, my phone spilling out onto the tiles. It's not broken but when I see more Double Take alerts on the screen, I just want to stamp on it, tell Mark it was stolen and get another phone with a different number entirely. But something forces me to pick it up, to check. I see my hand reach out – even though it doesn't look like *my* hand. I'm watching as an unknown woman logs in. Two new messages. Two new messages from Andy_jag.

But, before I can even read them, I lunge over the basin, my free hand pulling back my hair as my stomach clenches and tightens, not letting up until everything inside me has come up.

'So how have things been this last week?' I ask my first client of the afternoon, Carla, a quietly spoken woman a little older than me. She seems to have lost even more weight, which she can ill afford to do. My lip smarts as I talk. I'm forcing myself to be present for her, to listen to her fully, but it's taking all my effort.

After she's gone, after I've cleared away her tissues and put out clean glasses and more water, plumping up the sofa cushions, I flop down in my desk chair, staring at my phone.

So sorry about this morning, Abbi. Something annoying came up. Tell me when you're free next. I want to meet you. Your pics look divine xx

Something *annoying* came up? He's told Abbi that he couldn't meet her because something *annoying* came up?

That something was *me*.

Is this what he used to tell *her*, his lodger, when he left the house for those snatched afternoons with me last year? That I was an annoyance? I rest my head down on the desk.

'Oh God, Joe!' I jump up, knocking over my glass of water. 'Sorry… I mean, Joe, come in.' I drop back down into my chair again, mopping up the mess with a tissue.

'Lorna, are you *sure* you're OK?' he asks, coming right in, looming over me.

'Yeah, yeah, I'm absolutely fine, thanks,' I say, forcing a smile, thinking that's probably my biggest lie yet.

CHAPTER THIRTY-FOUR

Lorna

Freya's not going to her swimming lesson tonight. She was disappointed, and I promised her we'd go next week, but the thought of sitting in the poolside café waiting with the other mums from school, knowing they'll have been gossiping about me and my violent daughter, fills me with dread. I imagine them scooping up their kids, dragging them away from us in case Freya lashes out again. After the day I've had, all I want to do is curl up, hide away from the world. Mark has been understanding – more understanding than I deserve – and he's cooking dinner for Freya and Jack, while I told him I needed to catch up with some paperwork I missed doing this morning.

In the top-floor study I open up my laptop, logging into Double Take. I don't have enough guilt left to feel bad any more. It's a compulsion.

A green dot sits beside his profile picture. I type fast.

Abbi74: *Don't worry about this morning. Hope all OK and was nothing serious?*

He replies straight away.

Andy_jag: *Bit of a mess actually but nothing I couldn't deal with.*

So. I was annoying *and* a mess.

Abbi74: *You sound the capable type… I like that in a man.*

My fingers tremble as I type, making me have to go back and correct my words.

Andy_jag: *I am capable. But sensitive too. I believe in honesty and integrity. Don't you?*

Abbi74: *Of course I believe in honesty.*

I swallow down the bitter taste.

Andy_jag: *What's the worst lie you've ever told?*

Abbi74: *Ha ha you're funny.*

Andy_jag: *I'm serious.*

Abbi74: *I'd have to think about that…*

How can I tell him that *he's* my worst lie?

Abbi74: *Have you met any nice women on this site?*

Andy_jag: *That would be telling ;-). And you're changing the subject.*

Abbi74: *You married or in a relationship? Seems many guys are on here.*

That's true, at least. My inbox is stuffed with men wanting illicit hook-ups, others telling me their wives don't understand, or that they want a threesome.

Andy_jag: *A bit mistrusting, aren't you?*

Abbi74: *A girl has to be careful. So I'll take that to mean you're in a relationship.*

Andy_jag: *There's a woman. But it's not what you think.*

Abbi74: *That's what they all say* ;-).

Nothing for a few minutes.

Abbi74: *Why are you on here if there's a woman in your life?*

Andy_jag: *It's complicated.*

Abbi74: *Try me.*

Andy_jag: *We were in love.*

Tears sting my eyes.

Abbi74: *Sounds like you've been hurt?*

I daren't push too hard. There's no reply for a while, making me wonder if he's figured out who I am. 'Come on, come *on*,' I whisper under my breath, tapping my fingers on the desk. But then I hear someone coming up the stairs, making me quickly switch screens to a work document.

'Hi, love,' I say as Mark pops his head round the door. He stares at me for a moment, giving me a look. 'You OK?'

'Yeah,' he says, rubbing his hands over his face. 'Frey and Jack are eating. She's very subdued.'

'Did she talk about what happened at school?'

'We had a chat,' Mark says. 'She said Rosie deserved it. Said she was teasing her about… well, about coming here and seeing your mum and dad. Rosie's started rumours. You know what kids are like.'

'Oh God,' I say, flashing a quick look at my screen. 'Poor Frey. It was when Mum turned up unannounced. With Dad.'

Mark rolls his eyes. I don't need to say any more. 'What shall I cook for us?' he says, sighing, looking tired. 'And do we have any more fabric conditioner? No one's got any clean clothes, so I thought I'd put a load of washing on.'

Mark's never been one for gender-specific roles in our house, but it's always been me who does the laundry. Little by little, the things I always kept in order are slipping from reach. My fast-spinning plates are slowing, wobbling, falling to the ground.

'To be honest, I'm not really hungry,' I say. Mark stares at me, a sad look in his eyes. 'I'll get some more conditioner tomorrow. Just do it without for now.' I hate that my voice is dismissive, uncaring, but I just want him to go, which he does but then he stops, turning back, his arms braced in the doorway.

'Lorn, are you really OK?'

'I'm fine,' I reply, sick of people asking me.

He gives a little nod. 'You just don't seem… like you,' he says. 'And you're always up here working these days.'

I force a smile, making my split lip hurt. 'Really, I'm fine, love. Worried about Freya, of course, but I'll be down soon, and we can have a proper chat.'

Mark gives another small nod, a tentative smile and leaves. Only when I hear him back in the kitchen clattering the plates into the dishwasher do I switch back to the dating site.

Andy_jag: *I was hurt. It was tough. Still is.*

Abbi74: *Sorry to hear that.*

Andy_jag: *She was the love of my life.*

Then the strange, dizzy feeling sweeps through me again, making me grab hold of the desk. I close my eyes, tipping back my head, before replying.

Abbi74: *I understand that.* I pause, thinking what to type next. *So are you after a rebound relationship?*

It's my pathetic hope, of course, that he's just trawling to see how many unsuitable women there are out there for him, that no one could possibly live up to me, to us, to what we had. Even though we can never have it.

Andy_jag: *No. I'm not here for that.*

Abbi74: *So, what are you here for?*

My heart beats faster, praying he'll say what I want to hear. What I *need* to hear.

Andy_jag: *That would be telling…*

And then the green dot disappears, and he goes offline.

CHAPTER THIRTY-FIVE

Lorna

It's Good Friday but nothing much feels good about it. I should get up and go for a run, but it's the last thing I feel like doing. Apart from running away.

Mum is meant to be coming over on Sunday for Easter lunch, but I've not checked arrangements with her or if she'll be bringing Dad, let alone thought about stocking the fridge for the weekend. If I'm honest, I'm worried about the effect her visit might have on Freya. I haven't firmed up Mum's GP appointment yet either, or booked for someone to fix her conservatory roof or clean out the guttering, and she doesn't like the home help I found, so I need to search for someone else to come in several times a week. With Dad unable to do any of these things, it puts the pressure on me, making me feel like a terrible daughter, wife, mother.

But even with all these distractions, all of this normal, real-life stuff going on, my mind still snaps back to *him*, all the space he takes up in my head. I reach out to the bedside table for my phone, feeling around for it. It's not there.

'You looking for this?' Mark comes into the bedroom carrying two mugs of coffee with one hand. He tosses something onto the duvet. It lands on my stomach.

My phone.

At first I think he's throwing it at me – his face is stern and tense. But then he comes round to my side of the bed and puts the coffee down, giving me a kiss on the head. 'Morning,' he says cheerfully.

'Oh thanks, love,' I say, grabbing it. 'Where was it?'

'You left it in the kitchen.' He takes off his robe, his eyes fixed on me, and climbs back into bed, pulling the duvet up high.

'Did I? I thought I brought it up last night.' My cheeks burn.

'Nope,' he says. 'It was on the kitchen table. I thought you might want it.' He takes a sip, staring at me. 'Seeing as you're glued to it these days.'

'Am I?' I say, scalding my mouth on a large sip of coffee. I turn away, propping myself on my side with my elbow, looking at my screen, shielding it from Mark. At least I'd turned off all notifications, so it wouldn't light up or ping in the night.

My eyes go wide, taking a moment to focus on all the alerts on my home screen. How can that be possible? Mark would only have had to press the main button to see them all. We've always known each other's passcodes, but I changed mine a few days ago, telling myself I'd reset it once I've got my life back on track. In order. Tight and in control again, just how it was. Perhaps he's seen me entering my new code, figured it out over a few sly glances the last couple of evenings. I know how observant he is.

'Everything OK?' he says, touching my shoulder.

'Yeah,' I say, putting my phone face down on the bedside table. 'Everything's fine.' And I turn over, giving him a tender kiss, thanking my lucky stars when he responds, pulling me down under the covers and kissing me back.

But half an hour later, when Mark's in the shower, I grab it again, my hand shaking. It's what I have to do. What I *need* to do in the hope of making things better. This has all got to stop.

'Not hungry, mate?' Mark asks, watching as Jack pushes bacon around his plate. 'Lorna went to a lot of trouble cooking that.'

Jack watches me as I grab more toast from the toaster, juggling it as I bring it to the table, dropping it in the rack with the rest. I can't tell if he despises me or pities me. 'Have we got everything?' I say, grabbing the ketchup and putting it in front of Freya. 'There you go, sauce-monster.' But her expression stays neutral, her eyes down.

'We've got a right miserable pair here this morning,' Mark says, winking at me. I just want us to be a team again, even though he doesn't know we're not.

'C'mon, you two. It's a weekend full of chocolate, adventure movies and two weeks off school and college,' I say. 'Oh, and Mark, Cath's invited me to a last-minute spa day tomorrow,' I tell him, praying he won't mind. 'Her sister was going but can't make it now. Is that OK with you? It'll only be for a few hours.'

He looks at me, tiny crease lines forming around his eyes as he smiles. 'Sounds perfect,' he says, touching my arm. 'Just what you need.' Then his hand slips down to my tummy and he gives me a look, his fingers crossing over.

'Thanks, love,' I say. It's all arranged. And tomorrow afternoon *is* just what I need. The perfect chance to sort out my head once and for all.

'Eat up, then, you two,' Mark says to the kids, tucking into his food.

Jack makes a noise and starts to eat, though he doesn't look up. I try to forgive him these moody moments – on the whole, he's a good lad, and he works hard at college, determined to get a place studying IT at university. While I'm trying to be the mother he lost, it's easy to forget that he's dealing with being a teenager and all the angst that brings, as well as probably grieving a mum he never knew. It can't be easy, and I know it still affects him. It's not like he even has any memories of her to fall back on.

'Freya, love, aren't you hungry?' I say.

She looks up and manages a little smile, picking up her fork and eating a mushroom.

'Sweetie, we need to have a proper talk, but I want you to know that I got an email from the head yesterday. I only saw it late last night.' Mark looks up. I hadn't wanted to bring it up until we could be alone with Freya, but she's clearly in knots. *More* knots. 'Rosie's parents are being very understanding. They're not going to ask for any further punishment as her eye was fine, thank goodness. It was just a scratch that looked a lot worse than it was.' I don't mention the part where the head acknowledged that Rosie is a difficult child, that she likes to tease other kids, that she's got a track record of bullying. She almost implied she had it coming. 'But she did ask that you write a letter to her apologising. I think that would be a good idea, don't you?' While I agree she has to be held accountable for what she did, I just want to make her feel better. Or is it me who needs to be held accountable?

Freya gives a little nod, looking up from her plate again, a spark of relief in her eyes.

'Have you got your Easter bonnet all sorted, Frey?' Mark asks. 'Can't have whatshername from Sunday school beating you.'

She looks at him. 'I don't want to go to Sunday school,' she says, tears collecting in her eyes.

'Why not, darling?' I ask, though I already know the answer.

She kicks her feet against the chair rung, picking up a piece of bacon with her fingers and nibbling it. She shrugs.

'Is it because Rosie will be there?'

She tips her head sideways, pulling up her shoulders. *Kick... kick... kick...*

Jack groans. 'That's it,' he says, scraping his chair back. 'I'm off out.'

'Jack?' Mark says, his voice deep and serious. 'Sit down and finish your food.' He rarely loses his temper – never needs to, as though everyone instinctively knows how to keep the peace.

'What you gonna do if I don't?' Jack says, pushing back his shoulders.

'Jack, please sit down and finish your food,' I say, my eyes flicking between him and his father. I've never seen him quite this agitated before.

'I'm not hungry,' he says, standing his ground. Though I can tell by his face that a part of him wants to sit down and talk, even if the other part wants to storm out and slam the front door.

'You seem really upset…'

'I'm just sick of this fucking family and—'

Freya squeals, covering her ears and screwing up her eyes.

'Jack—'

'I'm just sick of no one ever telling the truth, yeah?' he says, his voice on the brink of cracking. He swipes up his plate and glass and takes them to the kitchen, dumping them on the draining board.

'Jack, come back,' Mark demands, swinging round in his chair. 'What are you talking about?' He glances at me, putting a hand on my leg under the table. I pray my cheeks don't show the flush that's burning from the inside out.

Jack returns, standing there, looking so much like Mark but with something else mixed in – his mother. I know she was very beautiful, with her long blond curls and Monroe-esque figure – the perfect match for Mark, whose classic good looks show no sign of fading.

'You think I'm stupid, don't you?' he says, staring at his father. The skin under his eyes twitches, while his lips try to form words he can't seem to get out. Then he turns to me, his hands resting on the edge of the table, his body leaning forward. 'You think I don't see what's gone on. What's still *going* on?' He can barely contain his anger.

My cheeks burn scarlet. Oh my God, he *knows*… Did he see my phone on the kitchen table last night, somehow manage to read my texts and messages? Or perhaps he's hacked into my computer and seen my online activity? He's a technology whizz and I'd never know if he'd done something like that.

'Jack, look… Calm down, love,' I say, flicking a look at Freya so he gets the hint. 'You seem really upset. We can talk about this, but not right now.'

He glares at me. I have no idea what he's thinking, why the look in his eyes shows hate and confusion. Even if I was his real mother, I still wouldn't know what to say.

'We can talk about this somewhere else, Jack. Just me and you, somewhere quiet.' I need to get him away from Mark. 'I'm a good listener.' I have to find out what he knows, reason with him, if possible. Bribe him if I have to. Anything but have him screw things up now I'm so close to sorting it.

'It's nothing I can't say in front of Dad,' he says. 'In fact, it's Dad who needs to hear it.'

Shit.

'I understand, Jack, really I do,' I say, stumbling over my words. My heart is pounding, my mouth dry. 'Though getting facts right first might be helpful. In case you've misunderstood something.' I give him a nervous smile, hoping he'll catch on.

'What, so you can twist my mind? I know what I know, Lorna, and I'm sticking to it. I'm not blind any more and I'm not stupid.' He makes a raging sound, covering his face to hide the tears. I don't think I've ever seen Jack cry.

'Enough,' Mark says, laying his hands flat on the table, half standing up. 'This is a family weekend, and I won't have it ruined. We'll go for that walk as we planned. It'll do us all good to get out in the fresh air. I'll hear no more of this, understand?'

Jack stares at him, with a look way more pitying than the one he gave me. He nods slowly, grabbing his phone off the table before leaving the room. The thud of his footsteps on the stairs drums into my head.

CHAPTER THIRTY-SIX

Nikki

There's nothing like a fun family walk. All rugged up against the chill with their cosy boots, coats and gloves. Woolly hats and happy smiles, cheek-to-cheek selfies, flattering filters and cute tags for Instagram. Pretending everything's perfect, pretending it's not all about to fall apart: #perfectcouple #lovemyman #family.

I watch them from a safe distance as they amble along, arm in arm, pulling in close, laughing, smiling, chatting. I wonder if her husband knows what she's up to? Well, *I* do. I know exactly what she's doing behind his back. #youdontfoolme #allfake #youllgetwhatyoudeserve #lyingbitch

I bite my lip, savouring the taste of blood.

Their little girl is on a scooter, whizzing up ahead of them until they call out, making her circle back round again. She scoots behind them, coming right up close to me so I can see how soft and fluffy her pink bobble hat is, even see the curl of her eyelashes.

Lorna looks back, not giving me a second glance as she sings out her daughter's name – *Frey-yaaa*. She doesn't notice me tagging along behind in my black beanie pulled down low, my thick grey scarf from Age Concern wound round and round my neck, covering half my face. My old coat hangs down low and my soft-soled shoes don't make a sound.

She's having an affair… I want to scream out. I imagine them both slowly turning, the shock on his face as it sinks in.

I saw her in a different park yesterday. The Therapist and the Lover. I laugh to myself – they sound like a pair of cards from a tarot deck. If she knew about me, I wonder what she'd call me – the Stalker, the Other Woman, the Lodger, perhaps?

Of course she didn't spot me there either, and neither did he, but I came close to giving myself away when I let out a shocked cry as she fainted. She hit the ground hard, making me clap my hand over my mouth, stifling the noise. I watched as he took her head gently in his hands, stroking her cheek, coaxing to her to wake up, talking to her. But she was out cold.

Something began to boil inside me. It's still simmering now.

Is that what real love looks like?

I hate them both.

She lay on the ground for a while, her head turned sideways, her body unmoving as he stared at her from above, not knowing what to do. But then he shocked me. He took his phone from his pocket and snapped pictures of her from all angles, quickly putting it away again when she began to stir. I was transfixed, trying to work it out, but had to rush off to get to the bus stop, or I'd be late for work. I'd splashed out on a taxi to follow her there in the first place and couldn't afford another one back.

Lorna and her family walk on, winding through the park. I hear a peal of laughter from her – sounding fake and put on, as if she's trying too hard. Mark winds his arm around her waist, and she flicks her long hair back over her shoulder. When she glances round again to check where her daughter is, I see she's got huge owly sunglasses on, even though it's not that bright. Perhaps to conceal the shame.

'Mummy, look – boats!' the kid squeals. She's jumping up and down next to Jack, who's got his earphones shoved in. She tugs on Jack's sleeve, making him hold her scooter while she runs off. Up ahead there's a small pond – just a shallow one with little slot-machine motor boats bobbing about.

I feel my feet start to drag, watching as they veer off towards their daughter.

'Can I have a go?' she calls out, clapping her mittened hands together.

My vision blurs as the tears come, but I can still make out Mark fishing about for some change, still see Freya's delighted face as she takes the coin. Then Lorna whips out her phone, snapping photos as Freya chooses which colour boat she wants.

But it's not the motor boats that make my hands tingle and my lips go numb. It's the other kid, what he's doing by the pond. My eyes are drawn to him.

I just need to get to the bench the other side of the water. Just need to sit down.

I watch, transfixed, as the boy walks round and round the pond, dragging his toy, his father standing nearby. My breathing quickens – short and sharp, burning my throat. I pull my scarf up further over my mouth to stifle it. I can't risk a panic attack.

I close my eyes, leaning back on the bench.

Breathe, breathe, breathe…

A sudden scream makes me jump, makes me grip on to the wooden slats as if I'm about to be hurled to the ground… but it's just Freya whooping in delight as her motorboat chugs off across the pond, her fingers frantically twiddling the knobs on the control panel.

'Oh-*ohh*, it's stopped already,' she says in a whiny voice a few minutes later as her boat docks itself. But Daddy to the rescue as he pumps in another coin.

I clamp my arms around myself as the panic subsides, rocking gently for comfort.

When the second coin runs out, the family continue with their walk. Jack lags behind, his hands shoved deep in his pockets, his feet scuffing the ground. He's the last one in sight as they disappear down the track. I don't feel steady enough to follow them further.

'Hi,' I say, trying to sound cheerful. The kitchen is warm and steamy, the air filled with the rich smell of something bubbling on the stove.

'Soup,' he says, winking. 'It's mushroom.'

'Smells delicious,' I say, bending over the pan and lifting the lid. He's always creating something, one way or another. 'May I?' I hold up the wooden spoon.

'Don't burn your lips,' he says, giving me a look that tells me he wouldn't mind if I did, that he'd have an excuse to kiss them better. I slurp some down, along with my thoughts. These days, I do what I have to do – to get by, to keep the peace, to keep a roof over my head.

'Delicious,' I say.

He flicks off the radio. 'Do you want some wine?'

'Sure,' I say, pulling out a chair at the kitchen table. His house is eclectic, like him. The walls of every room are covered in paintings, most of the floors littered with tatty rugs. It's what endeared me to the place when I viewed it – all the battered furniture, the mishmash of items collected over the years, nothing matching, most things worn out. It feels like a home – not *my* home – but the closest I've known to it since… I think back to when I was a child, before my father died. But I can't dwell on that. Trauma keeps me safe from the past. Everything locked up.

I dump my shopping bag on the floor, pushing it under the table. I picked up a couple of things on the way home from the park.

'Ah good, you got cling film,' he says, spotting it as the bag topples over. 'Well remembered.' I slide it further out of sight, taking the wine.

'You trying to get me drunk?'

'Maybe,' he says, winking. 'Where did you go off to so early this morning?'

'Just for a walk. Makes a change from working.'

'You're better than just flipping burgers.' He gives me a look, one that says I should get a proper job, one that pays more. Perhaps he wants me gone.

'It's that or I get a job as a stripper,' I say, laughing. 'Anyway, it's brass in pocket.' I pat my thigh.

'*My* stripper,' he says, dragging his eyes over me as he ladles out soup into two chunky pottery bowls, handing me a spoon. We eat in silence, the ticking of the clock above the cooker keeping time with my heart. 'Upstairs with you now,' he says, after we've finished, tucking his hands under my arms, pulling me up. 'You can give me my Easter present early.' He pulls at my sweater, exposing my neck, biting down on my skin.

'Of course,' I say quietly, knowing exactly what I have to do as he leads me upstairs by the hand.

CHAPTER THIRTY-SEVEN

Lorna's Journal

The others are downstairs watching something mindless on TV, something I can't be bothered with. I said I needed to catch up on some work, that I have to go over some papers for a practice meeting. No one batted an eyelid. Joining in with family life almost seems like a chore now, as if I'm not a part of it. Secrets have a way of doing that, of dividing and separating.

I ease open the door to Freya's room, the sound of the TV audible below. I slide the toy box out and pull up the carpet in the corner of the room. As ever, it comes up easily. I glace back over my shoulder to check there's no one watching as I prise up the end piece of floorboard. Underneath is the perfect hiding place. I've made a note of where the others are stashed in case I ever forget. Heaven forbid I should lose one.

I put the board, carpet and toy box back and creep upstairs to the study, praying I won't be disturbed. I flick on the desk lamp and start up my laptop, pulling up some work files to make myself look busy. Then, half hidden under the desk, I open the tatty notebook – a present the last-but-one Christmas ago.

27 February 2017

What have I done? Dear God, please help me. I know it's wrong and deceitful, so why does it feel so right?

My career is at risk, my marriage is at risk, my family, my home…
my entire life is under threat. So why am I compelled to carry on doing
this? Please let me find the answers as I write this down.

So. Yesterday. There was nothing romantic about checking into
that cheap motel, Andrew signing us in as the equivalent of Mr &
Mrs Smith, paying in cash, not meeting the receptionist's eye as she
handed over the key card. Yet it felt as though I'd been flown to Paris
in a private jet, wined and dined, proposed to by the Seine before
making love in a five-star hotel on the Champs-Élysées.

Of course, before we went, I made all the usual protest noises
that we couldn't, we shouldn't, I mustn't – but every time I made an
excuse, it seemed to lose its power, as if the protestations themselves
were wearing down my resolve. And I barely had any time. I couldn't
be late fetching Freya.

'I think that's called talking yourself into it, Lorna,' he said,
laughing, as we sat in his car. The engine was running, and the rain
was sheeting against the windscreen. He'd left the wipers off, so we
couldn't see out. But equally, no one could see in as I wavered and
hesitated in the car park about what to do. I looked at my watch.
He was right. If I hadn't wanted to, I wouldn't have got into his car
in the first place.

'I'm going to have you one way or another,' he said, touching my
face. 'It may as well be now.'

Was it his assertiveness that got to me? His confidence? I don't
think it was quite that, though I liked it, I admit. From the start,
he's known exactly what he wanted. Me.

'We could just go in and have a quick drink,' I suggested, convinc-
ing myself that would be OK. I even gave him a flirty smile.

'You think they have a bar in there?' And we both laughed, looking
at the dismal breeze-block place. It wasn't far from the M25, the sort of
bland hotel grey-suited salesmen might meet up at to discuss the price
of widgets or whatever. Or perhaps that was just a foil for their illicit
antics too. In my mind, I tried to believe that everyone did it, that

*having an affair was normal. Denying, distorting… I was throwing
everything into the mix to make it seem OK.*

'Shall we go in and see?' I said, my hand poised on the car door.
The rain was heavy, and I was ready to run for cover.

'Let's,' he said, though he may as well have said ready, steady go
because we were both suddenly outside, coats pulled over our heads as
we dashed to the cover of the reception area. Inside we were laughing,
drenched, my feet soaking in my work shoes.

'Look, it is a fancy place after all,' he said, pointing to a small bar
in the corner. Maroon velour chairs were set out around a handful
of varnished tables at one end of the foyer, the only customer a guy
sitting alone on a banquette with a beer, reading the paper. 'Gin and
tonic?' Andrew said, taking hold of my hand. Giving it a squeeze.

He got the drinks and we sat down, me with my legs crossed as if
that might somehow delay things. Just a drink in a hotel was fine,
surely? No worse – in fact, better – than kissing in a park, or him
coming to therapy and us not doing therapy at all. But we'd not gone
there yet. Not had sex. If we didn't do that, I told myself, then nothing
too bad had happened. I could claw my way back to level ground.
To normal life. Everyone has aberrations, don't they? My job is proof
of that every day.

'This isn't easy, is it?' I said, uncomfortable with our silence, even
though I often sit with clients through theirs – sometimes for an entire
session. My glass was slippery in my hand, covered in condensation as
I twirled it round. The bitter lemon slice and bubbles from the tonic
made me shudder.

'I know,' he said, reaching out, taking my hand across the table.
'You're very lovely,' he continued. 'Do you know that?' His eyes. The
way he looked at me. God.

I turned away then, focusing on the carpet pattern – small grey
and red squares repeating over a bottle-green background. I didn't
think I was lovely at all. Lovely women didn't do this sort of thing.
And then she was on my mind again: Maria. Almost as if she was

sitting at the table with us, shaking her head, looking disparagingly at me, a warning look in her eyes.

'She was always standing up for the underdog,' Mark once told me, a fond look about him. It's still hard to hear, though, even after all this time. 'She was always a voice for the weak, whether it was issues at Jack's nursery or unfairness at work.' I knew Maria had been an engineer and worked in a male-dominated environment, having to fight her way up the career ladder harder than her peers. From what I gather, she was a force to be reckoned with.

Perhaps that's why Andrew's kind comment in the bar did something to me, took the shudder from the bubbles and transformed it into a different feeling I couldn't place. A feeling of being wanted, perhaps? Needed. Cared for in a way that felt so foreign.

Of not being second best.

Anyway, my feelings don't make sense, given that I know Mark loves me deeply. He's the best husband. I know exactly where I stand with him, how to behave, the right thing to say, what makes him happy and what, on occasion, might make him upset and silent for a few days. Me and the kids are so attuned to him.

The guy drinking on his own swigged the last of his pint, folded his paper and got up, walking off, slowing down as he passed us. For a moment, I thought he was going to say something – did he recognise me, was he an old client? – but he didn't. He just walked on by, a tiny smile curling up the corner of his mouth. As if he knew what we were up to.

The barman wiped down the surfaces, polished the beer taps, put away some glasses. Then he came out and collected up the empty pint glass before returning to us with a tiny dish of nuts. There was music playing softly – just a selection of nondescript songs, some current, some from way back. That type of unidentifiable music hotels play. For some reason, it put me on edge.

'I should go,' I told Andrew, putting down my drink. 'I can't do this.'

But he didn't get to answer because suddenly, behind us, there was shouting and the thunk of fist on bone several times over. I jumped out of my skin, gasping, and turned just in time to see the newspaper guy hit the ground as another man took a couple of swings at him. He lay there for a moment, stunned, his legs caught up in the revolving door as the man who'd hit him went out, red-faced and yelling obscenities.

That's when everything swam before me – as if I was being dragged round and round the revolving door myself. Strange whooshing sounds reverberated through my head and flashing lights blinded me. I grabbed the arm of the chair, terrified. I've never been able to stand seeing violence.

'Christ,' Andrew said, laughing. 'Classy place.' I could hear him but couldn't see him properly – just his silhouette. I touched my head, willing it to pass. 'You OK?' Then I felt an arm around my shoulders.

I shook my head, but it hurt so much, made me feel even dizzier.

'C'mon,' he said. 'Let's go.'

And I allowed it. In that moment of shock and vulnerability, I allowed those strong hands to grip my shoulders, guiding me to wherever he took me because, by then, it didn't matter. I wasn't me. I didn't feel real. So I figured that neither were the consequences.

I stood there, hearing him book and pay for a room under a false name, making a joke about counting out the cash while I stood back, swaying in time to the music.

He took my hand then, holding me steady, leading me down a corridor, me walking obediently beside him, my footsteps quick – two to his every one pace, quietened by the carpet. I was going down a rabbit hole. A never-ending tunnel with so many doors leading off, and I could have taken any one of them, made my escape. But I didn't. I walked on as if I'd been drugged, Rohypnol in my gin, even though there hadn't been.

'This is us,' he said, inserting the key card. Every sound was magnified, every light bulb a solar flare. 'After you,' he said, checking up

and down the corridor before shutting the door behind us, putting the chain on.

It was dim inside. Thick netted drapes covering the gap between the half-closed curtains, obscuring the drizzly afternoon outside. He didn't bother with lights. I sat on the bed – him guiding me down with his hands pressed gently on my shoulders – and then he flicked on the TV with the remote. It was set to the hotel's channel – the welcoming text, the breakfast and checkout information. The same music as in reception was playing in the background. He left it on.

I felt myself being gently laid back on the bed, the tug on my feet as my shoes were taken off, then the awkward pull on my skirt that needed to be undone from behind. I was frozen, didn't make it easy as he undressed me. But I didn't try to stop it either.

His face was above me – the scar the only thing in complete focus while the rest of the room was like looking through a fish-eye lens. He was so close, the scent of him overpowering, smothering, drug-like and intoxicating as he pulled off his shirt, exposing his body. He was beautiful, I knew that, and I wanted him more than anything. But I still wanted to scream, lash out, hit the panic button, run for my life. Not that I could move. I was frozen by fear.

His hand swept down my body, pulling off my underwear, touching me, kissing his way down. I held the top of his head, nothing seeming real yet everything suddenly clearer, as though I'd been blind all my life.

My back arched, my fingers clawed, as I realised what he'd done to me, what was happening. Nothing else existed in that moment. He had complete power over me as he slid himself up me again, pressing himself down, working his way in, owning me as he tensed up, his muscles tight as I gripped him, allowing it…

I shudder as I read, clenching my teeth, gripping the journal tightly. There's more, but I hear movement downstairs, so I snap it shut and dash down to Freya's room, hiding it away under the floorboard again. 'Mummy, mummy,' I hear her calling out, then the sound of Jack grumbling, saying he's hungry, about there being no food in the fridge. Just as I'm going out of her bedroom, Freya comes in.

'Oh,' she says, looking surprised. 'What are you doing in here?' Even at her age, she doesn't like people in her room. But I deflect her question by grabbing her for a tickle, telling her it's bath time, that if she's good, I'll read her an extra-long story before bed.

CHAPTER THIRTY-EIGHT

Lorna

'Oh my God,' Annie says, grabbing my hand from across the table, her eyes going saucer wide. I flinch as she grips me, the pain shooting up my arm. 'Isn't that the guy from Cath's dating app sitting behind you?' Her expression tightens as she raises her eyebrows, looking beyond my shoulder.

I freeze, hardly daring to turn around, trying to hide the panic on my face. It's taken all my resolve to come out tonight. But surely she can't mean *him* – Andrew?

Mark turns around, slinging his hand on the back of my chair as he follows Annie's gaze. 'Cath's not still flaunting herself on that bloody site, is she?' he says, turning back again, shaking his head in disapproval.

'Her obituary will be on there, I think,' Annie says, laughing. 'She's always looking for someone or something better, never satisfied with the guys she meets.'

I pull my hand from Annie's grip, nursing it in my lap, looking at Mark and managing a smile when he catches me staring. After this afternoon, I was feeling different about everything, but now Annie's just put me on edge again.

'She should meet someone the old-fashioned way,' Ed says. 'In a sweaty club with a good dose of alcohol and bad judgement.'

'Didn't you and Cath see any hot men at the spa this afternoon?' Mark asks me quietly. He's joking, of course, but I can't help sensing a tinge of jealousy.

'We were too busy getting massages and facials,' I whisper back with a dreamy look. 'Though I think Cath was making eyes at some guy in the Jacuzzi.' I wink and give him a nudge, letting him know that he needn't worry.

'Look around now,' Annie says, still distracted and thankfully not listening to what we were saying. 'It *is* him, isn't it?'

My heart thumps again as I turn around slowly, making sure my hair and hand cover half my face. Two tables away there's a man with a petite blonde woman sitting opposite him. He's grinning widely, hanging on her every word. I let out a long slow breath.

'I've never seen him in my life before,' I say to Annie, turning back. Relief floods through me.

'Well, I swear his face is familiar. Maybe she's dated him, or been messaging him at the very least. C'mon, Lorn, you must remember. We're pretty bloody familiar with all the mug shots on that site now. It's as if *we've* been out with them all.'

'Oh, I see,' Mark says, raising his eyebrows. 'You personally vet all Cath's dates, do you?' He touches my arm, directing the question right at me. Now I'm unsure if he's joking or not. 'Should I be worried?'

I manage a small laugh, sipping my wine, grateful at least that it's not Andrew sitting behind me. That would have been unthinkable, as though there was no escape.

'Well, should I be?' Mark presses when I don't reply. His tone makes my heart miss a beat.

'Cath's just hopeless with dating,' Annie interjects. 'We have to look out for her, eh Lorn?'

'Do you now?' Mark continues, not taking his eyes off me.

'What's all this, then,' Ed chips in, putting down his phone and latching on to Mark's concern. 'You two girls dating vicariously?' He grins.

'No, of *course* not,' I say, rolling my eyes, giving a silly laugh.

Mark leans into me, giving me a little kiss, relaxing a little. 'You seem much happier,' he whispers in my ear. 'That spa session did you good earlier.'

I squeeze his leg under the table. 'It did,' I reply. 'I'm feeling super-chilled.'

'Oh-oh you're blushing, Lorn,' Ed says in a silly voice. I wish he'd just shut up. 'And we all know blushing means you're fibbing.' He laughs raucously, taking a large mouthful of wine, draining his glass before pouring more for all of us. 'Another bottle, please,' he says, flagging a passing waitress. 'It's Christmas weekend or something, isn't it?'

'Easter, stupid,' Annie says, poking him. 'Which is why Lilly wouldn't eat her supper before we left and then threw up just as the babysitter arrived. She'd scoffed three whole chocolate eggs by herself.'

Ed raises his glass. 'Happy bloody Christmas, then, to one and all,' he says loudly. When Ed gets going, he really gets going.

'Yes. Cheers,' Mark says, sounding flat in contrast. 'Here's to Cath finding a suitable man. As soon as possible,' he adds, not taking his eyes off me.

'You didn't have to go on about it quite so much, love,' I say, as we're getting ready for bed. Mark is hunched over the basin cleaning his teeth. He spits and rinses, staring into the mirror, watching me behind him as I brush my hair.

'Go on about what?'

'About Annie and me being interested in the guys on Cath's dating app. We're seriously not. We just don't want her to get hurt, that's all.'

He puts his arm round me, giving me one of his come-to-bed looks. 'But you do look at the guys on it, right? I bet you were swiping through it all afternoon with her at the spa.'

'Well, we looked a little bit. It was only to help Cath.' I poke him gently in the ribs, waiting for my cheeks to burn. Oddly, they don't. 'There's really no need to worry.'

'But you must feel attracted to some of the guys on there,' he says. 'Who's to say you're not contacting them?' He pauses, seeing the hurt look on my face.

'*I* say I'm not!' I reply as indignantly as I can manage, running a cleansing pad over my face.

'I'm just winding you up.' He pulls me close by the hands. 'Hey, did you hurt yourself?' He looks at the bruise blooming on the fleshy part of my thumb.

'Got into an argument with the weights on the bench press machine this afternoon,' I say, laughing. 'We did a workout too. Cath told me not to show off.' I roll my eyes.

'Well, I'm just glad you've come back all chilled and relaxed,' he says, giving my hand a kiss.

'Anyway, it's no different to you spotting a woman in the street and fancying her,' I say, thinking I should just drop the subject.

'It's very different.'

'How so?' We head into the bedroom – Mark pulling back the duvet while I flick on the lamps and turn off the main light. We climb into bed.

'Firstly, because I can't send a message to a random woman on the street, even if I did find her attractive.'

'Oh, so you would if you could?' I giggle as he runs his hand across my tummy, going down lower. We're both naked. 'Anyway, what's secondly?'

'Secondly, is that I wouldn't have a clue if she was single or not, would I? The men on Cath's dating app are there because they're single and looking.'

'Ha, I think Cath would dispute that.' I roll onto my side to face him as his hand slips between my legs.

I close my eyes for a second because, of course, it's *his* hand I feel... Tears well up, making me want to punch the pillow.

'She had one date where the guy was wearing his wedding ring at the start of the evening. Cath didn't say anything, but when he came back from the loo, he'd taken it off.'

'Careless,' Mark says, doing to me what he knows I like. I suck in a deep breath, closing my eyes, but it feels so wrong, as if I don't know who it is – Mark or *him*. I blink back the tears as he rolls on top of me.

Afterwards, I lie with my head on his chest, listening to his breathing, stroking his skin.

'Don't you want to know what comes third?' he says.

'Not really,' I say sleepily, kissing his chest, trying to feel content.

'Well, I'll tell you anyway. Third is that I wouldn't ever cheat on you – not even if the woman I'd passed in the street was gorgeous, single, loaded, handed me her business card and blew me a kiss. That's it, really.'

I pull him closer with my arm slung around his waist. 'I love you,' I say, screwing up my eyes.

I wake early, but this time for the right reasons. I lie there for a moment, remembering yesterday, before slipping out of bed. I go into the bathroom to put on my running gear, trying not to wake Mark. I haven't been for a jog in a long time. It's time to get back on track. Everything's going to be fine, just how it used to be.

He stirs as I leave the bedroom, stretching out, waking up, but I don't stop to speak. Instead, I go downstairs and open the living room door, sucking in a huge breath before the screams burst out of me – one after the other, over and over at the sight of the body on the floor.

It's not real... It's not real... It's not real...

I grab the door frame, my ears ringing as I see Jack lying on the carpet, his throat slashed. There's blood all over him, running down his neck, on his face, all over his arms and hands. My head explodes with pain as I scream, frozen to the spot, vaguely aware of Mark dashing down the stairs, running up beside me.

Oh my God, oh my God, oh my God… Please not Jack…

Sick forces its way up my throat as I retch at the sight of his body, covering my mouth.

Noooo! Don't be dead, please don't be dead… I'm so sorry… This is all my fault…

'What the *fuck*…' Mark is suddenly beside me, his robe half around him, bringing me back to the present as he grips my shoulders. He's surprisingly calm, given that his son is lying on the floor covered in blood. 'Jack?' he says from the doorway. 'Oh, *I* see…' Then he lets out a laugh. 'Very funny, mate.'

I scream again, burying my face against him. This can't be happening. I clap my hands over my ears, shaking my head from side to side, trying to make it all go away.

'Ha ha, April Fools!' Jack says, suddenly sitting up, spraying out laughter and shaking his head. 'Sorry, I couldn't keep it up any longer.' He stands up, his smile broad on his blood-smeared face.

I want to yell, kick and punch someone, some*thing*, but all I can do is stagger to the downstairs loo, shaking as I kneel in front of the pan, heaving up the remains of last night's dinner. My skin is cold and clammy. Then I hear Mark giving Jack a half-hearted telling off, followed by the pair of them laughing as I cradle my head in my hands over the sloppy water.

I go back into the living room doorway, shaking, unable to go right in.

'Love?' Mark says. 'You don't look well. I think you need another spa day already.' He's trying not to laugh.

'How *could* you?' I whisper, staring at Jack. I hug my arms around me, feeling as though I've been run over.

'It was just a joke, Lorna. It's April Fool's day.'

'Come here, you,' Mark says, drawing me close. 'He got you good and proper, didn't he? I thought there really *had* been a murder the amount you screamed.' He kisses my head. 'Come on, let's get some coffee and breakfast.' He heads for the kitchen, Jack following, but I stay frozen to the spot.

Freya, who'd been hiding and watching from behind the sofa, trots off behind them, telling her dad how she helped Jack do the fake blood and… and wasn't it amazing how Mum screamed so much, thinking he really was dead? And it was so funny when she was shaking and crying and, and, and…

I go back upstairs and flop down onto the bed. A moment later, my phone vibrates on the bedside table. I lunge for it out of habit, my heart skittering, but it's just Annie saying what a good evening last night was, that she was glad to see me looking more cheerful.

I put it back, face down, thinking what a good actress I must be, and curl up into a ball, sobbing for what seems like ages.

There's a knock on the bedroom door.

'Lorna, can I come in?' It's Jack. He opens the door a little, peeking round. He's still smeared with the fake blood, but I can see, now I've calmed down, that it's not very realistic.

'Sure,' I say, grabbing a tissue and blowing my nose. ''Scuse the state of me. Hormones probably.' I almost believe Mark's pregnancy hopes.

'Look, I'm really sorry about before,' he says, standing awkwardly at the end of the bed. 'I didn't mean to upset you. I thought you'd find it funny.'

I sit up, adjusting the pillows. 'Did Dad tell you to come and say that?'

He shakes his head, looking hurt. 'No. I wanted to.'

I nod, believing him. 'Thanks, Jack. It's OK.'

'I didn't think it through,' he says. 'Didn't know you'd fly off like that.'

'I'm sorry for overreacting. It was a shock to see you covered in blood on the carpet.' We both laugh.

'Sometimes I think you want that.' He sounds serious again.

'*What?* Oh, Jack, no. No, no *no*…' I frown, shaking my head. 'Of *course* I don't.'

'It wasn't even very good fake blood,' he says, shrugging. 'Anyway, after things got a bit tense at breakfast the other morning, I was just… just trying to do something to make us all laugh a bit. Guess it backfired.'

'Well, that was very thoughtful of you,' I say with a wry smile. Even though I'm still feeling shaken, I like that he's sought me out. Like it that he's now sitting next to me on the bed. 'Oh Christ,' I say, suddenly remembering. Jack looks puzzled. 'It might be April Fool's day but it's also *Easter* Day. Oh, poor Freya… I forgot to put out her chocolate eggs—'

'Don't worry,' Jack says, holding up his hands and grinning proudly. 'I made sure the Easter bunny came. I already did it. She's tucking in as we speak.'

I drop back against the pillows. 'There are some for you too, you know,' I say, relieved. But it occurs to me that he must sometimes feel sidelined by Freya, all the attention she gets. 'And thanks for doing that, Jack,' I add, wondering how he knew where I'd hidden the eggs. 'That was thoughtful of you. Unlike… *that*,' I say, pointing at his face and neck, grinning.

He laughs too. 'Actually, I thought Dad would get more freaked out about it than he did.'

'He's your dad. Of *course* he'd freak out if anything bad happened to you. And me. You do know that, Jack, right? I do love you just as much.'

He gives a coy nod, the glimmer of a smile. 'I didn't mean just because he's my dad. I meant because of…' He trails off.

I raise my eyebrows to encourage him, switching into therapist mode, hoping he'll continue. Jack rarely opens up, let alone to me. Besides, after his outburst on Friday morning at breakfast, I'm still not certain what he knows. It could be a chance to find out. 'OK-*aay*... That sounds cryptic. Like there's something you want to say but can't quite get out?' I swallow drily, trying not to show my fear.

He hesitates, scratching the drying blood on his neck. 'I thought Dad would be more upset at seeing me because of what happened with my mum. You know, my *other* mum,' he says, flashing me a look. 'I know it gets to him more than he'd ever let on, and he tries to be brave for me but...' He pulls a pained face. 'Sometimes I wish he wouldn't be.'

'I know, love,' I say. 'It's hard for you both.'

'Dad's always been good telling me things about Mum, being open and saying what she was like and stuff. He shows me photos of her, says how much she loved us, what a great mother she was.' He gives a little smile. 'But then I remember...' He trails off, looking even more pained.

'What is it, Jack?'

He shifts closer on the bed. 'I dunno, I've probably got it wrong. It doesn't matter.' He shakes his head.

'Got what wrong, love?'

'It'll just be my mind playing tricks. That can happen, right?'

'Well, yes, sometimes,' I say, not knowing where this is going. I'm just thankful he's not mentioned anything about Andrew, though I don't like to see him so troubled. 'Oh, Jack,' I say, seeing the tears in his eyes. I inch forward, in case he wants a hug, but he doesn't move. 'Have you ever spoken to anyone about this, about losing your mum and how you're feeling? I can tell you're hurting very much.'

He shakes his head.

'You're a therapist.' He looks up hopefully, eyebrows raised.

'I know,' I say, giving him a small smile. 'But I wouldn't be allowed to help you professionally. It's against...' The word gets lodged in my throat. 'It's not ethical to counsel family.'

He gives me a resigned nod.

'But we can still talk,' I say. 'Anytime you want.' I reach out and stroke his hand.

He nods, smiling briefly. 'It's just that… I actually remember things about my mum, Lorna.' He picks at the buttons on the end of the duvet cover, sighing heavily. 'But that can't be possible, right? Dad told me I must have got it wrong, that I was too young when she died to remember anything about her. Guess all I've really got are a few photos.'

'Sometimes our minds can fill in the gaps with memories that we'd *like* to believe,' I say, feeling bad I've not talked with him like this before. Another casualty of my affair. 'It can kind of help ease the pain of loss. So your dad's right in a way. Even though you were too young to remember your mum, there's still a grieving process to go through, Jack, and it doesn't sound like you've worked through it yet. I know it's hard.' I lean forward, trying to catch his eye. 'Really I do.'

He frowns, thinking about this. He doesn't seem convinced.

'No, you don't understand. I really *do* remember things.' He ruffles his hair, making a confused face. Then his shoulders slump forward. 'But… but then if *you're* saying it too, that my mind's playing tricks, then I guess that must be true. You're the therapist.' He sighs heavily. 'It's just that I've always wished so much that she was still alive. Wanted a real mo—' He stops abruptly.

I wince inside. Maria might as well be sitting in between us.

'It's OK, Jack,' I say, not wanting him to feel bad. 'I understand. I know I'll never be your real mum, but I hope I'm some kind of reasonable substitute.' I laugh, trying not to get too maudlin. 'Anyway, you're stuck with me, I'm afraid.' I give him a wink.

'Yeah, you're a good stepmum,' he says. 'Dad's lucky to have you. And so are me and Frey.'

I curl up inside from guilt, though it feels good to hear him say this.

'If only I could just get rid of this one memory,' he says. 'It's in my dreams too, sometimes. Or rather, nightmares.' He looks out of the window for a moment. 'Does that mean anything, do you think?'

'That you have nightmares?'

He shrugs and nods. 'You know what?' he says. 'I think I'll just hold on to the good memories, pretend they're real, even if they are false. And I'll try to forget the bad one.' He gets up and heads for the door, turning back to face me as he reaches for the handle. 'But…' Then he checks himself again, staring at me thoughtfully before shaking his head. 'Sorry again, Lorna,' he adds, wiping at the blood on his neck. 'And thanks for listening.'

'That's OK, Jack,' I say, giving him a little smile as he leaves, flopping back down onto the pillows when he's gone.

CHAPTER THIRTY-NINE

Lorna

'Mum?' I say for the second time. 'Would you like some more lamb?' She stares at me as if I've just asked her if she wants a trip to the moon. I hold up the carving knife, gesturing to the half-eaten joint of meat on the serving plate, flashing a look at Mark.

'Your father couldn't come,' she says out of the blue.

'I know that, Mum,' I say, trying not to roll my eyes or sound impatient. I carve her another slice of meat anyway. She doesn't look as though she's been eating properly. 'You already told me.' Frankly, I'm pleased he's not here.

'He doesn't like Easter.' She stares at the meat I put on her plate. 'All he does is sit in that bloody chair, the useless lump.'

I swallow it down, trying not to get angry with her. It's never easy dealing with how she is, but it was especially hard when I was a child. I constantly felt embarrassed, always making excuses and covering up for her behaviour. Once, at school, I pretended she'd died just to get some sympathy, make everyone stop teasing me. But I got found out, of course. In the end, I gave up having friends over because of what she was like. I know Freya's feeling similar repercussions too, but I don't want her to suffer like I did – have her childhood overshadowed by Mum. It affects us all.

'Let's not go there, Mum. Let's talk about something else.' I glance at Freya, who's thankfully not listening. She's immersed in her colouring book. I know I should be more sympathetic, especially given my profession, but sometimes it wears thin. We've all had to cope with Dad over the years – him sitting in that chair being the least of it. And then I catch Jack's eye as he holds up his plate for more lamb, and we exchange a knowing look, a sign of our connection earlier. I can't help thinking about what he said, about his memories, what's real and what's not. What our minds lock away to protect us, only releasing glimpses in tiny, manageable chunks when there's a chance of processing them. Or, worse still, when our minds fabricate things to compensate. It makes me feel bad for snapping at Mum.

'Whoa, Lorn, you OK?' Mark says, taking hold of my wrist.

I jump at his touch, every nerve on fire.

'You were really wobbling and shaking,' he says. 'Careful with that knife in your hand.'

'Sorry… I'm feeling a bit out of sorts.'

'Sit,' he says, gently taking the knife from me. 'That was a delicious roast, by the way.' He leans in to give me a kiss on the cheek. 'Did you do a test yet?' he whispers into my ear before carving the rest of the lamb.

I shake my head, mouthing *I will…* just to appease him.

Later, when Mum and the kids are ensconced in front of the TV watching *Jason and the Argonauts* for about the twentieth time, I tell Mark I'm going upstairs for a quick lie-down. His face lights up at the implication, knowing I couldn't keep my eyes open when I was first pregnant with Freya.

'I'll make everyone tea,' he says. 'You go and rest.'

I nod, watching him go into the kitchen, his body looking fit and toned beneath the black T-shirt he's got on over jeans. His hair is clipped short, showing off his strong neck, his broad shoulders. He's a good-looking man, I think, and I'm lucky to have him. Lucky to *still* have him.

I clutch the banister as I go up, feeling dizzy again. I stop outside my bedroom door, wanting to lie down, but I can't help glancing at the second flight of stairs leading up to the study. It's as though I'm not in control of myself, and something is drawing me up there, compelling me to open up my laptop and log into that damned dating site. Like I'm a robot, pre-programmed. An addict getting her fix.

As ever, there are many messages – from the usual 'Hello sexys', to men giving me their Kik username, Instagram handle or phone number, to some actually vaguely normal-sounding approaches. I delete them all quickly, my heart sinking when there are none from *him*. A pain stabs through my heart as I read back over the last exchange between Andy_jag and Abbi74.

I hold my head in my hands, sighing, knowing I never can meet him again, and certainly not in the guise of Abbi. I'm nothing better than a catfish, soon to be forgotten, sinking to the bottom of the pond.

You're the only man I've ever truly loved… but why? I type in the empty grey message box, hating myself, watching the flashing cursor. Then, of course, I delete it without sending. I drop my head down, sobbing quietly, not realising that Freya has come upstairs, that she's standing right beside me.

'Mummy, what's wrong?' I feel her little hand on my back. 'I thought you were lying down? Is it because of Nana?'

'Oh, darling,' I say, sitting up, forcing a laugh and wiping my eyes. 'Nothing's wrong. I'm fine.'

'No, you're not. Why do adults always lie?'

I shrug, unable to answer without fibbing. 'I'm just a bit tired, that's all. But I'll be OK.'

'I don't believe you,' Freya says, staring at my screen.

Shit…

Quickly, I switch windows to a clothes website that was left open.

'What was that?' she asks. 'That other website?'

'Oh, I don't know. Probably just some silly pop-up advert or something.' Freya won't know anything about dating sites. But then there's a quiet bleep in the background as the site tells me a message has come in.

'No one's watching the movie with me any more and it got really scary,' Freya says, her finger on the trackpad, idly scrolling through the clothes on the screen. 'Nana's fallen asleep, Jack's gone down the road to meet a friend and Dad's washing up. Everyone's boring. I want to play a game.' She folds her arms and pouts.

'I'll play a game with you,' I say. 'Why don't you go and wake Nana up and I'll be down in a moment?'

She nods, going off downstairs again, her slippered feet dragging slowly.

When she's gone, I check the message. It's not from him, of course, but my heart still sinks, even though I know it has to be over between us. I take a deep breath before typing one last message. *I love you. I always have… and I always will…* Words I could never say to his face. Then I click send.

I log out and go downstairs to find Mark setting out a board game with Freya, while Mum's head is lolling against the side of the sofa. The front door opens, banging loudly again. A waft of cold air precedes Jack.

'Daz wasn't in,' he says to no one in particular. 'Is there any more chocolate?'

I can't help the smile, can't help the warm feelings as my family unwittingly glues together the shreds of my heart – a heart that doesn't even know why it's been broken, or if it even deserves to be mended.

'There's tons of the stuff in the kitchen,' I say. 'Bring it all in. Let's gorge ourselves and play silly games.' I want nothing more, I think, as I watch us all doing what families do best – muddling along – than to spend time in their company, their warmth, their love and, for just a couple of hours at least, shut out all the mess in my head. Pretend like none of it happened.

'You seem perkier already,' Mark says as we sit at the dining table, everyone choosing what colour counter they're going to be. 'But you didn't get much of a rest.'

'Freya came up,' I say, rolling my eyes, flashing him a grin. 'It's fine. I'm OK.' Mum wakes and joins us then, somehow sensing that Mark has got out the port left over from Christmas.

'Ooh, don't mind if I do,' she says with a chuckle, sitting down next to Freya. I hold my breath as Mum looks puzzled. 'Move up, chicken,' she says. 'Your granddad's going to sit there.'

Freya shoots me an awkward look, opens her mouth to speak even though nothing comes out. She shifts up a place anyway, leaving a larger gap than needed between her and Mum.

'Mum, Dad's not here today, remember?' I say loudly, even though she's not deaf. But it somehow feels appropriate to hammer the message home. As much for Freya's sake as anything. 'You know that.'

'Isn't he?' she says, looking around. 'Where is he, then?'

I sigh, giving Mark a look. He gives me an encouraging nod. 'Dad's at home, Mum. Don't worry. He's fine. It's what he wanted. You'll see him later when we take you back.'

Mum thinks for a moment, taking one of the pencils Freya is handing out. The soft powdery lines on her face gradually change to what look like hardened cracks, mud that's baked in the sun too long. And the neat bow of her mouth, never without lipstick, puckers into a mean grimace – so different to the affable smile she usually wears.

'It's what he wanted?' she says, as if she doesn't believe me.

'Yes, Mum,' I say, knowing there's no point elaborating.

Mum thinks some more, her teeth clamped together, the pencil gripped between her white-knuckled fists before she snaps it clean in two.

CHAPTER FORTY

Nikki

'I'd like to make an appointment, please,' I say after the receptionist answers. The words make my heart thump with anticipation. Today is the day, as though the planets are somehow perfectly aligned, some cosmic force at play in the heavens. I knew I'd recognise it when it happened.

'I'll check availability for you. Is this a self-referral or have you been asked to call by a medical provider or other service perhaps?'

I hear her tapping at a keyboard.

'Self-referral,' I say. 'And I'd like to see a female therapist, please.' That will narrow down the field a bit, funnel me closer to her. I don't want to sound insistent.

'I have an assessment slot free with Julie a week on Thursday at eleven fifteen. She's a new therapist here. How does that sound?'

How does it sound? It sounds not fucking like *her*.

'I'm sorry, I can't make that time. Do you have anyone else? Something sooner?'

'Most of our female therapists are busy until…' I hear her tapping away again. 'Oh, actually, it looks like there's been an email cancellation come in over the weekend. Let me just check when…' She makes a thoughtful noise, tapping away some more. 'I don't suppose there's any chance at all that you can make it to the clinic this afternoon, is there? I know it's short notice but—'

'Who is the appointment with?'

'Her name is Lorna Wright. She's very experienced and normally has a long waiting list, but I can see that one of her regulars has cancelled for later. It's at three o'clock this afternoon. Can you make it?'

'That's perfect,' I say, wishing she knew how much I actually meant that. 'Absolutely perfect.'

'Great, if you can just give me a few details, I'll book you in.'

Then she explains how I'll have to pay for the assessment session today and how future billing works if I should come regularly after that. I don't tell her that just the one session is all I need.

CHAPTER FORTY-ONE

Lorna

'There's no easy way to say this, Lorna, but there's been a complaint against you.' Joe sits opposite, stony-faced, not offering me a coffee like he usually would when I have a supervision session with him. It's our first day back after the Easter break.

'*What?*'

I feel numb, unable to take in what he's saying.

'Who from?' I ask, terrified of what's about to be revealed, of what's already been said. I can see by his pained expression that Joe isn't enjoying this any more than I am. 'A complaint… about *what?*'

'Inappropriate behaviour, I'm afraid.'

Christ. I knot my fingers, twisting my knuckles until they hurt, staring at my feet. 'What kind of… inappropriate behaviour?' I brace myself, waiting for him to shoot all the allegations about having an affair with a client at me. One of the most heinous and potentially damaging things a therapist can do.

Andrew's weekly appointment is scheduled for this afternoon, Tuesday, as we were closed yesterday, which is going to make things especially difficult. He must have complained last week, before Easter.

It's OK, I tell myself, trying to think. *You can deal with this, just like everything else…*

I can see Joe's mouth moving, see the pained expression on his face, but I can't hear him. He's no doubt explaining that I'll be suspended, that questions will be asked, statements taken and submitted to my professional body while they decide what to do with me, reviewing the case, all the ethical guidelines I've breached. It'll be written about in their monthly publication for all my colleagues to see, I'll be held up as an example, unemployable in psychotherapy, and no doubt the tabloids would like a sniff at the story too: *Therapist at Top London Clinic Struck off for Affair with Client…*

And there'll be no hiding from Mark what I've done. Not like last time.

'Joe, I'm so, *so* sorry,' I say, sucking in a large gasp of air, knowing nothing else is appropriate. There is no defence. Disclosure is my best tactic. 'I never meant for any of this to happen. After last year, I thought I had it under control, thought I had dealt with it but…' I trail off. Joe is frowning, looking perplexed, as though I've gone mad.

'Look, Lorna,' he says. 'The upshot is that Tom's mother is willing to hold off further action if—'

'Tom's mother?'

'Yes. She feels the last session was unproductive because of you checking your phone. She said Tom didn't complain because he didn't want to hurt your feelings. You've said yourself the lad trusts you, that you've got a good relationship with him. He's beginning to open up, from what you say. Anyway, she's willing to let it go, this time, if we offer her three sessions free of charge. I've only ever had to do this once before, Lorna, and it's not something I want to make a habit of. In this case, I've agreed and only because of the progress you've made with him already. His mother's not disputing that.'

'But…' I clap my hand over my mouth.

'Lorna…' Joe makes a different face now, one of puzzlement. 'Have you actually been listening to a word I've said?'

I resist the explosion of relief, force myself not to fold in two, burying my face in my hands and letting out deep wails and laughs combined. 'Absolutely, and I understand, Joe. Really, I do. Checking my phone in session was totally stupid and not cool and it will never happen again. If it hadn't been for Freya being ill, if I'd got some backup in place and—'

'Yes, yes, I know all that,' he says. 'But I have a condition too.' He keeps his eyes fixed on me as I look pained, raising my eyebrows, bracing myself. 'That you talk to me. *Now.*' He looks at his watch, then folds his arms. 'We've got forty-five minutes left.'

I sit there, nodding slowly, biting my lip. My eyes close momentarily, wanting nothing more than to spill everything out, but one thing's for sure: I can't. I can't tell anyone. *Ever.*

'I've not been sleeping well,' I begin. 'Stuff on my mind.' I dredge up a skeleton of my problems, enough to keep Joe happy.

He nods, unfolding his arms, getting into a more relaxed position in his consulting chair. Part of me feels as though I want to lie down, to be analysed, psychodynamic style, picked apart, everything dragged back to my childhood so the blame doesn't lie with me, so that I can pass it on, hide behind excuses, while another part of me wants to be sectioned, locked up in a secure psychiatric hospital, drugged and plugged into an ECT machine to get what I deserve.

'Mum's been on my mind a lot too. I don't think she's been eating properly, and all she does is go on about Dad. You know the score there, Joe.' He nods sympathetically, knowing about my parents. Maybe it's affecting me more than I realise, though I have no idea why. It's been that way since forever. I should be used to it. In fact, I can't remember a time before it, or if I've ever questioned it, the deeper reasons for it. The *whys*. As an only child, I just thought it was how families were. It was only when I hit my teens that it began to seem odd. For the most part, I brought myself up, escaping to a bedsit and a dead-end job as soon as I turned sixteen. Mum didn't try to stop me.

'She's just so stuck in the past,' I continue, wondering if that's really more about me than Mum. 'She rarely goes anywhere without Dad, yet she hates him. In fact, I was surprised she came to ours alone at Easter. Plus, I think Freya's been affected by it more than I thought and has been in trouble at school. And Jack seems really confused about stuff from way back, to do with his real mum, and… and…' Tears collect in my eyes as Joe's expression mirrors my pain. He understands, he gets it. I just wish I could expunge *everything*.

'And on top of it all, my poor husband doesn't get much of a look in these days,' I say with a guilty laugh. 'There's a lot I need to deal with, to be honest, Joe. It's like I'm not me any more, as though… as though I'm becoming someone else.'

'I understand,' he says. 'Like someone you don't recognise?'

'Yeah, exactly,' I say, the relief of the client complaint not being from Andrew still flooding through me. 'But maybe it's the *real* me, and I just forgot her. Anyway, the long weekend helped. I went to a spa for a few hours on Saturday, had dinner with friends afterwards…' I force a smile, trying to convince him it's easy as that – four days off work and I'm right as rain.

'Self-care is important in this job, Lorna, but I don't need to tell you that. And while supervision is essential for your caseload, I'm going to strongly recommend you undertake a course of personal therapy with an independent practitioner. It's not something we'd want to touch on here at the clinic.'

'Of course,' I say, willing to agree to anything right now.

'It sounds to me that rather than facing issues in your life, you've chosen to bury them, maybe even kept things from yourself?' Joe's tone of voice is coaxing, lulling, comforting. He has the kind of face that makes you feel safe just from making eye contact.

'Maybe,' I say, thinking it through. Though we both know our minds keep stuff locked away for a reason.

CHAPTER FORTY-TWO

Lorna

'I've called his mobile twice and it goes straight to voicemail, I'm afraid,' Sandy tells me later that afternoon.

'Can you try again?' I say, stepping impatiently from one foot to the other by the reception desk. I check my watch again. It's twenty minutes past Andrew's appointment time and he's only been late once before. It's his last one, and I just want to get this over with.

Sandy does as I ask, putting the phone on speaker as it connects. There's no one else in the waiting room and, sure enough, his mobile goes straight to the standard voicemail recording.

She leaves a quick message, then hangs up. 'I've got a landline number for him on file here too,' she says. 'Shall I try that?'

'Yes, yes, of course,' I say impatiently, frowning. 'It was his last appointment today.' I can hardly tell her that I've heard nothing from him the last couple of days either – not as Abbi74 or myself. Then I think back to those last messages, shuddering at the thought of being found out.

'It's ringing,' Sandy mouths at me, the handset pressed to her ear. 'Oh hello, is that Mr Carter?' she says, but then pauses, looking puzzled. 'Taylor? No, I don't think so,' she says, glancing up at me. Reluctantly, I jot down Andrew's real name on her notepad for her to see, giving her a thumbs up. She knows clients often book in under another name to protect their privacy. 'Oh yes, actually I am calling about Andrew Tay—' she says slowly, but is interrupted. She doesn't say anything for a while. Gradually, her eyes widen, and her mouth drops open as she listens, staring at me. 'Oh… oh dear. Oh my goodness.' Her face goes pale and she makes a twisted shape with her mouth. 'I see. That's terrible. I'm so sorry to hear that.' More silence as she listens. 'Me? No, I don't know him personally… I'm calling from the Grove Clinic actually, about an appointment he had today. He was a client, yes. I was checking to see if he was still coming, but obviously…' She trails off. 'OK. OK, yes, I understand.' Sandy then gives out the clinic's details while I grip the reception desk, waiting for her to get off the phone. A moment later, she hangs up.

'What? What is it?'

She looks up at me, trying to find the right words, her mouth opening and closing. 'Just a moment, Lorna love, there's something I need to run past Joe.' She holds my gaze as she gets up from her chair, giving me a little smile before she disappears into the staffroom, ignoring my questions.

It seems like forever but eventually Joe comes out, gently ushering me by the elbow through to my office. 'What's going on, Joe? Why won't Sandy tell me what's happening?'

'Sit down, Lorn,' he says when we're shut inside. For the first time ever, I sit on my clients' couch, facing Joe as he sits in my chair. It doesn't feel natural, yet strangely fitting.

'Just to be clear, I asked Sandy to call my client because he's late. If he's a no-show, I wanted to get on with some report writing instead. I did everything right, Joe. I didn't contact him myself, I swear.' My mouth is so dry, I can hardly speak.

'I know, Lorn, I know that,' he says kindly. 'Look, there's no easy way to say this. I know as well as you how attached we become to clients and how the relationship we develop with them can throw up all sorts of feelings. Which makes this all the harder to say—'

'It's not like that!' I say, almost yelling, almost in tears. Truth is, it's way worse. 'I was literally just getting Sandy to check—'

Joe raises his hands. 'Lorna, it's OK. Really, I understand—'

'No! How can you understand?' I can't even cry. I'm way beyond that. I drop my head down into my hands. For the second time in a day, it feels as though my career is about to be over.

'Lorna… I'm afraid your client is dead. I'm so sorry.'

Slowly, I raise my head, staring at Joe, my mouth open, my eyes wide. His face is a mix of pity, compassion and sadness.

'*Dead?*' I say so quietly I wonder if I've even spoken.

Joe gives a small nod. 'I'm so sorry, Lorna. It's never an easy thing to hear about a client. The relationships we forge in therapy aren't one-sided. We're as involved and invested as they are. That's what I was trying to say before.'

'How?' I say, my voice shaking, barely a whisper. 'I… I don't believe it. He can't be *dead*…' My hands go over my mouth.

'When Sandy called his landline, a detective answered. He didn't tell her much, but your client was found deceased in his house over the weekend. It's being treated as suspicious.' Joe pauses, rubbing his face, feeling my pain. Pain that I can't show to its full extent because of everything. 'Apparently, there's a murder investigation underway.'

'*Murder?*' I whisper, shaking, trying to take it in.

Joe nods again. 'That's what the detective told Sandy. It's dreadful to lose a client this way. I'll stay with you for the rest of his session if you like. I know he was a newish client, and we've all lost them to illness or suicide over the years, but however it happens, it can still feel as if you failed them.'

I'm nodding, agreeing with him, though I can't take it in. I stare at the floor, focusing on anything except the thoughts filling my mind.

'Dead…' I whisper, repeating myself over and over. 'Murdered? But *how*?' Unanswerable questions flood through me. 'Sorry, Joe, but I just don't believe it. *Can't* believe it. Poor, *poor* man.' I fight against my grief, forcing myself to hold it inside to an acceptable level. If I let the full force of it out now, it will look suspicious. In Joe's eyes, I didn't know him that well. 'Did they say what happened?'

'We know very little. I suppose it might be on the local news later. But don't torture yourself with details, Lorna. Focus on yourself right now.'

The *news*. I hadn't considered that. I nod again, my mouth hanging open, a thousand questions waiting to come out. Questions Joe can't answer.

'Sandy said the detectives will be coming to the clinic in the next few days, to talk to you. She's given them our details. I can be with you if it helps.'

'But what about client confidentiality?' I say, feeling the panic rise. I can't stand the thought of him being dead, but I also can't stand the thought of having to talk to the police about how I knew him.

'You know the score, Lorna. If they come with a court order, which they will, then we will have to disclose. His records are up to date, I take it?'

I nod again. 'Yes, yes, I think so,' I say, thankful I put in the work to catch up with my paperwork.

'Do you want a cup of tea? Some water? You look really shocked.'

'Thanks, Joe. Tea would be good,' I say, trying to act as if the news is only mildly disturbing because he was a new client, rather than devastating because he was my lover. I close my eyes, resting my head down on my knees, my face buried in my hands while Joe's gone.

But all I can see is *him*… imagining how his body would have looked to whoever found him; wondering *who* found him.

'Here you go,' Joe says, handing me a mug. 'I put an extra sugar in it.'

'Thanks, Joe,' I say, sniffing, just managing to hold back the tears.

'Look, Lorna, given what we talked about earlier, what you're going through anyway, how about we reschedule your client list for the next few days, so you can take a break?'

'I'll be fine, really,' I say, even though it's a lie.

'I just had a quick look in the diary and noticed you've got a new assessment booked in next…' He glances at his watch. 'In about half an hour. How about I take her instead? She's your last client today.'

I pause, thinking. 'You know what? I think it'll do me good to carry on. I just need to keep going, Joe.'

He nods. 'You know where I am,' he says a while later, getting up to go.

When he's gone, I put my tea on the table and lie down on my couch, pulling the grey blanket over me. I'm shivering, even though it's not cold. I screw up my eyes, determined to keep the tears away. Instead, I cry inside, still unable to believe what's happened.

'Lorna, your next client is here…'

Startled, I sit up. I must have fallen asleep. Sandy's voice rings through my intercom. I dash to my desk, pressing the reply button. 'Two secs, Sandy,' I say, forcing myself awake.

After I've quickly brushed my hair, fixed my make-up and plumped up the sofa cushions, I go out to reception. There's only one client there – a dark-haired woman reading a magazine. She looks up as I approach, returning my smile.

'Nikki?' I say. 'Please, come through.'

The usual routine. I've done it hundreds, if not thousands, of times over the years.

Nothing out of the ordinary.

Apart from Andrew being dead.

'Have a seat,' I say, pointing to the sofa. She slips off her coat – a dirty old thing – to reveal ripped jeans and a sweater underneath. She pushes her hands through her short hair, which doesn't look as though it's been washed in a while.

'Excuse the state of me,' she says, giving herself a look up and down. 'I've just come from work. It's not the most glam job.' She laughs then, exposing straight white teeth that almost look out of place in her elf-like, angular face. I try never to read or judge someone by appearance, but if she wore some make-up, dressed up a bit, had her hair styled – well, I can see she'd be very beautiful. For a moment, I wonder if I've seen her before, as if I recognise her from somewhere – maybe the street. Just for a fleeting second, her face looks familiar.

CHAPTER FORTY-THREE

Nikki

'Excuse the state of me,' I say, unable to take my eyes off her. 'I've just come from work. It's not the most glam job.' I can't believe we're sitting only a few feet apart, finally talking to each other. The contrast between us is stark yet oddly appropriate. I was going to smarten up but didn't expect an appointment so soon. 'I flip burgers. In a van. It's greasy.' I laugh then, already finding this much easier than I was anticipating.

It's sort of the truth, but I can't explain what I *actually* did right before I came here. She wouldn't like it. Not one bit. But the thrill of getting that key from under the pot copied while they were all out, the excitement of testing that it worked in the lock – a plausible story at the ready should her neighbours challenge me – was too much to resist. I'm getting bolder by the day. I only intended poking my head into the hallway, seeing what it was like, how it smelt, perhaps a glance at the mail on the mat. But curiosity took over and something drew me further on down the tiled corridor, into the living room, through to the kitchen. Upstairs, I looked through her clothes, her make-up, took a couple of items for myself. I doubt she'll ever notice.

I had to stop myself smashing everything up.

'That sounds like you're being a bit hard on yourself, Nikki,' she says with a warm smile. I've heard her voice before, of course, but it's never been directed at me. There's a look in her eye, though, almost a look of recognition, making me wonder if I've been too cavalier with my watching.

'At least I managed to put on some lippy,' I say, rolling my mouth together. I did it especially for her, when I was in her bedroom just before I came here – using that one I'd found by the burger van a while back. My landlord always likes – *liked* – me wearing a bright scarlet colour, and on my nails too. He said it made me look like his dirty whore. I wonder if he ever made her put any on? She doesn't look like the type, but then she doesn't look like the type to have an affair either.

'You look absolutely fine,' she says, smiling, holding a clipboard and pen. She waffles on then, taking extra details from me – most of which I fake – then she goes on about some stupid contract, how the session is confidential, who she'd have to tell if she thought I was a risk to myself or anyone else.

It's not me who's at risk…

'Perhaps you can begin by telling me what brought you here today, Nikki.'

Her shapely, slim legs are crossed, her knees just showing from under her tasteful skirt. But then I'm imagining those legs wrapped around *him,* doing all the things to her that he used to do to me. It's a good thing she can't see inside my mind.

'I was hoping you'd be able to tell *me* that,' I say. I'm not going to make it easy for her. She taps her pen on her lip a couple of times.

'OK, so it sounds like you want me to figure out what's bothering you, what's wrong in your life?' Her tone is way too smug for my liking. 'A lot of people have misconceptions about what therapy is or isn't, Nikki,' she goes on. 'It's not about me telling a client how they feel or what they should do—'

'Money for old rope, then,' I say. 'If the client has to do all the work.'

She smiles, looking slightly awkward. 'Well, that's exactly right actually – apart from the old rope bit.' She gives a little laugh. 'The client does do most of the work, yes. They know more than *anyone* how they feel, even if they find it hard to express. They know far more about themselves than any therapist. And they also know what they need to do to become happier or more fulfilled… or whatever they want to change. It's not my job to *tell* them these things but rather to help them explore and uncover these feelings and needs, to reconnect with themselves in a way they perhaps wouldn't do otherwise.'

'I see.' I take a moment to think about this, hating that it actually makes sense. No one's ever put it like this before, that *I* might actually know what's best for me.

'So, would you like to tell me about yourself, what brought you here today?'

I think for a moment, trying to find the right words.

'Even though I don't know you yet, Nikki, you're looking quite upset right now, as though something's really troubling you.'

I shrug, staring at my feet, suddenly feeling like a little kid.

'I understand how hard it is, taking the first step to come to therapy. And opening up to a stranger can seem very… unnatural,' she says, her voice oddly soothing. 'Whether someone's suffered trauma or abuse of any kind – anxiety, depression, or a general feeling of discontent they can't actually put a finger on – the hardest step can be getting it out there in words. I just want you to know this is your safe place, Nikki. A place to share what's on your mind. There's no judgement here.'

No judgement. She's already warned me about what will happen if she thinks I'm a risk to myself or anyone else, that she would have to tell her supervisor, the authorities, maybe even the police.

I take a deep breath. It needs to come out. 'Have you ever done something so… so *bad*, so against the very essence of the person you believed you were, that it actually felt *good*?' It doesn't sound like me speaking, as if I'm a different person. As if being in this room is changing everything about me. 'Something so bad it actually felt *liberating*?'

'That almost sounds as though…' Lorna stares at the ceiling a moment, trying to find the right words. She doesn't seem at all shocked. '… as though by doing something so wildly out of character, it's allowed you to discover a different part of yourself? Perhaps even a part of yourself you like? And had maybe ignored or forgotten?'

'Yeah, yeah, that's exactly it. And the part I discovered *was* a part of me I'd forgotten. A piece of me I'd stopped myself remembering.'

Lorna is nodding, listening intently.

'Is that possible?' I ask. 'To forget stuff?'

'Absolutely,' she says.

'Does your mind do that on purpose, or can you force it to happen?'

'It's an automatic response. You can't really force it. If a person experiences something very disturbing or traumatic, especially in younger years, then the mind will often block out those memories to protect the self. However, it's not a foolproof mechanism. Things or events later on in life can trigger these unprocessed memories, causing the feelings of the trauma to be re-experienced. Even something as simple as a sound or colour or smell can cause flashbacks. And they can be extremely powerful and frightening.'

She doesn't look very well as she's speaking, the colour gradually draining from her face. She touches her temple and I swear she's got tears in her eyes.

'What if I'd killed someone?' I ask. 'Hypothetically, of course,' I add with a laugh.

For a second, she looks horrified, but then her face loosens into a small smile. 'That would certainly be distressing enough to set off post-traumatic stress disorder, yes, though it depends very much on the circumstances – for example, if it was self-defence in a terrifying situation.' She pauses. 'What are you telling me here, Nikki? I have to ask.'

I shake my head, keeping a neutral expression. 'The reason I'm here is because someone died,' I say. 'Someone really important to me.' I think about this and realise it's actually true twice over – once a long time ago, and once more recently.

'I'm very sorry to hear that,' she says. 'Grief is a complicated emotion.'

'I was actually responsible for his death.'

'OK, Nikki, you're telling me some pretty big stuff here, and I appreciate your honesty. I'm wondering if we can explore a little more about this… this *death*. Guilt is a weighty—'

'But what you really, *really* want to know is if I killed someone, right? So you can call the police, have me arrested?' I tip back my head, laughing.

'Is that what you're saying?' she asks, swallowing.

I stare at her for what seems like an age before leaning forward, elbows resting on my knees. 'When I was a little kid,' I begin, 'I lost my father.' She's about to say how sorry she is, but I put my hands up to silence her. 'It was my fault he died. It was a hideous and grotesque death. I was the first one to see his body, all limp and lifeless. Imagine that,' I say. 'Knowing that it was because of *you* that your father was dead. I loved him. Loved him dearly. I was his little princess, followed him about everywhere.' I feel the sting of tears in my eyes.

'Sounds like you've been carrying a lot of guilt about this, Nikki—'

'Sounds like? *Sounds* like? Is that all you can say?' I cup my hand to my ear, tilting my head around, making my eyes go wide. I must look demented.

'And anger, perhaps?' she says, looking more and more nervous. I stand up and walk to the window, staring out at the little park opposite where I've sat and watched her countless times. I pull back the blinds, revealing Cigarette Man on the bench, rolling a joint. If it wasn't for him, I'd be homeless now too. I can hardly go back to my lodgings. Not after what's happened. Not after what I've done.

'Of course I'm fucking angry,' I say, swinging round. 'Wouldn't you be?'

'Anger needs to be worked through, but can also be a place of stuckness, Nikki. If thoughts and feelings aren't processed, then—'

'You go on about all this processing stuff but what does it really mean?' I walk across to her, looming over her. 'I lost the man I loved.' I take a deep breath. 'To another woman.' I spit the last bit out.

Lorna makes a sympathetic face, her eyes fixed on me, but I can tell she's nervous. Her voice remains calm and soothing, but I still hear the quiver in it. She's probably got a panic button somewhere in the room. 'Why don't you sit down, Nikki. Have some water.'

'Water?' I say, spinning round on my heels, reluctantly sitting down. I hate that she has this effect on me, seems able to placate me, get through to me, even though she knows nothing about me. 'Sure,' I say. 'I'll have some water.' I reach across and pour a glass from the decanter. 'Would you like some?'

'Thank you,' she says, relieved I seem to have calmed down.

But, instead of pouring another glass, I take mine and stand up again, chucking the lot in her face. Then, while she's gasping, shocked, wondering how to react, I reach into my bag and pull out the kitchen knife I brought with me, hurling myself at her, plunging the blade into her heart, her throat, her eyes, over and over again until we're both covered in blood. She stares at me, coughing up red spit, her grip on my arms getting weaker and weaker until she's finally dead.

But then I realise I didn't do any of that. That it was all in my imagination and I'm still sitting on the sofa. I pour a second glass and pass it over to her, giving her a little smile.

'Thank you,' she says, taking a sip. 'Now, why don't you tell me about the man you loved, and, of course, this other woman?'

CHAPTER FORTY-FOUR

Lorna

When I get home, Mark is already in the kitchen. He texted me several hours ago to say he'd finished work early.

'Hey,' I say, giving him a kiss. I feel drained. 'Thanks for picking up Freya from the childminder. What's all this, then?' I smile as best I can, holding him round the waist from behind, resting my head on his broad back. He smells good – familiar, comforting, safe.

I feel the lump in my throat. I don't know how I'm going to get through the evening without breaking down.

'Thought I'd give you a night off from cooking,' he says, turning and reciprocating the kiss. 'You look worn out, Lorn. Bad day?'

'You could say that.' I pull away as the tears well up. It's been happening about every two minutes or so, the longest I can manage without thinking about *him*. I catch sight of myself in the mirror by the back door. The grief in my eyes is deep and dark. 'God, I need a drink.'

'Do you think you should?' Mark says while throwing some red peppers in with the chicken he's frying. 'You know, in case…' He glances down at my stomach.

I stop, my hand on the fridge door, bottle in hand, closing my eyes for a second. I put the wine back in the fridge. 'You're right,' I say, smiling. 'That smells so good.'

'Fajitas,' he says proudly. 'Freya's idea. We picked up ingredients on the way home.'

'I'm starving,' I say, wondering how I'm going to force anything down. 'And thanks for cooking.' In reality, it makes me feel even more wretched, even more guilty that Mark is so good to me. If he knew the truth, he'd be chucking my stuff out on the street, changing the locks, filing for divorce.

I still feel numb from the news.

But then something hits me. *Fuck.* I should have thought of it before.

'So, you going to tell me all about it, then?' Mark says, moving quickly between the cooker and the worktop, chopping garlic and chillies, tossing them in the pan. I stare at him, squinting, my mind elsewhere. 'About your bad day?'

I run my hand through my hair, closing my eyes briefly.

'Sorry, what?' I stare at him, distracted. 'It was just one of those days. You know. Full on.' I try to make it sound like no big deal when, in reality, it's been the worst day of my life.

Nearly the worst day of my life.

I choke back the tears as another wave hits me.

'Talking about stuff helps, you know,' Mark says with a wink.

'Funny,' I reply. 'I'm going up to change. Is Freya in her room?'

'Hanging up her uniform, I hope,' he says, and I feel the burn of his puzzled stare on my back as I leave.

On the landing, I stop and smile, hearing Freya singing to herself. But instead of going in, instead of seeing my little girl, asking about her day, pressing my face against her sweet-smelling hair, I creep past and go up the second flight of stairs to the study. I'll see her properly on my way down, spend some quality time with her.

I flick on the light and stare at my laptop on the desk, dragging my hands down my face. I can't risk letting it all out. If I did, I don't think I'd ever stop crying. For now, numbness will have to suffice, at least until I've done what I have to do.

I open up my computer and go straight to various news websites, scrolling through dozens of local reports. It doesn't take me long to find it. *Local Artist Found Dead in Bed* one report claims.

Sex Game Tragedy: Up-and-Coming Artist Dies in Suspicious Circumstances

I put my hand over my mouth.

Extreme Art – Bondage Horror as Nude Artist Found Murdered

I can hardly stand to read – *Bondage Horror?* – but click on one of the stories anyway, my eyes flashing across the words. There's a picture of his house – a red-brick villa with a flash of yellow crime scene tape across the front gate. An officer stands guard at the door. Bile rises up my throat from my empty stomach, burning into my mouth.

Detectives were called out to a house just off Lavender Hill, Battersea in the early hours of Easter Monday where the body of a 45-year-old man was discovered. Not yet officially identified, he is believed to be a well-known artist with works regularly displayed in prestigious Chelsea galleries. His pieces are mainly of nude women in erotic poses and have recently fetched upwards of £10,000 each.

Detective Inspector Peter Carney from Scotland Yard said: 'It was a particularly gruesome attack on a well-respected local man. We're treating the death as suspicious. The deceased was found naked, bound to his bed, and asphyxiated with cling film. If anyone has any information about this horrific crime, please call the police hotline.'

I can hardly breathe myself as my eyes flash over the words, all the horrific detail. I read another report, this time the words *electrical cable* and *strangulation* making me want to throw up. My hand goes to my throat.

Oh dear God... Andrew... Please, no...

And then the tears come. Hot and forceful from the very core of me as my heart aches. I can't stand it. I really can't stand the thought of him dead. I didn't even get a chance to say goodbye, to tell him that I loved him. There were so many things I wanted to say but couldn't. And now it's too late.

I bang my fist on the desk, making my laptop jump. My head drops down onto the wood but whips back up again as I remember what occurred to me in the kitchen. If the police are all over Andrew's house, then they'll be all over his phone and computer too. Which means they'll see he's registered on Double Take and no doubt be able to get the details of the people he's been in contact with. If they follow up, if they find Abbi74, then Mark will know about everything. And perhaps Cath will be involved too, seeing as she also sent him a message.

'Oh God, and all the texts between us on his phone. What if he didn't delete them?'

Shit, shit, shit...

Quickly, I log into Double Take. There's a fresh batch of messages since last time I logged in, so I quickly delete them all, making sure to keep the string of messages Abbi exchanged with Andrew. I want to give them one last read before I block him and delete the lot – delete the fake photos and then delete the account as if it never existed. I can't risk the police finding it. I have no idea if it will erase the messages in Andrew's account too, but it's worth a shot. More tears come, blurring my vision, as I read through our exchange one last time, saying my goodbye.

Then an alert flashes up in the corner of my screen.

You're proving popular today! You have a new message from Andy_jag.

CHAPTER FORTY-FIVE

Lorna

At first, it doesn't register who it is or what it means. In fact, I barely glimpse it, ignoring it until it slides off my screen, along with a couple of other alerts: *so-and-so has viewed your profile… liked your photo… sent you a wink…*

Tiresome, especially as I was only ever on the site to talk to Andrew to find out about *her* and to test his love for me. I didn't achieve either.

But something snags in my mind about that last pop-up. Something that doesn't seem right, making me click back on my list of alerts, showing me everything in one go.

And there it is: *You have a new message from Andy_jag.*

'Fuck, *what*?' I whisper, covering my mouth. '*Andrew*? But… but that's not possible,' I say under my breath as my heart catches up with my brain. For a second, I almost feel hope – pathetic hope that he's still alive or that there was a terrible mistake and the police identified the wrong person. But then the realisation sinks in and my skin begins to crawl, the hairs on my arms standing on end.

Andrew is dead. It was in the newspapers. The police confirmed it to Sandy. So *who* the hell just sent me that message?

'Shit,' I whisper, standing up, then sitting down again. I tear my fingers through my hair, not knowing what to do with myself. With a shaking hand, I open it up, hardly daring to read it. Whoever sent it is still online.

Andy_jag: *Let's play another game.*

'Game?' I whisper. What the hell is going on? My hands are sweating as I type a reply.

Abbi74: *What kind of game?*

I wait anxiously for a message back, keeping one ear on the landing in case Freya or Mark comes up.

Andy_jag: *Last time, I asked you 'What's the worst lie you've ever told?' but you evaded the question. So this time, I want you to…*

Oh God. What if it's the police toying with me, trying to catch me out in case they think Andrew met his killer online? I heard about a case like that once, an online dating hook-up gone wrong, ending in tragedy. It's what we've all warned Cath about.

I lunge for the waste bin under the desk, retching into the plastic liner. Nothing much comes up because I haven't eaten all day, but the spasms still grip my middle, squeezing the life out of me. I wipe my mouth as another message comes in.

Andy_jag: … *this time I want you to tell me a secret.*

Christ, I think, as my finger hovers over the block and delete button. I should ghost him, as Cath calls it, disappear without trace and delete my account. If it's the police fishing, the last thing I need is to be associated with this.

But what if Andrew *is* still alive? What if it's really him?

Abbi74: *If I told you, then it wouldn't be a secret any more, would it? Why don't you tell me one instead?* I type, trying to be evasive like before.

As I wait, tears well in my eyes as I stare at Andrew's thumbnail profile picture. It's one of my favourite shots of him, taken at a gallery opening last year. I found pictures of it online after the event, scoured them for glimpses of him with the lodger to see if she was there with him, wishing he could have taken me instead.

Then another message appears. I hardly dare read it but take a deep breath as I click on it, the blood draining from my head.

Andy_jag: *The only secrets I have to tell are yours, Lorna…*

CHAPTER FORTY-SIX

Lorna's Journal

10 March 2017

The point of a journal, apart from purging, is to show movement, change, the fluidity of ourselves and our lives. Feeling stuck, up to our necks, in at the deep end with no chance of a way out… these are all familiar predicaments in the human condition. But a journal takes those thoughts captive, saving them for later, bottling our feelings for a future time – whether that be in a week or a decade – giving a context to the movement and personal growth that otherwise might seem non-existent. That's why it's as important for a therapist's self-development as it is for that of a client. It shows me how far I've come, how far I've got to go. A way of looking back to measure the distance between then and now. A change I wouldn't otherwise see…

What a load of fucking bullshit that was, I think, hiding the notebook under a towel that was left draped on the radiator as I sit, shaking, on Freya's bedroom floor. I've got the towel over my knees, the journal hidden beneath. I only have a couple of minutes before I'll have to go down for dinner but couldn't resist coming in to see my little girl, give her the cuddles I've missed all day. She was in the bathroom when I came into her room, so I quickly prised back the carpet and pulled out the journal. There are only a few pages left to read and, for my own sanity, I need to finish it.

'Hi, darling,' I say as Freya comes back. 'Did you wash your hands?'

She holds them out, still slightly wet. 'Do elephants eat cookies?' she asks while holding a plastic zoo animal. She gives a quick look at the towel draped weirdly over my knees, the notebook concealed beneath so only I can read it.

'Mmm, cookies are their favourites,' I say, turning back to the handwritten pages as Freya sets out some play dough food she's made. 'Are you hungry, darling?' I say. 'Daddy's been cooking something yummy. Can you smell it?'

Freya nods, making some comment about fajitas being her favourite, but I'm already engrossed in the words again, taking myself back to last year...

So much sex. Just sex all the time. It's all we do. Whenever and wherever we can. I feel like the luckiest, dirtiest girl alive. I admit it, I get high on it. High on him. He always pays cash for the cheap hotels, never allowing me to fork out. Sometimes we go back to that place near the M25, but other times it's just a grim boarding house with a wonky b. & b. sign somewhere south of the river. I think he likes the seediness of it, the illicit tinge that the unwashed sheets and grimy bathroom give our already illicit encounters. Once or twice it's been a chain hotel near Euston, and we've even done it in his car a couple of times, as well as the wooded area of a park after dark.

But it's never been at his house. I'm never allowed there because of her. *It burns into me, the jealousy cutting deep, reminding me of something I can't identify. And of course, in return, he keeps reminding me that he can't come to my house either.*

So I decided to change that, in the hope he might one day do the same.

'You sure it's clear?' he said, standing in my doorway, glancing up and down the dark street. It was the first time I'd seen him vulnerable. Then his eyes flicked up and down the short, clingy dress I'd put on. It was actually lingerie – a classy grey satin thing Mark had given me for Christmas. I saw his eyes widen at the sight of my stocking tops, my ridiculously high heels, the scarlet lipstick I'd put on especially for him. I knew he loved it.

'Wow,' he said. 'So are you going to invite me in?'

I stepped aside without saying a word. Kicked the door shut behind him as he lunged for me, throwing me back against the wall. We staggered, bumping against the hall table, knocking off the lamp (the one Mark bought for me. I had to pretend I broke it while vacuuming), me walking backwards towards the stairs with him holding my head, my breasts, kissing me so hard I couldn't breathe. I tore his clothes off as we went, leaving a trail of them in our wake. But we only made it halfway up the stairs before he'd had me, making me feel like an animal.

When we finally did make it to the bedroom to start all over again, he paused for a moment, pulling open the wardrobe doors.

'Andrew, don't,' I'd said, looking away at the sight of Mark's shirts hanging there – all arranged neatly, evenly spaced, the way he likes. His underpants and socks were on a couple of shelves to the right, and I always smiled when he commented that I didn't put them away neatly enough, laughed when he told me I was untrainable. Then Andrew looked in my side of the wardrobe – equally as neat, but sparser. Mark sorts through my stuff several times a year, getting rid of the things he doesn't like to see me in, making me to do a fashion parade for him, telling me if I look frumpy or not. The stuff he hates goes to charity. Nowadays, I've learnt it's easier to ask him if he likes an outfit before I buy it.

I closed my eyes, dropped back on the bed. Then I heard the door click shut. 'Why did you do that?' We lay between the sheets, him on top of me. My body was on fire again and I could hardly talk.

'Do what?' he said, breathlessly, clawing at the pillows behind us. Mark's pillows.

'Look in the wardrobe?'

Andrew said nothing but went at it harder then, owning me, making me forget myself. Perhaps that's what it is about him: he takes me away from the person I am. The person I don't know. The person I don't want to be. Since forever, there's been someone hiding inside. A terrified child. Never speaking up.

Afterwards, we lay together – entwined, exhausted, me sweating guilt – but only briefly because Mark was due back any time. 'You have to go,' I said. 'I need to shower.'

He looked at me, hoisted himself up on his elbows, kissed me. 'Don't shower,' he told me. 'And don't change the sheets.'

'I remember that night,' I say quietly. 'What a fucking idiot I was.'

'Ummm… you swore,' Freya says, covering her ears and giving me a stare.

'Sorry, darling. I didn't mean to. Look, why don't you be a really helpful girl and go downstairs and set the table?'

'OK,' she says, standing up to go.

'I'll be down in a few moments.'

She scampers off, and when she's gone, I put the journal back in its hiding place, taking a few moments to compose myself before I go downstairs too.

CHAPTER FORTY-SEVEN

Nikki

'You want onions with that?' I ask, glancing down at him from inside the sweltering van.

'Please, love,' he says, pulling some cash from his pocket. 'And a can of Coke.'

'Cheese as well?' I say, scraping the blackened griddle as a waft of smoke billows up. 'It's a pound extra.'

'Yeah, all right,' he says, beckoning over his mate. I assemble his burger and wrap it up in a neat packet of waxy paper, putting it in a box. I grab his drink from the fridge behind.

I've only got an hour before my shift ends, before I'm not squashed in this tiny space with fat Denny. Denny's Burgers, that's what the sign on top of the van says in lurid ketchup-red and mustard-yellow scrawl. Denny's OK, treats me well and pays me in cash. And even though we're stuck inside this tiny space for hours on end, he's never once put his hands on me. He even urges me to get home safely when I'm on a late shift and puts me in an Uber if it's past midnight. But I try to do as few hours as possible now, just enough to pay the rent.

Not that paying my rent matters any more.

'Five eighty-five, please,' I say, handing across his food. He gives me fifteen pounds.

'Can I get another one for my mate? The same again please, love. Take it out of that.'

I nod, eyeing his friend who's approaching the van. A couple of builder types on their lunch break. They'll probably come every day for a week or two, then I'll never see them again when they move to a different site. It goes like that. Faces coming. Faces going.

And then I spot him.

Cigarette Man. Or Nigel, as I now know he's called. He's holding me to my word.

He strides up to the van, giving me a broad smile, flashing his missing teeth.

'Y'all right?' he says cheerfully.

'Yeah, not bad, thanks.' It's a lie, of course, though since my session with *her*, I've been mulling things over, thinking about everything she said. I didn't expect it to go like that, for it to actually make sense. For me to see things differently. For her to *help* me.

'Come for the free burger you promised, ain't I?' Nigel gives another toothless grin, clapping his arms around his body, shifting from one foot to the other. There's still a chill in the air, despite the spring flowers and buds everywhere.

'Denny's are the best,' I say, making sure Denny hears as I give him a playful nudge. 'And don't worry, Den, it's on me,' I say. 'Nigel's my friend and I owe him.'

And that's true. I really do. Nigel has turned out to be one of those rare people who senses when someone's in need and doesn't ask questions. Probably because he's been in the exact same situation himself.

'Just paying it forward,' Nigel told me when he first took me back to his new place on Saturday. I couldn't possibly have gone back to my lodgings; couldn't return to where it happened. And even after only one therapy session, I know I did the right thing.

'I've only been living here a few days meself,' Nigel had said. 'So it's not up to much yet. But it's a roof and four walls, right?' He said I could have the couch for as long as I needed. I didn't tell him why I'd suddenly left my place and he didn't ask, just like I'd never ask where he got all those new watches from or the couple of boxed TVs over in the corner.

'Want cheese and onions on it, Nige?' I say after I've wrapped up the other man's burger and they've left. Several others are waiting in the queue now. When we're parked here, there's always a steady flow of customers.

'Yeah, please,' he says, still fidgeting.

He cooked for me my first night at his flat. Well, I say cooked. We had microwaved pasta. But I was grateful for anything – anything other than homemade mushroom soup or whatever else *he* used to tempt me with, trying to make our situation seem OK, acceptable, normal, when I knew he was playing me for a fool. No one gets away with that.

What was it Lorna said towards the end of our session? *You need to re-parent your inner child, Nikki. Learn to love her again...* It was as though she really understood, almost as though she'd experienced my pain first hand. It wasn't sympathy. It wasn't pity. It was compassion, empathy, understanding. Of all people, I hated her for giving me that.

Anyway, as soon as I'd left my room – hurriedly packing up all that I owned and getting the hell out – I'd headed for the little park opposite the clinic. It wasn't to watch *her* this time – it was Easter weekend, after all – it was to find Cigarette Man. The only friend I had in the world and I knew he'd be there at some point, meeting a mate or two. He never judged or asked awkward questions, and I always made sure to give him some smokes or a half bottle of something from the corner shop. It was a hopeless bond, really, and all the stronger for its desperation.

When Nigel arrived, I told him I had nowhere else to go, which was when he offered me a place to stay, saying his flat had come good a couple of days ago.

'Here you go, Nige,' I say, handing across his burger. 'Enjoy.' I give him a wink and go to put a five-pound note in the till on his behalf, but Denny stops me.

'Any friend of yours,' he says, folding my fist around the money. 'On the house.'

I feel the tears prickle my eyes at the thought of having two friends now. 'Thanks, Den,' I say, and get on with serving the other customers before I break down completely.

CHAPTER FORTY-EIGHT

Lorna

I am receiving messages from a dead man.

Last night, as Mark and I watched the late evening news, there was a short local report on Andrew's death. As soon as it came on, I went out to make tea, get water, go to the loo – anything so I didn't have to hear the details or see the news crew standing outside his house. Especially not with Mark sitting beside me.

'That was terrible. Did you hear about it?' Mark said after I sat down again. 'Some poor sod got it mid-fuck, by the sound of it.' He sprayed out laughter. 'Still, if you're going to go, it's gotta be the way.' He sipped the large whisky he'd poured for himself, flicking the channels. 'Shame we don't have any of his art. Prices will shoot up now.'

'No, I… I didn't see it,' I said quietly. All I wanted to do was sob and punch the cushions. And I wanted to deactivate my phone too – close all accounts, erase it, stamp on it and throw it in the river. Anything to go back to how things were.

Because Andy_jag is still contacting me, knows my name. Which means, whoever he is, he knows my secret too.

The last message came in today just before I left work. I hadn't heard anything since last night, a message I was too scared to reply to. Now he says he wants to meet me, take me out for a coffee, have a meal, lunch, a walk by the river…

I have no idea who it is.

My hands shook as I tucked my phone back in my bag and left the clinic for home – a part of me still hoping it really was Andrew. Either way, the nightmare I thought was over, isn't.

'I really *am* going mad,' I say, not meaning to, covering my mouth quickly. The others are all chatting away and I don't think they heard. We're at Charlotte's this week, her perfect living room looking as though it's straight out of an interiors magazine. You can tell she doesn't have kids.

'Oh the irony, Lorn,' Cath replies, pulling her socked feet up underneath her. We all have to take our shoes off when it's book club at Charlotte's. 'There's no hope for us lot if you think *you're* going mad,' she says, laughing. 'More wine is the answer, love. And a good fuck.'

I'm about to reply, cover myself by saying that it's because I nearly put the cereal in the fridge this morning, or was about to fill my petrol car with diesel – that everyday kind of 'mad' we all know – but Annie chips in. 'Sounds like the dating site's going well, then – eh, Cath?' My skin goes cold at the mention of it.

'I thought you'd never ask,' she says through a wide grin, rubbing her hands. 'And yes, actually, it is.'

'Oh, do tell,' Megan says, the others all focused on Cath now.

But Charlotte moves closer, her eyes fixed on me. 'Going mad?' she says, laying her hand on my arm. 'Lorna?'

She's pressed up beside me on her huge white L-shaped couch. We never bring red wine to Charlotte's.

'I'm fine,' I reply quietly as the others carry on talking, whooping and laughing at Cath's recent dating stories. 'It's nothing.' I'm so used to saying this now, I almost believe it myself.

'Doesn't seem like nothing to me,' she says, squeezing my arm with a perfectly manicured hand. 'I wasn't going to say anything, but you don't look well. Is…' She hesitates. 'Is everything OK at home, between you and Mark?' I'm sure she's noticed the dark circles under my eyes, my crumpled top – the first thing I grabbed off a pile of discarded clothes in the bedroom – and my unwashed hair, pinned up to hide the fact.

'Absolutely fine,' I say. I know how close she and Mark are, know they talk regularly.

'It's just that Mark and I had a little chat,' Charlotte says, shifting even closer so I can smell her perfume. I breathe in deeply, hoping to achieve the same sensation as when I was with Andrew, pick up on the same earthy, woody notes of whatever it was he wore. But there's nothing. Nothing at all except a pleasant smell.

'He's worried about you too,' she continues. 'He mentioned about…' She glances down, reaches out and touches my tummy. 'I'm so happy for you both,' she says. 'But I've heard it can send your hormones crazy, making you behave like a different person—'

'*What?*'

'The baby,' she whispers in my ear.

'But there is no baby,' I say, not meaning to snap. My jaw is tight, my teeth clenched. Though I almost wish there was. Andrew's.

'That'll just be your hormones talking.' She laughs excitedly. 'Mark's so happy but we'll keep it in the family until you're three months gone at least and—'

'Charlotte, read my lips,' I say, more loudly now. 'I… am… not… pregnant. OK?'

Everyone looks around.

'Oh,' Charlotte says flatly. 'Are you sure?'

'Yes!'

'You'd better tell Mark that you lost it or something, then. He *really* thinks you're expecting.'

'But I didn't lose it,' I say. 'I didn't lose *anything*.'

Except myself, I think, escaping to the loo.

I decide to walk home rather than take the bus. I need the air, the time alone, space to think. Instead of sticking to the main roads, I go the longer way, through the park. The park where Andrew and I shared our first kiss last year. If I look hard enough, I convince myself, I might still see the sparks in the air.

I break down as soon as I get inside the gates, sitting on a bench in the shadows as it all comes pouring out. I can't hold it in any longer. Tears stream down my face as my body convulses, making me double up. It's the first time I've properly cried since Joe told me what happened. 'Please, *please* don't be dead… Oh, God… I… I can't stand it…' I wish I'd just had a chance to end things properly, not have it happen like this. It's all gone so wrong.

I blow my nose again, folding the tissue over and over. Then my phone pings an alert, making me whip it out of my pocket. Double Take. I haven't deleted the app yet.

When I see the name, it makes me want to throw up.

Andy_jag: *Meet me. Saturday morning. I insist.*

My knuckles are white from gripping my phone, and my heart thumps wildly. My fear knows no bounds.

'Think, Lorna, *think*,' I whisper, glancing around nervously. It's dark and deserted in the park, and I could even convince myself that I'm being watched. I should never have come this way home. Then, out of the shadows, a couple walking their dog come past, nodding at me but looking away quickly when they see the state I'm in.

Who *are* you? I stare at my phone.

I type out a reply. I have to find out who it is and what they know.

Abbi74: *OK. Bishop's Park 9 a.m. Saturday, at the corner entrance.*

I'll watch from a distance, wait to see who turns up. And I'll wear my trainers for a speedy escape if necessary. My breathing is heavy as I get up and carry on walking through the park, briskly now to get out of the shadows. Several times, I stop and turn around, thinking I hear someone behind me, but there's no one there. Just the deserted park. Then something that new client, Nikki, said comes to mind, making me walk even faster.

Have you ever done something so bad that it actually felt good?

I hum to myself as I walk on, which somehow makes me feel not quite so scared. It reminds me of when I was a kid – how I'd sing to myself when I was frightened and alone. All those times I was locked outside in the back garden for hours on end, sometimes late into the night. Singing helped it not seem so bad then too.

I stumble and trip, throwing out my arms as I go down, the impact of the fall jolting up my arms and into my shoulders.

'Ow, God…'

Stunned, I drag myself up, more shocked by the resurrected memory than by tripping over. My right knee is bruised and painful as I walk on, limping, my jeans and hands covered in dirt.

Locked out, I think, trying to remember, to work out why. It's almost as though it happened to someone else, but I'm convinced it was me. *Hammering on the back door… wailing for someone to let me in…* I didn't understand why, didn't question it. I was a good girl – *oh God how I tried to be one of those* – always doing as I was told. I'd just wanted my mum, but she was never there when it happened. I felt so alone.

And then the fragments of memory are gone, as though they never existed at all.

'Lorna, what happened to you?' Mark asks. He's at the front door the second I come in, taking me by the shoulders, looking me up and down. 'I was worried sick. I was expecting you back ages ago, so I called Charlotte and she told me when you left. I was just about to come out and look for you.'

'I'm sorry,' I say quietly. 'I decided to walk.' I stare at the floor, slipping my coat off my shoulders. 'The long way.'

'And this?' he says, pointing to my filthy jeans.

'I tripped.'

'Your face?' Mark says, tilting up my chin. 'You've been crying.'

'I'm OK,' I say, swerving his touch and heading to the kitchen. I pull open the fridge and grab a bottle of wine. I can't think of any other way to get through this.

'Should you be doing that?' Mark asks, coming up beside me, touching my stomach. 'You know…'

'Mark, for fuck's sake, I'm not pregnant, OK?' I snatch a glass from the cupboard, knocking the cap off the bottle and pouring it right up to the rim. '*OK?*'

He stands there, staring at me, his face blank, his eyes heavy. I'm hardly able to look at him as I glug it down, nearly finishing it in one go.

'Well, whatever, you still shouldn't be drinking like that, especially as I know you'll have had wine at Charl—'

'Mark, will you leave it? I'm not four years old. You'll be fucking checking if I've cleaned my teeth before bed next.'

'OK, fine,' he says, hands up in surrender as he backs off, a hurt look on his face.

'Shit, Mark, I'm so sorry. Truly… I… I…'

He stops in the doorway, staring at me, shaking his head before turning to leave.

CHAPTER FORTY-NINE

Lorna

'I'm so glad to see you much brighter, Lorna,' Joe says at the start of our Friday supervision session, handing me a coffee as I sit down opposite.

I smile. It physically hurts to act like this, but I do it anyway. *Fake it till you make it*, Cath once said. Never before has it seemed more appropriate.

'Did you arrange personal therapy yet?' he asks.

'Oh, yes,' I say, sipping my drink. 'Yes, I did.'

I can tell by the look on his face he's not convinced, but it wouldn't be in the nature of person-centred therapy to question me, to make me feel guilty or irresponsible. That's my job, and I'm doing fine at it.

'And how are things at home, with Freya?'

'Yep, all fine there too,' I say, deciding not to tell him that Freya's wet the bed the last couple of nights. She's not done that since she was potty trained. 'It was just a blip,' I add, forcing a smile. I can hardly tell him that I think some of her upset has been caused by my change of mood and behaviour, that I'm threatening the very fabric of her security by not being the mother she knows and needs.

'OK,' he says slowly. 'So let's get onto Tom. You saw him this week?'

Samantha Hayes

'Yes, I did,' I say, relaxing into more comfortable ground talking about clients. 'We discussed his mother's complaint, of course. It would have been weird not to bring it up. He didn't seem bothered at all, said it was her wanting to complain all along. That she's always been controlling, minimises his worries, doesn't listen to him, treats him like a kid.'

Joe nods, listening.

'Anyway, the upshot is he's moved out of his parents' place and into a friend's flat until he can secure university accommodation. He's decided not to quit his degree and has seen his tutors. There's a plan in place. It's early days with his therapy still, but he's making progress.'

'How did his parents take the news about him moving out?'

'You can imagine,' I say. 'Of course, they're blaming me.'

Joe nods.

'He's opened up a lot more about his past.'

Joe makes a sad face, closes his eyes a moment because he knows what's coming.

'It started way back. His father in his room every Sunday night, climbing into bed with him. The mother knew, Tom said, but she did nothing. Turned a blind eye because of what would happen if she interfered.'

'So her way of dealing with her lack of control of the situation was to... well, be strictly in control of other things. Like Tom.'

I nod, referring back to my notes. 'Tom's alluded to characteristics that suggest psychopathy and narcissism in the father. To quite an extreme. He and his mother have lived in an abusive situation for many years – psychological as well as physical. They were so manipulated they were unaware of what was happening. We're just scratching the surface yet. Anyway, I talked to Tom about the ISVA service, how they can help him legally. With their support, he wants to go ahead and report his father. Said he's kept all these secrets too long.'

'OK,' Joe says, nodding in approval. 'Has he been referred on already?'

'All done.' I nod, taking a breath. 'But you know what? Tom had no idea any of this was wrong, that it wasn't normal. He just thought it was the way his life was always going to be. For ages, the only person he felt he could blame was himself.'

And, for the rest of the session, I'm fighting back the tears.

After our meeting, I go back to my office to write up some notes, prepare for my next client. But I can't focus. Not after what Joe told me just as I was leaving the room, a stack of files clutched to my chest. It stopped me in my tracks.

'Oh, and Lorna,' he'd said. 'The police are coming on Monday at ten, so if you can make sure Andrew's file is up to date and ready for inspection that would be great.'

'Of course,' I'd said, trying to stay calm.

'I'll be with you when they interview you, so no need to look so worried.'

'No, no, I'm not worried,' I said, forcing a smile. 'I've done this kind of thing before.' And indeed I have – for a couple of clients who took their own lives at my previous clinic, several who were involved in crimes, another who'd gone missing.

But this is different.

I stare at my computer screen, at the cursor blinking, ready for me to type up client notes. I scan down my list of appointments for the rest of the day and see Nikki's name last. Sandy told me she'd booked her in again after her assessment, but I hadn't realised it would be so soon. I've lost a few clients these last couple of weeks and I'm trying not to think about why they left, but I'm pretty certain it's because I've not been focused, that I'm not giving them my full attention as a therapist.

I drop my head in my hands, thinking about Andy_jag and whether I should go through with our meeting tomorrow morning. It could be dangerous. I've gone over our Double Take messages a thousand times, trying to pick them apart, overanalysing every word, trying to figure out who has hacked his account.

Then, right on cue, my phone vibrates, making me jump.

Andy_jag: *Don't be late...* is all he says, making a chill run the length of my spine.

‹Nikki, come in and sit down,' I say. She looks different this week, as though she's been taking better care of herself. She's wearing make-up and her hair is washed; her clothes, perhaps new, suit her better. ‹I wasn't actually sure you'd be back to see me,' I add when we're both settled.

‹No. Me neither.' Her voice sounds a little terse though, her body mirroring this with tensed-up shoulders. ‹Actually, I had no intention of coming back but...' She trails off, as if she can't find the right words.

‹OK, is that because you felt therapy wasn't for you, or because you might find it too painful opening up?'

‹Neither of those,' she says, tilting her head.

‹Do you want to tell me why?'

‹Sure. It was because I'd already decided that I wouldn't like you.'

‹Oh. I see,' I say. It's not the first time I've heard this from a client. ‹But something changed that?'

‹Kind of,' she says, sounding embarrassed. ‹It was when you said about me knowing best about myself, that it's not your job to tell me how I feel. Well, that chimed. Struck a chord.' She looks pained, as though she doesn't want to be saying this but can't help herself.

‹I see,' I say, letting her continue.

'My whole life, people have been telling me who I am, how I should act, making me feel a way that suits *them*, not me. And I don't like it one bit.'

'I hear you,' I say. For some reason, her words cut deep. 'When you say *people...?*'

'It makes me angry now, even though I didn't realise what was happening at the time. I feel dirty and used, left with a rage burning inside – the kind of fury that could drive a person to, well.... Do you understand?'

I narrow my eyes, watching her every move. 'Drive a person to what?' I ask. 'Kill, maybe?' I add when she doesn't reply. I don't like putting words in her mouth, but I need to pursue this.

She gives a barely noticeable nod.

'Those are powerful emotions, Nikki. Are you referring to someone close?'

'You mean, as in a lover?' She laughs then – a bitter laugh – before turning away.

'I'm sensing some strong... I don't know, *resentment* here, Nikki? Am I right? It's as though it's knotted into you.'

'Oh, you're good,' she says, smiling in a twisted way, exposing her white teeth. 'Resentment, anger, bitterness, hate, frustration... you name it, I'm knotted up with it.' She takes a moment, thinking. 'It's not just resentment and anger, though. It's regret too. A deep ache that I've lost the person I loved most in the world.'

'OK,' I say slowly. 'You mentioned a lover last time...' I say, hoping she'll run with it. I've had clients talk about rage-venting murder before – it's not uncommon and almost always hypothetical. But I still have to check it out in case she actually *did* kill someone, or is planning on it. I don't need to be in any more hot water with Joe if I don't flag that something's going on.

'Lover... such a nice-sounding word, isn't it? It makes me think of warmth, caring, closeness, bodies touching, passion, someone

who's got your back. But it's got a dirty side too, don't you think?'
She gives an overly knowing giggle.

I swallow, staying focused, kicking the personal trigger into
touch.

'You probably think I don't look the type to have a husband
or a partner, a regular everyday guy, do you?' she continues. 'That
someone like me is only ever the *other woman*?' She whispers the
last part.

'No, Nikki, I… I…'

She reaches over and pours herself a glass of water, taking three
long, slow mouthfuls, her slender throat rippling as she swallows.
'But don't forget,' she says, wiping her mouth with the back of her
hand. 'An illicit lover is usually another woman's man.'

CHAPTER FIFTY

Nikki

'So you mean lover, as in an affair?' Lorna asks. She's not looking that great today – pale and tired – as if she's got things on her mind, hasn't been looking after herself.

'Affair. There's another funny word.'

'Funny?' she replies, coaxing me to elaborate. She has a knack of drawing me out.

'I always think it's a bit of a coy way of putting it. *Affair*. You know, like we all have affairs: bills to pay, jobs to go to, rent to take care of…' I can't help the throaty growl at that last one. 'But affair… it doesn't really capture the gut-wrenching betrayal, the misery, the depression, the low self-esteem, the loneliness or, well, the anger. Does it?'

She shakes her head slowly. Hanging on my every word.

'In fact, I'd say *betrayal* was a far better word. "Oh, I'm having a betrayal with the window cleaner" or "I left him because he had a betrayal with his secretary". You get what I'm saying?'

Her eyes are wide and unblinking. 'I do,' she says flatly. 'You… you seem quite passionate about this, Nikki. Almost as though you've had personal experience?'

I can't help the slow nod, my eyes heavy. I never intended on telling her any of this stuff, of course, never thought for one moment that she'd get through to me, reach me in a way no one else ever has. Maybe even help me. 'Yeah,' I say, sipping more water. I blow my nose, not crying, but close.

'I'm really sorry to hear that. Your pain seems very raw.'

'Thing is,' I say. 'It's not like I've got anywhere in life. No fancy job, no big house or expensive car or happy kids or a wonderful marriage. Do you know what I do? I work fifteen hours a week in a burger van. Guess how much I make from that?'

She shakes her head.

'One hundred and ten pounds a week. Cash. Sometimes the occasional tip. But who tips for a burger, eh?' I laugh again. 'And now you're wondering how I get by, living in London on that wage, aren't you? You're wondering if I have a rich relative supporting me, or if I steal or live rough. And you're probably wondering how I'm even going to pay your bill.'

'Well, if it's to do with your emotional well-being, Nikki, then yes, I'm interested in your finances and how that's affecting you. But you don't have to tell me anything you don't want, and I'm sure you're responsible enough to pay our—'

'You know everything there is to know about my finances now. Well, nearly everything.' I lean forward on my elbows, my chin thrust out. 'Do you want to know where I've been living?' I don't wait for her to answer. 'In a rented room in a house. It's not far from here. Quite a posh area, actually. All bohemian and arty. My room was on the top floor of an old place – tiny, quirky, cold in winter, and often there was no hot water. My landlord lived there too.'

'I see,' she says, still hooked on my every word.

'I bet you're wondering how I could even afford a *cupboard* in that neighbourhood on a hundred quid a week, let alone an entire room, aren't you?'

'Well, I... no, I wasn't—'

'I'll tell you how, Lorna.' I say her name slowly, letting it linger on the tip of my tongue. Then I stand up, go over to her desk and pick up a glass paperweight, turning the globe around in my hands. I perch on the edge of the desk. 'I was a lodger with *benefits*,' I whisper, not taking my eyes off her. I put down the paperweight and pick up her designer glasses instead. I see her frown, her mouth twitching to speak, but she says nothing.

'I had to fuck my landlord, Lorna,' I say quietly. 'Fuck him whenever, however and wherever he wanted it. No questions asked. He said "fuck" and I said "how hard?" For that, I got next-to-nothing rent.' I put her glasses on, tilting my head and cupping my face in my hands. The room goes blurry. 'What do you think? Do I look like a therapist now? Or a hooker? Or maybe even the other woman?'

Lorna is silent for a moment, but even through fuzzy lenses, I can see that her cheeks pink up and her eyes turn teary.

'A lodger…' she says as if she didn't mean to, as if the word is a bitter pill.

'Yes,' I say, sitting back down, folding my arms. 'Thing is, it all went a bit… a bit wrong.' I pull a face.

'Wrong?'

'Yes, I had to… end it,' I explain. I take her glasses off, setting them down on the desk, going over to the window and pulling back the blinds. It's raining and there's no sign of Nigel. He told me he was going down to the job centre today.

'I'm almost getting the feeling you're afraid to be loved, Nikki.' She swallows drily. 'As if you put yourself in situations which you know are wrong for you. Like a protection, a defence against being loved genuinely so you can't get hurt. Things from our pasts can have an odd way of manifesting in the present.'

'Oh, those pesky little things from our past,' I say, flashing her a look before sitting down again. 'How they simmer away in our unconscious minds.' I lean forward. 'Then boom!' I clap my hands together, making her jump. 'Something explodes. Something so big happens, so unexpected that everything just clears like a fog lifting and it's as though you can suddenly see things as they really are.'

Lorna is silent again, biting her lip, staring at me, then at her notepad, not knowing where to look.

'And it's in that flash of clarity that you know exactly what to do to make things right. Even if it means doing something so terrible, so dangerous, so hateful and messed-up you feel as if you won't be able to live with yourself ever again.' I sip more water, eyeing her over the glass. 'Does that make sense?'

She gives a tiny nod, barely perceptible.

'Because sometimes you have no choice.'

And deep in her eyes, I see that she understands me perfectly.

CHAPTER FIFTY-ONE

Lorna

'Lilly! Lilly!' Freya says, jumping about in the hallway when her friend comes inside. It's good to see her excited for a change.

'Come on, Frey,' Mark says. 'Let everyone get in.'

She grabs Lilly's hand and leads her upstairs to her bedroom, leaving me wondering how two little girls can make such a noise on the stairs.

'Lorn,' Annie says, with an almost pitiful look on her face, her head tilted. 'How are you doing?' She reaches out for a hug.

Her tone makes me feel like a patient, wondering what everyone's been saying about me behind my back, discussing my mood, my looks, why I haven't seemed myself lately. But tonight, I've made the effort. I have to appear normal for everyone's sake. For *my* sake.

'I'm well, thanks,' I say, hugging her and Ed. I take their coats and the wine they've brought, and go through to the kitchen with Annie following behind. 'Actually, I feel pretty great,' I say, forcing a smile, testing out the words. 'And it's Friday.' I reach a couple of glasses down from the cupboard. 'Yay.' It comes out a lot flatter than I'd intended.

'Cheers to that,' Annie says, raising her glass. 'I'm happy to see you looking so much brighter. Nice top, by the way.'

I chink glasses with her as Mark rummages in the fridge for beers, going back into the living room where Ed is. A moment later and he's got the vinyl on and I hear them in deep discussion about music. Annie and I sit perched on stools at the island worktop.

'Thanks,' I say, smoothing down the sheer fabric. Truth is, I'm a bit behind with the laundry and it was the only thing I could find in my wardrobe that was clean and not made of Lycra or sweatshirt fabric. It's killing me to wear it, though. Why I bought it, who I wore it for, makes me want to scream.

You look stunning in that, he'd said. *Shame I'm going to have to take it off you…* It was that night on the boat.

'Ooh, someone's got some fancy ideas,' Annie says, sliding some brochures across the counter. 'Booking a holiday?' She flicks through one – the blue skies, slivers of white sandy beaches and beautiful people relaxing, laughing, holding hands, turning my stomach.

'All Mark's doing,' I say. 'He came home with them today. He wants just the two of us to go away. And soon.'

'How romantic,' Annie says, nudging me. 'Though you don't sound very enthusiastic. Look at all the activities and water sports in this place.' She glances at the front again. 'Antigua. Tell me you're not turning down scuba diving and sailing in the Caribbean? I really *will* think you've lost your mind then.'

I force the laugh, allow the smile. 'It's a nice thought but there's work, my clients… I can't just let them down at a moment's notice.' Then the other morning flashes through my mind, when I cancelled a morning's list to see Andrew. 'Anyway, I can't exactly ask Mum to look after Freya while we go away. She's got her hands full enough with… well, you know.'

'Your dad?'

I nod, rolling my eyes. 'Nothing changes.'

'Anyway, you don't need to ask your mum, stupid. Not when you've got me. Duh.' She makes a silly face and sips her wine, helping herself to the olives I put out. 'Lilly would love it if Frey came to stay for a week or two. I'm her bloody godmother, Lorn. What use am I if I can't give you and Mark some alone time?'

'Thanks, Annie, that's kind,' I say, considering the idea for a moment. I'm Lilly's godmother too, and Annie's the only one I'd truly trust with Freya should anything ever happen to me and Mark. I know she'd have a good home with Lilly as a new sister – and, I sometimes wonder, a *better* home given how things stand here now. But, if the worst should happen, it makes me worry about what Jack would do, not having his own mother or any godparents. He's not quite eighteen and seems a mile off being independent. I suppose Mark's mum and dad up north would take him in, though he barely knows them.

'Try not to look quite so morose about it, Lorn?' Annie says, rolling her eyes while flipping through another brochure. 'Wow, look at this place. Pure luxury.'

I give it a quick glance, unable to get excited about a holiday when Andrew is lying in a morgue somewhere. I think about his relatives, family, friends – how they were told, who's making arrangements. I knew so little about him, or what he represented in my life, why I was so attached to him.

Then the thought of meeting whoever Andy_jag is tomorrow makes my heart race, my palms sweat. I glug back some wine to dull my nerves, just as Freya and Lilly tumble into the room – a welcome distraction.

'Mummy, is it time to order pizza yet?' Freya says, jumping up and down. They've both got scarlet lipstick daubed on their mouths and are each wearing a pair of my heels.

'Oh Christ, I hope that's not Lorna's best Chanel lipstick, you girls,' Annie says, covering her face and laughing.

'Don't worry, I don't own such a thing,' I say, grabbing a menu from the drawer.

'It's this one, Mummy,' Freya says, sounding as though she's going to get a telling-off. 'Is it OK to use?' She holds out a little tube with the end all gooey and wound right out. It's as scarlet as scarlet comes. I don't recognise it.

'Oh,' I say, taking hold of it. 'Did you get this from Annie's bag? It's not mine.'

'And definitely not mine,' Annie says, laughing. 'You wouldn't see me dead in that colour.'

'It was on your dressing table, Mummy,' Freya says, looking worried. 'Please don't be cross.'

'It's OK, darling,' I say, hating that she almost looks scared. 'No telling off. You both look gorgeous. Just mind your ankles in those shoes.' I open my iPad, pulling up the pizza menu. 'Here, choose what you want, girls.' I turn to Annie while they discuss toppings. 'That's odd,' I say, looking at the lipstick. 'I've never seen this in my life before. It's just some cheap brand, look,' I say, showing her the logo. 'I might not be a Chanel girl, but I certainly have my standards. I've never bought this type before.'

'It's amazing what you keep buried at the back of your cosmetics drawer,' Annie says. 'But at least Freya and Lilly are having fun.'

'No, Annie, you're not hearing me. This is not my lipstick.' I glance through to the living room. Mark and Ed are engrossed in conversation. 'I have no idea where it's come from.'

Within the hour, the six of us are sitting around the table – the girls tucking into Hawaiian pizza, while we adults share out a Chinese.

'Sorry it's just another takeaway,' Mark says to Annie and Ed. He gives me a look. 'Lorna, perhaps you could do that lamb dish next time they come over? A home-cooked meal.'

'Nonsense, this is just fine,' Annie says, touching my arm, before I can reply. 'That's why restaurants have delivery services,' she says, passing me the rice.

'I'm sorry,' I say, freezing with the serving spoon halfway to my plate. I catch Mark's eye from the other end of the table. 'I'll cook next time, for sure.'

He stares at me, pausing before giving me his trademark smile, eyes creasing, lighting up. I breathe again.

'Ed, you should see where Mark's taking Lorna,' Annie says. 'The Caribbean.'

'Nice for some,' Ed replies, laughing and almost choking on a prawn cracker. 'Did you remember to book Butlins, love?'

'All sorted, darling,' Annie replies, blowing a pouty kiss across the table. 'And Frey-frey, how do you fancy coming to stay with us while Mummy and Daddy go on holiday? Jack too, if he wants, though I suspect he'd rather stop at home.'

I watch my daughter's face and, for a moment, she glances at me, looking scared, a little lost, but then, when she realises what it means – lots of sleepovers at her best friend's house – she beams approval.

'Then you won't feel sad any more, will you?' Lilly says, grabbing another slice of pizza. 'For not having any friends. But don't worry, cos I'll always be your friend and it'll be like we're sisters and stuff, and you can even share my mummy and nana if you like, then you won't have to worry.'

Freya stops eating, her bottom lip quivering.

'What do you mean, not having any friends?' I ask Lilly, biting my tongue about Freya sharing her mum and grandma.

'Since Freya hurt that girl Rosie, no one at her school will be her friend,' Lilly mumbles with a string of cheese stretching out of her mouth. 'But you can come to my school instead if you like,' she says matter-of-factly, chewing.

'It was only cos Rosie told everyone about Nana,' Freya snaps back with a scowl. 'She deserved it.' She crushes the remains of her pizza slice between her fingers, tears pooling in her eyes. 'But I wish Jack had never told me to hurt her,' she says, just as her big brother comes into the dining room, striding right up behind her. His smile falls away and his cheeks burn scarlet when he hears what Freya just said.

'Hi, love,' I say to him, trying to ease his agony. It's not the right time to discuss this. 'Would you like some food?'

'No, thanks,' he says quietly, giving Freya a look and shaking his head. He sighs heavily and goes off upstairs.

'Christ,' I whisper, glancing at Annie. I put my napkin on the table and go after him. 'Jack... Jack, wait—'

'Abbi, just leave him be,' Mark says firmly, making me stop in my tracks, the hair on my arms standing on end.

I turn around slowly. 'What did you just call me?' I grab the door frame.

'I said, "Baby, just leave him be".' He stares at me, smiling kindly, no doubt wondering what's got into me, why I seem so on edge and anxious. 'Come on, sit down and enjoy your meal, Lorn, before it goes cold.'

CHAPTER FIFTY-TWO

Lorna

I'm not going. I can't possibly go. It's dangerous, foolhardy, risky and reckless. I've been awake since 4 a.m., wishing I hadn't drunk quite so much wine last night. My head thrums.

Mark shifts beside me, groaning, reaching out a hand to me, finding my skin beneath the T-shirt I'm wearing. Even though his eyes are closed, I see the smile spread on his face. He presses up close, letting me know how he's feeling.

'Morning,' I whisper. He leans in for a kiss, wrapping his arms around me. 'I'm going for a run soon,' I say, incapable of giving him what he wants right now.

'Noo,' he says, holding on tight.

I tense. I can't do it. Not with everything on my mind. I switched my phone off overnight, making sure it was in my bedside table drawer rather than left downstairs. I hardly dare turn it on for fear of there being more messages from Andy_jag, perhaps cancelling. Perhaps worse.

'Love, I need to get up,' I say, stretching, trying to pull away. But Mark's holding on. 'I haven't run in ages and I'm losing my fitness. I want to go on…' I hesitate, hating myself all over again. '… on quite a long one today. Will you just hang out here with Freya for a bit?'

'You know what?' he says, backing off and sitting up suddenly with a grin. 'I'll come with you. Jack can stay with Freya. He won't mind, plus there's leftover pizza for their breakfast. You know how much they love that.'

'You want to come with me?'

'Sure. We hardly ever run together. It'll be fun. You can show me your favourite route.'

'Well… I was going to try out a different one today. And… and actually, I'm meeting Cath and we're going to get a smoothie along the way. Have a natter.'

'Cath? Running?' Mark laughs, stretching his arms out before putting them behind his head.

'She's trying to get fit,' I say unconvincingly. 'For her new dates. We'll just be chatting about girl stuff.'

'Fine,' he says, eyeing me. 'I'll leave you two to it, then.' And he throws the duvet off, getting up and heading for the shower.

It's a bright morning and, thankfully, being Saturday, the park is busy. I pull my sunglasses down off my head, covering my eyes as I approach, glancing all around, suspicious of everyone. Mums and dads with pushchairs, toddlers in hand, are everywhere, as well as other runners, people meeting up, couples out for a morning stroll. It's all so normal, all so unthreatening and regular, yet every face I see sends fear through me – especially when someone catches my eye, like the man who just wheeled his bicycle past, staring at me for a moment too long.

Was that him? Was that Andy_jag?

I'm dressed in my running gear, so Mark didn't get suspicious, and my hair is swept back and covered by a dark grey bandana. My sweat top is zipped up to my chin but, try as I might, I can't hide my entire face behind sunglasses and the collar. Anyone who knows me would still recognise me. I'm keeping away from the spot I suggested we meet at, choosing to wait, as inconspicuously as I can, a little bit removed but where I can still see the park gates. Still able to run for it should

I need to. And if it's the police setting me up, it wouldn't look good if they knew I showed up here, the location mentioned in Andrew's Double Take account. Not with them coming to see me on Monday.

I check my watch yet again. Twenty minutes to go.

'What are you *doing*, for God's sake?' I whisper under my breath, pacing about, checking my phone for the hundredth time. There haven't been any more messages and he's not been online since I agreed to meet. 'This is madness. Just prolonging the pain…' Tears collect behind my sunglasses, and I'm thankful no one can see. If I was sensible, I'd go home and forget it, get on with my life, get the therapy Joe suggested.

'Oops, sorry, sweetheart,' someone says, startling me. I nearly scream as they bump into me.

'Oh… that's OK,' I say, relieved it's just an old man. I pace about, catching site of a food van out in the street not far from the gates. It looks as though it's just set up and could be a good place to watch from without looking suspicious. A couple of people are waiting to be served. A coffee would be a good distraction to pass the next fifteen minutes – each one dragging like an hour. I stare at every single face going in or out of the park gates as I head over towards the van, joining the queue.

At first, it doesn't register who's inside, who's casually tossing burgers and sausages on the griddle, shovelling onions around with a spatula. Probably because I'm too busy staring at the passers-by, hoping, *praying* to see Andrew, by some miracle, still alive.

But something has snagged in my mind, making me even more anxious. It doesn't fully hit me until the other customers have left with their coffees, until I'm up against the counter, staring up at her with no chance of walking away unnoticed.

'Hello!' Nikki says brightly, instantly recognising me. 'Fancy seeing you here. Isn't it a lovely morning?' She's alone in the van.

'Oh,' I say, desperate to turn and go. I don't want to risk engaging with a client outside of work again, and certainly not

now when I'm preoccupied. Plus, I don't want to miss Andy_jag.
'Hi, yes, lovely.' I step away, deciding against the coffee.

'What can I get you?' she says, stopping me in my tracks. If
I'm rude and ignore her, she might say something to the clinic.
And she did speak to me first so, technically, talking with her very
briefly is OK.

'Just a coffee, please,' I say quietly. 'Black, no sugar.' I keep my
eye on everyone coming and going from the park.

'Live around here, then, do you?' she says, scraping the hot-
plate, adding more burgers. I glance up at her briefly.

'Er, no. Yes, kind of,' I say. 'Not really.'

She laughs again, her broad, white smile seeming different now
she's outside of the therapy room, as if she's much more comfortable in her domain: the burger van. 'You don't sound too sure?'

I smile, not replying, stepping from one foot to the other, my
eyes flicking about. Chatting to a client was not on the agenda.

'Been for a run?' Nikki asks, not giving up. There are no other
customers left to distract her.

'Not yet.'

'Fancy some breakfast? I do a mean bacon and egg bap.'

'No, that's fine, thanks,' I say, looking away again.

'Coffee won't be too much longer,' she says, pointing to the
huge urn. 'Takes a while to heat up.'

It looks as though it'll take the rest of the day, judging by the
size of it. I'm tempted to abandon the coffee, but I don't want to
seem rude or make her have any reason whatsoever to grumble to
the clinic. One more complaint and I'll be done for.

'So, what brings you round here then if you're not local?' Nikki
says, leaning on the counter, wringing out a dish cloth before
quickly glancing at her phone. Her face is make-up free, her skin
fresh and bright, making her appear less troubled than when I saw
her at the clinic. She dries her hands.

'Just a change of scene, really,' I say, turning and catching sight of a tall man about the same size as Andrew approaching the gates. My heart thumps as I hold my breath. He stops, pausing, looking around as if he's also waiting for someone. He gets out his phone, tapping something into it. I've never seen him before and have no idea who he is. But he definitely looks as though he could be an undercover officer, maybe even calling for backup as I'm watching. My mind is in overdrive.

Then he looks my way, catching my eye for longer than necessary, making me gasp and turn back to face Nikki in the van. Then my phone pings, sounding an alert.

When I look, it's an alert from Double Take. From Andy_jag.

'Anyway, it's *such* a coincidence we should bump into each other like this,' Nikki says, smiling, not taking her eyes off me. 'Don't you think?'

CHAPTER FIFTY-THREE

Lorna

'Mum?' I call out from the hallway after I've let myself in. 'It's just me…'

Nothing.

I take the shopping bags through to the kitchen, still shaken from my experience in the park this morning. As soon as I got my coffee from the van earlier, I left and chucked it in the nearest bin. I went home, wondering what the hell I was thinking – waiting, alone and vulnerable, to meet a stranger. A stranger posing as a dead man.

'Go and find Nana, Freya,' I say as she follows me through to the kitchen. 'She's probably fallen asleep in front of the TV.'

Freya hesitates, and I can read the fear in her eyes. *Do I have to?* But I don't want her relationship with her nana breaking down because of some stupid, judgemental kid from school. 'Would this help?' I say, holding out Mum's cake tin.

Freya grabs a chocolate roll, Mum's favourite treat to offer her, and a little grin forms as she runs off. I set to unpacking the few groceries Mum asked me to pick up, but my heart sinks when I open the fridge. Most of the food I brought with me last time is still sitting on the shelf, untouched. I check the packaging of the microwave meals. Four or five days past their use-by dates. I take them out and chuck them in the bin. No wonder she looks so thin.

'Mummy!' I hear Freya squeal from the living room. 'Mummy! *Mummy!*'

Shit.

I drop the shopping and dash through to find Freya standing with her hands cupped over her mouth, her eyes bursting wide. Mum's head is lolling off to one side, her tongue poking out from between her pale lips. Her skin is ashen.

I let out a long breath, taking hold of Freya. 'It's OK, sweetie,' I say, not sure if my nerves can take much more today. 'Grandma's just asleep.' Mum's chest moves steadily up and down, her fingers twitching on her lap.

'No, no, Mummy!' Freya squeals again. 'It's *Granddad*. What's happened to him?' Tears begin to flow down Freya's cheeks as she points across the room.

'Oh *God*,' I say, when I see Dad lying there. 'OK, darling, why don't you go in the kitchen and put the rest of the food away? I'll sort this out. Don't you worry, Granddad will be fine.'

She does as she's told, giving a last look back at my father lying on the floor. He's a mess.

'Mum,' I say, crouching down beside her chair. 'Mum, wake up, it's me.'

Slowly, she stirs. She's been crying. She's obviously had one of her fights with Dad. It looks worse than ever this time.

'Lorna?' she says, bleary-eyed, straightening herself up and wiping the drool from her chin. 'Oh, Lorna…' she says, as if everything's just coming back to her.

'It's OK, Mum,' I say, cradling her. 'I'm here now. We can sort this out.'

'Your father,' she says, staring wistfully across the room. 'I didn't mean to…' She covers her face, sobbing. 'I just got so angry with him.'

'I know, Mum. I know you didn't mean it.'

'Will you clean him up, make him better?' she asks, sniffing and pulling a tissue out from her sleeve.

'Of course I will,' I tell her. 'He's fine for the moment.' We both stare at him lying there. 'You're OK, aren't you, Dad?' I say in a loud voice, mainly for Mum's sake. 'See?' I say a second later. 'Now, why don't you tell me what happened?'

With a cup of tea in hand, Mum is finally able to talk about it. Freya's in the kitchen watching a cartoon on my phone so she doesn't overhear.

'I'm afraid I lost my temper,' she says. 'I couldn't take any more of it. It was like a switch flicked inside me.'

'I know, Mum.'

'He just sits there, never doing anything. Whatever I say to him, whatever I do for him, wherever I *take* him – nothing. It's been the same for as long as I can remember.'

'So you wanted to change that? To show him how angry you are about it?'

'Yes,' she said. 'To be honest, Lorna, I've been sick of the sight of him sitting in that bloody chair for a long time now. Day in, day out, unless I moved him, of course. It's time to accept that it's over, isn't it, Lorna? That things aren't the same any more.' Mum sounds as though a fog has cleared around her. She bursts into tears again, letting it all out. 'But what do we do now? Look at the state of him. Will I get into trouble?'

'You've been brave, Mum. You've done what's right for you. Things will start to feel better now, I promise.' I've wished for this moment for a long time, but Mum's always been stubborn. I never thought it would end quite this violently, though, and it's the last thing I need to deal with right now. But it's also oddly fitting, strangely well-timed.

'Maybe you can join the bridge club now, and that walking group you always fancied being a part of,' I say. 'Dad's not going to hold you back any more. It's your time now, Mum.' I make it sound easy – as though getting over someone, moving on, happens in a flash.

'Drink up,' I say, stroking her hand. 'I put in an extra sugar to help with the shock.' She's still shaking but looking calmer. I glance over at Dad on the floor. 'And don't worry about that,' I say, tipping my head towards him. 'No one need ever know, right? Our little secret.' Mum gives a timid nod, the glimmer of a smile. 'Good,' I say, giving her a kiss on the head as I stand up. 'Right, I'm going to clean him up. Make like it never happened.'

Mum smiles, tracking me as I head out to the kitchen and return a moment later with a dustpan and brush. 'It won't take a minute,' I say, getting down on my knees and sweeping up the bits of broken urn and the fine grey ash that seem to have gone everywhere. I tip it all into a plastic bag. It'll have to do for now until I have time to get the Hoover out, probably a wet cloth too.

'There,' I say, standing up. 'All done.' I eye the chair where Dad's been sitting for as long as I can remember. He must have taken the full force of Mum's swipe.

'We could take him down to the sea, couldn't we?' I say, holding up the plastic bag. 'Scatter him there.'

Mum gives a little nod.

Then Freya comes running into the room, holding out my phone to me. 'Mummy, mummy,' she says. 'You just had a message on your phone. Who's Andy_jag?' she says, staring at the screen. 'It says "Don't ignore me. I asked if you enjoyed your coffee this morning…?"'

And that's when the bag of ashes falls to the floor, sending out a cloud of grey dust all around me.

CHAPTER FIFTY-FOUR

Nikki

Maybe this therapy stuff really does work, I think, staring at the grubby bathroom mirror at Nigel's place, concentrating on my make-up. I look different, I feel different, I sound different, and I'm even behaving differently. Perhaps I'm all fixed! 'And it only took two sessions,' I say with a slightly crazed smile, opening my eyes wide as I apply mascara. 'A bargain!' Not that I intend paying, of course. She owes me that much.

The highlighter on my cheekbones catches the light, just as the woman said it would. I spent an hour in a department store getting a tutorial on how to apply foundation and concealer (though didn't tell her I'm already an expert at concealing things), and then she showed me how to contour and shadow my eyes so they pop. Her words, not mine.

'Oh, eyes *will* pop,' I considered saying, but kept the joke to myself. I wasn't in the mood for explaining. Afterwards, she tried to sell me a load of stuff, but I didn't buy anything. I've got a make-up bag of my own now. I didn't think it would hurt to pinch a couple of things when I was at *her* place. She's got so much of the stuff, all top brands, that I doubt she'll notice a few bits missing. I was in a hurry to get out and stupidly left my one and only lipstick on her dressing table. I need to get it back, which gives me the perfect excuse to go inside again. I'm getting bolder and bolder. It feels deliciously dangerous.

'I got me an interview later,' Nigel says when I come back into the living room. He's scooping Rice Krispies into his mouth and sitting on the arm of the grubby sofa. 'As a packer in a warehouse,' he says proudly.

I smile, giving him a nod as I put on my coat. 'It's going to be a good day all round, then,' I say, grabbing my shoulder bag and leaving.

The police pull up outside the clinic not long after I get to the square. It's been the usual trickle of clients into her practice over the last twenty minutes or so. When she arrived, she was wearing black trousers, a pale blouse with that grey coat, her usual leather bag, and smart flat boots, the ones she wore on Friday at our appointment.

There are two officers – a man and a woman – and they stand outside the building for a few moments, discussing something between them before heading up the steps into the Grove. It makes me smile, as though they're going in for therapy. I'm sure, in their job, they need it. Cleaning up after all the despicable things people do. People like me.

I know Lorna's been sitting at her desk since she arrived – the vague shape of her visible through the blinds. But now she's standing, going across the room towards the three people who've entered – dark shapes in the background. Two of them are the police – I can just make out the bright flashes on their uniforms – and there's another man in there too. I've seen him coming and going enough times to know he works there.

I rub my hands together, heading back over to the bench, almost as if I want to leave them in private, preferring to imagine what's being said in there rather than knowing for sure. I light a cigarette and sit down to wait.

An hour later, the police car pulls away and I'm back at the hedge, watching Lorna with the other man in her office still, talking, him pacing about, Lorna sitting at her desk, tracking him as he goes from one side of the room to the other. Then, when he leaves and she's all alone again, she lays her head down on the desk, staying like that for ages. A part of me almost feels sorry for her.

Then, oddly content, strangely calm inside, I head away from the clinic. It's only a short bus ride. I swipe my Oyster card as I get on and sit down, pushing my hand into my pocket to check. The key is still in there, cold and jagged in my palm. I stare out of the window, thankful it's such a beautiful, sunny spring day. I glance at my watch. I've got hours before anyone's home.

CHAPTER FIFTY-FIVE

Lorna's Journal

I've brought the journal into work today, to finish reading the last pages between appointments. After this, I can't stomach any more – to face the truth about how it happened, how the lies grew, how fake smiles and made-up excuses turned into such betrayal. And now it's happened *again*. I've been an idiot and it doesn't feel good. Makes me want to smash things.

13 April 2017

I've told him it's over. Told him I can't do this any more. My body aches for him, but my mind hurts worse. It's as though a bomb has gone off in my brain, obliterating everything good and leaving only the bad. I don't know how I will go on without him, but I have to. For the sake of my family, for the sake of me. If Mark ever found out, it would destroy him. He'd kill me. Not literally, obviously, but it would finish us off. I'm not going to write any more about it. I'll start a fresh journal and hide this one until I'm ready to get rid of it. Until the pain lessens. One step at a time to save myself, to get back to the place I need to be.

After telling Andrew it was over, I handed in my notice at work. There's no way I can continue at the Medway. It's too risky now. When I told him it had to end, he seemed to accept it at first, though he was upset, of course. His eyes hung heavy, but he was a man about it. There was no anger to begin with. I told him all the reasons – that I still wanted to be with Mark, how him being a client was a huge risk to my career, how he'd never allowed me to go to his house, how I felt he was lying to me about his lodger. But he didn't truly understand that I felt shut out. That I was crazy jealous of her. Ironic, I know, and I don't even understand it myself. In the end, things got tense between us and, at one point, I was afraid he really would tell my boss. Which is why I'm leaving my job now, before he destroys my career as well as my marriage. It's just too risky.

So as of today, I won't see Andrew again. It kills me to write it; kills me to think about it. I've already applied for several other jobs, saying to Mark that I needed a change, that the practice was badly run, that I could get a better salary elsewhere. As ever, he understood completely, even saying that if I needed time off, then he'd support me. He earns good money and we're not hard up. In fact, he was so good about it he pretty much insisted that I don't go back to work at all, that I'd be better off staying at home for Freya. And, of course, if we have more children, then it would be ideal. But I explained that my job doesn't work like that, that I need to keep up my practising hours to stay a member of my professional body, that I have to attend development courses regularly. He wasn't convinced, though I suppose one day soon I'll have to give it all up if we want more children.

Anyway, after that I deleted all the messages Andrew and I ever exchanged, erased his number and reset my secret phone, ready to sell. The SIM card is cut up and in the bin. I don't want it any more. From now on, my life will be ordered, tight, controlled. Everything back to normal.

No one will ever know.

I snap the notebook shut. Enough is enough. I glace at my watch – my next appointment is in fifteen minutes. I won't be taking the journal home – it's evidence, after all – though it's probably just as risky leaving it here at work. But I can't hide it back under the floorboard in Freya's room. I don't want it in there, contaminating her space. All these disgusting secrets seeping out, fouling the house.

I open the lockable drawer in my desk, sliding it under a stack of paperwork. It will do for now, until I get a chance to destroy it. Besides, no one's going to be looking for it, not here. Not in a million years.

I sit at my desk, tapping my pen on the wood, my jaw clenched, my neck tense. One slow tap after another, falling in time with the ticking of the clock.

Tap… tap… tap… My anger builds.

I swing round as the door opens, sighing out in relief when I see it's Mandy.

'Hi…' she says sweetly. She has that look in her eye as she stands there in her short uniform, fiddling with her hair. Just the look I need to see right now.

'Shut the door,' I say. 'And lock it,' I add. She gives me one of her smiles – one side of her mouth turned up, a glimmer of her perfect front teeth showing. I unfasten my belt, raising my hips and pulling down my trousers a little way. 'Come here,' I tell her.

She does as she's told, lifting up her dress, grabbing on to my shoulders as she straddles me.

'Do you want me?' I say, staring up at her. I need to get out the rage.

'Oh yes,' she says, her sweet smell smothering me. 'Always.'

'Tell me… tell me how much… you want me…' I grab her breasts as she settles on, arching her back, not taking her eyes off mine.

'Oh, Mark, I want you so much, baby… You know I do. Every time we do it, it just gets better and better…'

CHAPTER FIFTY-SIX

Lorna

The police have gone. And now Joe has gone too. I sit at my desk, drained, head down on my arms, thinking. Too exhausted to even cry.

They took Andrew's notes away with them. I was careful from the start to make sure I didn't write much, keeping the information to the bare minimum. It met our practice guidelines, of course, and the contracting details were solid, but my general notes were basic, unemotional, brief. They seemed satisfied, though I doubt it will throw any light on their case.

But what they asked almost sent me into meltdown.

'When did you first encounter Mr Taylor?' the female officer said. I can't even recall her name, barely took in anything about them, I was so nervous.

'He… he first came for an assessment on Monday the twelfth of March,' I say, glancing at his file to check, nodding when I saw the date. 'And he booked in under another name. David Carter,' I said, wanting to bring this up before they did.

The officers stared at me for a moment before making notes. They looked to Joe, who gave them a shrug. 'It happens sometimes,' he said, backing me up. 'Clients can be nervous or even ashamed about coming for therapy. They don't necessarily want to reveal their real names. And we understand that need for privacy.

As long as contact details are accurate, in case a safety issue arises, we don't have a problem with this.'

'And when did you get to know his *real* name?' the male officer asked, looking at me.

I glanced at Joe, who gave me the tiniest of nods. I had no idea what it meant, whether I should tell the truth – which Joe doesn't know anyway – or not.

'I realised quite soon that he'd come under an alias,' I said after a pause, figuring that was at least the truth. 'Maybe it was because of his job. I understand that he was getting fairly well known as an artist.' Then Andrew's nude paintings were on my mind again, those skilful brushstrokes depicting other women's bodies. It made me want to scream.

'It only became clear to Sandy, our receptionist, that there was a different name involved when she called Mr Taylor's landline after he was late for his appointment last Tuesday,' Joe added. Neither of us has actually answered the officer's question.

'My notes show the name he'd used to book in,' I add, covering myself.

'So, the twelfth of March this year was the first time you'd ever met Andrew Taylor?' the officer went on, seeming more concerned with dates than his name.

'Yes,' I said, digging my nails into my palms.

'And how did he seem? How was his mood?'

I looked at Joe again, who gave me an encouraging nod. 'Well, not very open to talking to begin with. As if he was struggling with the idea of admitting he needed help. Even though he'd obviously decided he did, for some reason.'

'And what did you believe that reason was?' the female officer asked.

I pause, unsure what to say. 'I think… um… I think he came regarding relationship issues,' I said, knowing it wasn't far from the truth.

'And did he mention any other therapy he may have received in the past?'

My mouth went dry then. 'No, I don't think he did.'

'OK,' the male officer said, flashing his notebook at his colleague, exchanging nods. 'So he didn't mention anything about the Medway Clinic?'

I couldn't help that my cheeks flushed then, that it felt as though the ground had shifted beneath my chair. 'No,' I said, flicking my eyes to the ceiling. 'No, I can't recall that he did.' I pretended to skim down his notes then, though my eyes wouldn't take anything in. I wasn't thinking straight, unsure if it was tears or fear blurring my vision. I folded my hands in my lap, trying to stop them shaking.

'OK. It's just that from his bank details, and then following up with the practice manager there, we know Mr Taylor had a number of sessions at the Medway Clinic last year.'

'Oh. OK,' I said, shrugging, trying not to sound too surprised. 'He may have done. It's not unusual for a client to switch therapists.'

Joe gives a confirmatory nod. 'Happens occasionally,' he said, backing me up. But then he touched his chin, frowning slightly, rubbing his fingers through his short beard as though something rang a bell.

'Fair enough,' the female PC said. 'So you didn't know that he'd been a client at the Medway?'

'No. No, I didn't,' I said, wishing I could backtrack, untangle the lie.

'And if you had a client come back to you a year or so later, would you be likely to remember them?' the male officer asked.

'Oh for sure,' Joe said, chipping in before I got a chance. 'You may not remember every specific detail, but in this job it's all about the relationship. Any decent therapist would remember a client they'd worked with only a year ago. Don't you agree, Lorna?'

'Oh, well, yes. I suppose. Maybe.' I fiddled with my hair then, not knowing what to do with myself.

'Perhaps you can explain then, Lorna,' the male officer went on. 'Why you haven't remembered that Andrew Taylor – aka David Carter – was a client of yours for a few months last year at the Medway Clinic? That was your previous place of employment, wasn't it?'

'Oh…' I replied, my mouth feeling completely frozen. 'Yes, maybe… I mean, yes, it was but I'm not sure if I recall him.' I looked to Joe for support, but he was also staring at me, eyebrows raised, his arms folded, eagerly awaiting my explanation. 'I can't say that my memory is infallible.' I forced my mouth into a pathetic smile that didn't get reciprocated.

An hour after they've gone, after I've been over and over everything a thousand times, I buzz through to Sandy, requesting that she cancel all my clients. I feel sick to the core, ill, wiped out as if a virus has swept through me, destroying my ability to function. I just need a day or two off, some time to recover, time to hide away. I know, under the circumstances, Joe will understand. He'll have to. I send him a quick email explaining I don't feel well. I've got to get out.

Then I phone Mark, but there's no reply on his mobile so I call the dental surgery.

'Oh hello, Lorna,' the receptionist says. I've known her for years. 'I'll put you through to his office, hang on a moment.' I wait as the on-hold music plays. 'Sorry, but there's no reply from his room. I think I saw Mandy go in there not long ago. They're probably busy. Can I get him to call you when he's free?'

'Sure,' I say, thanking her and hanging up.

I'm heading home. Not well. See you this eve I text to Mark instead, adding a couple of kisses.

Then I message Annie, asking if she can fetch Freya from the childminder on her way home from work later, if she can go back to hers for a play date with Lilly. She replies almost immediately, telling me no problem, that Lilly will be excited.

I pull on my coat, grabbing my bag and keys, dashing out of reception before I get collared by Sandy, giving her a quick wave as I pass. Thankfully, there are several people in the waiting area and she's on the phone so I'm able to leave without fuss.

I step out into the bright spring sunshine and head for my car. The only place I want to be right now is home – even though I know I left it in a terrible mess this morning. I just want to hide away for a while. Curl up and die.

CHAPTER FIFTY-SEVEN

Nikki

I go up the front path, unlocking the door of number seventy-four, letting myself inside as if I own the place. Bold as brass. They should have been more careful, leaving that key under the flowerpot.

'Oh,' I say, going into the kitchen, staring around. Last time I came in, it was clean and tidy, the washing-up done, the surfaces wiped. But today it looks as though they left in a hurry – breakfast things everywhere, last night's cooking utensils and plates on the draining board. The rubbish bin is overflowing and there's a stale smell in the air.

I wander through into the living room – all dark greys with chunky, expensive furniture, bright ornamental pieces splashed around for contrast. It's not my taste. I straighten a large framed photograph on the wall – one of those posed family shots with each of them in a white cotton shirt, jeans and bare feet, their brilliant smiles flashing. The beautiful family. The perfect family. A family to be envied. When you look from the outside.

But from within, the cracks are plentiful.

I pick up a couple of colourful velvet cushions strewn on the floor, plumping them up and placing them back on the sofa. I close a couple of women's fitness magazines, putting them on the wooden chest that serves as a table, and collect the couple of wine glasses that have been left there. I take them through to the kitchen.

'You're letting things go, Lorna,' I say, pulling on bright yellow rubber gloves and running a bowl of hot soapy water. Meantime, I load the dishwasher and tidy away all the packets and other things left out. When I've washed up, wiped down the surfaces and taken out the rubbish, I open the kitchen windows for some fresh air. I light a couple of scented candles too. It really stinks in here.

'Right,' I say, grabbing my coat and bag, heading upstairs. 'Lets' see what we've got up here.'

CHAPTER FIFTY-EIGHT

Lorna

I pull up outside our house, easily finding a parking space in the middle of the day. I turn off the engine and sit staring at the place for a while – the freshly pointed brickwork, the bright red front door, the two bay trees. I remember when Mark first brought me back here, a while after we'd actually first met. He usually came over to my flat, saying it was more convenient. I was delighted to finally see where he lived. Despite everything going on, I manage a small smile at the memory. I'd followed him around the place, looking at everything as he showed me each room, learning more about him, hoping to get a glimpse of the man I was falling in love with. They were heady days. By that point, he'd won me over entirely.

The sun is warm on my back as I get out of the car, go up the front path and unlock the front door. I go inside, knowing almost immediately that something is wrong – although it's not the kind of wrong that bothers me. In fact, it's a relieved kind of wrong, a sort of reprieve as I realise I didn't leave the kitchen in quite as much mess as I'd thought. In fact, it's in no mess at all. It's gleaming. I was expecting to come back to a load of dirty plates when all I want to do is crawl into bed, hide from the world, but that's far from the truth. I take off my coat, draping it over the kitchen chair, slowly staring around.

'No,' I whisper, shaking my head. 'No, this isn't right.' I think back to this morning. Mark definitely left before me, calling out that he wouldn't be home until about ten tonight because of a late clinic, and then he was going straight on to squash and something to eat with his mates. I was relieved, I remember, because it meant I wouldn't have to rush this morning to clear up the house, that I could do it later before he got home. I didn't want him to know I'd left it in a mess.

But now, all the washing-up is done, and the windows are open – both sashes pulled up, the spring breeze gently airing the room. And the candles are lit – the white jasmine-scented ones Annie gave me. Plus, someone's taken the rubbish out and put a load of washing on. It's still churning in the machine.

I swallow as the sound of blood whooshes in my ears.

Then there's a noise. From upstairs?

The hairs on my arms stand on end, a shiver running down my spine.

'Mark?' I call out from the hall. 'You up there, love?'

My stomach lurches at the thought of him being annoyed by how I'd left things this morning. No reply. Nothing except the sound of running water.

I put my foot on the first step, realising that it's the bath taps I can hear as I go further up. Mark rarely takes baths, preferring to shower, and I know for a fact Jack has gone on a field trip to a science museum with college. Freya is at school and, besides, she'd never come home alone.

'Hello?' I call out, reaching the landing. The air feels steamy, perfumed like my new bath foam. I glance into mine and Mark's bedroom – the bed is made, which I didn't get a chance to do earlier either. A couple of my dresses are laid out on the bed.

There's a coat and a bag I don't recognise draped over my dressing table stool.

Christ… someone's been in my house. Someone is *still* in my house.

I reach in my pocket for my phone but it's not there. That's when I remember I left it in the car, plugged in to charge on the way home.

Shit.

I'm about to venture into the bathroom, my heart thumping, but the door suddenly swings open. There's a naked woman standing there.

I scream, jumping backwards.

She doesn't move or say anything.

'Fuck, fuck, *fuck*,' I say over and over. I raise my hands defensively, yelling obscenities at her. 'What the hell are you doing here? What the *fuck*… You shouldn't be here! Get some clothes on! What the hell…?'

Nikki stands there calmly, her short hair tucked behind her ears and her arms down by her sides, making no attempt to cover her breasts or anywhere else. She stands with her feet a little way apart, showing no embarrassment or guilt. In fact, there's no emotion or expression on her face whatsoever.

'What are you *doing*?' I say again, shaking not so much from physical fear now, but rather that a woman – a *client* – is naked in my house.

'Taking a bath,' she says, as if it's the most normal thing to be doing on a Monday lunchtime. 'I cleaned up for you,' she says, offering a tiny smile. She walks past me into my bedroom, taking off her watch and dropping it in her bag. 'You're back earlier than I expected,' she says almost accusingly.

'*What?*' I say, following her into the bedroom, getting up close and trying to intimidate her. I want to grab her, shake her, throw her naked onto the street. Though I can already hear Joe's harsh words: *You were violent to a client who's clearly vulnerable and mentally unstable?* I need to call the crisis team now – as well as the police. If she's not arrested for breaking and entering, she'll be taken in for a mental health assessment at the very least. 'This is my house, Nikki, and you most certainly should not be in it. You scared the life out of me. I'm going to have to ask you to get dressed and leave immediately. There are people I can call to help you, OK?'

She tips her head to one side before padding back to the bathroom. 'I'm not leaving. Not yet,' she says with a sweet smile. She lifts one leg up, toes pointed, and steps into the bathwater. A second later she's sinking beneath the bubbles, giving me a look before closing her eyes. 'Mmm, this is lovely,' she whispers.

My mouth hangs open, my entire body shaking with anger, rage and, I admit, something like relief that it wasn't actually a burglar. 'I've asked you nicely, Nikki, but I'm very concerned about your mental health right now.' Not to mention my personal safety, I think, though don't tell her that. I don't want her to know that I'm nervous. 'I'm going to get my phone from the car and make a couple of calls. When I come back inside, I want you dressed and ready to leave, OK? And to explain why you're here,' I add, waiting for a response. But there is none.

I stare at her for a moment, not knowing what to do, so I turn to go, heading down the stairs. I don't want to leave her alone even for a second, but I have no choice. I need my phone. We gave up having a landline handset a while ago.

'I know what you've been doing,' she sings out.

I freeze, halfway down the stairs.

'With Andrew,' she adds in a high-pitched, tormenting voice.

I close my eyes, grabbing the banister rail to stop myself falling.

'And here's you thinking I was just another nutjob. The girl from a burger bar. A lowly *lodger*,' she says, spitting out the last word as if it has a stigma attached to it.

I grip the handrail, forcing myself to turn around, to go back up even though each step feels like a mountain as the realisation of who she is dawns on me.

'I know everything about you, Lorna. And by that, I mean *everything*.'

I hear the water slushing as she washes herself. She's sitting up now, rubbing her arms with my sponge as I stand in the doorway. She gives me a huge, satisfied smile.

'What are you talking about?' I say, barely audibly, holding on to the door frame.

'I don't think there's any need to explain, is there?' She plunges the sponge underwater, washing herself everywhere, unabashed. 'I thought I could make us some lunch. Thought we could talk.'

'Lunch? *Talk?*' I say, hating the quiver in my voice. She's obviously in a dangerous mental state and, for some reason, has seen fit to take it out on me. I've had clients form unhealthy attachments to me before, one or two checking me out on Facebook and other social media, some asking where I live, if I'm married, if I want to be their friend. A couple have been more zealous and determined than others, but I've only had to ask a supervisor to step in once or twice to refer them on to another therapist. But *this* – this is like nothing I've ever known before.

It's more than just an unhealthy obsession.

'Talking can be good,' I say, humouring her. I need to find out what she knows. What her intentions are.

'I do a mean eggs Benedict,' she says. 'I saw you have all the ingredients in the fridge.'

I give a tiny nod. 'I can help you, if you like,' I say, smiling, having no intention of doing any such thing. I need her out, gone. 'Why don't you get dry now?' I reach for a towel, holding it open.

Nikki gives me a warm smile, her eyes not leaving mine as she stands up, her breasts bobbing as they leave the support of the water. Foam runs down her as she takes the towel, holding it at arm's length. I can't help that my eyes sweep up and down her body.

She's beautiful and I hate it; hate that her figure is different to mine – curvy yet slim, shapely and alluring. Unpretentious and unselfconscious almost in a childlike way, yet with the confidence of a grown woman.

I forget the brushstrokes on the paintings. Forget the mental image I've conjured of her over months and months, torturing myself, hating every inch of the woman I'd never even met, yet who's caused me so much pain.

Because here she is, naked, standing right in front of me. Andrew's lodger.

CHAPTER FIFTY-NINE

Lorna

'Nikki, cover yourself up,' I say, turning away. '*Please*, just get dressed. You're not thinking straight, and you need help.'

'Oh, that's so thoughtful, Lorna, but I think *you're* the one in need of help right now. And I'm thinking very straight. I've been practising,' she says, pulling her shoulders up to her ears in an ingratiating way, flashing me a smile.

I hear her step out of the bath, feel the waft of air as she dries herself, drops the towel on the floor and goes into my bedroom again.

'But you can't just…' I want to scream at her but have to stay calm. I follow her through. 'How did you get *in*, for God's sake? This is not normal behaviour, Nikki.'

'Which one do you think?' she says, holding up two of my dresses against her.

'*What*…? Nikki, Listen to me. Put your own clothes back on and—'

'I like this one best,' she says, looking at the burgundy dress, throwing the other back down on the bed. 'It's more of a forgiving colour, don't you think?'

She goes to my underwear drawer then and pulls out a pair of black knickers, stepping into them. I stand there, watching her, my mouth hanging open, hating that I don't know what to do to stop this.

'Do you mind?' she asks, coming up close and turning around, holding her bra straps for me. Unbelievably, I find myself hooking her up.

'Nikki, you need to—'

'I used to have a dress quite like this,' she says, ignoring me, sliding it over her head, wiggling it down her body. '*He* bought it for me. Did he buy this one for you?'

I shake my head, not knowing what to say. 'No, Mark bought it,' I reply quietly, lowering my head, terrified of angering her. I just need to get her out. Then decide what to do.

Nikki zips up the side and slips on her ankle boots, giving me a twirl. 'What do you think?'

'It… it looks nice,' I say quietly, indulging her, wondering if I should have a weapon to hand. But all I can think of are my nail scissors in the bathroom, and they're not going to do much. I stare at her, wondering if I could actually stab another human being if it came down to it. I cover my face at the thought, hating everything that's happened, including that the dress looks way better on her than it ever did on me.

I take a breath, composing myself, as Nikki grabs my brush from the dressing table, using it on her hair, working it into dark, tousled spikes with some spray. It doesn't look as though it's been properly styled in a long time. But she's still undeniably attractive, though different to how I imagined. Andrew's paintings were abstract, and the faces were never designed to be recognised.

'Won't be a moment,' she says brightly, taking a make-up bag from her handbag and quickly touching up her cheeks. 'I hope you don't mind, but I borrowed a few things when I was here last week—'

'Last *week*?' I say, almost screaming, coming up to her and swiping back my compact. 'I wondered where this had gone.'

'But I did leave my lipstick here by mistake. You're welcome to borrow it.'

'The one that Freya used…' I whisper, trailing off as the realisation hits me.

'Ah, little Freya. How is she?'

'*What?*' I touch my forehead, feeling faint again.

'And Jack, of course?' She rolls her lips together, looking at herself in the mirror, satisfied she's done a good job. 'Right, I'm starving,' she says, taking my hand and leading me downstairs. 'Aren't you?'

CHAPTER SIXTY

Nikki

'Nikki, I really think we need to talk about Andrew,' Lorna says when we're in the kitchen. She's shaking, looks very pale, very fragile, as though she might pass out at any moment. That would be annoying. 'We should talk about what you know, what you're intending on doing.'

'If you like,' I say, smiling.

'Perhaps get a few things straight,' she adds. 'Clear up any misunderstandings. But first, I need to get my phone from the car. Why don't you put the kettle on, eh? We can have some tea.'

She slides her hand from mine, making to leave the room.

'Oh, I agree. There are definitely things we need to get straight. But no, you won't be needing your phone,' I say, grabbing her wrist. 'Really. Don't go outside.' She hesitates, the look in her eyes showing me just how scared she is, that she knows I'm serious, the damage I could do with one phone call. 'Sit down, Lorna. I was thinking we should have something stronger than tea.' I open a few cupboards, eventually finding a bottle of cheap brandy in the cupboard next to the cooker.

'Glasses are over there,' she says, resigned, dropping down onto a stool at the kitchen island, not taking her eyes off my phone on the worktop.

'I know,' I say, getting a couple out. 'This *is* nice, isn't it?' I pour two large measures. 'Now, drink up.'

'What is it you want from me, Nikki? Is this something to do with our therapy sessions? How can I help you?'

'Cheers,' I say, ignoring her questions.

'Look, about Andrew. I don't know what it is you think you know about me and him, but you're wrong.'

She takes a large slug of brandy then, wincing as it goes down.

'Oh, I don't think I am,' I say. 'I've been watching you for a while now. I know everything about you, and him. And all about your family too.' My turn to wince then, and not just from the alcohol. '*Everything*,' I add in a whisper.

'You've been *watching* me?' she says, incredulous. 'Watching me do *what*?' She has tears in her eyes, making me feel sorry for her. Almost.

'So,' I say, leaning on the worktop across the island unit from her. 'You're the other woman…' I give her a long, hard look. 'I always knew there was one. Right from when it started, actually. But I was too stupid to notice. Too wrapped up in everything, too invested in making a life for myself, making things work between me and *him*. Believing what I wanted to believe, only hearing what he told me, rather than what was actually happening right under my nose.' I take a deep breath, allowing the feelings I've been suppressing for so long to flow through me, absorbing the shock of them. 'Did you ever fuck him in our house? In *my* bed?'

'No!' she says, turning away. 'Look, for what it's worth, it's over now,' she says. 'Obviously.'

'What? Don't play me for a fool, Lorna.' I say, smiling sweetly. I go to the fridge, taking out the eggs, a packet of prosciutto slices, an avocado, a lemon, a jar of Hollandaise and a bunch of fresh parsley, placing them on the worktop one by one. 'Why don't you put some toast on? Cut it thickly. It's nicer that way.'

'I… I'm not hungry,' she says. 'What the fuck are you playing at, Nikki? Cooking in my kitchen…' She gestures to the food, her voice wavering, on the brink of tears. 'I've told you, it's over between me and him so why don't—'

'Such a cliché, isn't it?' I say, glancing at her as I gather utensils. 'The other woman. The bitch-battle, the catfight. But don't worry, I'm not about to pull your hair or scratch out your eyes. See? I'm cooking you a nice brunch.' I instinctively scoot around the kitchen, slugging some oil in a frying pan, putting some water on to boil for the eggs, placing the parsley on the chopping board. 'The toast?' I say, waving my phone at her, pretending I'm about to dial someone, spurring her into action. This time, she does as she's told.

'If it's any consolation, I'm sorry,' Lorna says, sitting down again. 'He was always vague about you. I didn't know.'

'Honesty was never his strong point,' I say, laughing drily. 'Whatever he did say about me, I'm sure it was unpleasant. Nothing short of vicious, I would imagine.' I stare at her, trying to read her as if I'm the therapist now. 'You'd have ended up the same as me in the long run – put down, belittled, controlled, lied to, cheated on, deceived. I'm actually doing you a favour. You'll realise one day.'

'What?' she says, looking confused.

'I bet you were made to feel like the most cherished woman in the world, as if you were the only one? Trust me, it wouldn't have been long before you felt crazy, suspicious, spying on him, driven to extremes to get proof, as though it's *you* who's been unreasonable, not him.'

I recognise the look in her eye; can see she's in denial.

'But not this time. I've seen to that,' I say, taking a large cook's knife from the block. Lorna's wide eyes track my every move, watching as the blade glints in the sunlight streaming through the window. I grab the parsley with one hand, scrunching it up, bringing the knife down through it in satisfying hacks.

'It was his charm that drew me to him in the first place, how he could beguile the pants off anyone,' I say, fighting back the tears. 'But when I found out about you, it tipped me over the edge, made me hate him. Hate *you*. Made me do something reckless. He always denied your existence. Said I was crazy.'

'And that's why you're here?' Lorna says, knocking back more brandy, looking fearful. 'Because you want revenge or something?' Her eyes flick down to the knife.

'Why don't you pop the prosciutto on to fry? Get it nice and crispy,' I say, cutting the avocado in half. I scoop it out into a bowl, adding a squeeze of lemon juice before mashing it up ready to spread on the toast. 'Isn't this nice?' I turn to her, reaching out and touching her shoulder. 'Us cooking together. Like mates. We have *so* much in common, Lorna.'

'Yes, yes, it is,' she says, swallowing, frowning, half smiling all at the same time. She gives a quick glance to my phone lying on the worktop. I slide it closer to me, out of her reach. 'Nikki, I don't know what it is you want from me, or how I can help you, but…' Her face contorts, looking agonised, as she moves away from the sizzling pan, leaning on the counter beside me. The candle flickers between us in the breeze, the jasmine fragrance mingling with the scent of lemon and brandy. 'But if it's money you want, then I can help. We can sort something out. Just tell me how much you need. But please…'

'Please?' I say, raising my eyebrows, looking up at her, the knife in my hand.

'Yes. *Please*. And I mean it, Nikki. I really mean it. I had no idea about you and And—'

'You think after everything that's happened, everything I've been through, that I'm going to listen to your fucking pathetic *please*?' Spit flies from my mouth as she jumps at my raised voice.

'Then tell me. I'll listen. I know you've been through a lot, Nikki. You mentioned about someone dying, about it being your fault. I'm still your therapist. I can help you work through it.'

She's humouring me, I know. Trying to appease me until she can get rid of me, have me locked up. But that look on her face, the same look when she gave me her full attention at the clinic, when she listened to me like no one ever has – it does something to me. I can't help myself. 'It was my father,' I say, a couple of sharp, involuntary breaths making me shudder. 'I was the first one to get to him after he died, the first to see his body. I was only a kid. The horror of seeing him like that has never left me.'

'Oh, Nikki,' she says, her hand reaching out slowly towards my phone. I know she's trying to distract me, upset me, grab it when she gets the chance. 'I'm so sorry to hear that.' I think she means it.

'We were in the car and it was raining hard. I was only little and chattering incessantly in the back, pestering my dad, begging him to look round at my broken toy. He did, quickly, but suddenly veered off course, swerving, trying to avoid the truck we were about to hit head-on. We went straight into the ditch, slamming into a tree. He hadn't got his seatbelt on and flew through the windscreen. I was bruised and battered but managed to crawl out of the car. I found his body ten feet away, barely recognisable.' I bow my head, covering my face at the memory. 'I've tried so hard to block it out.'

'That's horrific,' she says, shuddering.

When I look up, her hand is on my phone.

'No!' I scream, swiping it away from her, hating that I opened up to her. 'Don't fucking play games with me!' I'm panting, breathless and upset from the memory of the crash. But I need to stay focused on the now. 'You have not one *clue* about the shit I've been through because of *him*. Because of *you*. But not any more. Not any fucking more, Lorna Wright, oh-so-fucking-entitled to help herself to another woman's—'

'But I didn't know for certain what was going on between you. He was always so vague,' she says, getting up close, her expression pleading. Her fingers bend as they grip the worktop, her arms shaking. There are tears in her eyes as she hiccups back her sobs. I raise the knife, looking at the blade as it glints between us. I take a deep breath and start chopping the parsley again.

'I know you didn't, Lorna,' I say calmly, pouting at her, tilting my head. 'I know you didn't. And it's OK. It's not your fucking money I want.'

'Then what *do* you want?' she says, sniffing. 'Are you going to tell Mark about…' She hesitates, so I look at her, making an encouraging face. 'Are you going to tell Mark about me and… *him?*'

'Why would I care about…' I say, but trail off. We both whip round at the same time, each of us frozen.

A noise.

From the front door.

A key in the lock.

Fuck. This wasn't in the plan. If, indeed, I had one.

CHAPTER SIXTY-ONE

Lorna

The noise again. It's definitely the front door. I wipe my hand across my cheek in an attempt to hide the tears. Trying to compose myself, trying to look normal.

I'm here, in my kitchen. With a friend. Cooking.

Just cooking. Cooking brunch with a mate. Perfectly normal.

'Mark?' I say, catching sight of him in the hall before Nikki does. She draws in a sharp breath, as though she hadn't expected this either, but there's no time to beg her, no time to plead with her to act like my friend.

Please, dear God, don't mention Andrew…

'Lorna?' Mark shouts, banging the front door closed. Nikki starts chopping again – chop, chop, chop – while humming a little tune. I glance at her, wondering if she's decided to play along. 'I got your message saying you'd come home poorly. I have a couple of hours free so wanted to see if you were OK.'

Footsteps in the hallway, getting closer… closer.

And then he's in the doorway, filling the gap with his broad body, his legs apart, his shoulders back. At first, he looks at me, but then his eyes flick across to Nikki.

She looks up at just the same moment.

There's silence – just the sizzling in the pan behind me and the sound of my heart thumping in my ears. They stare at each other for what seems like an age, no one moving. Then Mark's mouth opens but nothing comes out. He takes a step closer. I've never seen his face look so blank, so shocked, so confused. It's as if a mask has fallen off him and he doesn't know who to be. Exposing a man I don't recognise.

'Hello, Mark,' Nikki says, almost brightly. 'I didn't expect you home until later. We're just making eggs Benedict. There's plenty, if you'd like some.' She keeps on chopping, beaming a smile, glancing up a couple of times as though everything is completely normal.

Mark stares back hard, his eyes narrowing, deep furrows forming as he frowns. His head shakes from side to side as if his brain is telling him one thing, but his eyes are telling him quite another. He edges forward, approaching her as if she's a feral animal, drawing up close the other side of the island unit, studying her. Beads of sweat glisten on his top lip, the muscles in his jaw are clenched and tight. His dilated pupils make his eyes turn black.

He looks like he's seen a ghost.

'How have you been?' Nikki says brightly, staring him out. 'Fancy a drink? We've been really naughty and got the brandy out, haven't we, Lorna? But what the heck, eh?' she says, laughing. 'You only live once. Right, Mark?'

I look from one of them to the other – back and forth, back and forth – until Mark crushes me with one word.

'*Maria?*'

Nikki stands dead still, holding the knife. 'So,' she replies, her voice not so bright now. 'How have you been?'

'*What?*' I say. 'What do you mean – *Maria?*' I stagger back, catching on to the worktop behind me. 'Tell me!' In my head, I'm screaming it out, but in reality, my voice is weak, nothing more than a pathetic squeak. They both ignore me.

I watch Mark's expression change, recognising the telltale signs – his colour draining away, his shoulders tensing, his teeth clenching together. I haven't seen him look like this in ages.

And then everything Nikki – *Maria* – said works its way through my mind again. It takes me a few moments to work it out, but when I do, it makes me feel sick.

Belittled… controlled…

She was talking about *Mark*, not Andrew.

Mark's breathing is shallow and fast, his whole body seething with anger. 'What the *fuck* do you think you're doing?' he roars. His fists are clenched down by his sides. 'How the hell… what the…' He paces about the kitchen – two steps one way, three back the other – tearing at his hair. He's barely able to spit out the words.

'I'd have thought "Oh thank God, Maria, you're *alive*!" would be more appropriate, don't you?' Nikki swings round to me, pulling a silly face. 'Some men can be *so* fucking rude.' Then her face turns venomous, making me want to back away, get away from the pair of them. I don't know who to believe, who to trust.

'I'll be honest, I didn't expect things to play out like this today,' Nikki continues. 'But I always try to look on the positive side now, especially after having such good therapy.' She turns to me again. 'And after only a couple of sessions too.'

'What? You've been seeing Lorna for therapy?' Mark spits out, his eyes burning between the pair of us. 'Lorna, how long has this been going on, you gullible idiot? You have no idea what you're dealing with here or what she's capable of. This woman is mental, as you've no doubt found out.' He comes over to me, his demeanour suddenly changing when he sees me reeling from the insult. 'I'm sorry… sorry, love. I'm just shocked. Naturally.' He wraps an arm around me. 'Don't worry, I'll protect you from her. She needs locking up.'

He pulls me closer, reaching into his pocket for his phone, waving it at Nikki… Maria… whoever she is. 'I should report you to the police, you… you lunatic. What you've done is nothing short of fraudulent and—'

'Fine,' Nikki says, pointing at his phone with the tip of the knife. 'Go right ahead and call them. Call whoever you want. You can't control me any more, Mark. I may have been dead to you for the last eleven years but—'

'*Eleven* years?' I say, shocked, thinking, working it out. 'You said Maria had been dead for fourteen years, that she died when Jack was only three, several years before we met?' I look at him, willing him to explain, to do something, *anything*, but he just stands there looking torn, his face twisted.

'Oh, he's good, Lorna. He's very good. Get used to everything he's ever said to you being a lie. He started seeing you while he was still married to me. While I was *very* much alive and living here. Wake up, woman.'

'*What?*' I look up at him.

'He kept us both in the dark. Neither of us knew to start with, but when I found out, he began trying to get rid of me, trying to make out I was crazy and have me locked up in a psychiatric hospital. Anything to get shot of me,' she continues. 'By that time, he wanted to be with you, not me. I was devalued, discarded, thrown away like a piece of trash.'

'None of that is true!' Mark yells. 'You can see how unstable she is, Lorn.' He gives me a squeeze.

'Then came our sailing holiday in Scotland,' Nikki goes on, ignoring him.

'Yes… yes, I remember you going on a sailing holiday, Mark,' I say, trying to think back to exactly when that was. It was when he sent me that picture of him and Jack, the one I keep on my phone. 'But you're wrong. He went with some mates. He took Jack too. It was a dads' and sons' trip.' She's lying. She has to be.

'No, Lorna. He went with *me*.' Nikki taps the knife on the chopping board. 'Mark told me it was suitable for Jack, a gentle trip for his first sailing holiday, but we should never have taken him. He was far too young for the treacherous waters Mark took us out in. It was terrifying.' She pauses, watching my reaction. 'Has he suggested a nice holiday alone with you lately? A quiet romantic break by the sea? If so, I wouldn't go if I were you. Just saying.' She laughs then, glancing over at the holiday brochures lying on the side.

I can't take it in, what it all means. My mind searches way back, to when Mark and I first met. We didn't live together for a while, of course. It was three years before that happened, during which time we took it slowly, mostly meeting at my place. It's possible he could have had a separate life, I suppose, with Maria still living here.

I glare at Nikki, watching her every move. 'No, you're wrong!' I yell, huddling closer to Mark. 'You're just jealous. Mark, tell me this isn't *your* Maria? Tell me that it's someone else, that she's messing with us, or it's some kind of crazy mix-up, a practical joke even?' I choke out a desperate, hysterical laugh as I study her, unable to accept any of this. Her hair's completely different, but her face... her cheekbones, her eyes. There could be some similarity, though she doesn't look anything like the photos I've seen. But then they would have been taken at least fifteen years ago, maybe more. Was this why I felt a flash of recognition at the clinic?

'Mark, but you said she *died*. I... I don't understand. Just tell me this isn't her!' I grab hold of him, searching his eyes with mine.

'Shut up a minute, Lorna. Let me think,' he says. I can smell the sweat breaking out on him – not the usual healthy smell, but fear oozing from his body.

'You have to listen to me, Lorna. I *am* Maria, Mark's not-so-dead wife. I would shake your hand but...' She trails off, glancing at the knife, shrugging. 'Anyway, it seems a bit late for pleasantries.'

'But... but Mark, why would you tell me she's dead when she's not?' I try to pull away from him, but his arm is clamped around my shoulder.

'She *was* dead!' he yells, tearing at his hair with his free hand.

'In truth, I was dead to him a long time before I *actually* died, Lorna. Why don't you tell her what happened, Mark?'

My mind races all over the place, partly wondering, of course, what Nikki… Maria, whoever she is, knows about Andrew, about Andy_jag. Then it occurs to me – I was looking for a *man* the other day at the park, when really I should have been looking for a woman. I cover my mouth as it hits me.

She was there – Nikki. At the burger van. Then came the two messages from Andy_jag – one while I was there at the park, and another chasing it up when I was at Mum's later that afternoon.

I hope you enjoyed your coffee this morning.

Her. It was Nikki. Maria.

CHAPTER SIXTY-TWO

Lorna

'Oh God, no, *Andrew*…' I say, my face crumpling, my hand covering my mouth as I say his name out loud. Mark is beside me, his breathing fast and laboured.

'I'd not feel too guilty about *him*,' Nikki says, unfazed. 'Mark won't have been faithful to you for more than five minutes anyway. Isn't that right, Mark?'

'But… but you hated me being with Andrew,' I say to Nikki, trying to make sense of everything even though it's too late for hiding behind lies. I barely know what's real or not any more. 'And oh, God, you must *really* hate me. I've been the other woman *twice* in your life now.' Nikki is still holding the knife, so I edge behind Mark, hoping he'll provide some kind of protection. The tears flow then, hot and heavy, when I realise what I've done.

'What are you talking about?' Nikki says, her face blank for a moment, her eyes twitching until something registers. 'You think… you think this Andrew person and *me*… that we were…?' She makes a face – a glimmer of a smile – rolling her eyes, shaking her head as if she's way ahead of me.

I nod, sniffing, waiting for her to continue. Bracing myself for Mark's reaction.

Nikki laughs. 'I've never met Andrew whoever-he-is in my life before,' she says. 'He means nothing to me. I've seen you two hooking up, though. Been with you on enough of your dirty liaisons to know what you got up to. Frankly, I applaud you, Lorna. I wish I'd done the same.' She walks around from behind the island unit, waving the knife at us as she approaches.

'*What?*' Mark says, turning and shoving me away. The look of hatred in his eyes nearly kills me. 'You're a dirty fucking whore. And you think I didn't know anyway?' he says. 'I found one of your pathetic journals a few weeks ago, when I was checking for a leaky heating pipe in Freya's room. I've read all of it. I know what you got up to last year, and I know what you've been doing recently. You dirty bitch.'

'No, Mark, it's not like that. You don't understand. Really, you have no idea what it's been about, why I…' I reach out to him, begging, even though I can't possibly tell him. I hate myself even more.

'Oh, I can assure you, I know *exactly* what it's about. And I know all about you on that bloody dating site too. You must think I'm fucking stupid. I saw you on Cath's profile, flaunting yourself. And you're glued to your phone all the time.'

It's as though I've been punched in the guts. 'The dating site? I… no, Mark, you don't understand that either. I need to explain—'

'Why don't you explain it to Andy_jag, then?' He slaps me across the face, making me stumble backwards, stunning me. Then he jabs at his phone, bringing up a familiar screen.

Double Take.

'You stupid thick bitch,' he spits out, forcing me to look at an account, a profile – a profile that *he's* logged into. The screen name makes my heart split in two.

Andy_jag.

'*No…*' I whisper, tears pouring down my face.

'Yes, Lorna.'

'You're Andy—'

'I knew you'd take the bait when you saw his picture,' he says, a smug look on his face. 'I knew you were always on it at Cath's and wouldn't be able to resist if you saw your bastard lover on there. Photos of him were easy to find online, and I knew enough from your journal and those articles to choose a screen name that would fit, to write something plausible. Plus, it was easy to recognise you when you messaged him as Abbi. Lucky for me you were too stupid not to delete the cookies on your laptop. Your username wouldn't have shown up on the login screen that night if you had. You weren't quite quick enough getting rid of it.' He laughs then, his fists balled by his sides.

I grab on to the worktop, feeling sick at what it means, what I've been doing all this time. What I've *done*.

'Anyway, when you said "ditto", I knew it was you,' he goes on, his voice filled with hate. 'And here's me thinking it was *our* special word.'

'Oh my God, no, no, *no*…' I can't stand it. The tears come hot and fast, the sobs rising up from my broken heart. 'Those messages you sent,' I say, looking at Mark through swollen eyes. 'The things you said… you have no idea what you've done.' Then I turn to Nikki, clawing at my face. 'You're not Andrew's lodger?' I say. 'Not his lover?' My voice is weak, thick with snot, not wanting to believe the truth.

'No. Sorry, Lorna,' Nikki says, almost sympathetically, edging closer to Mark with the knife. He moves further away. '*My* landlord is a dirty old letch in his sixties called Ken. But this isn't news to you, surely? I already told you this story. I was left with no choice but to degrade myself, to service the dirty old fucker so I could survive.' She jabs the knife towards Mark, making him jump back. 'It's what I'm used to, after all, being treated like shit. But last weekend, he… he…' she trails off, closing her eyes for a beat. 'He crossed the line, he forced me to… It was disgusting. I had to get out. I'm staying with a friend now. I just wanted to be near Jack, so I could see him. That's how it all started, me wanting to be close to my son again. I missed him so much.' She fights back the tears.

'But how could you leave Jack in the *first* place?' I hear myself saying, dropping down onto the stool again fearing I'll pass out. 'I don't understand. Why would a mother do that?' I pick up my brandy glass and swirl the liquid round, knocking it back. I pour out another large measure, the heat of the candle hot under my wrist, warming the glass.

'You think I *wanted* to leave him?' Nikki says, pointing the knife at each of us. 'When the boom swung across the deck on that fucking boat, knocking me into the water, I thought I was going to die. Do you know what that's like, Lorna, to literally have everything you love and cherish flash through your mind, knowing you're never going to see your son again? That sailing holiday was the most horrific, isolating and terrifying experience of my life. Apart from Jack, I was alone with *him*. We should never have gone out in that rough sea.' She jabs the knife towards Mark. 'The trip was meant to fix our marriage, but I felt helpless, abused, ridiculed, and was forced to have sex with a man I felt nothing for – and all with our little boy within earshot. I was stuck at sea with him, terrified for Jack and no idea how to get away, let alone sail or use the radio. He was trying to break me.'

Tears roll down my cheeks as I sip more brandy, swirling it round in the glass, conscious of the candle flame. 'Nikki…' I say, wanting to listen to her, sit with her, hear her story. The therapist in me coming out even now.

'This is all total bullshit,' Mark yells, taking a step towards her, but she raises the knife, forcing him back.

'That sudden tack was no accident either. Mark timed it perfectly without warning me, sending the boom across the deck, hurling me into the freezing water. Jack's face in the cockpit, where he was strapped in, was the last thing I saw as I went over.

He witnessed everything. He probably still remembers it. I was wearing a life jacket, but the weather was bad, the swell big, pulling me under time and time again. I couldn't breathe. And Mark knew that I wouldn't survive long in those temperatures. I screamed out to him for help, watching as the boat sailed further away. Mark was standing at the helm, staring back at me, holding a steady course in the opposite direction. He made no attempt to swing round or rescue me. He knew the drill, could have at least tried to turn back or throw in a lifebuoy, but he left me for dead. Jack was crying out for me. He was six.'

'Christ, Nikki, oh *Nikki*,' I say. I might be caught up in this whole mess, but her story is horrific. One of the worst cases of abuse I've ever heard as a therapist. I think of the trauma Jack must be harbouring, how it's been coming out, him doubting his memories, upsetting Freya. The lies his father told him are unforgivable.

'You need to get out now, you crazy fucking bitch,' Mark shouts, suddenly lunging towards Nikki. She jabs the knife at him, darting back behind the island unit. 'I don't know what the hell you think you're doing but just get out of my house!' He's red-faced, sweating, his fists clenched by his sides, shoulders hunched.

'It's strange, but a kind of peace came over me after a while,' Nikki continues, ignoring him. 'As though I was resigned to my fate. That was when I decided to die, to never come back. It was an escape. All I could think about was Jack, how I'd never get to see him grow up. But then I realised that no child wants to see their mum crazy all the time, depressed, drinking too much, in and out of psychiatric hospitals. I knew Mark loved him dearly, saw him as a mini version of himself, and I had no doubt he would look after him. In those terrifying, freezing moments, I convinced myself my son was better off without me. Convinced myself I *was* actually crazy. That I hadn't even been worth fishing out of the water.'

'You were in hospital because you *were* mad,' Mark spits out. 'And you drank because you… you were an alcoholic. So yes, you *are* crazy! What more proof do you need?' He's shuddering, filled with rage.

'Shut up!' I scream at him as something flicks inside me. 'Let her speak!' I'm shaking, watching Nikki, overlaying her story on my own. It feels as though I'm drowning too – choking on memories of Mark. *I always get what I want*, he'd told me.

'I don't know how long I was in the water or what happened because I must have passed out. But the next thing I knew, I was in a boat. A foreign fishing boat with a couple of men who didn't speak English and who were warming the life back into me. I've no idea how long it was before we reached the shore, but I refused to let them take me to hospital. I convinced them I lived locally, insisted they leave me alone at the harbour. I never saw them again. Mark had to call the coastguard, of course, report me missing, no doubt telling them how he'd tried and tried to save me, to go back and locate me. But by the time he'd bothered to raise the alarm, the mayday signal would have given out a completely different GPS location for the search. They never found a body. As far as Mark and the rest of the world was concerned, I was dead. And seven years later, officially so.'

'Oh, Nikki… *Maria*,' I say, breathless from her story. 'Why didn't you tell the police, the doctors, anyone?'

'I'd tried to get help in the past, but no one ever believed me. In the end, I knew there was no point. Besides, apart from not seeing my son, I'd never felt so free in my life. I had nothing, I was a nobody, but it was a chance to start again. Without *him*.' She glares at Mark. 'Over the years, I laid low in Scotland, got by with cash-in-hand, live-in jobs, recovering, getting my strength back – emotionally, you understand. In time, it became clear that there was nothing wrong with me. There never was. It was all *him*. I stayed in Scotland for years, knowing Mark would never look for me. He was too preoccupied with you, Lorna.' She draws in a deep breath. 'It was the hardest thing I've ever done, yet the most liberating too. If I'd stayed, I'd have lived my life feeling dead inside anyway. It was always in my plan to come back for Jack. I was just never sure when. Or if he'd even want to know me. The only person I ever killed was me.'

'What is it you want from me, Maria?' Mark growls. 'How much to get rid of you once and for all?'

'I don't want your fucking money,' she says. 'I just want my son back. Did you know he smokes weed, hangs out with a bad crowd? I even saw him shoplift once.'

I hang my head. I've tried to bring up Jack well, tried to be the mother he never had. I feel so bad for him that his memories were denied over and over by Mark, so he eventually believed the lies he was fed. But Jack's unconscious mind has never quite allowed him to forget, never fully let go of the horror he saw, how his father left his mum for dead.

Deep down, he knew.

Then the horror of my own reality hits me again, making me want to retch.

Denying, distorting…

'Jack won't want anything to do with you,' Mark spits out.

'That's not true!' I say, standing up. 'Jack's always loved his mum. I *know* this.'

'You're both crazy bitches,' Mark shouts, lashing out with his arms at us. 'And you, you cheating whore,' he says to me. 'You can go fucking hang yourself, for all I care!'

That's all it takes.

His words echo around me, vibrating through every cell of my being, through the years. Waking me up.

Again.

For a second, the world goes quiet, all my senses numb, protecting me – perhaps like Maria's moment of calm in the sea when she thought she was going to die.

But then one quick tip of the glass is all that's needed for the candle to ignite the warm brandy, sending blue swirling flames out of the top. Before he knows what's happening, before I can stop myself, I chuck the whole lot in Mark's face, dousing him in the flames. I'm fuelled by anger, driven by that rotting place deep inside.

Mark screams, clutching at his face, his neck, his clothes as the burning alcohol seeps down, the flames spreading over his skin, scorching him more and more as his hands spread it around. He can't put it out. It's everywhere. He drops to his knees, yelling, shrieking for help, crying in agony. His clothes are alight, his hair on fire, the skin on his cheeks and neck blistering as the alcohol burns.

All I can do is watch.

And when Nikki rushes up to him, plunging the knife into his back, I don't do anything. Don't even try to stop her. I just watch as she stabs him over and over as he writhes, helpless, on the floor from the flames and the pain.

Blood spreads quickly, pooling around his twisting body as he squirms and thrashes. Nikki pants and screams as she keeps on stabbing him front and back – even when his movements subside, even when blood streams from his mouth, his eyes, and even when his body finally stops moving, she's still sinking the knife into him. She's covered in blood, hysterical, her face contorted with hate and rage. She kicks him, spewing out all the malice stored up inside her.

He twitches. A final groan.

I let her have this.

Let her get it all out.

It's good therapy.

CHAPTER SIXTY-THREE

Nikki

I'm breathless, spinning, out of my mind. He was right – I *am* a crazy bitch! What have I done…

Oh my God, oh my God, oh my God…

'Nikki, Nikki,' she says, grabbing my shoulders. 'It's OK. Stop now, calm down. Stop, please…'

I feel her breath on my face, her hand on my wrist as she gently takes the knife from me, dropping it on the floor. I look down, seeing the last of the flames on Mark die out.

Along with him.

She pulls me close, not caring that blood gets all over her. I'm sobbing, convulsing, blood, tears and snot all over my face and hair, smearing it all over her as she holds me tight.

'It's OK,' she says. 'Breathe. It's OK, just breathe. Let me think. We'll… we'll sort this somehow.' Her voice wavers. She's as terrified as I am.

We rock back and forth, standing in the kitchen, our feet paddling in the mess around us. Mark's blood. Each of us can feel the thumping heart of the other – two lives synchronised, attuned, somehow understanding.

I don't know how long we're like this. It feels like an eternity.

'You need another bath,' she says, holding me at arm's length. Then the laughter. Not proper laughter, but hysteria fuelled by shock. We're shaking uncontrollably – our legs, bodies, arms, heads. Not knowing what we're doing. Freezing and scared.

We drink more brandy. From the bottle.

'I told you this dress was a good colour,' I say, my voice broken, warped, not sounding like me. Stupid things coming out. Nothing real.

'Let me think,' Lorna says, releasing me, pacing about. But there's an air of defeat about her, as if she already knows our fate. 'I want you to wash, Nikki. Wash well. Take everything off in here and go back up to the bathroom and scrub yourself. Get some clothes from my wardrobe.'

'What?'

'Just do it,' she says, pulling at her hair, hugging herself. Her face is white.

I look down at Mark, his body unmoving. I can't take in what she's saying.

'Do it,' she says more sternly, looking me square in the eyes. 'I'll sort this. I just need time to work it out.'

'But—'

'Nikki – *Maria*,' she says earnestly. 'Please.'

I don't know what she means.

'No, *I* should deal with it. I did it. And… and I'm already dead,' I say, clutching her arms.

'Exactly,' she says. 'So do as I say.'

The bath is still warm, but the bubbles have gone. I step in, sinking down under the water, rubbing my hands through my hair. When I resurface, the water is pink. I scrub myself with the sponge, adding soap, using a brush to get the blood out from under my nails, around my cuticles. I end up draining the water, whipping the curtain closed and showering. I need to be clean. Really clean.

Afterwards, I dry off and do as Lorna said, finding some clothes in her wardrobe. I take out some sweatpants, a T-shirt, a zip-up top. Her feet are a size bigger than mine, but the trainers fit OK. I lace them up tightly.

I grab my old clothes, the clothes I came in, and stuff them in my bag. Somehow it doesn't seem right to put them back on; would have felt like stepping back into my old life. Now, it feels as though I'm striding into Lorna's. What I wanted all along.

Just as I'm leaving the room, something on the dressing table catches my eye, something on a pretty china dish glinting in the sunlight. I pick it up.

'My necklace,' I whisper as the white gold chain slips through my fingers. I clutch the diamond pendant in my fist. He gave it to me when Jack was born but must have since given it to Lorna. I shove it in my pocket, knowing how much he paid. The money will be useful.

Downstairs, nothing much has changed except Lorna has lit a fire in the living room hearth. The smell makes me gag. 'Your boots, underwear and my dress,' she says, pointing to the flames. She's tracked blood all over the carpet, not seeming to care. 'Don't step in it,' she says, catching me looking. 'You weren't here. Ever. OK?'

I stare at her, no idea why she's doing this. '*What?*'

'My mind's made up. I want you to go to Jack's college at six this evening. His coach is due back then. He's been on a trip. Go to him, Maria. Explain who you are. Tell him everything, like you told me. What you do after that is up to you, but please, look after him. He's your son, but he's been my son too. He's a good boy.' She seems determined, urgent, no stopping her. Tears fill her eyes as I go to hug her, but she holds up her hands, halting me. She's still covered in blood.

'I'll write down the college's address for you.'

'I already know it,' I say with a small smile. 'But what are *you* going to do?' I ask, my eyes flicking back to the kitchen.

'Maria, trust me,' she says, glancing at her watch. 'You should go now. The longer you're here, the riskier it is. In time, your story can come out. People will understand. You've done nothing wrong. As long as you keep quiet about *this*.' She points to the kitchen.

I stare at her, having no idea what she's planning. Then she shoos me towards the hallway. We stand near the front door, staring at each other.

'I know what it feels like to be dead inside,' she says. 'Hiding things from yourself, denying what's there, what's happened in the past. But all it does is prevent you from having a future. I want you to go and have yours, Maria. Because none of this ever belonged to me.'

Our eyes stay locked for a few moments – hers glistening with tears. It's equivalent to the hug we'd share if it wasn't for the blood. And then she opens the door, hiding behind it so no one in the street sees her. The sunlight streams in through the gap, and I step out – leaving her in the darkness.

CHAPTER SIXTY-FOUR

Lorna

I close the door, not bothering to lock it or put the chain on. I stand in the hallway for a moment, my heartbeat slow now, strangely calm as I listen to the echoes of our lives here – the children, their friends, our friends, my family, Mark and me. Feet thumping up and down the stairs, bags and clutter left in the corridor, mail on the doormat, the smashed lamp, friends round for dinner, play dates for Freya, Andrew grabbing me, not even letting me get upstairs before he'd had his way.

I cover my face.

I loved him.

And now it's too late.

Shaking, I go back into the kitchen, my stomach turning from the stink of congealing blood and scorched flesh. Mark's face is red and blistered, his eyes open with his cheek pressed on the floor as he lies half on his side, his arms and legs splayed out.

I nudge him with my foot. There's no need to check his pulse. I can see he's dead. The kitchen knife is still on the floor, so I pick it up and wash it thoroughly in the sink, rubbing away all traces of Maria's fingerprints. Then I take the handle, getting my prints all over it instead, gripping it, smearing some of Mark's blood on it again.

I lay it back on the floor where it had been and grab the brandy bottle, swigging from it, relishing the searing heat down my throat.

When I've wiped down everything Maria touched with a tea towel, I slide down onto the floor, sitting in the blood beside Mark, my knees drawn up as his face leers awkwardly at me, his fingers splayed out close to the knife. 'We fucked up good and proper, didn't we?' I say, knocking back more brandy, pulling a face, almost expecting a response from him. 'Bloody hell, I can see why I saved this for cooking.' I look at the label, wiping my mouth with the back of my hand. 'It's a bit shit.' How stupid to think of something so trivial as I sit in the aftermath of my husband's butchering.

I gaze around my kitchen: at Freya's paintings taped on the fridge, Mark's sticky note saying 'Get toothpaste' underlined a dozen times, Jack's shoes left near the back door, and my lunchbox on the counter – I forgot to take it to work this morning.

Then I remember the police coming to my office earlier. It seems an age ago that I lied to them, twisted the truth. I bet they'd like to speak to me now.

'You know, I really loved him,' I say to Mark, hating that I'd never told Andrew. I'd always held back, not allowing my true feelings out. Some kind of pathetic attempt at guilt management. I gulp down more brandy, then make my way out to my car. I don't care who sees me any more. I need to get my phone.

I stumble back up the front step, feeling drunk, banging the door back too hard against the wall. There are a few missed calls – just work. Plus, a couple of texts. One from Mark earlier, saying he's coming home to check on me as he had a quick break. Another from Annie asking if Freya can stop over the night.

That's when the sobs come. A deep, painful eruption for my little girl. My eyes feel as though they're going to split open from the pressure as the tears stream down my cheeks.

Great idea, I text back, my hand shaking, hardly able to see the screen. *Actually, would you mind if she stayed with you for a little while? Calling on her fairy godmother here! Will explain soon xx* I gulp up a couple of erratic breaths as I tap send. It has to be done.

Then I drop down onto the floor again next to Mark, his hand midway between me and the knife now, making me wonder if he's moved. I prod him. Nothing.

'Freya will be fine,' I tell him, hearing myself slurring. 'She's better off without the both of us.' Then I tap out a text to Jack. *Someone else picking you up from college later. Please listen to her. Please trust her. Please do as she says. I love you, Jack. L xx*

I stare at my phone, my eyes fixated on the yellow and pink Double Take icon. I open up the app, going to my messages with Andy_jag. With *Mark*. I scroll back, my eyes swimming with tears as I read. Then I find them. *Those* messages, from over a week ago.

Andy_jag: *I've got some trouble going on in my life. Stuff needs sorting.*

Abbi74: *Oh, sounds serious?*

Andy_jag: *If I tell you a secret, do you promise to keep it?*

Abbi74: *Of course. You can trust me.*

I remember how much my heart thumped then, as I finally thought I was going to get a glimpse inside Andrew's mind, unravelling the man I loved.

Andy_jag: *I've been seeing a therapist.*

Abbi74: *That's OK. Lots of people do.*

I'd smiled to myself, wondering what he was going to reveal about me – wondering if he was going to tell Abbi that he was in love with me, that he couldn't live without me, that he'd do anything to be with me.

Andy_jag: *Trouble is, my therapist is obsessed with me. Won't leave me alone. Stalks me day and night. She's a nightmare.*

I'd gone cold then, shaking, a sense of disbelief washing through me. I couldn't bring myself to reply before the next message came in.

Andy_jag: *I'm going to report her to her boss. She's done enough damage. Her career will be over. Her personal life too. She's going to get what's coming to her.*

I'd shut my phone down after that, dropping onto the couch in my office. I was too numb for tears. I didn't understand. I stared at the wall for ages, trying to take in what he'd said. I knew I needed to talk to him. As me, as *Lorna*. It was ridiculous – I wasn't stalking him. What we had was wrong, but always mutual. And whatever happened, I had to stop him reporting me to the clinic, reason with him, make him see sense. I couldn't run away a second time.

'You know what,' I say, looking down at Mark's body as he swims in and out of focus. I wipe my nose on my sleeve. 'I thought things were shit then.' I laugh, swigging the last of the brandy. 'I had no fucking idea, did I?'

All I'd wanted was to go to Andrew's place to talk, to work something out, to gauge his mood, to see if he really was going to report me. Persuade him otherwise. I couldn't believe he was actually doing this.

'I didn't really go to the spa with Cath that day,' I confess to Mark, hiccupping. 'Just so you know.' It was always a risk, I realise, with seeing Annie later that night, but thankfully she hadn't spoken to Cath for a couple of days. I blustered my way through the lie.

I already knew where Andrew's house was. I decided to surprise him with a visit, perhaps even catch him out with his lodger, have something to throw back at him for a change. It was always a battle of wills, despite our passion. But that wasn't the main reason for my visit. Truth was, I was scared. I had to smooth things over, convince him not to destroy my career – even if that meant carrying on with him in some way if he insisted or, hopefully, ending it calmly.

I tap the first number.

9

'He was shocked to see me, of course,' I say to Mark, prodding him. 'But pleased too. He eventually invited me in and I couldn't see any sign of the lodger. He said she was out. Kept saying he didn't know why I was so hung up about her, why I couldn't just leave it be, why I had to go on and on and on about her.'

I drink more brandy, nearly emptying the bottle, tapping the next number.

9

'He told me he thought she was unattractive, just some farm girl trying to make it in the city. Not his type. But I wouldn't believe him. *Couldn't* believe him. It was ingrained and stuck. From somewhere.' I trace my finger through Mark's thickening blood on the floor, my hand close to his. Close to the knife. 'He said he hadn't wanted me at his house because he didn't want you finding out where he lived, in case you followed me. He said he did it for my sake, but still, I didn't believe him. Besides, I couldn't forget what he'd said to Abbi about reporting me to the clinic – even though I now know it was really *you*.'

I spit on him before resting my head back on the side of the kitchen island, my finger tapping out the final number.

9

It connects instantly. 'Emergency, which service do you require?'

I pause.

'Hello, which emergency service do you require, caller?'

'Police,' I say, but then the scream comes, and I drop my phone. His hand is quick, lunging for the knife, grabbing it, raising it towards me, his half-dead eyes staring at me as he bares his teeth. Mark drags himself half up, sliding in his blood, taking a stab at my leg. He misses but tries again and again – me pulling myself out of the way, pushing myself back across the floor with my feet, frantically slipping in the mess. He's getting closer, wheezing, coughing up blood, his eyes demented. I scream again, my back pinned up against the cupboard as he reaches me.

He sinks the blade into my leg.

'Oww… nooo… you fucking bastard!' I kick his hand hard, pulling the knife from my muscle, yelling in agony. Then, with one swift stroke, I plunge it into his throat, hitting his artery first time. What little blood is left in him drains out, his head finally hitting the floor.

'Fuck, fuck… oww, oh *God no*… help me. Someone help me, *please*.' The pain in my calf is unbearable, ripping through every nerve. I slide across to my phone, panting, breathless, shaking. I grab it, holding it to my ear.

'Hello… caller, hello, are you there?'

'I'm… I'm here,' I say, sobbing uncontrollably, knowing what I have to do. 'I… I want to report a murder…' I cry. 'I just… I just killed my husband.'

CHAPTER SIXTY-FIVE

Lorna's Journal

3 May 2018

It's not like my journal before, of course, but it's all they allow me in the cell – a few sheets of paper and a pencil. Guess they don't think I'm a suicide risk, about to stab myself with the point – but then I know exactly the right things to say. Anyway, writing this helps pass the time. And God knows, I've got plenty of that while I wait for the trial. Bail was refused several weeks ago.

I once wrote that journaling is the best therapy for the therapist, for self-reflection, for personal growth. A measure of change. And I stand by that. I never expected Mark to find any of my diaries, let alone the one about what happened with Andrew. I should have destroyed it last year, but I didn't. I couldn't. I thought I'd hidden it well enough. It was me clinging on, unable to let go. Not moving forward at all.

But life doesn't always go the way we expect. If it did, I'd have been out of a job long ago.

It wasn't until I got to Andrew's place that day, the day I was meant to be at the spa with Cath, that it all came back, hit me head-on like a high-speed train.

An eclipse of everything.

Though I still didn't see it, even when it was coming at me full speed. Some things are too close to focus on clearly. Besides, there was no time to get out of the way. (Keep your writing legible, Lorna. You know what your solicitor said about this being used in your case. He's going down the mental health plea route. ~~Ironic.~~)

Andrew let me in, eventually, though he was reluctant. The way he looked at me standing on the doorstep, I could see he was torn between wanting to rip my clothes off and sending me away. He didn't like that I'd turned up unannounced.

'I'm working,' he'd said, looking pained. I noticed his hands were covered in paint as he glanced up and down the street. 'But you'd better come in.'

'Are you alone?' I'd asked nervously, my eyes flicking around his hallway.

He nodded, that look in his eyes. And the scent – the scent that had driven me wild since the first moment we met – was stronger than ever, as if his entire house was steeped in it. No wonder it was always on him. After only a few breaths, I felt giddy, drunk, as if I'd been transported to a completely different place. A different time. I remember wobbling as I took off my coat, holding on to the wall to steady myself as he hung it up.

'Come through,' he said, a smile turning up one side of his mouth, as if he was getting used to the idea of me being there. And the scar – oh God the scar – creasing upwards, sending me into more of a meltdown. I prised my eyes away.

'What do you think?' he said, gesturing to the large canvas on an easel. 'My latest.' As I followed him into the room, my senses were on fire. I felt disorientated. The small studio was cluttered with paintings in all stages of completion leaning against the walls, and there were tables littered with tubes of paint, pots of brushes, bottles of all kinds containing different coloured liquids. The wooden floor was splattered with what looked like years' worth of spilt paint. A huge, dried-up palette. A record of his work.

'It's not finished,' he'd said. 'I didn't want you to see it yet.'

'Wow,' was all I'd said, staring transfixed by the canvas. 'It's…' I turned my head sideways to see if that would help my brain make sense

of what I thought I was seeing. His pictures were always bold, daring, almost violent in nature – some of the nudes I'd seen online had hateful angry faces set over stunningly slim, perfect bodies, while others had grotesque and distorted bodies with the face of an airbrushed model. But this was different. This was intrusive, private, almost voyeuristic of someone else's pain.

The painting was of me.

'Do you like it?' he said. The likeness was uncanny – he'd captured a side of me I didn't know existed, painted me in a way no mirror or photograph ever could portray. But as for liking it, I didn't know.

'I…' I went closer, wanting to touch it, but I could see the paint was still wet. 'I'm bleeding,' I'd said, stating the obvious. A glistening red trail led from my lips. 'And I'm on the ground. Naked.' It took a moment to realise, and even then it was only because a couple of printed-out photographs of me were clipped to the edge of the canvas.

'You took photos of me when I fainted?'

'You looked so beautiful,' he said. 'I couldn't resist.'

Then I heard a noise. 'What's that?' I jumped, terrified his lodger would come back, fearful of the consequences. I didn't want to meet her, didn't want to see the face of the woman I hated so much, who'd caused me so much pain, who had unconditional access to the man I loved when I didn't. 'Is it her?' I felt the panic rising in me, déjà vu choking me. 'Is it Paula?'

'Who the hell's Paula?' Andrew said with a laugh, amused. 'It's just the back door blowing shut in the wind,' he said, coming up to me. 'Anyway, my lodger's name is Beth, and I have no idea why you're so hung up about her. She's nothing to me. She was just a fling, pays her rent.'

I still didn't believe him.

As he took hold of me, it was like a fog gathering in my mind, obscuring all sense from my consciousness. Or rather, unveiling my unconscious bit by bit. We staggered backwards as his mouth came down on mine, his hands all over me. 'No, you're lying,' I said, mumbling as he kissed me harder. He didn't hear. Didn't care that my heart was racing, that a sweat was breaking out on me. He had no idea that I was losing myself, that I was transforming into someone I didn't recognise. I still had no idea why.

I kissed him back as he tore at my clothes, hoping it would somehow ground me. We crashed into a table, everything spilling, falling to the floor. He didn't care. He swept stuff aside, pushed me down. My face was in the mess, the spilt liquids, inhaling the heady vapours from the bottles, making me feel high.

And then that single, indefinable smell again – so strong now it almost hurt. The same scent that was always on him. Mixed up with his aftershave, it passed as something intriguing, beguiling, attractive. But now, with my face pushed close to the source, I felt sick, terrified, as if something bad was about to happen. There was something oily and slick on my cheek. Nothing pleasant about it.

'No!' I screamed, but he didn't stop. The scream wasn't for him, anyway. It was for another time, another place.

'I want you, Lorna,' he said, his mouth against my ear, his body rammed hard up against me. I was almost gone by this point, even though I didn't see it at the time. Couldn't fit together the final pieces of the puzzle. Some were still missing, lost, hidden away. The eclipse wasn't yet total.

We went upstairs, me staggering as though I was drunk, yet happy that I was finally inside his house, that I meant something to him. And, as ever, I blocked out the guilt, convinced myself it would be the last time I'd see him, that I'd come to call things off, end it all calmly. I hadn't even dared to mention about the clinic at that point, ask if he was going to report me. That could come afterwards. Our need for each other was too strong. I was intoxicated. I wanted him one last time. I sensed it was going to be the best yet.

'Tie me up,' he said as we went into his bedroom. It was messy, strewn with his clothes, more paintings, boxes of stuff everywhere, his bed was unmade, the sheets all over the place.

'*What?*' *I said, trying to raise a smile. He pulled off my top, undid my bra. I thought he was joking.*

'*I want you to. We've talked about it.*' *He took off his clothes then, lying down on the bed. 'Do it for me.*'

'*Really?*' *I was so lost in it all that I'd have done anything he asked.*

'*Really,*' *he said seriously, pointing to some ties lying in a tangle on the floor.*

When I saw them, I said something about being well practised, about him doing it with the lodger, but I can't really remember how it came out as I bound up his wrists and ankles to the metal bed frame, tightening the knots more than was warranted. Then he'd joked about me being the expert. But my jealousy was still burning deep. There would be no loosening or getting away. I made sure of it, my eyes fixed on him as I worked. Part of me hated that he looked helpless spread-eagled like that – less of a man – but something in me ignited. As if he deserved to look pathetic.

'*Good girl…*' *he said.*

Good girl…

My head swam at the words, warped my brain with even more confusion. I felt like a kid, drowning in the past, but trying to stay in the present. It wasn't working. I was losing my grip.

'*Draw the curtains,*' *he said. 'I want it dark. And put some music on.*' *He flicked his eyes over to an old record player, a stack of vinyl propped beside it.*

'*Oh, cool,*' *I'd said, loving that he was into all that. I was learning more about him now that I was in his home, soaking up the real Andrew, the one I'd always wanted to get to know, as though I'd been allowed a private viewing of his mind. This was his domain. His stuff. His life. I felt special. Better than her.*

Better than Paula.

My eyes flared with bright lights. Someone else's bedroom. Someone else's woman.

A gin bottle smashing against the wall.

I grabbed hold of the bed.

'Just play what's already on there,' he said. 'It's one of my favourites.'

When I steadied myself, I dropped the needle, turning it up, waiting to be surprised. I was back on the bed as the first track played. I teased him, making him writhe, doing what I knew he loved – as well as some stuff he didn't – until he couldn't control himself any longer. I wasn't particularly listening to the music, even though I knew the artist. But something was flickering deep inside still, nagging at my unconscious mind. Tugging at threads. Waking up the past.

'You look ridiculous,' I'd said afterwards, kissing him, feeling powerful as I loomed over him. I'd giggled some more as we kissed again, me stroking his skin, straddling him. Showing him I was still in control.

'I love you, Lorna,' he said, looking up at me, but I didn't reply. Not even when he asked me if I loved him back. Over and over. He wanted to hear it so much, but I couldn't. Something was happening to me and I wasn't sure what. I felt as though I was coming out of my body. It was terrifying, like a raging illness taking over. For a few seconds, I literally couldn't breathe. My throat closed up. I felt like someone else entirely.

Then it came out of nowhere.

The song.

The trigger pulled.

The gunshot.

I screamed. It was like an explosion – a nightmare ignited, but it wasn't just in my head. It was real. All around me. The past colliding with the present.

No stopping it.

I was living it, though I didn't realise it at the time. All I knew was that I was terrified, and I had no idea why.

'Fuck, no!' I clawed at my face, staring at him, screaming over and over, covering my ears, trying to block out the music. Then I hit him, lashing out, hating him, the loathing spewing out of me. I

couldn't help it, couldn't hear his protests even though I could see his mouth moving, begging me to stop. The look of horror as his expression changed from pleasure to pain.

All I could hear was that song cutting right through me. It wasn't music any more. It was a wormhole to memories I'd long forgotten. A past blocked out.

I was back there.

More real than reality.

'No, no, nooo…' I heard myself screaming. It didn't sound like me. I was above him, my arms thrashing wildly, my nose on fire with the smell – it was in my hair, on my face, on him. It burnt my nostrils.

Sandalwood cologne mixed up with the stink of linseed oil, turpentine – the smell of him.

My father.

Good girl…

The spillages in his workshop. Me passing out, waking up in it. The stink up my nose.

The grotesque dead birds hanging around him.

Paula. My parents' lodger. That night in his bedroom.

My mother… blaming me, leaving me for months, the remains of my cremated father kept ever since as her sick prize. Rarely letting him out of her sight. Untrustworthy, she said.

'I hate you, I hate you, I hate you…' The words spewed out of me, even though I wasn't really me any more; didn't know what I was doing.

The man I saw in front of me wasn't Andrew either – he'd long gone. His face and body had morphed into the grotesque image of my father hanging by his neck – his body naked, the blood pooling in his groin.

His thing *sticking up.*

A total eclipse.

A full set of triggers.

And it ripped everything out of me that I'd hidden from myself all these years – the trauma I'd never been able to process was being played out right in front of me, set in motion by things I had no idea about until now. It was my unconscious's way of dealing with it. Of processing the past. My brain doing what it had to do.

Unlocking itself.

An explosion.

Except it was Andrew – the man I loved – not the one I hated for what he'd done to me and my mother, for abandoning us, for blaming me in the most horrific of ways.

This is what happens when you watch people, when you tell secrets… It's your shame now…

I couldn't control myself. I didn't know what I was doing.

(But no one will believe that in court, Lorna. You deserve everything you get.)

I was pouring sweat, raging, desperate to get out all the things I should have said to my father when I'd caught him with Paula that night.

She lived with us, paid my parents to rent a room because they needed the money. To help clothe me. Feed me. Send me to ballet class.

The lodger.

My mother had no idea about their affair. She often worked nights in a factory. When she got a sniff of things, when she forced me to tell her what I knew, it destroyed her. I pulled back my arm and thumped Andrew hard in the jaw at the memory. He let out a cry, but all I could see was his scar. I wanted to pummel it into oblivion, never have to think of it or him *again.*

It was in exactly the same place as the gash my father ended up with on his lifeless face when our neighbour raced next door to see what was wrong. He'd heard me screaming when I'd found my father hanging in the workshop. He grabbed a Stanley knife from the workbench and cut him down, accidentally slicing into my father's lip as he hacked at the cable round his neck. It didn't matter. He was already dead.

Little nine-year-old me stood there helpless, watching, knowing it was all my fault for spying, just as his note had said. And he was right. I've carried the guilt ever since.

Beneath me, Andrew begged for me to untie him, to calm down, to get a grip of myself. I could see he was smarting from the blow. The bed rocked from him struggling but he was bound fast. I barely knew what I was doing when I pulled the extension cable from the wall, barely noticed the hypnotic melody of Elton John's 'Tiny Dancer' on the turntable as I wound the cable around his neck. I pulled hard for as long as I could, watching his cheeks go red then purple, his tongue bulging out of his lips as he coughed and choked, his bursting eyes staring up at me, imploring me to stop when he couldn't speak any more. Coughs and spit bubbled up his throat.

I had no idea what I was doing. All I knew was that if I didn't do it, the pain inside me would be stuck in there forever, would never go away. It wasn't me – it wasn't Lorna the daughter, the mother, the wife, or even the lover acting out. It was the child within me – the little girl who'd been imprisoned for so long.

She was mad as hell.

When the thrashing and writhing slowed, I knew I had to make sure he was gone for good. I wanted the rot out of me. But I could still see the tiny tick of an irregular pulse at his throat, the occasional twitch of one of his tied-up hands, his eyes rolling in his head. Panicking, I tore round the house, searching in the lodger's room, the bathroom, the living room and studio… for what, I had no idea. Anything to finish the job. Then I saw it in a kitchen drawer.

Back in the bedroom, I bound the cling film round and round his head – layers and layers of it – making certain he wouldn't be able to breathe. I wasn't quite strong enough to strangle him to the end, but there was no way he'd survive suffocation. When I'd finished, his features were unrecognisable through the plastic. He could have been anyone. Except he wasn't.

He was my father.

Afterwards, I sat on the bed beside him, panting, sweating, staring, not knowing who or where I was, or even what to do next. I'd not thought that far ahead. All I knew was that the puzzle was finally complete. And, for a time, it felt good. I felt free. Purged of the pain and trauma. To me, it made perfect sense.

I'd revisited my childhood. Put things right. Good therapy.

Then reality slowly hit. Like drunkenness wearing off, I was gradually sobering up, realising the consequences. I'd killed a man in cold blood. Andrew. The man I loved.

I sat with him for a while, dazed, staring at him, praying none of this was real. But it was. I thought about turning myself in there and then, calling the police. The guilt and self-loathing wrung out my insides. How could I carry on with my life after this? But then I thought of Mark, of Freya and Jack. How they needed me. Besides, I knew I was good at keeping secrets – other people's as well as my own. I'd done it all my life. This would be the biggest one yet.

I don't even know how I got home later that afternoon, but, gradually, I turned back into me, got dressed, gathered my stuff. I cleaned Andrew's body with a wet towel, wiping all traces of me off him. I took the towel with me, dumping it in a skip on the way home. Threw up in the gutter. Sat on a park bench, thinking what to do, gathering myself. I felt myself turning numb from the inside out.

Self-preservation yet again.

I didn't realise it then, of course, but it was because of Mark that I killed the only man I've ever truly loved – him, posing as Andrew, saying he was going to report me. I'd never have gone to his house otherwise. And Andrew died not knowing I loved him back.

And now I pray every day that the baby inside me is his, not Mark's, that they'll let the baby have a paternity test, though I may never know for sure. If I go to prison, which I will, they said that I'll be able to keep my son or daughter for eighteen months if there's a place at a mother and baby unit. After that, I don't know what will happen.

So this is my confession, the last journal entry I will ever make. There's no looking back for me now. No reflecting. No forward movement or change. No personal growth or bettering myself. Just stasis. One day blurring into the next as I watch myself get bigger and bigger. I'm not asking for forgiveness by writing this, so don't pity me. Whoever reads it, whoever hears my story, if you truly listen to me, all I'm asking for is ~~understanding~~.

And one day, if Freya finds it in herself to visit me here, I'll tell her my story – explain why Annie has to be her mummy now, help her comprehend why I'm locked up – even though the little girl inside me has been set free. I'll explain how secrets from long ago sometimes stay buried, lying dormant, festering, hidden, waiting for the perfect conditions to strike. And how the worst kind of secrets are always the ones we keep from ourselves.

A LETTER FROM SAMANTHA

Dear Reader,

I'm so pleased you chose to read *Tell Me a Secret*, and I do hope you enjoyed the time you spent with my characters. I'd love it if you signed up here *www.bookouture.com/samantha-hayes* to keep up to date with all my latest books and forthcoming releases. It's really easy and ensures you don't miss out!

Tell Me a Secret is a book filled with complex and troubled characters. At its core lies a very demanding yet rewarding profession – psychotherapy. And it's a subject very close to my heart, not least because my brother is an experienced therapist working within the health service. Of course, he's extremely professional and confidentiality is paramount to him, but learning about therapy in general over the years heightened my interest in the subject.

That, along with experiencing excellent counselling myself just when I needed it, I felt driven to undertake a course, and I was lucky enough to be accepted onto a four-year degree programme in psychotherapy. The first year was eye-opening, rewarding and challenging.

As a person-centred course (the modality pioneered by Carl Rogers), the training, as well as the therapy itself, is a journey of self-discovery rather than a destination. The whole ethos and effectiveness of person-centred counselling is based upon relationships. At the heart of good therapy lies the unique connection between the therapist and client.

And of course, as an author, it got me thinking. Therapy of all types is extremely helpful to many people, but what if it goes wrong? What if the therapist fails at her job? What if her own troubled past, as in Lorna's case, catches up with the present? So I made this unique client–counsellor situation the core of my story, which as you found out, leads to a devastating and heartbreaking outcome for Lorna. Therapists are human too, after all.

Tell Me a Secret is a book steeped in relationships – from Cath's more light-hearted dating disasters and the women's friendships, to the controlling dynamic between Mark and Lorna, to the sometimes difficult relationship between a step-parent and step-child. And not least, the tragic love story between Lorna and Andrew. But, of course, the most important relationship we will ever have is with ourselves – the most complicated love story of all!

Finally, if you enjoyed my book, it would be wonderful if you could write an online review. I genuinely value your feedback and, of course, it helps spread the word! And I'd love you to join me on Facebook or Twitter too, or take a look at my website for details of all my other books. The details are below.

In the meantime, I'm busy working on my next story and can't wait to share it with you!

Sam x

 samanthahayesauthor

@samhayes

 www.samanthahayes.co.uk

ACKNOWLEDGEMENTS

Once again, it's time to give my sincere thanks to a wonderful team of people who have helped shape my book into the best it can be. Writing it is only the beginning of the process, so I must again give huge thanks to Jessie Botterill, my amazing and insightful editor, for all her hard work and passion. Couldn't do it without you! And of course, my heartfelt gratitude and thanks to all the wonderful team at Bookouture for getting my books 'out there' – not least the tireless and enthusiastic Kim Nash and Noelle Holten. Your energy and passion for bringing amazing stories to readers is boundless! Plus, a big thank you to Séan and Catherine for your eagle-eyes and hard work, and also to Maisie for being an early and very helpful reader.

Agent extraordinaire, Oli Munson… what can I say? Thank you! You're the best and I love being in 'Oliver's Army' and part of Team A.M. Heath. Big thanks also to Jennifer Custer, Hélène Ferey and Alexandra McNicoll for everything you do, and have done, over the years.

Tell Me a Secret has a very important and often difficult profession at its heart, so I'd like to give sincere thanks to my brother, Joe, a very experienced therapist. All our late-night chats and brainstorming were incredibly useful and your knowledge and input invaluable. Any errors or, indeed, indiscretions by my characters, are either fictitious or my own mistakes!

No acknowledgements would be complete without a special mention of Tracy Fenton and THE Book Club on Facebook – along with her incredible admin team and amazing members. How does this one fare for 'In Your Pants'?

Finally, as ever, a massive thank you to all my readers around the world – I love hearing what you think of my books! And finally, finally, love to my dear friend Debbie, whose listening ear over the months of writing this book rivalled any therapy! And of course lots of love to my dear family, Avril and Paul, Graham and Marina, Joe, Ben, Polly and Lucy – for everything.

Made in the USA
San Bernardino, CA
24 March 2020

66192956R00199